CHRISTOPHER D. OCHS

Anigrafx, LLC
Emmaus, PA

Published by: Anigrafx, LLC
                Emmaus, PA
                www.anigrafx.com
Printed by: KDP

ISBN-10: 0-9981726-1-X
ISBN-13: 978-0-9981726-1-3
Library of Congress Control Number: 2020912846

Diversity Editor: Danielle Fields
Editor: Dianna Sinovic
Chameleon Art: Adapted from tattooimages.biz
Cover Photography: Adapted from Alessandro Oliverio, pexels.com
Book & Cover Design, Formatting: Christopher D. Ochs

ACKNOWLEDGMENTS

Danielle Fields

Thanks for your patience while correcting my misconceptions and answering awkward questions about diversity and racism, after the tragic deaths of George Floyd and Breonna Taylor. Thanks for helping me grow.

Rosalind Wiseman

Thanks for your eye-opening work on the psychology and social dynamics of girl-vs-girl bullying, "Queen Bees & Wannabes."

My "Reference Library"

Thanks to my pool of volunteers, for your guidance in your respective fields of expertise.
> A. Lee Levengood, attorney
> Susan K. Monroe, librarian, teacher
> Richie Sullivan, NYPD detective, Ret.
> Laura Trexler, teacher
> Gail Zapf, school administrator

The Bethlehem Writers Group

Thanks for reading, followed by your critiques, corrections, suggestions, pushes and prods, discussions and laughter.

My "Quibble & Nibble" Critique Partners

Thanks to Charles Kiernan and D.T. Krippene, for your wit and wisdom, critiques and pointers, and off-the-cuff remarks that often inspired even greater weirdness ... And new recipes!

i

ALSO BY THE AUTHOR

DEDICATION

Dr. Marvin Brubaker	Clark Ferguson	John Hnatow
Dr. Johanna Ott	Dr. Jack Ridge	Dr. Ed Roeder

Mentors, teachers, and professors who taught me
The love of learning
How to teach myself
The need to always be open to learn
The obligation to pass it on

MY FRIEND JACKSON

CHAPTER ONE

Jasmine steeled herself against the piercing stares as she ran laps. She had managed to evade the seven pairs of curious eyes while she waited in Coach's office, but there was no escape here under the lens of the open gymnasium.

From the safety of the basketball court's far side they peered at her, darting their gaze away when her eyes met theirs. The barrage of wary glances stood out like spotlights beaming out from sweating girls' faces that ranged from light chestnut to deep mocha.

Some of the girls were vaguely familiar, dredged up from wisps of memories from the season's games she had played for her previous school. But two faces stuck out from the crowd.

Coach Garcia had an enigmatic smile, stretched thin under probing eyes. Something underneath—the angle of her stormy eyebrows, the tilt of her head—told Jasmine that the debate inside Coach's head might be leaning in her favor.

The second stare was less friendly. A wolf sizing up her next meal would have been more reassuring.

Oh, right. She's the team captain I fouled early this season. Elbowed her, knocking her on her butt during a layup. Got a nasty scratch, too, when she hit the floor. Wonder if she remembers that?

Coach sounded a blast on her whistle, sweeping both arms together in a gathering motion. The eight girls broke from their laps around the court. They assembled in front of Coach, who strolled with authority onto the nearest foul lane.

"Okay, ladies. Before we get into warm-up drills, it's time for introductions." She pointed at Jasmine, who took a solid step forward from the semicircle.

Jasmine held her chin high enough to show she wasn't cowed, but not so high that she came off as a show-off or poser.

"This is Jasmine Price." A sporadic stream of unenthusiastic "hello"s were muttered around the circle. The team captain's glare didn't waver. "Your turn, team. Intros all around. Call out your name, from left to right."

Madison, Akilah, Trinity, whatsits, whosis, and …?

Jasmine gave up on pinning the flock of names to their faces as they flew past her ears. The only other one that stuck was the last one —Nevaeh, the team captain.

Nevaeh stood out with that unmistakable air of authority, borne out not only from her station on the team, but more. Her stance, the way she held the basketball against her hips with disdainful nonchalance, a uniform two shades brighter than anyone else on the team, and a pair of the latest designer kicks made it impossible to miss who was top of the pecking order. She thrust out her neck, showing off a sports necklace holding a man's heavy steel and gold ring, and a perfect set of blinding-white teeth behind darker-than-dark collagen-plumped lips. Then there was her long black hair tied in a sports bun, wrapped with a braid tinted with the school colors of blue and gold.

Oh, brother. Heaven forbid anything get in the way of Miss Rah-rah McMoneybags.

"Jasmine's transferred from Eastside," said Coach.

Jasmine blinked away a growing unease when she was peppered by a ring of playful but disapproving "ooh"s. Somewhere in the dying echoes poked out a pair of bitter whispers.

"The Projects?"

"*That* shit-hole?"

Jasmine resisted the urge to spot who dissed her, focusing instead on the mischievous curl in the team captain's snarl.

"All right, knock it off." A pinch of Coach's contralto bullhorn slipped in, giving the command the right pinch of *oomph*. The grumblings switched off fast as a radio. "She's with *us* now, and we're lucky to have her. Her stats are good, I've watched her moves in our Eastside games, and Coach Evans had nothing but good things to say about Jasmine. Though her old team is ticked off that *we* got her."

A handful of chuckles bounced around the gymnasium. Nevaeh wasn't one of the few joining in. Her sour-lemons expression stomped the last hint of her smile into oblivion.

"Okay, team. To start, we'll try a couple of drill exercises. Jasmine, you're in first squad. Akilah, you move over to second squad for now." With a deafening clap, Coach signaled court was adjourned.

The one who looks like she just got slapped must be Akilah.

"First squad, to the far basket. Nevaeh, you run 'em through pivot shots. Akilah, run your girls through a V-cut drill here." Two short pipes on her whistle, and the squads scattered.

Jasmine settled into the drills' give-and-take. Glances from her new teammates lost their leery edge with each repetition of catch, pass, shoot. They were gradually replaced with respect, and even a weak smile or two.

Except for Nevaeh. Her gaze never shifted from stiff coolness, like she was watching a mouse running through a maze.

Jasmine tilted her head in search of Coach Garcia. She, too, gave her the eagle eye while tapping her whistle against her chin.

Let Coach and Nevaeh watch. Concentrate on the game. The rest will take care of itself.

With a flick of dismissal in her shoulders, Jasmine dove into the warm-ups. The distinctive drum of the ball on the boards and the shrill squeak of sneakers on polished wood were a song to Jasmine's ears. She eagerly lost herself in their rhythms. After several rounds of passing, dribbling, and faking exercises, Coach piped her whistle.

"Heads up, girls. Time for a quick game. And for once we have even teams." Coach stabbed her index finger into the heart of the first squad. "Trinity, you head up the second string against Nevaeh."

The girl with raspberry tints at the end of her short, angled bob flashed a goggle of surprise that soured into displeasure.

Trinity, check. So, what's she got against me?

Nevaeh handily nabbed the tip-off against Trinity. Jasmine wasn't sure, but she thought she caught a wink between the two of them.

Akilah was Jasmine's shadow. Anytime Jasmine got the ball, Akilah ran her down, her arms swinging like windmills in a storm, blocking every shot. Trinity's shrill cackle slipped in from the far side of the court. Jasmine flipped a knowing smile to herself when she spotted Nevaeh flashing signals to Akilah.

Running both squads, huh? Okay, I get the lay of the land.

Another trill of the whistle announced a break. Coach signaled to the short pudgy girl on the second squad. "Madison, switch with Akilah on first squad." Exasperation exploded on Akilah's face. As they trotted to their newly assigned places, Nevaeh glowered at Coach with hot displeasure.

Coach chirped out two whistles, and the scrimmage resumed. Jasmine grabbed every opportunity passed to her and ran with it. Watching, all the while. After a few minutes into the session, she picked up on everyone's favorite moves. Most notably, the team shrimp, Madison. She was way too eager to be rid of the ball. With her thunder thighs quivering, she'd pass it like it was a ticking bomb.

No time to think about that. Keep your head in the game. You're being tested here.

Settling back in herself, the three-point shots came easy. Jasmine beamed a cheek-busting smile after she aced a layup, arcing like a ballerina past Nevaeh's attempt to block. Switching to defense, she intercepted the ball from Nevaeh, who was more interested in showing off than passing. Jasmine dribbled back to her side of the court and leaped for the perfect nuthin-but-net ...

"You!" Coach Garcia bellowed at full blast. Everyone on the court screeched to a halt.

Jasmine scowled at her spoiled shot bouncing off the backboard. As she caught the rebound, she swore the bleachers rattled from Coach's shock wave.

"Yeah, *you*—Caleb!" Coach stomped down the sideline, her arm flailing at someone blocked from Jasmine's view by Nevaeh's head. "What the hell you doin' in here? This is girls' basketball, not prom night. Get you and your crap outta here, before I call security."

Jasmine stepped to the side, moving from behind Nevaeh. Holding the ball with her fingertips, she cocked her head at the intruder.

If trouble had a face, it would have been his. He was bad news personified, dressed in black jeans and a black jacket with a large letter "C" over his heart and its sleeves jammed up to the elbows. Sporting a backward black baseball cap, and tattoos the length of his neck and forearms, he strutted past Coach like he was carrying.

Yeah, I seen his type a lot at the Projects. Tho' kinda surprised he's not wearin' gang colors.

"Move your butt, Caleb … *Now!*" blasted Coach with a rock-steady arm pointing toward the nearest door.

He blew a sloppy, noisy smooch at Coach that sounded more like a raspberry. Cocking his cap forward, he waved a quick farewell in Nevaeh's direction.

With her hand welded to her waist, Nevaeh returned a covert wave in the homeboy's direction.

Jasmine bit her lip, stifling the guffaw that wanted to burst out.

You gotta be kiddin'. The captain and that douche?

Jasmine lobbed the ball to the nearest girl and folded her arms over her diaphragm, hoping to clamp down the laughter it was still trying to push out. The ball drummed loudly on the baseboards once, before Madison caught it.

Jasmine inhaled, the urge to explode having vanished, when she spied the young stranger staring at her.

A hungry leer splashed across Caleb's face. He blew a silent kiss, this time with his eyes locked with Jasmine's, and his hand pointing straight at her like a finger gun. His crooked smile never wavered as he ambled toward the exit.

Nevaeh followed Caleb's line of sight, spinning to face Jasmine with an expression that could blister a cactus. Jasmine deflected it with a curt shrug of indifference, before turning away in search of the ball.

Madison lumbered past, spinning the ball in her hands. With her chin pressed down so hard, her already impressive jowls squished further out, she muttered, "Don't get between those two. Caleb's bad news. And Nevaeh ain't gonna stand for it."

"Yeah, I can see that."

"*Vaminos.* Keep movin', ace," Coach goaded the dark figure as the door closed behind him. She blew a long trill on her whistle and faced the squads, trying to paste a happy face over her lingering anger. She pulled the ball from Madison's sweaty palms. "Okay, girls, back to it. Show me whatcha got."

Coach signaled to Nevaeh and Jasmine. The second they took their face-off positions, she tooted a fast couplet on her whistle, and threw a high tip-off.

Nevaeh jumped a full hand above Jasmine, copped the ball and zoomed down the court, with Jasmine in close pursuit. A quick dribble was followed by a feint, then a pass to one of the teammates whose name Jasmine had missed from roll call.

Spotting her opening, Jasmine dove in and intercepted the ball when the girl tried to pass it back to Nevaeh for the layup. Smiling at the cusses spilling from Nevaeh's mouth, Jasmine angled sharply and dashed back down the court. With a quick two-step, she soaked in the wondrous moment when she reached her sweet spot just outside the three-point line.

A rip along her arm, and sharp poke in her ribs knocked her out of the zone. Tripping one foot over the other, she rolled onto her side. Glancing up, she spotted Trinity and her blocker from first squad, both were dodging for position and swinging the arms high, blocking Coach's line of sight.

Nevaeh's designer kicks dashed past her head. She aimed a derisive giggle at her fallen opponent. Dribbling the ball down the court with any defense far behind, she sank her own two-point shot with ease.

Coach's loud and long screaming whistle trounced the chorus of sneaker screeches on the floorboards. "Awright, who fouled Jasmine?"

Jasmine frowned at the sudden vacuum. No one spoke as she hauled herself upright. Her ribs barked with a stabbing squeeze. She rubbed at the red scratches along her outer shoulder.

I guess Nevaeh does remember that game. Okay, sweetness—we're even. But that's all you get.

"Who's got the ball? Take your foul shots, Jasmine."

Jasmine was satisfied with two out of three foul shots made, and relieved that the remaining minutes of practice were uneventful.

Coach blew a long song-like warble on her whistle and gathered the eight girls together. "Okay, team—good practice. I saw a lot of hustle out there. I'll post the new arrangement for next game's first squad and fill-in tonight. Now hit the showers."

Jasmine showered quickly, uncomfortable under the pressure of another round of searchlight stares in the locker room. A few curt "see-ya"s were exchanged, but Jasmine found she could finally exhale only after she was dressed and out the door. Her ribs reminded her not to exhale like that again.

I had to stand my ground and represent, but I think I made more enemies than friends. Maybe next practice will be better. Gotta make nice tomorrow, or it's gonna be a bitch.

CHAPTER TWO

Jasmine stomped around the kitchen table, her threadbare pink bathrobe flapping around her legs. She strangled an outdated flip-phone in one hand, while her homework fluttered in the other.

No one's gonna help me, not after yesterday.

She convinced herself that her supposed friends at school already had paragraphs filled out for each question on yesterday's assignment. Jasmine's answers stared back at her—a phrase here, a half-sentence there. And all of them clear evidence that World History was still her worst subject.

And no one from Eastern could help me. Not even if they wanted to. I thought they'd be happy for me, getting outta the Projects. But they turned ugly on me. Not the happiest of partings.

She shook her head to rip out those cobwebs. Glancing once more at her phone, worry stretched Jasmine's lips thin. Although she had pleaded for help by text several times last night to any student who had bothered to trade numbers, not a single answer had come back. She frowned at the stove clock—less than an hour until the last metro bus before the school doors closed.

Mrs. Fieldings, a slender woman with salt-and-pepper box braids and a mahogany face aged by a cruel and relentless sun, sat at the table.

She blinked as she followed Jasmine stalking a circle around the kitchen.

"Sit, child. Or you'll make poor ol' Bibi dizzy."

Jasmine glanced at Bibi. Before she could stop herself, she plopped in the metal tube and plastic chair across from the old woman. The two patches where the pink fuzz of her bathrobe had worn down to bare nylon mesh chilled her rump.

Bibi's eyes fixed her with an arresting gaze and a half-smile that bespoke the Wisdom of the Ages. Bibi's "Look," a gentle but compelling exclamation point, made her request an irresistible command.

Ma has her Look, but Bibi's gets me every time.

Jasmine dangled a spoon above her bowl of cold oatmeal and stared between her flip-phone and her frayed history textbook. The phone came to life with a ping, displaying the name "Akilah" across a large crack in its screen. Her hopes of help with homework evaporated.

Cripes. She's not gonna help. She's Nevaeh's flunky, and the last person I want to talk to. Not after yesterday.

Wondering what new torments awaited her at school, her pleading eyes wandered across the kitchen table past Bibi. With her chin resting in a cupped hand, Jasmine exhaled a petulant sigh overflowing with melodrama.

Bibi's reply was a raised single gray eyebrow while pouring herself a steaming mugful of white whisper tea. She studied the moping girl across from her, then plonked down the teapot, startling Jasmine.

"Out with it, *Jazz-meen*, dear," she said with a wink. "You can tell ol' Bibi."

Jasmine returned a "whatever" shrug of her shoulders and shoveled a soggy glob of oatmeal into her mouth. She slid her homework and books into her backpack.

Bibi lifted a jar of honey out of a large woven handbag, with a cross-stitched pattern depicting a lioness peering above tall grasses with a small multi-colored lizard crouching on its shoulder. She ladled a spoonful of honey darker than roasted cinnamon onto Jasmine's breakfast, then another into her tea as she regarded the pouting youngster.

"Or you can tell your *muuther* when she gets home." Her Tanzanian accent made it sound both like a plea and punishment. It was Bibi's turn to shrug when Jasmine's phone bleeped again, announcing a new text had arrived, this time from Nevaeh.

Crap. She and her gang's gonna ride my butt. All day.

Jasmine swiped its screen to open the messages, but withdrew her hand as Bibi's thin, woody finger levered the top of the flip-phone closed.

"It is them again, isn't it? The ones who *say* they are your friends."

Jasmine flashed indignant eyes at Bibi for daring to intrude on her electronic Holy of Holies, but she relented. She could never stay mad at this gentle, happy woman from downstairs. In the two weeks since Jasmine and her mother had moved into this apartment complex, Bibi charmed her way into heart and home, becoming the grandmother she never had ...

"Just call me Bibi," Mrs. Fieldings had insisted when Jasmine returned from that first day at the new school to find this strange woman chatting with Ma over this very table. "That's what I called my *grahnt-muuther*—she was my *bibi*," she said with a nostalgic grin.

The Projects had taught Jasmine to mistrust anyone and everyone. But with a wave of her hand, Bibi could sweep all the problems of the world out of sight and out of mind. These days, it would be unusual if Bibi wasn't sharing breakfast with her until Ma got home ...

"Yeah, it's them again," Jasmine began with a plaintive sigh. "Yesterday was bad. I tried to make nice all day, but nobody wants to be around someone from the Projects." Her words tumbled out faster and faster, like a stream toward a waterfall.

"Some kids got on my case 'cause we're so poor. They dissed me 'cause I got Ma's cheapo phone. Then at lunch, everyone saw I got the crap meal—the one you get when you can't buy the regular one. I sat with Akilah, 'cause she's on my basketball team. But you could tell she wanted to be anyplace else." Jasmine stabbed her oatmeal with her spoon. "I tried to talk about practice the day before yesterday, but she pretended nothin' happened. I switched to classes, trying to find out what she likes, hoping we could help each other out. But all she wanted to talk about was boys. It was like she wanted to make me feel low on purpose, 'cause she and Nevaeh have so-o-o many friends, and I'm the new kid and don't know nobody. Then Nevaeh and the rest of her posse piled in, and all she talked about was her boyfriend, Caleb. More like she was warning me away. I can't figure out why she's worried about me. I don't want nothin' to do with that bozo. He's bad news."

Bibi stopped swirling her tea. "What do you mean?"

"He made eyes at me during practice the other day, and that got me on Nevaeh's bad side. Then there's the stuff I picked up in the halls. He's got a hard-on for anyone with tits."

Bibi made a small burbling sound in her tea, and a drop dribbled down her mug.

"But that's not the half of it. Nevaeh brags he's in a gang, one of the really nasty ones. Dunno which one, he never wears colors. But I heard he was in a buncha robberies. Maybe even a murder. Everyone says he does drugs, sometimes the heavy shit."

Bibi rapped her spoon on the table. "*Jazz-meen* Price! Don't let your *muuther* hear you talk like that. Remember what she said yesterday. 'Only people with a four IQ use four-letter words.'"

"Sorry," rushed out of Jasmine's mouth. "But why would Nevaeh think I want anything to do with that assho– ... that jerk?" She stuck out her tongue and mocked a retch. "If I wanted to hook up with any-one like him, I woulda stayed in the Projects."

Bibi looked at her bag with a pensive frown, then petted the diminutive lizard on the lioness' back with her index finger. "Sometimes girls are attracted to bad men," she said with a faraway stare aimed at her open hand.

Jasmine's eyes were drawn to an age-old scar that cut diagonally across the folds of Bibi's palm.

With a shake of her head, the placid Bibi returned, inhaling the vapors of steaming tea laced with honey. "Oh, never mind him. You were talking about lunchtime. Then what happened?"

"Seven of us were squeezed at our table. Then a teacher stops by and says there were too many. 'Who was the last to arrive?' she asks." Jasmine planted her cheekbone against her fist and sulked. "They all pointed at me, even Nevaeh. But I was there before them!"

"Oh, the young people there just don't know you like we do."

"They know enough." Jasmine pulled aside the flap of her bathrobe, and rolled up the bottom of her T-shirt, revealing an angry purple blotch. "I transferred to this stupid school just two weeks ago, and I'm already on a ton of people's shi– ... not-their-favorite list."

Bibi's eyebrows knit together in a harsh downward arrow. "Child, where on earth did you get that from?"

"Practice two days ago, after Caleb gave me the eye. Nevaeh elbowed me to the floor when I was doin' a layup. Of course, Coach didn't see who did it." Jasmine gingerly rubbed her robe over her injured ribs with a wince. "The girls on the basketball team are the worst."

"Nevaeh again?" Bibi leaned forward in her chair with her arms folded. She projected the fervor of a lioness protecting her cubs.

"But that wasn't all. Akilah, Nevaeh, and the others picked a fight with me after school."

"Why? Because of Nevaeh and her boyfriend?"

"Nah, because of basketball. I hoped I was going to be on first squad, but Coach put me on fill-in for tonight's game. Nevaeh and her posse wanted to make sure I know my place." Jasmine set her shoulders firm in a defensive hunch. She lifted the sleeve of her robe, uncovering day-old scratches that still glowed red and tender. "Like I said, the girls in basketball are the worst."

"Oh, my. That looks terrible. Your *muuther* seen those, or your bruise?"

Jasmine shook her head. "She put some ice on my ribs, but it didn't help much."

The front door squawked open, and down went Jasmine's sleeve. She leaned back from the table to see her mother closing the front door.

Ma shambled in, as dilapidated as their kitchen. She greeted them with a warm smile, but a hint of desperation glistened in her wet eyes.

Jasmine had seen that look before, when Dad was deployed overseas. Ma's hard-as-nails determination had taken one too many hits, and even the strongest dam will break under enough pressure. Jasmine's toes curled in anticipation of bad news.

"Missus Price, you're home early," Bibi said, between sips of her tea. "Your boss let you come … *Ai*, honey, what's wrong?"

Ma shrank an inch as her brave face abandoned her. She hung her day bag on the back of the chair between Jasmine and Bibi, and sat.

"The workshop was shut down."

"What?" Jasmine and Bibi exclaimed in unison. Bibi set her mug on the table with a harsh *thunk*.

"ICE bust in. They took half the workers. Said they were illegals. So many of them were women I was just getting to know. I hoped some could be good friends. Now they're gone, just like that," she said, with a distracted snap of her fingers. Ma looked at Jasmine with sorrow-filled eyes. "Then the cops carted away the boss, too. The whole shop is shut down. Locked up. So they don't need no seamstress no more."

Ma broke down in a pile of sobs, propped up by shaky elbows.

"There, there," said Bibi, squeezing Ma's arm. She tried to console her with a musical lilt wrapped around sweet inspirations leading onward and upward toward a brighter future. Jasmine abandoned her breakfast and hugged her mother.

Ma's smile would surface for a moment or two, only to submerge back into an ocean of tears. "No way I'm gonna get paid now. How am I gonna make ends meet? I gotta find me another second job again. But I can't take time off from my daytime job to do that." Her sadness was infectious. Jasmine fought back her own weeping with a fence of sniffles.

"I *so* needed that day job. The hotel work doesn't pay enough. Housing at the base is all taken, and Damon's pay is already garnished, so it barely covers the new rent. And Jasmine—I wanted her to have a better school, and away from … If we gotta go back to the Projects …"

Her last word pitched headlong into another cascade of wailing emotion.

"Don't worry yourself none, Missus Price. Things will work out. That's what Bibi is here for. There ain't no Mr. Fieldings no more, so I have plenty of time to help out." Bibi put her wiry arm around Ma and hugged her close, nudging her until they rocked back and forth. "We have each *uuther*, and we never give up."

"One foot in front of the other. Right, Ma?" said Jasmine in a breathy whisper. "I could skip school and find some—"

"No! Don't you dare!" Ma barked, her face streaked with wetness. "You wanna end up like Dad and me? We work hard at cruddy jobs because we dropped out. No way you're doin' the same."

Bibi gazed at Jasmine and cooed with a reassuring nod over Ma's sniffles. "We all got problems, child. But first things first. We'll sort out your *muuther*, then see what we can do for you." A decisive nod of affirmation, and Bibi's attention returned to Ma.

"Tell you what, Missus Price—I'll walk Jasmine to her bus stop, and fetch today's paper from Parker's Corner Store." Bibi gave Ma's shoulder a playful tap, and her voice blossomed with renewed optimism. "Then you and I, we'll go through the want ads, and find you a new job."

After a few hurried clicks, Jasmine held up her phone to show Ma. A list of job agencies printed on its screen, slow as a snail. "We can also look at these places. My phone's too old to do much online, but we can try the computers at the library."

"Good idea." Bibi squinted at the tiny cracked screen. "But I'm no good with those gadgets. We'll try the library, if we first can't find anything in the paper."

Bibi fussed around Ma and Jasmine like a bee about her hive—getting tea, straightening up the kitchen. And smiling, always smiling.

When Ma's trembling jowls signaled another fall into despair, Bibi brought out her dog-eared wallet photo album. She leafed through the collection, until she found a picture of her son embracing his wife and daughter.

"They're gonna have another *beh-bee* in a few months," she beamed. "Won't that be *grahnt?*"

The photo helped cheer up Ma, but it dredged up an emptiness deep inside Jasmine. She brought up her only family picture on her hand-me-down phone. Her shoulders slumped with a sigh. The flip-phone's screen was too small, too grainy, and its crack splayed directly over Dad's blurred face.

"*Ai*, look at the time, child," said Bibi. "Change your clothes for school, while I go downstairs to collect my purse and things. We have so much to do before you catch your bus." Bibi put her honey jar back into her bag, and let loose a single chuckle at the sight of Jasmine wolfing down the dregs of her breakfast.

"I'll be right back with the paper after I see Jasmine off, Missus Price. Don't you worry none. Take a shower, you'll feel worlds better. And ol' Bibi will be back before you know it." Opening the front doorway, Bibi pointed at the small pile of junk on a tray inches from her hip. "And don't forget your keys again, Jasmine."

Jasmine swept into her bedroom, threw off her ratty pink bathrobe and changed into her only pair of jeans and the cleanest top she could find. Checking her scant makeup in her bedroom mirror, she frowned at her hair. Frizzed and unruly, the best she could do was bunch it together with an old hairband. She breezed through the kitchen and planted a quick peck on Ma's cheek.

"It'll be okay, Ma. I'll do good in school. Promise." Jasmine wondered how comforted Ma would be, considering how hollow her words sounded in her own ears.

Shouldering her backpack, Jasmine cast a worried eye at her mother. Ma's hang-dog trudge toward the bathroom answered her question. Down three flights of stairs like a whirlwind, Jasmine whisked to Bibi's ground-floor apartment, bounding down the last five steps in a single leap.

Bibi opened her door, midway through donning her spring jacket. "Come in, dear. I'm a little slow. Just a few more things to collect."

Jasmine stepped in, closing the door behind her.

Jeez, how long does it take to get ready for a bodega run?

Bibi's apartment smelled like old person. Something else lingered there, too, covered by layers of old lavender, wintergreen, and disinfectant. But compared with her and Ma's grungy apartment, Bibi's front room was surprisingly bright, decorated with equal parts tried-and-true Americana and colorful items that spoke of Bibi's home in Tanzania. Throughout the apartment were a smattering of plants, the likes of which Jasmine had never seen before.

"But first, I have a confession to make, *Jazz-meen,*" Bibi said through a sheepish grin. "There's another reason I asked you down here. I have a little friend who would like to meet you." She stood next to a squat table holding a glass terrarium the size of a breadbox. Filled with miniature versions of the plants that graced her apartment, the diminutive forest devoured what little light it could glean from the living room window barricaded with a rusting exterior grate.

Jasmine's stomach twinged with uneasiness. "We're not allowed to have pets."

"Ho-ho," Bibi dismissed the thought with a chuckle and a wave of her gnarled hand. "What the Super doesn't know won't hurt him. Besides, my friend almost never comes out. And I don't bring him out, except to say hello to new friends."

Jasmine inched warily over to the glass enclosure and peered down through a coarse hardware cloth screen weighted down with a thumb piano—a *mbira,* Bibi called it on the one occasion she brought it to breakfast. Bobbing her head back and forth, Jasmine peered through the metal mesh and glass. The only sign of movement was a large fly skittering inside the front glass wall.

There's moss, some orchids, a small log, a water dish, but nothing else. Wait ... that log moved.

Jasmine jumped when a flash of glistening pink, half the length of the log, shot out. It slapped against the enclosure, pinning the fly against the glass wall. Just as quickly, the slimy pink flesh popped back into a waiting V-shaped umber mouth. Jasmine's ears twitched when its jaws clamped down on the bulbous fly with a strangely satisfying crunch.

What Jasmine took to be part of the log changed from a lifeless brown to battleship gray. Three horns protruded from the front of a lizard's head, above a wide gaping mouth that ended in a slight frown as it munched on the fly's carcass. A saw-toothed ridge ran down its back, and four five-toed claws gripped the log. Two beady eyes, sunk into a pair of leathery pebbled cones, darted this way and that.

Jasmine's mouth hung open at the sight of those swiveling eyes— first one eye up and the other down, then the right eye pointing ahead while the left swept backward. Intrigued by this impossible animal, she continued to gape as it swallowed the mangled remains of the insect. Before her eyes, it changed from dull steel gray to a tantalizing lumines-cent green that brightened the whole window.

"Cool, did you see that?" Jasmine blurted with wonder. "It changed colors! What is it?"

"A *ka-mee-lay-ohn*. He changes colors all the time. That's how he communicates ... well, one of the ways." Bibi shook her head as though to shake away a mental cobweb, before her gentle smile returned. "Green means he's well fed."

"Where did you get it ... uh, *him*?"

"Oh, he came with me from my home, when Mr. Fieldings brought me to America. We're not to bring such things through cus-toms, you understand. But there he was, hiding in Mr. Fieldings's suit-case, curled around a leather belt. In my country, he's called a *kinyonga*, but my *bibi* named him *Roho Kinyonga Mlin*—" Bibi's jaw shut with a clack loud enough to make Jasmine's own teeth ache.

"*Ai*, I bit my tongue." Bibi dabbed her mouth with a finger, inspecting it for blood. "Oh, it makes no matter what we called him. I doubt you could pronounce it, anyway. Whatever name you come up with, it won't make no nevermind to him," she said with a nervous tit-ter. With a smile and her Look, she added, "Now hold out your arm ..."

Jasmine's left arm floated up from her side, as though it had a mind of its own. Bibi lifted the *mbira* and screen off the cage and dug her hand into the leafy tapestry. "Come on out now, you little trickster. Say hello to *Jazz-meen* properly."

Jasmine scrunched up her face, giggling with trepidation, as the chameleon latched on like slow-motion handcuffs. Two rear claws clamped on her wrist, and a thick sandpaper tail slowly coiled around her thumb. Front claws the size of a quarter grasped either side of her arm near her elbow.

"Ooh, that feels weird," Jasmine warbled as a thrill ran up her back. She raised her arm to look the chameleon straight in the eyes—one of them, anyway. "Hello there," she said with a bashful snicker.

The curious lizard flashed to a full radiant yellow.

"Oh-ho, he's taken a shine to you," Bibi said between chortles. "Yellow means he's happy."

As the creature inched past Jasmine's left elbow, its plodding, methodical gait mesmerized her. She thought it might even be smiling at her.

"He ate a huge fly just now. What else do they eat?"

"All sorts of things, child. Bugs, worms, snails. Even humming-birds, the poor dears." Bibi's head drooped to stare at an end table piled with knickknacks bookended by a pair of framed photographs. Her smile sagged to a thoughtful frown. "All ... sorts of things," she trailed off wistfully, ending with a hitch in her voice.

Bibi stood silently, her shoulders sagging. Glum as a funeral mourner, she seemed to age ten years. She took a step toward the table, her shaky hand reaching behind a framed picture of a young man dressed in a graduation gown and mortarboard. Jasmine smiled with recognition at Bibi's son, his broad toothy smile spreading ear to ear under high cheekbones that were unmistakably his mother's.

From behind that photograph Bibi pulled another picture—a faded photo of memories past, bordered by a black walnut frame. Jasmine tried to snatch a peek of the photo, but Bibi held it close to her heart, and the beginnings of a sob made her bosom twitch.

The chameleon's eyes flitted, pointing backward, fixed on the black picture frame. His fore claws pinched Jasmine's arm, and the serrated ridge along his back stood at attention while it shifted to a mottled red.

She blinked at Bibi with concern. "What's wrong?"

The weathered woman placed the frame face down on its table. Her momentary sadness vanished, replaced by a stern gaze that pressed her lips flat and bloodless. "Nothing, little one."

And just as quickly, her steely mask was whisked away with a sniff of her nose and a click of her tongue. "*Ai*, look at me, getting all mushy when you have a bus to catch. And I still have to lay my hands on my purse." Her voice faded as she disappeared into her kitchenette, as small as Ma's but with touches of bright colors that made it happier and homier.

Jasmine nearly jumped out of her socks when something gripped her other arm.

Looking down, Jasmine blurted, "What the—?"

The chameleon had moved.

His head rested on the back of her right hand, and his tail wrapped around her elbow.

Jasmine winced as the lizard's claws pinched her forearm. His vibrant yellow and red hide had transformed to a blue so brilliant, it seemed to contain its own light.

"How did you switch to my other arm?" she said with a startled laugh.

"What was that you said, child?" came Bibi's carefree reply from the kitchen between the clatter of utensils being shuffled about.

"I said, he somehow moved to my other arm while I wasn't look-ing," Jasmine called out, craning her neck toward Bibi's voice, but keep-ing her eyes riveted on the curious lizard.

Bibi emerged out of the kitchen, all smiles and dropping a small purse into her lioness handbag. Her familiar laugh rang out, "Oh-ho! You'll find that trickster can do some amazing things." She skidded to an abrupt stop. Stark eyes like Ping-Pong balls fused on the sapphire-hued lizard.

Jasmine's own smile fizzled. She tentatively raised her wobbly arm toward Bibi while she glanced between the chameleon and the old woman. Clearing her throat with a tremulous note of uncertainty, she asked, "Umm, what does blue mean?"

Bibi blinked and took a deep quivering breath. "I … I am not sure, child," she said. "I have only seen that once before."

The roar of a diesel engine with one misfiring piston rattled the window.

"*Ai*, here we are dawdling, and your bus will be here any minute. We must hurry." Bibi pried the lizard off Jasmine's arm with both hands. Jasmine rubbed the four indentations on her forearm—the skin itched but was not broken.

Bibi held the chameleon to her face and said, "Now you behave, you little troublemaker." As if she might be laying a baby in its crib, she deposited the chameleon on his log. Once she placed the *mbira* back on top of the metal screen, Bibi became energy personified—locking her front door and scooting Jasmine outside the apartment building. "Now, let's hurry along."

With a lighthearted grin, Jasmine gave the chameleon a small wave through the grated window. It stared back like a taxidermist's prize display.

Jasmine marched along in a springy quickstep, but every half-block she paused to wait for Bibi to catch up. She pouted at the old woman who was a conundrum wrapped in contradictions.

First she's in a hurry, now she's sauntering along while she soaks in the sun. First she's happy and carefree, then has those weird flashes of mystery.

Jasmine said a nervous "hello" to a group of classmates as they walked by. Most of them had their noses buried in their cellphones, though one girl telegraphed an unmistakable "you're-gonna-get-it" smirk straight at her.

She was one of the girls that squeezed me off the table. How many soljahs does Nevaeh have?

Jasmine jogged ahead of Bibi to the end of the block, halting at the bus stop in front of Parker's Corner Store—a rundown bodega that was the last holdout surrounded by rows of "Out of Business" and "For Sale" signs. She took out her flip-phone and waited for the old relic to connect to the bodega's free wi-fi. After a few faltering mis-spelled attempts, the phone dribbled out a few photographs of chameleons. They loaded at such a tortured pace, they might have been hand drawn faster. Scrolling through the meager results, she spotted a three-horned critter just like the one that had clamped on her arm.

Trioceros jacksonii—the Jackson's Chameleon.

She showed the phone to Bibi the moment she caught up. "How's this? I'll call him Jackson."

"Oh-ho, that's fine, *Jazz-meen*. I like that name, and I think he will like it too." Her words were almost drowned out by the grumbling of a poorly maintained engine and hiss of air brakes of the approaching metro bus. It stopped in front of the bodega, and a crowd of students and grown-ups crammed around its doors.

"Now you hurry along and have a good day at school. Don't let those wannabe friends get under your skin. And don't you worry about your *muuther*. I'm sure we'll find something in the paper." With her all-knowing wink, Bibi added with a farewell wave, "I believe we might even get her an interview today. Which means we'll need some new makeup. Maybe I'll lend her mine ..."

Jasmine waved from the lowest step, and her smile persisted as she swept her school card though the metro reader.

However, Jasmine's happy demeanor evaporated when she looked down the aisle for empty seats.

Nevaeh, Akilah, Trinity, and two others of their exclusive circle were planted in the back row. They all wore smug sneers, except for Madison, who was saddled with a worried frown.

Jasmine caught herself staring too long at Nevaeh's tricked-out clothes that walked straight out of an Abercrombie & Fitch storefront. Her envious eyes danced over Nevaeh's new gold chain necklace, adorned with the heavy steel and gold ring emblazoned with a large letter "C," and a flawless chocolate complexion framed by black hair relaxed to perfection with just the right touch of curl at the ends, tinted with blue and gold. Clothes, bling, the glam, and a perm—all together, it had to cost more than a month's rent.

I wish … Aw, no way Ma could spring for any of that.

Jasmine pulled down the edge of her out-of-fashion blouse culled from a charity thrift store. She rubbed the back of her neck, chasing a self-conscious itch that crawled up her spine. The chaotic frizz of her unkempt hair, bunched up by a too-small hair band, irritated the back of her hand.

Where the heck does she get the dough for all that?

Nevaeh pierced Jasmine with a contempt that could melt her flip-phone. Akilah glanced in her direction for only a moment, but her expression screamed disdain. Trinity peered with laughing eyes over her notebook, labeled proudly with her name. Both of the I's were dotted with little hearts.

Jasmine plunked herself down in an empty window seat, with her back to Nevaeh and her minions.

Boxed in by strangers, she imagined the weight of the eyes of every student pressing down on her—except for the kids within speaking distance, who focused on their cellphones as if their lives hung in the balance. Jasmine had little doubt they preferred to hide in the safety of the internet, rather than risk eye contact or actually *talk* to the new kid. With a sigh, she extracted her own worn-down phone from her pocket and joined the circle of silence. She tried to coax more information about chameleons from the doddering old device, but its molasses-in-Alaska progress ground to a stone-cold halt a block away from Parker's.

Her phone pinged with a new text message from a number she

had never seen before. It rang again and again in rapid succession. Jasmine's heart sloshed into her stomach when she opened the messages.

"No Projects ho's on b-ball"
"Head lice epidemic on the b-ball team"
"With that hair, Jizz-min must be Patient Zero"
"If we lose tonite, it's Jizm's fault"

A chorus of giggles from the back of the bus was drowned out by the roar of the diesel engine. She clapped the phone shut and shoved it in her backpack's pocket. Right next to …

Great. The start of another wonderful day. And I forgot my keys again.

CHAPTER THREE

The bruise over Jasmine's obliques screamed whenever she jumped to shoot or block. Her shots bounced off the rim. She couldn't keep up with the opponents she was assigned to guard. But what stung worse than the side-sticker where Nevaeh had jabbed her was that Coach Garcia benched her the last half of the night's inner-city league game.

Her cheers from the sidelines were anemic as well, thanks to her aching ribs and the gym's humidity sucking her meager energy out of her. Jasmine's team barely held it together when she was on the court. And despite the best efforts of short and chubby Madison, they lost by a landslide. The spirits of everyone on her team were miles away from festive.

Between plays, Jasmine scanned the audience for Ma.

Nah, she's probably still at her interview. It's just as well, the way this game has gone down the toilet.

After the final buzzer, Nevaeh sidled over to Jasmine as she trudged back to the home team locker room. "I'm sorry about yesterday," she said nodding toward Jasmine's ribs as she toweled sweat from her neck.

Jasmine stopped in her tracks at the end of the bleachers, as the departing crowd of students and parents milled around them.

Nevaeh is being ... nice to me?

Team shrimp Madison squeezed her way past the two girls toward the locker room, followed by the tail end of the first squad. "Way to go, Fatty-son," they grumbled behind her back.

"I really feel bad about it, Jasmine. Caleb drives me nuts sometimes. I feel like I made you lose the game." Her sweet voice and disarming smile tugged at Jasmine as they walked to the lockers. "I'll make it up to you. I'll ask Coach about putting you back in first squad for next week's game. If you're feeling up to it, of course."

"That would be awesome," Jasmine said. Somewhere in the back of her head, something didn't add up. Nevertheless, Jasmine scrambled for a compliment to offer in return. "You were really hot with your rebou—"

Nevaeh split off down her row of lockers, unheedful of the olive branch Jasmine had offered her. Instead, she dove into an animated conversation with other squad-mates.

With a shrug and an *I-shoulda-known-better* half-smile, Jasmine continued to her locker. She peeled off her sweaty uniform and headed toward the showers.

At the end of her aisle, she was snagged by another girl. Jasmine blinked with surprise at Akilah—she had already changed into her street clothes.

She must've sprinted through the shower.

"Wow, Nevaeh apologized?" Akilah said, her eyes wide with wonder.

"Guess so. She said she was sorry."

"That's amazing. What else did she say?"

Jasmine recounted the conversation in a stumbling manner, while Akilah listened with intent concentration, prompting her repeatedly for more details.

"Then what did she say?" Akilah asked.

That's the fourth time she's asked that.

Not only was Akilah's stream of questions shallow and repetitive, but Jasmine picked up the same vibe from her that she got from Nevaeh. Her eyes narrowed to size up Akilah's ulterior motives.

"Tell ya later. I gotta wash up and get home."

Nevaeh and a few other girls left the shower room as Jasmine entered. Nevaeh flashed Jasmine her magazine model smile, but the other girls were too busy chatting to pay her any attention.

She rushed through her shower. She still didn't feel very clean, as most of the soap had been used up. Jasmine grabbed a towel and returned to her locker aisle, but was met with a line of empty benches —the girls in her row were already dressed and gone. Her fists squeezed tighter than her stomach when she spotted her combination lock. It was undone, and the locker door was ajar.

She tightened her towel around her midsection and dashed down the aisle, her sopping wet feet squishing the non-skid mats against the concrete floor. She flung the locker wide open, fearing that everything would be stolen. But a quick rifling through her stuff found all her things were still accounted for—blouse, backpack, flip-phone, socks rolled in her shoes, jeans ...

Jasmine pulled out her panties from the crumpled jeans. Her lower lip trembled.

The crotch of the panties was soaked red. They cradled an open vial filled with food coloring. The bright red stain had leaked onto the front of her pants as well.

A snicker echoing over the wall of lockers grew into an avalanche of sadistic belly laughs. Jasmine ran between the bench and lockers to the end of the aisle, only in time to catch the locker room door click shut with finality. The receding laughter and name-calling by Nevaeh, Akilah, and who-knows-who-else filtered under the doors.

Crying in silence except for the occasional strangled sob, she tamped out her clothes in extra towels to squeeze out the last wetness and prevent the stain from spreading further. She dressed, pausing before putting on her jacket, instead tying its arms around her waist over the patch of red.

Jasmine crept close to Coach's office window. Not wanting anyone else to know the cruel joke played on her, she held her breath as she padded past yellowed blinds louvered halfway shut. Coach Garcia faced her chalkboard, writing names and stats.

It wasn't the embarrassment alone that angered Jasmine—it was the added frustration that whining to Coach would only make things worse in the long run. Holding a pile of crimson-splotched towels at arms' length, she dropped them into the hamper.

Jasmine trembled, her fists clenched with resolve, in front of the locker room doors. When she could stop shaking, she wiped her face dry and opened the door.

They will not see me cry.

With her head down, she zoomed past a janitor tackling the Herculean task of cleaning up mounds of post-game trash and rivers of spills around the bleachers. A few girls from the opposing school still filtered out of the visitors' locker room. As each turned the corner to the street exit, they ran the gauntlet of Caleb's radar.

Aw, dammit. Him, too?

His easy smile drew their attention away from his lust-filled eyes as he chatted up every pair of legs that strolled, jogged, or paraded by. Jasmine searched for another exit, but not before she cringed at Caleb's shout echoing throughout the gym.

"Jasmine—Hey, girl, where you goin' so fast?"

"Home," she replied flatly, burning him with a scowl intended to scream "Go Away" to anyone with half a brain. Nevertheless, after Jasmine did a U-turn, Caleb's kicks squeaked on the court floorboards catching up from behind. Before she could make it to the far exit, Caleb jumped in front her, his arm barring the way.

"By yourself? Now why's a fine lookin' beauty like you headin' home all alone?"

Jasmine wanted to shove past him, but the dampness beneath her jacket reminded her to play it cool. She gritted her teeth with a quiet growl as she focused on the exit behind Caleb.

Through their doors stormed Nevaeh. Her expression transformed in a heartbeat from surprise to raw hatred. Though her eyes bounced between the two of them, Jasmine couldn't mistake Nevaeh's glares of unfiltered malice reserved for her.

Jasmine nodded past Caleb's shoulder. "I think there's someone else who wants to talk to you."

He spun around. Jasmine held back a snicker at the garish, stylized "C" logo on his cap glowing with gold embroidered thread.

With open arms, his best smile, and without a tinge of shame, Caleb beamed, "Babe! There you are. We was lookin' for you."

Jasmine took advantage of the distraction to double back again. She smiled at the argument pitching to a rolling boil behind her.

They deserve each other.

At the corner of the school, a pair of sweating parents corralled a foursome from the home team into an idling metro bus. A smaller group from the other team and their apprehensive chaperone thought better of sharing the crowded ride and waited for the next bus.

I really don't want to deal with anyone from either team right now. And I'm screwed if Caleb and Queen Nevaeh get me in a squeeze play here. If the rest of the team shows up, they'd probably be on Nevaeh's side too.

She turned her head to glare at the antiquated cameras angled to cover the meager courtyard and the crowds it contained.

And those things are no good. It's the school's worst-kept secret that their security system goes up and down like a yo-yo.

With a stiff inhale to steel her resolve, Jasmine set off on the long walk home. She gave the residential block around the school the once over, clenching her jaw at the deceptively innocent beginning to the gauntlet ahead of her. At least, by following the bus route, she wouldn't get lost in the darkness of her unfamiliar new neighborhood.

A scant number of well-kept house façades soon gave way to crowds of boarded-up windows. Broken glass crunched under her shoes. Within the span of one block, flattened energy drink cans were replaced with empty beer cans.

Spasmodic fluorescents from Mom-n-Pop stores made the streets jitter against the late Saturday evening sky. In a neon collision of rhythms, barrooms flashed the names of brews that their regulars had vomited into concrete stairwells, or whizzed into side streets. Krylon tags of artists and gangs making their mark in the world shouted across every vertical surface.

Compared to the Projects, this is a cakewalk.

But I can't let my guard down. Gotta stay on my toes.

Jasmine gripped the straps of her backpack. Her forearms burned from the effort, almost as much as her ribs ached during the disastrous game.

Another city bus rolled past Jasmine, and the welcome stink of diesel drowned out the acrid odors oozing from the stairwells and alleys. She scanned the faces of passengers in the pallid bus interior lights as they flashed on by. A few team members straggled inside this bus, but neither Akilah nor Nevaeh was in her usual rear seat. And no sign of Caleb.

Maybe they caught a different bus. Or they're still arguing.

While she waited for a crosswalk light, Jasmine's phone hummed against her thigh. She pulled it from her pants pocket, careful not to move the tied jacket and expose the red secret it hid. She responded to the unknown number on the screen with a skeptical sneer.

If this is another of Nevaeh's goons, I'm gonna—

"I got the job!" Ma's voice blasted out of the tiny speaker.

Jasmine grimaced and jerked her head away from the saw-toothed squeal of victory. "What? Where?"

"One of those upper end coffee places. It's a dream come true! Whaddya think of that?"

Before Jasmine had a chance to reply, Ma's excited voice continued to rattle out of the phone.

"I can't talk long, Jazz. They want me to start tomorrow night. Isn't that great? Oh, but Jazz, I'm sorry I missed your game, my interview ran late. Oh, and you forgot your keys at home again. Just wait for me at Bibi's. I'll be back as soon as I can. Oops—my new boss needs his phone back. Gotta go." The call ended with Ma's tinny laugh.

"That's great, Ma," Jasmine said without enthusiasm to a dark phone.

Yeah, great—she got the job. More nights home alone with no one to talk to.

The light changed, and seemingly endless lines of cars squealed to a stop. Their impatient engines revved as though they were doing the pedestrians a favor by permitting them to cross. Behind the shadows of a mom and her kids, Jasmine hustled across the intersection. She winced at the side-sticker that wouldn't go away.

Past the homeless who shuffled their carts of ill-smelling treasure, past addicts with unfocused eyes swimming in the throes of their chemical dreams, past their comrades whose greedy darting gazes searched for their next score, Jasmine hastened her pace. Her momentary burst of speed soon dropped back down to the fastest limp her side permitted.

A shot rang out half a block behind her. A stampede of yelling strangers forced her forward. The press of the crowd became stifling when, two row-homes ahead, four prostitutes scarcely older than herself brought traffic to a honking standstill. The yowls of their hair-pulling, cloth-tearing cat fight vaulted over the gasps and cheers of gathering spectators.

Three men tumbled out of a bar directly in front of Jasmine. Shouting obscenities, two of them threw drunken punches at each other and a bouncer twice their size. A second gun blasted thunderously behind her. Jasmine pinched out a yelp of surprise when a nearby window chirped with a ricochet.

Jeezus—was I ever wrong! This is just as bad as the freakin' Projects.

Blocked from front and behind, Jasmine dodged into the nearest side street. She hustled without breaking into anything faster than a brisk walk, squinting to adjust her vision to the hungry darkness that blotted out the neon behind her.

Diving into an alley's not the safest, but it's better than that crap back there.

Jasmine quick marched, weaving through the obstacle course of garbage cans, dumpsters, and scampering rats. Backtracking from a dead end and trying to keep her bearings in the labyrinth of brick, she hoped the next street looked familiar. It didn't. She tried the next side street that promised it would point her in the right direction.

Gotta get back to the bus route before another detour gets me totally lost.

Halfway down the latest alley, her ears pricked up at the sound of a footstep. Before she could turn around, her world went blinding white with pain.

Jasmine doubled over in the back doorway of a Chinese food joint, gasping for air between two dumpsters reeking of rotting meat and burnt soy sauce. Her ribs were aflame and the back of her skull felt like it had been split by a jackhammer. She reached for her searing scalp, and her backpack tumbled off her shoulder, clanging against the dumpster.

"Bitch, I told you to stay away from Caleb. He's *mine!*"

Jasmine gathered her rubbery legs underneath her to stand, steadying herself against the nearest dumpster. Her vision returned, rippled with wet blurs that might have been tears, snot, or blood.

In the long shadows cast by distant streetlights, Nevaeh's face burned out of the darkness, livid with rage.

Jasmine's abs clenched, trying to squeeze behind her spine, when she recognized the signs of a girl prepped for a throwdown. Earrings gone. Hair tied tight behind her head. Face slicked with a sheen of Vaseline to deflect blows and scratches.

What the hell do I do now?

The oversized heavy steel ring emblazoned with a prominent gold initial "C" no longer hung from her necklace. It was on the middle finger of Nevaeh's fist. A tuft of Jasmine's frizzy hair dangled from it.

That ring—it ain't her bling, it's Caleb's.

The tendons of Nevaeh's knuckles quivered, taut as bridge cables. She shoved Jasmine backward against the wall with her free hand.

Jasmine whimpered as her head thumped against brick. The

world's loudest gong clanged in her ears. Her legs buckled, helpless against the ground that seemed to spin under her. She kept her eyes glued on Nevaeh's burning scowl, the only thing that kept her consciousness from tumbling upside-down.

Jasmine's accusing stare only infuriated Nevaeh even more.

"Can't you take a fuckin' hint? Don't you know you ain't wanted, *ho*? Our team don't want you. Caleb don't need you. And I sure as shit want you *gone*!"

Nevaeh raised her fist again. "Die, bitch!" Putting her full weight behind it, she swung, aiming Caleb's ring straight for Jasmine's face.

A glistening blur of dark umber shot out from behind the other dumpster. It wrapped around Nevaeh's head, and a muffled scream flooded Jasmine's ears. Nevaeh clutched at the glistening slimy blob, but her attempts to claw the suffocating mass away from her face proved futile.

A split second later, Nevaeh's whole body snapped away like a rag doll.

Caleb's heavy steel and gold ring clattered on the asphalt.

Nevaeh's strangled gurgling made Jasmine's gut twist. Somewhere beyond the dumpster came a slurping rasp, as if from a giant bowl of ramen. The sound of tearing cloth and rending flesh was followed by the sickening crack of bone.

Jasmine curled into a ball, raw terror forcing her knees into her chest. Her feet twitched with every shallow ragged breath. She clamped her head between her hands, but the horrific sounds still reached the spinning pit of her darkest fears.

The dull murmur of the streets had reclaimed the alley, and her sense of up and down returned. Righting herself against one dumpster, she wiped the stinging sweat and tears from her eyes and squinted into the murky light.

What the fuck just happened?

One timid step from between the two dumpsters, then another. Jasmine peeked around the reeking metal containers. Emboldened by the silence, yet expecting Nevaeh to lunge out of the darkness, she took another step into the center of the alley, backpack in hand as a makeshift shield.

She was alone in the shadows.

"Nevaeh?" Jasmine said tentatively.

What the hell am I doing! Do I really want to find her? Or whatever that thing was?

The faraway rumbling of engines was the only reply. She called the name of her attacker again, her throat constricting tighter with each syllable.

Something that mimicked a grotesque voice slithered above her head, hissing like wet leather on a griddle. Jasmine craned her neck, peering in the direction of the nightmare sound.

Nothing but brick wall, dumpsters, rusted and crumpled gallon containers of cooking oil, and garbage bags piled high into mounds of uncollected trash.

The voice scraped out a hideous rasp that came close to speech, from some horrible mouth that was never meant to form human words.

"Mah lin zee. Koo lin da. Jasss-meen."

CHAPTER FOUR

Jasmine dashed blindly from the alley. Down a street. Away. Any-where-but-here away. Gone was any sense of time, place, or people. From the chaos arose her single driving thought—Home.

Panic sizzled down Jasmine's spine, energizing her tired legs, until the stabbing in her rib cage focused her bearings into razor-edged clarity. She blinked with astonishment at the front of her apartment building, as if it had fallen out of the sky.

After wrenching her arm nearly out of its socket on the locked front door, she fumbled for her keys that weren't there. She pounded on her building's intercom buttons, yelling into the grating.

The intercom buzzed, and she yanked open the door.

Her hand still clutching the jacket over the pants' crotch of bright red, Jasmine stumbled to the door closest to the entrance—Bibi's apartment. Her other arm held her backpack against ribs that felt like they wanted to explode.

"Good God, child. You're a sight. What happened to you?" Wrapped in a glowing turquoise and tangerine knee-length shift, Bibi swept Jasmine into her apartment.

Jasmine tried to answer, but her jaw hung agape. Choking sobs punctuated pain-filled gasps for air.

"Something," she wheezed, gulping for oxygen. She peeked around the door jamb at the lit entrance into the dark street beyond. Fearing what might stare back at her, she recoiled into the nearest corner. "Some *thing* … after me."

Bibi banged the door shut with enough force to make the walls rattle. She twisted the deadbolt and looked Jasmine straight in the eye.

"You're safe now, honey," Bibi said, followed by a parcel of Swahili muttered under her breath.

Jasmine dimly sensed Bibi's gentle hands coax open her clenched fist, and she let her jacket fall about her ankles. Bibi's cry of surprise rang throughout the room, pulling Jasmine from the brink of unconsciousness. Her eyelids snapped from half-shuttered to wide open.

"*Ai*, child—What happened?" Bibi shuddered as she started to undo Jasmine's belt. "We must get you some help. Do you need a doctor?"

Jasmine's hand flashed to her hips and grabbed her belt buckle away from Bibi. "Okay—I'm Okay." She tried to swallow, but her dry tongue clung to the roof of her mouth. "Stupid prank. Food coloring."

"Okay?" Bibi demanded. The Look of the lioness lurked somewhere behind her eyes, as she pressed a soft flat palm on Jasmine's stomach. "You sure you don't need a hospital?"

"I'm sure," she replied firmly. Her breaths came a little easier, but now other parts of her began to hurt. Jasmine shook her head to clear her watery vision and whimpered at the throb pulsing around her skull with every heartbeat.

"Who did this to you, child?"

"I … don't know," she mumbled, not sure if she answered the right question.

"Uh-huh," Bibi replied with unbridled disbelief. "Where are you hurt?"

"Everywhere," Jasmine groaned.

"Well, you ran here. So your legs must be all right." Bibi examined Jasmine's arms first, gently kneading the flesh, searching for broken bones or sprained joints. Jasmine winced when Bibi got close to her ribs.

"Ah, yes. That one again." Bibi said. "Now hold your breath, child." She cupped her wrinkled hand against Jasmine's side and pressed tentatively. Jasmine's groan jumped to a high-pitched whine. "Ah, good. Not broken," Bibi said with the smallest smile of relief.

Bibi probed Jasmine's shoulder blades and the back of her neck until she found the swelling lump under a cable of hair. The furrows in Bibi's forehead deepened while she probed through hair coated with brick dust.

"*That's* no prank. Who gave you that?"

Jasmine wasn't sure gravity pulled from the right direction. She dropped her backpack and flailed for something to hold onto.

"*Ai*, sit down, child," Bibi's voice swam about Jasmine's head. Jasmine felt hands guide her into a chair filled with velvet plushness. Her nostrils filled with the familiar scent of old lavender and wintergreen as she sank into the comforter that lined Bibi's TV chair.

Oh, God, that feels good.

Jasmine blinked, squinting at the human blur of turquoise and tangerine splotches hustling away from her. Bibi's voice echoed from the kitchen, followed by the squawk of a faucet and the splash of water. "Don't fall asleep. Keep talking. Tell Bibi how this happened."

Jasmine muttered the first words that came to her, strung together in disjoint phrases. "Basketball," "shower," "pretended to be friends," "pants in locker" reverberated somewhere between her mouth and her ears. It seemed like she watched and listened to herself talk from another part of the room. For a moment, Jasmine wondered who this girl in Bibi's chair was, who sounded like a frog with a head cold.

Bibi's voice sliced through the shifting haze. "No, not the mess on your pants, honey. Tell me how you got *this*." Bibi pressed a bundle of ice cubes wrapped in a dishtowel against the welt at the base of her skull.

Jasmine yelped, then drew in a sharp breath between clenched teeth. The fresh sting of pain brought the world back into focus, and she was back in her own head again. By degrees, she rested against the delicious ice-cold pillow and the oh-so-sumptuous comforter.

"Nevaeh after the game … cornered me in the alley." Jasmine's voice cracked into splinters. She coughed dryly, then winced from the recoil of misery stabbing at the back of her head and in her ribs.

Bibi sloshed a glass of ice water inches in front of Jasmine's eyes. "Drink some of this. Sip, don't gulp." She examined Jasmine's face with concern, waiting for the clinking of ice cubes and her voice to register with the girl.

Jasmine spied the glass and grabbed it. Bibi's shoulders relaxed. "Good—no concussion. You're out of the worst, then. Now tell me, how on earth you got this way. Slow and clearly, this time."

Jasmine took a swig and coughed a fine mist. The coolness at the back of her throat was heaven. After taking another full mouthful of blessed cold wetness, Jasmine stared upward, replaying her dark and blurry memory on the ceiling.

"The streets got bad after dark. Fights in front, shots from behind. Went down the nearest alley. Got lost. Nevaeh ambushed me. Beat on me, knocked me on my head. Used Caleb's ring like a set of brass knuckles. But then …"

A flood of slick pulsing umber, darker than dried blood, crowded everything else out of her recollection, and Jasmine dropped her pleading gaze to Bibi. "She disappeared. Something grabbed her."

Her gut tensed, and her ribs complained in reply. "It got her. She disappeared. Then those sounds." She winced at the memory. "Omigod, I think it *ate* her."

She lunged forward, and the ice slid between her shoulder blades. Jasmine's ribs punched back at her, commanding her to sit back and breathe slowly. Bibi dug behind Jasmine to reposition the ice pack.

"I looked for Nevaeh, but she was gone. It was gone too. Both of them."

Bibi pulled up a chair and sat eye to eye with Jasmine. "Did you see what *it* was?"

"No," Jasmine began, unsure of herself, tilting her head away from the throbbing. "But it said … *tried* to say something."

The echo of the scaly, slithering voice tugged at her, like she should know the word from somewhere before.

"'Mah Lin' … sumpthin'?"

I should know that sumpthin'. I know I should …

"Then it said my name … I think." She shivered at the recollection of her name rasped by something so utterly inhuman.

The lioness in Bibi's face melted into an emotionless mask. Bibi stood and went over to the terrarium, her back toward Jasmine. She gave her head the slightest of nods, adding with a whisper, "So you were right, you little trickster. *Jazz-meen* needed you, after all."

She plunked the *mbira* and the mesh screen behind the terrarium. The *mbira's* metal tines sang an amorphous chord that rattled between Jasmine's ears. Bibi's body sidled back and forth as she searched the glass cage. The rhythmic swaying of her brightly patterned dress made Jasmine's vertigo threaten to return.

"Ah! There you are, *Mlinzi*, you troublemaker." Bibi reached into the terrarium and lifted Jackson out. Displaying a dark mossy green, he turned bright tangerine and hissed at Bibi as she hefted him onto her bosom with one arm. His eyes twitched back and forth, tag-teaming between the two people in the room. When Bibi turned to face Jasmine, she was wrestling something metallic from his neon-bright claw. "What's that you have? Let it go, *Mlinzi* … *Now*, I say."

Prying the item from his grasp, Bibi wrapped her fist around it. Jackson sulked from orange to ashen gray. She draped Jackson along the top ridge of the sofa opposite Jasmine. "Now you behave, *Mlinzi*. You've put our poor girl through enough tonight."

Bibi took her seat again, as Jackson faded into the beige wall behind him, his leathery hide immersing itself into the texture of the old paint crazed with age.

Now I remember!

Jasmine's eyes blinked and grew two sizes.

"*What* did you just say, Bibi?" Jasmine tried to swallow, but her throat refused to move. "'*Mah lin zee*'—*Mlinzi*. That's what that … that *thing* said."

Her jaw clamped, and she tried to stand, lifting herself a few inches only to collapse back into folds of soft lavender. A light sighing of air from the overstuffed pillows around her hips resounded in her ears, overtaken by a hissing from across the room that grew rough and heavier with each passing second.

Jasmine's calves twitched like crazy.

I gotta get outta here.

She tried once more to stand. The bundle of ice slid down the small of her back, and a firm hand on her shoulder urged her back down. "*Jazz-meen*, child, hush. There's no one here that will hurt you." Bibi glanced over her shoulder at the couch, a sober frown puckering her jowls. "Isn't that right, *Mlinzi*?"

The wall above the entire length of the sofa shifted, undulated, pulsed. Under a ponderous weight, the top of the sofa bowed and its frame creaked. The reassuring scents of lavender and wintergreen were swamped by stale air, redolent of moss and things left in the refrigerator too long.

Jasmine struggled to prevent her insides from turning to sludge.

Above the furniture, the crazy-quilt of cracked wall paint melted into a coarse darkening leather. An oval of forest green formed in its center, rolling outward in rhythmic waves. A giant triangular head lolled over one sofa arm. A muscular tapering tail, its base the width of a dinner plate, wrapped around the opposite end. Larger than a tiger and growing larger as more of its bulk shed its camouflage, the thing looked like it could crush the old furniture between its dark green claws and tail with ease.

The monster raised his torso inches above the couch's back. It turned its three-horned head, one eye focused on Bibi, the other pointed straight at Jasmine. The beast's mouth opened, emitting a soul-curdling hiss that made Jasmine's innards quail.

"*Jack ... sss-o-ohn*" spilled out of its quivering maw. Its bulbous umber tongue beat like a malevolent heart. The creature closed its mouth again with the sound of a body bag zipping shut.

"Jackson?" Jasmine shrieked. Her eyelids fluttered, and gravity went sideways again.

Bibi squeezed Jasmine's wrists and shook them. "No, no, child. You stay awake. Mustn't fall asleep, concussion or no," Bibi chided, like a lecturing teacher.

"Run, Bibi," she croaked, grasping Bibi's hand. Groaning with effort, Jasmine pulled herself forward. Her glass of water tumbled to the floor. "That thing got Nevaeh. Run!"

Bibi stood, calm as a mountain lake. She replaced Jasmine's ice pack with a fresh pillow. Her patient hands eased Jasmine back into the warm comforter. Sopping up the spilled water, and with a strange resignation in her voice, sighed with a long-suffering smile.

"I know."

"You ... *know?*" Jasmine panted while she stared at the behemoth poised across the room. It gazed back at her, slowly tilting its head like an inquisitive dog, until its eyes locked a bead on Bibi.

She had resumed her seat in front of Jasmine. Instead of the dishtowel, she now held the black picture frame from the end table in one hand, and opened her other palm, revealing a heavy steel and gold ring.

"That's Caleb's ..."

Unable to complete the thought, Jasmine's jaw went slack. She regarded Bibi with her eyebrows steepled in forlorn defeat. Her shoulders sagged, and she sank deeper into the comforter. The pain from her injuries no longer registered past the shock.

"You knew," she repeated in a whisper.

Bibi slipped the ring into a deep pocket in her colorful shift and turned the picture frame to show Jasmine.

The black walnut frame contained a photograph of a Caucasian man and a younger Bibi, arms about each other's waists, standing in front of an old-fashioned jet from an airline long since out of business. The picture's faded colors, blanched by time to sallow sepias and weak cyans, couldn't erase the carefree warmth in their smiles and the love in their hearts.

"That's Mr. Fieldings. He was a volunteer in your country's Peace Corps. He and others from a nearby mission came to my village in Tanzania. They dug a well, built a small hospital and a school. The missionaries left a doctor-priest with us, and Mr. Fieldings stayed to teach us math and English."

She turned the picture back to herself and whooshed a deep sigh. "We both knew such things were frowned upon by many in the village, but we fell in love. The priest married us, and at the end of Mr. Fieldings's service, he brought me to America." Resting her cheek on her hand, Bibi sighed with a weight of uncounted years, then wiped at eyes brimming with dampness. "He was so hand-*suum* and strong and kind, and we were so happy. But my *bibi*—my *grahnt-muuther*—she was not pleased." Bibi chuckled to herself. "It mattered not, we were so much in love."

In the space of a heartbeat, she stiffened her neck, and the watchful lioness returned.

"But our love that began so strong in Tanzania sputtered. After a few years in America, something changed—*we* changed. Before I knew it, Mr. Fieldings and I simply tolerated each other."

After a wistful sigh, Bibi mumbled to herself, "My *bibi* had wisdom I chose to ignore. Wise old Bibi Rakotomalala, she always knew what was inside people." Bibi rose out of her distant stare and fixed Jasmine with soul-searching eyes.

"We thought having a child would bring us closer together again, rekindle the love we had somehow lost—but we were wrong. The arguing just got worse.

"Then, one year after our son, Rendell, was born, Mr. Fieldings got laid off. He could not find good work, only odd jobs here and there. Soon he started staying out all hours every evening. Most every night he came home with liquor on his breath. And that was when …" Her voice trailed off, and the lioness retreated into herself, biting her lower lip as she gnawed on her emotions.

Shame, remorse, or anger? Jasmine couldn't tell.

"That was when he began to hit me." Bibi rubbed her jaw and grimaced, as though revisiting the memory of an old injury. "*Ai* ... I had almost forgotten for how long the beating went on."

The remembered pain was whisked away by a stern resolve. "Then one night, Mr. Fieldings came home stinking to high heaven. There was murder in his eyes. He twisted my arm out of its socket. Then he grabbed a kitchen knife and screamed at me, saying he was going to kill me. And I believed him." Bibi's head bowed, and her voice sank to the barest whisper. "That's when *Mlinzi* came."

"But ... he was already here. He came with you. From Tanzania. He hid in your luggage."

"Yes, child. Little *Mlinzi—Jack-suun*—had been here with us all that time." Bibi clicked her tongue and let escape a sigh that oozed sadness. "My *bibi* gave me Little *Mlinzi* as a present, a blessing on our wedding. She had the strangest intensity in her eyes when she held him up to us. Cupped there in her hands, he looked at me and turned blue—as bright and deep as the spring sky."

A weak grin of reminiscence traveled across her face, then evaporated as quickly after a glance in Jasmine's direction. "We kept him, but we thought, like any untamed animal, he would wander away. He never did. He tagged along no matter where we went. When we came to America and Mr. Fieldings found Little *Mlinzi* in his luggage, we thought he just stowed away by accident."

Bibi's eyes clouded over with a faraway look again. "We had no idea back then what he was. But Bibi Rakotomalala knew—she *knew* I would need the real *Mlinzi* sooner or later."

"What happened to Mr. Fieldings?" Afraid of the answer, Jasmine shivered from a fearful coldness stiffening in her core. She wrapped her arms about herself tightly, ignoring the complaint from her ribs.

"You already know. From what you described, the same thing happened to Nevaeh." Bibi rose with a sigh and placed the frame back on its place of reverence on the end table. *Mlinzi*'s right eye followed her, but his left eye remained riveted on Jasmine. "Mr. Fieldings was gone, never to be seen again."

Jasmine pressed back into the folds of her chair, wishing she could completely dive into the blanket and avoid the giant reptile's cold piercing stare.

"Like you, I was scared out of my mind. I did not know what to think. I was afraid of my own shadow for the longest time. But then, two years ago, some nasty man broke in and tried to rob me." Bibi stroked *Mlinzi*'s giant head and rubbed one of his horns. She pursed her lips and sat in front of Jasmine once more. She patted Jasmine's hand, drawing her out of her cushioned fortress.

"One minute the robber had his gun pressed against my head. I closed my eyes and prayed for ... for I don't know what. Help, or a quick end." Bibi scrunched her shoulders in a small shiver. "The next moment, I heard him choke and the gun was gone. When I opened my eyes, there was *Mlinzi*, munching away. Swallowed him whole, all but one shoe."

Bibi took both of Jasmine's hands in hers. Jasmine shivered when her fingertips touched the old scar slashed across Bibi's palm.

"That's when I knew what he was. When I finally understood the blessing my *bibi* pronounced over me on my wedding day." Bibi purred like a lioness that discovered catnip. "*Roho Kinyonga Mlinzi*—spirit chameleon protector. *My* protector."

"But why is he here? Why did he ..." Jasmine gulped. "Why did he kill Nevaeh?"

"I told you, child. He's here because of Bibi Rakotomalala—my *bibi*." She patted her hand over her heart, and a dreamy gaze cast over her eyes. "My *bibi*, she knew the ways of our people, our land, and more. All those years ago, she knew what Mr. Fieldings would become. So she gave me a protector."

Bibi smirked with a mild reproach aimed at the ceiling and patted her chest. "To tell the truth, she wasn't giving him to *me* on our wedding day. She offered me to *him,* and he accepted me."

"That doesn't make sense," Jasmine replied, her voice cracking with despair.

Bibi shrugged and took a quick breath. "As for Nevaeh, she said she was going to kill *you.* And you believed her, no?"

A meek whisper of a "yes" was the only response Jasmine could summon.

"There you have it." Bibi tapped the tip of Jasmine's nose with the lightest touch. "*That* is why he did what he did."

Jasmine gawked at the woman in gray box braids, stupefied by how matter-of-factly she dispensed her revelations that threatened to destroy Jasmine's world, her sanity, her—

A polite knock at the front door made Jasmine jump like she heard a gunshot.

Bibi rose and straightened her dress. "Besides, *Mlinzi* is no longer my protector. He's yours. He's accepted *you* now." She regarded Jasmine's confused stare with thoughtful sadness and a fatalistic shrug of her shoulders.

"I'm so sorry, child—I really am. It is such a burden." Bibi caressed the line of Jasmine's jaw. "I almost wish it wasn't you ... but then, you wouldn't be alive now if *Mlinzi* didn't choose you. Might as well face it, little one. He's yours, and you are his." She went to the front door and squinted through the peephole.

"Mine?" Jasmine whined, drowning in her confused helplessness.

"*Ai*, it's your *muuther*." She undid the deadbolt, pausing before she turned the doorknob. She regarded Jasmine with a gentle smile, but a resolute warning in her eyes. "We shall speak of this later. Mind you, tell no one of *Mlinzi*, not even your Ma. Don't even try. Even if you *could* tell, she wouldn't believe you—she simply couldn't. She would think you're crazy."

Jasmine drew a deep breath. Every inch of her wanted to yell at Bibi, to spill her guts to Ma and maybe the whole world. Fragments of "Are you *shitting* me?" and "I'm stuck with ... with a monster? A real live fucking *monster*?" ran laps in her skull, yearning to burst out of her mouth.

Something shifted from the corner of her eye, and she snapped her head toward the sofa.

Mlinzi was gone.

Recoiling from a sudden onslaught of spinning dizziness, Jasmine managed with difficulty to turn in her seat toward the terrarium.

Jackson—the right sized Jackson—sat unperturbed upon his moss-covered log.

CHAPTER FIVE

Covers that held no warmth, no matter how hard she clutched them. Twitching legs that would run off into the night, were they not attached. Stabbing pulses of bone-deep ache every time she shifted in a futile search for a comfortable position in which she might relax.

Instead, a never-ending parade of silent screams suspended Jasmine in the twilight between fitful sleep and comfortless silence. A relentless roulette wheel of emotions chittered away between her ears.

I hate Jackson.

Whenever she closed her eyes, unbidden memories replayed: the petty cruelties inflicted by Nevaeh; the galling laughter of her teammates; the dark alley that promised safety but delivered none; twitching against the cold alley walls in cowardly silence; wrapped in a blanket drenched in lavender and wintergreen, while Bibi explained away her injuries, her nervousness, her panic to Ma. Each troubled memory was slashed by the umber rush of Nevaeh smothering under *Mlinzi's* tongue before being snatched away with the irrevocable swiftness of a switchblade.

I hate Bibi.

Deep down she knew she shouldn't—she didn't. Not quite.

It was something else—a gray festering that lay between disappointment and betrayal. Disappointment, at how easily the old lady she trusted like family weaved a web of misdirection around her mother, as glibly as a used-car salesman unloading a clunker. Betrayal, that she dumped some family curse on her—and tried to make it look like a blessing.

"She just had a bad night, Missus Price," Bibi's spectral voice wafted alternately from within the pillow and the bedroom ceiling. "First, a rough time in tonight's game. Then those terrible girls playing such a horrible prank on her, and look—a perfectly good pair of pants ruined. Then, worst of all, a bad mess with all the violence in the streets." She put her hand over her mouth in feigned surprise. "My goodness! So close to a fight and a shooting. Is it any wonder she's such a bundle of nerves?"

But nothing about Nevaeh.

Or the thing that killed her.

All this misdirection coming from the woman she trusted—*loved* —as much as a grandmother? How could Bibi hide Jackson all this time, then unleash that hulking monstrosity *Mlinzi* on Nevaeh? And then foist it on her as though it were a lost kitten? And what was that crap about the stupid lizard *choosing* her?

A nauseating lump burned in her chest, where boiling anger and betrayal built up pressure against a wall of guilt.

Jasmine curled into a shivering fetal ball whenever the roulette wheel stopped once more on the most unpleasant of the night's revelations.

I hate myself.

But was it truly hate she directed at herself? Or was it fear? Or might it be guilt, desperation, or loathing? Or was it the thing Ma tried to explain in Dad's last letter from Afghanistan—"survivor's guilt?"

Another ache led to another turn, another shudder, another hate.

Run away. Leave all this shit behind.

No sooner had the thought popped in her head, the recollection of the prostitutes fighting in the street answered in rebuttal.

Girl, you know what happens to the girls who run away. Even here, same as the Projects. Remember that street whore cat-fight?

When sleep found a way to worm its way in, elusive dreams were filled with breathless stumbling through tall vegetation in the savanna night, running blindly from the hoarse pants, grunts, and growls of a lion on her heels. Heavy paws rustled scrub just beyond the shoulder-high curtain of swaying grass. Jasmine fell prostrate at the edge of a clearing, under the flimsy canopy of an enormous but leafless rain tree. Scattered around its dead trunk were a wasteland of fallen limbs and broken branches. Above the remaining bare limbs soared the Milky Way from one horizon to the other. Hanging low in the cloak of night, a waning moon grinned cruelly.

The crunch of dry stalks crackled from every direction. Her ankles shouted with sudden pain, struck by a heavy, wet warmth. She struggled to right herself and free her bloodied legs from the grasp of the great cat's claws.

She scrabbled to seize a fallen branch. Rolling over and wielding it like a club, she faced the creature. She squinted into the feeble moon-light, ready to strike at anything that resembled fur. Her breath caught in her throat when a glistening umber tongue shot out from the forest of grass and wrapped around her ankles. From within the tall reeds slithered a vile reptilian hiss. "*Mah lin zee. Koo lin da. Jass meen.*"

The tongue squirmed its way up her body, and two lizard eyes swiveling in scaly neon-blue cones poked through the grass.

Jasmine whimpered herself awake, as the constricting tongue was replaced with sweat-soaked sheets plastering her arms tight against her torso and twisting around her ankles. She untangled herself from the corded python of damp linen and stumbled out of bed. Her back and shoulders shivered from the clammy T-shirt clinging to her skin.

She grabbed her tattered pink bathrobe hanging from a closet doorknob and huddled inside its threadbare fuzziness. Still rubbing the sand from her eyes, she staggered out of the bathroom. Two familiar voices and the clinking of spoons stirring mugs echoed down the hall-way from the kitchen.

She stalled behind the straight-edged shadow thrown by the naked bulb above the kitchen table. She watched the distorted shapes of an arm's shadow slide back and forth along the hallway floor as they conversed. The tinny drone of the TV's Sunday sermon pulsed in rhythm with the steady tick of the stove's cooking timer.

"I got the call early this morning, Missus Price," Bibi's voice qua-vered. "My son, Rendell, is at the hospital. His missus gave birth to a daughter nine weeks too early. The poor *muuther* and child are both so sick. She's doing so poorly. Had a heart attack during labor and now is in intensive care. The little one is in a glass box, just to stay alive. They need my help to care for their firstborn, my dearest Cheta, while ..."

Jasmine stared at the shadows in disbelief.

Is Bibi crying?

Bibi's guttural sobs ended as swiftly as they began, elbowed out of the way by her familiar chuckle. Happy but nonetheless forced, the lioness tried to keep a brave front.

"I still have some packing to do, and I must dig out my rainy-day fund from the coffee can for the bus ticket."

"Surely, we can help," said Ma. The unzipping of a handbag was followed by the snap of a purse.

"Oh, no, you don't, Missus Price. You keep your money. You need it more than me. You're just getting your feet back on the ground. I can make do."

"Surely there's something we can do for you. Can we look after your apartment while you're away?"

"Thanks ever so much, but I've already made arrangements. My neighbor from 1C will water my plants—only she can't abide my pet. He's much too close to a snake for her liking."

Jasmine's jaw dropped, and she pressed herself hard against the wall. Her knees began to shake.

No no no. Don't you dare say it.

"Besides, Jasmine's already given him a name—*Jack-suun.*"

"Well, that settles it then," Ma punctuated with a rap on the Formica table. "Jasmine will be happy to take him while you're away."

That monster ... here?

Jasmine launched herself out of the shadow and planted her feet in the doorway between the hall and the kitchen. Her fists shook by her side. "*No!* I won't ..."

Ma wore an expression of unabashed astonishment, in stark contrast to Bibi's lopsided plaintive frown. Between their mugs of tea lay a packet of snapshots. On top lay the picture Bibi had shown before to cheer up Ma—a man with a barrel chest, a woman with skin darker than his, and a little boy whose smile could brighten the whole world.

Jasmine's stern glower melted into a shiver of embarrassment under the weight of Ma's unyielding scowl.

"Jasmine *Emily* Price!" Ma plunked down her spoon on the table with the force of a judge's gavel. "After all Bibi has done for us? 'Specially after last night? You apologize, right now, young lady."

Jasmine fell back on her tried-and-true '*I-wanna-stay-out-late*' whine. "But Ma-a-a, you don't know what ..." Bibi's words echoed behind her eyes like a remnant from her dream. *She'll think you're crazy.*

She tried anyway. "Mah Lin—" her tongue welded itself to the roof of her mouth. "Jack— ... Ja—" she stammered before her jaw slammed shut.

"Pay her no mind, Missus Price. Poor Jasmine is still turned all around from last night, and she hasn't had anything solid in her for almost a whole day." Bibi stood, and her chair's legs scraped a metallic staccato across the linoleum. "I'll fix her something while you finish getting ready for work."

"Al-l-l right," Ma reluctantly agreed. She aimed a stern squint at Jasmine, followed by a wag of her finger. "No more of your 'tude, Jazz. You may think you're too old for me to put you over my knee, but you just try me." Ma swept out of the room, snatching her hotel uniform draped over the back of the chair. She snapped off the TV, leaving the mumbled trail of her "Never in all my days" soliloquy to fill the vacuum.

Bibi placed a bowl of cold oatmeal topped with slices of browning apple on the table. She pulled out a chair for Jasmine, patting its seat as she settled effortlessly into her own chair again. Jasmine shuffled to her seat and stared stone-faced at the snapshot of Bibi's son and his family on the center of the table.

"I'm sorry to burden you with *Jack-suun*, child. But I simply must help my family," she said with quiet straightforwardness.

"So I heard," Jasmine replied as cold as stone. Her fists bunched around the rim of her seat.

"I know the problems you have, child. I had them too, long ago. But consider my predicament. I be in a real bind as to what to do—go to my son, Rendell, or stay here—even with *Mlinzi* looking after you."

"Don't say that thing's name!" Jasmine hissed. She focused her hatred on the untouched bowl of oatmeal. She couldn't bear to look Bibi in the eye. Her stomach ached like a drill was boring into her gut, and the lump on the back of her head throbbed anew. "You're leaving me alone? With that ... that *monster?*"

"Child, you know he won't hurt you. I told you so. You saw for yourself as well." Bibi reached out to stroke Jasmine's shoulder.

She flinched away, glaring ever more sternly at her oatmeal. "But you can't ..." Her eyes darted to ensure Ma was out of earshot. "You can't just give him to me. I don't *want* him."

Ma skirted past the table, swirling her coat about her as she collected her handbag. She halted inches from the table and turned to flash one last authoritative grimace at her daughter. "Is everything all right here?"

"Fine," champed Jasmine.

"Yes, everything's dandy, Missus Price. You get along. Don't want to be late for work."

"All right," Ma repeated with a skeptical cadence. She hugged Jasmine, who remained frozen in concentration on her breakfast. "You be safe on your trip, Bibi. I'll keep you and your family in my prayers."

Bibi waved, thanking Ma as she scurried out the front door. Once alone with Jasmine, her omnipresent smile waned. "I didn't give him to you, *Jazz-meen*. I told you before, he chose you. It's no longer a matter of what *you* want."

Jasmine fumed in silence. Heat flooded across her cheeks, and blood pounded in her ears, drowning out Bibi's words.

This is getting worse by the minute.

Bibi sat back, inhaling deeply, rebuilding her concerned composure, and folded her hands on the table. "You told me *Mlinzi* spoke to you back in the street. Do you remember what he said?"

Frowning silence was Jasmine's only reply. Her arms ached from clamping the sides of her chair for so long. She forced her eyes to remain welded to one slice of apple floating in oatmeal. Despite her attempt to remain as unyielding as cold steel, Jasmine could not repress a shiver at the memory of *Mlinzi*'s voice, nor the wretched words he hissed.

"Did he say something like … '*kulinda*'?" asked Bibi.

Jasmine swiveled her head at the mention of the word, refocusing her bubbling frustration on the old woman's relentless prodding. She scowled at Bibi for a moment, but hints of recollection and uncertainty cracked her mask of anger.

"There, you see? He said so himself, did he not? He said '*kulinda.*' That means 'protect,' *Jazz-meen.*" Bibi caressed Jasmine's shoulder once more.

This time, Jasmine did not flinch. Her shoulders relaxed and her head bent down, yielding to gravity, exhaustion, and resignation.

Bibi's kind lioness returned. "This is what I've been telling you all along, child. Bibi did not give him to you, he *chose* you. *Mlinzi* knew your need, and he chose."

Anger against love, fear against trust, betrayal against acceptance, confusion against understanding—they all battled against one another in Jasmine's heart.

"There are many tricksters in this poor world, little one. They lie to everyone, sometimes even to themselves. But *Mlinzi* is not like that. Oh, he may change color, change size, change from meek and mild to frightening and ..." Bibi paused with pursed lips. "... and yes, even deadly. But he has never lied."

She leaned toward Jasmine, tilting her head to peer directly into Jasmine's faltering glower. "And he did not—*will* not—lie to you. He said 'protect,' and he meant it."

Jasmine rose out of her chair, swung her arms around and clutched Bibi in a sobbing bear hug. She rested her chin on Bibi's shoulder, and the words tumbled out.

"I can't take it. I just can't take it. I'm all alone. Everyone at school hates me. Ma is never around. And now you're *leaving*? Sticking me with that damned lizard?" Her whole body shook with a sob that echoed in every corner of her soul. "That thing has screwed up everything worse. It took ... it killed ... it *ate* Nevaeh. I don't care what you say—'he likes me, he chose me.' Fer cryin'-out-loud, Bibi, I'm scared of the damn thing."

She lifted her head and overflowing eyes pleaded with Bibi, searching for any life preserver she might throw her. The roulette wheel of emotion clacked away again in her head. "What the hell am I supposed to do? I can't talk to Ma at all, or she'll think I'm nuts. I couldn't talk to you. How could I? You brought it here, fer Chrisesakes. And now you're going away? Leaving me *alone*—with a monster that *kills*!"

She violently shook her head until Bibi patted it with a reassuring coo.

"There, there, child. I am so sorry, believe me. I am sorry I must leave. Even more, I am sorry for the grief I and *Mlinzi* have caused you." Bibi took Jasmine by the shoulders and held her fast once more with her Look. "But one thing I am not sorry for. If I had not shown you to *Mlinzi*, you would be dead at the hands of that horrible girl Nevaeh. You *do* understand that, do you not?"

Jasmine couldn't decide if she wanted to bawl her eyes out, hold onto Bibi until her arms fell off, or slap that suddenly irksome patient smile off her face. Pressure from the three desires squeezed out another spasm of blubbering.

Bibi embraced Jasmine. Without a word, Bibi breathed with

unhurried patience and patted Jasmine's back with every exhale.

Jasmine inhaled the scent of the lavender lioness and let her anger dissolve away. She wasn't sure why the fear and indecision faded away—and she didn't *care* to understand it.

Bibi took Jasmine by the shoulders and guided her back into her seat. She fixed Jasmine immobile with her gentle gaze and wise smile. "I wish I could stay here, little one. But my son needs me badly. You feel alone, but my son *is* alone. His wife is alone, dead to the world. My *grahnt*-son and new *grahnt*-daughter are alone. If I could stay here with you, you know I would. But I must go where I am needed most." Bibi sighed and shook her head.

"You are strong, Jasmine. But you are not alone. *Never* alone. You have your Ma. True, often she is not here at home. But all she does, she does for you. You think she does not feel alone, as well?

"Talk to her—she will listen. Tell her what happens at school, at *basket-y-ball*. Tell her the bad, but don't forget to tell her the good, too. Tell her, and you will find you are not as alone as you fear. She just might surprise you. And you just might discover one day, maybe one day soon, you can even tell her about *Mlinzi*."

A chuckle made Bibi's whole body shake. "Until then, talk to *Jack-suun*. He's a good listener." She lifted Jasmine's chin with an index finger and winked at her. "He interrupts only when he must."

The cooking timer rattled out an obnoxious cracked plastic chime that wound down to a strangled clunk.

"*Ai*, child. Eat your breakfast, take your shower, and get dressed. The bus to my son's city leaves this morning, and I surely would appreciate your help with my carry-all."

Jasmine gobbled down a few mouthfuls of oatmeal and apple, but slowed to a methodical munching when her stomach sent a quivering reminder that it wasn't quite convinced everything was peachy.

She rushed through a shower, not allowing herself the luxury of pondering her situation under the lukewarm water. The spray went ice cold, and every muscle in Jasmine's body tensed, squeezing a small yelp of aggravation from her and ending her rinse abruptly. When Jasmine emerged from her room, dressed in a loose shirt, a pair of baggy pants Ma had pulled out of an unpacked moving box, and her hair bound high in a sports bun, Bibi was clearing out a space in front of the living room window.

"*Jack-suun* likes to watch the street. It will be a nice change for him, to see so much more from up here."

Jasmine couldn't shoo away the last of her misgivings. "Do we really have to keep … Jackson here?" *There, I said his name.* "Can't I take care of him in your apartment?"

"No, dearie. I only have one spare key, and my neighbor in 1C has that. Besides, he's *yours* now. You *know* that, surely?" Jasmine's shoulders tensed upward, and she stared at the empty window table. "Come on, let's go fetch him. Help me bring *Jack-suun* upstairs, and get him settled in."

Jasmine lugged the terrarium against her hips as she climbed the stairs, but shimmied it away with an uncertain grimace when one of Jackson's eyes pivoted toward her. She puffed out an exhale of relief as she deposited the heavy glass enclosure on their window table. Jackson held his head upward, its three horns pointing directly at her. His leathery hide turned a dirty yellow as his mouth wrinkled in a curious expression.

Is that a smile?

"You see? He likes it there," Bibi laughed. She placed a paper with a short, scribbled list on top of the terrarium's screened lid. "Here's instructions on how to care for him. Keep the window open when it's warm enough and no rain. He'll eat anything that flies in. If he doesn't change colors over the course of day, it means he's hungry, and you'll have to get him some other food."

Jasmine shivered and squeezed her eyes shut. The unwanted image of Nevaeh's head wrapped in a glistening tongue burst in on her recollection.

God, no. She couldn't mean …

"Here's an address for a pet store. Tell the owner you need crickets for *Mlinzi*, and he'll give you a bag for free. Clean his cage every two weeks—"

"Weeks!" Jasmine exploded, an exaggerated pout on its heels. "How long are you going away?"

"As long as Rendell and his family need me. And I told you, child. *Mlinzi*'s yours now. Even if I were at home downstairs, he'd still find his way up here where *you* live. So his box might as well be up here with you anyway."

Jasmine regarded Jackson with a humorless frown and half-hearted harrumph. He responded with a leisurely step forward, acknowledging her with a molasses-slow tilt of his head, not unlike that of a sun-bathing cat.

Jasmine peered upward through the window. Blue sky striped with wispy streaks of sun arched overhead, and she cracked open the casement window. Sounds of the awakening city rumbled and honked from below. She folded her arms and locked eyes with Jackson.

"Okay, you stupid lizard. But you're on probation," she pronounced, trying to imitate the authority she often heard in Coach's voice. Trouble was, Jasmine wasn't even remotely sure what she meant.

"Not the happy ending I hoped for, but a truce will have to do." Bibi clapped her hands together and smiled broadly. "*Ai*, get your jacket. I have to collect my things from my apartment. Then you can help me with my carry-all to the central bus station."

The air outside was cool, refreshing, with a gentle breeze that whisked away the fumes of the ever-present crawl of traffic. Jasmine was distracted by the rhythmic trundling of the carry-all wheels bumping over the sidewalk seams, until the scent of over-brewed coffee wafted out of Parker's Corner Store.

A handful of kids and their parents in their Sunday clothes hovered around the street corner pole laden with a bewildering array of traffic and bus route signs. Jasmine let slip a silent sigh of relief after she assured herself neither Akilah nor any other of Nevaeh's friends were drifting about.

"One of these buses goes to your son's city?"

"No, dear. But the next one goes all the way to the main terminal, where I catch the bus I need."

A city bus with "Central" on its marquee trundled next to the pole like a leaky tugboat sidling up to its pier. The lumbering vehicle rocked to a stop, its air brakes hissing through grimy wheels. A weak chorus of grunts resounded from the kids before they dug in their pockets for their metro passes, herded by their parents in front of the folding doors like prisoners going to their cells.

Jasmine was next in line to board when Bibi mumbled under her breath. "*Ai*, I almost forgot." She delved into her coat pocket and dropped a nugget of metal into the green mesh trash basket clamped to the pole. Jasmine, with a nervous shudder, glanced at the remaining crowd, hoping no one spotted Bibi dumping Caleb's ring. She was safe —they were shuffling into their seats, the kids swiping across their phone screens, and the adults reminding their offspring to behave in church.

Jasmine and Bibi climbed in and took seats near the back facing the curbside. The bus grumbled to life as it merged back into the stream of traffic. Jasmine settled into her seat and tried to relax, but the moment was choked short when she turned to look out the rear window.

Trotting to the bus stop shrinking behind them was Akilah, dressed to impress, but definitely *not* for church. Slowed by her designer flats, she flailed her arms in a futile attempt to hail the bus. Once she reached the street pole, Akilah bent over, leaning on the trash container, to catch her breath. She did a double take and fished out a hunk of glinting metal from the basket.

Oh, crap.

CHAPTER SIX

Jasmine collapsed into her seat moments before the bell rang for first period's Earth Science class.

Having survived the gauntlet of the morning bus, the cramp in her shoulders loosened, and the knot in her chest unwound. The countless sneers and snickers directed at her wardrobe, consisting of a ragged tunic mismatched against Ma's baggy pants, were bad enough. The jibes and abuse texts from Akilah and Trinity, and anonymous shade from the rest of their gang, were worse.

If their looks could kill, Jasmine would have spontaneously combusted in the school halls. But without the guidance of their queen bee, the hive was utterly disorganized.

But Akilah found Nevaeh's ring. She's gotta suspect something.

Jasmine closed her eyes and sighed, letting the teacher's voice wash past her, embracing her island of relaxation.

But such luxury lasted only one period. History class wiped the last shred of serenity out of Jasmine.

Like a hungry wolf with a cock-eyed crew cut, Mr. Wyatt smelled fear. He zeroed in on Jasmine, selecting her most every time the class's response of dead quiet to his questions lasted too long. It threatened to give Jasmine a headache that went straight down her neck to her heart.

The time between classes was a worse ordeal. It started small, beginning with furtive glances in her direction from cliques of girls huddled along hallway walls. Every single one of the clusters dispersed into nearby classroom doors as she approached them, scattering like rats scurrying to their nests. It worsened throughout the day as the groups found their courage. Snippets of interrupted conversations, ending with "haven't seen her since she went after you-know-who," and "bitch doesn't even have a fuckin' scratch on her," were breathed just loud enough for their intended target to hear, accompanied by accusing glances. If Jasmine had any doubt about whom they were yakking about, it disappeared when she overheard her name in the last of those faltering whispers.

A curious zipping sound from behind, and her backpack slipped off her shoulder, tumbling to the ground behind her. She turned to a sight that made her gawk with surprise.

Akilah picked up her bag, dangling it by the strap neatly sliced in two.

"Whoa, careful, girl. I almost tripped over this. Those cheap things fail at the worst time. Never know what might break …" She handed the bag to Jasmine. She sneered as her hand under the bag opened to reveal Caleb's ring—the one Bibi had thrown away. "… or what might fall out."

A whirlpool of undigested stress flushed down Jasmine's stomach.

Trinity strolled past her with a sickeningly satisfied smile. She hummed while tending to her nails with a bright chrome file. The glint on its edge, honed down to razor sharp steel, hinted at what its true use was. Akilah giggled with her head cocked at a taunting angle as she sashayed away alongside Trinity.

If history period was bad, math class at the end of the day was a lost cause. Jasmine's blood roared in her ears like a freight train filled with tigers. Her jaw clicked with a pop that rang in her skull like a cannon when she spied Caleb's hard-bitten face through the classroom door window. He stared at her like he might at a dead sewer rat.

She wondered if her impending dread would ease up in basketball practice. *I need to work off this nervous energy. Show Akilah and Trinity that they can't upset me.*

Her hopes were dashed once she caught the glances of worry and the snatches of fear whenever her teammates' eyes met hers. That and the glares of unblinking malice from Akilah and Trinity.

Coach Garcia blasted her whistle. "Okay, where's Nevaeh?"

Jasmine stood in the mill of six other girls, all of them frozen in mid-throw or mid-approach, looking at each other as if they were caught with their hand in a cookie jar. Most of the team's shoulders shrugged, while the rest bleated a chorus of half-hearted "ah-dunno"s.

Jasmine stood stony silent, eyes wide open, hoping she could gather a decent poker face. Akilah and Trinity kept glancing in her direction with daggers in their eyes.

"Tough for her—she knows the rules," Coach barked. "If she can't be bothered to show up for practice, I may have to get a new captain for this weekend's game."

She clapped her hands once with authority. "First string to the right, second string to the left."

A flurry of short trills on her whistle punctuated the order. Sneakers squeaked and balls bounced on the polished wood floor, their echoes diminishing as two lines formed on either side of Coach. Jasmine scampered to the leftmost position.

Coach glared at the vacant rightmost position. She scanned the two small squads of youthful faces.

"Jasmine, how's your ribs today? You think you can play better than that lame performance you gave us the other night?"

Trinity and Akilah scowled under vicious eyebrows.

"Yes, Coach," she said, not too loud, not too confident.

Coach took a menacing step toward Jasmine, her fists planted on her hips. "Then say it like you *want* to beat Crosstown High, dammit," she hollered.

"Yes, Coach!"

Coach clapped her hands. "That's better. All right then, Jasmine moves to first squad." A couple of more pulses on her whistle screeched, ringing endlessly in the near-empty gym. Naked shock was plastered on Trinity's face, while Akilah boiled with disgust. Her eyes squinted so hard, Jasmine would not have been surprised if blood spurted out of them.

"Okay, first string, V-cut drill. Second string, weave passing." Coach inhaled deeply, followed by a "*Today*, ladies!" that made the rafters shake.

The first squad zoomed to their half of the court. They circled the inner court in an eggbeater of passing, cutting, shooting, and blocking, each player taking her turn at the basket. By the fourth cycle into the drill, Jasmine smiled, finally able to lose herself in the flow and leave all thoughts of trouble behind. No Nevaeh, no Caleb, no Jackson.

A sudden yelp of pain rang out in the court. Trinity tripped and rolled over, holding her knee. Coach skittered over to the girl rocking on the floor, kneeling over her and offering assistance. The windmill of the squad's activity skidded to a halt. Jasmine stared in confusion at Trinity, not being able to piece together who tripped her up.

Stars of pain exploded from the right side of Jasmine's skull. The echoes of the distinctive *pong* of a basketball impact rang in both ears. She staggered a few steps to the left.

Akilah proffered a smarmy smile of apology, saying in a singsong falsetto, "Ooh, sorry Jasmine, I thought you were ready for my pass."

Jasmine fumed. She pressed her lips flat, stern with anger—until the vision of Caleb's ring in Akilah's grasping fingers tumbled into her recollection, quenching her fire with cold guilt.

"Nothing's wrong with you, Trinity. Stop being a baby," Coach scolded as she helped the girl to her feet. "This isn't a European soccer team. Get back in the drill."

Jasmine dove back into the drill, warily eyeing Akilah every time they trotted past each other. During a lame attempt at a layup that resembled a wounded bird, Akilah stumbled and landed face down. Under Coach's shrilling whistle, Akilah yowled a string of four-letter words. They didn't sound heartfelt to Jasmine's ear.

Jasmine's head recoiled with another snap to the side, to the boom of the basketball striking her squarely in the ear. A swirl of dark ocher threatened to topple her over until she steadied her forehead in her hands.

This time it was Trinity who held an open palm to her mouth, scrunching in a fawning curtsy like an apologetic Southern belle. "Ooh, sorry Jasmine, I thought you were ready for my pass."

How original. Okay, I get the point.

Jasmine ground her teeth until they squeaked against one another like nails on a chalkboard. She scooped up the ball, her fingers digging into the ball's rubber pebbles. Her footfalls pounded toward Trinity. She halted at the screech of Coach's whistle, able only to glare at Akilah's stumbling form thrown back into the mix.

"What is with you girls today?" cried Coach. "Get your friggin' act together, Akilah. And what the heck was that *walking*, Jasmine?"

Her whistle shrieked again as she sang out a fresh set of orders. "First squad, guard breakdown drill. Second squad, wing layups. Make it sharp, we'll need perimeter action against Crosstown." Trinity knelt to tie her shoes, keeping one eye on Coach.

Jasmine's squad formed a half-circle inside the three-point line and began their weave. Out of the corner of her eye, Jasmine caught exactly what she expected. Trinity pretended to take a gainer over her loose shoelace. Jasmine swiveled her head to locate where the next alpha-bitch attack would come from.

She spotted Akilah in mid-throw follow-through, with the ball hurtling straight at her head.

Jasmine's arms shot up like lightning. The ball thrummed in her hands like a tight tom-tom drum. Twisting her whole body, she put her entire weight behind rocketing the orange meteor back at Akilah's face.

The shock in Akilah's eyes disappeared behind the ball in a flash. She toppled back into a tangle of arms and legs on the floor, as the ball bounded away into the corner.

God, that felt good.

Coach's whistle pierced the sudden silence of both squads. "Jasmine, what the f—" she sputtered at top volume. "*You!* Hit the showers and wait in my office."

Dashing to the fallen girl, Coach Garcia pried open Akilah's eyelid between her thumb and forefinger. She fumbled in the pockets of her team sweatshirt, pulled out a small paper straw and broke it in two. As she waved it over Akilah's nose, the snap of ammonia wafted past the gathering group of girls.

Akilah's eyes fluttered, and she coughed harshly.

Coach held three fingers steady in front of Akilah's face. "How many fingers do you see?"

Akilah spluttered a weak reply.

Coach sighed a small whoosh of relief, but immediately shot a furious glare at Jasmine. "What are *you* still doing here? I said hit the showers and park your butt in my office. Everyone else, back to work. *Move it!*"

Jasmine wheeled, storming back to the locker room. Coach and Trinity leveraged Akilah back to her feet, guiding her to the nearest bench despite the girl's protests that she was all right. Pacing back and forth in the locker room while mumbling to herself, she peeked through the gym door. Squinting her eyes through the window's wire lattice,

Coach's and Akilah's backs were turned toward Jasmine. Akilah sobbed a string of syllables with a whimper, and Coach responded by putting her arm across her shoulder.

Whatta suck-up. What crap is she telling Coach now?

She showered while the sneaker squeaks and hammering of balls on the floorboards resumed beyond the gymnasium doors. Jasmine practically ran between the drops in the shower—she sure as hell was *not* going to be caught with her pants down in the locker room twice. While dressing, she slammed every door she could—the trash can, the lid to the towel bin, and her locker. With each wham, she envisioned a disfigured version of Akilah's or Trinity's head between the door and its frame.

Her last audible act of revolt was ramming Coach's door open against the masonry block wall. Plopping down in front of Coach's desk hard enough to make the chair legs splay out with a squeak, Jasmine corralled her backpack between her shins. She folded her arms and scrunched her face into her fiercest scowl. At least the stench of bad perfume, athlete's foot, and yeast wasn't so bad in Coach's office.

A series of whistle blasts and a long string of Coach's cajoling signaled the end of practice. The doors into the locker room banged open, and the titters, laughter, and whoops of the team filled the ranks of lockers. A single shape passed the louvered blinds and loomed in the doorway. No amount of wishful thinking could misinterpret the grimace on Coach's face. She was ticked off in a major way.

It was Coach's turn to slam the door shut. The blinds on the window fluttered from the blast, before she pulled their cords to lay them opaque against the window. She laid into Jasmine at full volume, though little of her verbal abuse penetrated Jasmine's scowling defense. The blood pounding in her ears was an effective shield, as she hunkered down in her chair.

Then the room became quiet.

Jasmine looked furtively under down-turned eyebrows at Coach. She was not met with the hateful glower of an ogre about to tear into a helpless victim, but the pouting half-frown of a grown-up facing a distasteful chore. "Okay, that tirade should throw the vultures off the scent for a minute or two," she said at half-volume without the slightest hint of emotion. "What's really going on, Jasmine? That sob story of Akilah's was a total crock. Then she lays down some crud about how she's afraid of *you*."

"Afraid of *me*?" Jasmine blurted. Her arm stabbed at the door. "They, Akilah and Trinity—"

"Yeah, I know. I'm not blind. Any idiot could see they were trying to rope-a-dope you and get you in hot water. She even rattled off some nonsense you're going to do to her what you did to Nevaeh."

Jasmine grabbed the tarnished chrome arms of her chair. Her fists clenched the metal tubes with anger, and her eyes went wide with fear. "... what *I* did?"

"Look, Jasmine. I have an idea of what's going on between you and Nevaeh." Coach strolled over to the metal closet across from her desk. "You're the new girl, and an easy target. It doesn't help that you're good enough to make first squad. The girls who're used to being on top are nervous."

She clicked open the closet door and pulled out a towel criss-crossed with crusty swaths of dried red food coloring.

"Nervous enough to put you through the wringer. I haven't seen them use this trick in a long time." Coach tossed the towel back into the closet and closed it again. "But the next time they goad you on the court, don't take the bait. Or I'll have to do something about it."

Coach stared at the ceiling for a moment, rubbing one knuckle across her mouth. "Now I gotta get serious. Nevaeh's missing. Do you know anything about that?"

Jasmine shifted uncomfortably in her chair. She didn't want to lie, but she couldn't tell Coach the truth either. Bibi's warning swirled between her ears—*She'll think you're crazy.*

"C'mon Jasmine. Nevaeh and her friends have it in for you. From the scuttlebutt I can piece together, you walked home after the game. After you left, Nevaeh slapped her boyfriend hard, then chased after you. My guess is she was jonesin' to nail your butt to the wall. That was the last anyone on the team saw Nevaeh. What happened?"

Jasmine focused on a crack that meandered across the concrete floor—unrepaired, but slopped over by battleship gray paint. "She trapped me in an alley, slammed me against the wall, and punched me—hard. I spotted an opening and ran as fast as I could, straight home. I didn't lay a hand on her. Honest. That's all I can tell you."

Without sounding nuts, that is.

Coach folded her arms, regarding Jasmine with unblinking eyes. At first, she looked like she might believe Jasmine—until her mouth worked into a frown that made it plain she suspected she wasn't getting the whole story. After a sigh and a shrug, she surrendered with "All right, have it your way. Akilah's gonna raise a stink about your stunt today, but it's up to you whether you get a slap on the wrist or thrown off the team." She sidled up to the door and glanced though the gap between the blinds and the window. "Hang tight here, until I clear everyone out. We're gonna get to the bottom of this."

She cleared her throat, squared her shoulders, and let loose a thunderous bluster that would have made a Marine drill sergeant proud. "Don't gimme that crap! Sit right there until I get back, young missy. Or you're gonna be in detention until all your eggs drop out." Coach wrenched open the door and tromped out of the room like a rutting bull. "And what do *you* clowns think you're doing? You want some too?" she bellowed.

A pair of girls stumbled back from the door, squealing an eek of surprise as they cinched their wet towels tighter around themselves, then scrambled for the safety of their lockers.

Minute after sweaty minute ticked by, and the bustle of showering, dressing, and primping diminished—but not fast enough to avoid trying Jasmine's patience. One after the other, Akilah then Trinity paraded past the office door, their malicious smiles drinking in their anticipation of what was in store for their common archenemy. Jasmine returned the favor by grinning sweetly and flipping them the bird.

More minutes of frustration. She twiddled her fingers, tapped her foot to a song she tried to play in her head, tried to think what pearl of wisdom Bibi would say at a time like this. Or what Ma would tell her. Or how disappointed Dad would look, when he'd roll out his old standby, "One foot in front of the other." His face would … it would …

Oh God, I can't remember what Dad looks like.

Her stomach felt worse than if it were torpedoed by a volley of Akilah's and Trinity's basketballs.

She pushed herself out of the chair, slung her backpack with its remaining strap over one shoulder and fidgeted next to the doorway.

So, Coach is in my corner, but she smells something's off. I can't stay here. The more she presses, the more I'm afraid I'll slip up.

The coast was clear—no sign of the Troublesome Twofer. She slunk out of the locker room through the gym and into the outer hallway, but not before she caught the dim echo of Caleb's hushed rasp.

"Hey, Akilah, c'mere. Where d'ya think *she's* going?"

What the hell are those two up to?

Jasmine bolted through the steel and wire-reinforced glass doors into the street. A metro bus pulled up to the corner half a block away.

Stifling a cry at the bus to wait, she sprinted through a thin cloud of the idling bus's exhaust. She sidestepped through the door just before they louvered shut. Swiping her card under the gaze of the impatient bus driver, she grabbed the nearest seat and pressed the side of her face against the grime-streaked window.

Caleb and Akilah popped out of the school gym's street exit. Caleb stamped his foot, punched the closing door and screamed a curse drowned out by the rumble of the diesel engine. Akilah's face was an open book that shouted "this ain't over."

Jasmine exhaled through lips stretched taut.

Made it. For now.

CHAPTER SEVEN

Jasmine munched absently on a stale doughnut her mother had rescued last night from the coffee-shop's expired goods. She stared half-asleep at the empty chair across from the kitchen table. What should have been a sweet breakfast seemed tasteless as yesterday's oatmeal without Bibi's laughter and light filling the kitchen.

Like a mouse in a desperate search for cheese in a maze, Ma scurried from bathroom to bedroom in a state of undress, then through the kitchen to the front room, mostly dressed. She juggled her breakfast while shoving a packed lunch into her bag and keeping her eyes riveted to the local news on the tiny television. Mumbling an unintelligible expletive around a piece of dry coffee cake, she stopped dead in her tracks when a new headline flashed on the screen. The announcer's words were lost behind the static crackling out of the speaker, and the spasmodic screen flickered his skin from a pale green to blazing red.

With her fist, Ma rapped the cracked plastic housing of the ancient appliance scavenged from a neighbor's junk pile. After a firmer second knock and a jiggled cable connection, the TV settled back into normalcy.

She tore the food out of her mouth, spraying out a shower of crumbs.

"Of all days! A bus strike?" She leaned over Jackson's terrarium and squinted through the window at the threatening sky. "And it's raining, too. Just what we *don't* need," she groaned.

Ma slid open the closet opposite the front door and pulled out her rain jacket and a crinkled sheet of plastic. She snapped open the neon orange poncho and draped it over Jasmine's bag.

"Aw, Ma. Don't make me wear that cruddy thing."

"You *will*, 'cause we don't have Bibi here to take care of you when you catch cold."

"I feel like I have a target on my back when I wear that."

Bigger than the one I already got.

"It'll be wet outside, and there's gonna be a mess of extra traffic, Jazz. You'll need this, so those idiots on the road see you. I seen 'em all night in the coffee shop. Their heads are in their phones and up their assho– ... their you-know-what's. You'll *wear* it, young miss."

"Will you stop calling me that."

"I will, when you don't gimme grief about everything. Honestly, is this what Bibi had to put up with each morning?" Ma tucked the back of her work shirt into her pants and her work shoes into her bag, puffing like a sprinter unaccustomed to the rigors of a marathon. "Now finish your breakfast, clean up, and get to school."

She pointed to Jasmine's backpack with an accusing finger. "And don't forget your keys again. I'm working an extra shift, and Bibi ain't here to let you in." She swirled her coat around herself, the trail of a faint "Iluvya" trickling through the doorway on her way out.

Jasmine stifled a sneer and raised her glass of milk, but gagged when she caught a whiff of sourness. Choking down the last bite of pastry made her mouth dry as desert.

With a growl of frustration, she ambled around the rooms faster and more haphazardly than Ma had done. Rinsing the dishes was followed by putting on shoes, turning off the TV, and a dozen other minutiae as she shuffled from room to room. She cracked open the casement window above Jackson's cage, though she doubted even insects would venture out on a day like this.

She came to a sudden stop as she frowned at the orange poncho. Her nose crinkled at the hint of old mildew that drifted up at her.

Jasmine stomped out of the apartment building, playing the part of an angry Day-Glo nylon duck to the hilt. She glanced up, grimacing at the misty drizzle. It wasn't a proper rain, rather only a clinging dankness that chilled down to the bones in no time flat—what Ma would call "a raw day."

She trudged past the bus stop, sneering at the poor slobs that stood next to the sign pole, soaking up dampness, waiting for a bus that would never come. The thoughts of what tyrannies might await her at school were interrupted again and again by the honking of the over-abundance of cars that swarmed the streets. Jasmine kept away from the sidewalk's edge with her head down, out of the fine sprinkle of rain, and away from the showers that dribbled out of clogged gutters and runoff that tires sprayed out of potholes.

Seconds after a rainbow sheen of oil-slicked water washed up around her feet, she froze at the sound of a speeding car hydroplaning into a skid. Her street-smart eyes zeroed in on a car swerving half a block ahead of her.

The auto careened, spinning counterclockwise after it clipped the corner of the pickup truck braking in front of it. It bounced to a stop across the sidewalk, mortally wounded and steaming. Traffic ground to a splashing halt, followed by a chorus of honks, brays, and blasts over-riding the yells and curses of their drivers. Pedestrians soon fell into their predictable pattern, rubbernecking and blocking the entire street. They tried to shoulder and struggle past one another, clogging every passage.

Jasmine zigged around idling cars and zagged between stalled delivery trucks. Holding her ears against the deafening horns blasting out of their grates as she zipped in front, she darted into a pedestrian chute. Enclosed by scaffolding pipes holding tarps taut against the weather, it huddled under a building façade that looked like it had been under repair since before she was born. Crowds, like cattle stampeding away from the accident, squeezed her in as they clogged the walkway. A gangway only inches wider than herself, closed off by a severely man-gled chain link fence, made a T-intersection off to one side. A rip in the fence was folded up like a tent flap, inviting her to make a quick escape.

She gathered the poncho about her and ducked through the opening. The scent of rotting wood and sewer gas assaulted her nose the moment she finagled her way through the opening.

The alley squeezed between two buildings, dilapidated husks of faded brick and crumbling stucco towering on either side. The walls were shadowless, their ancient features barely discernible from the fee-ble slit of gray sky dribbling down on her. Sheets of moldy plywood were nailed over windows that otherwise would have stared at the wasteland of disintegrating masonry. The walls were almost free of graffiti—only an occasional tag of distorted initials appeared here and there. At the far end of the alley, a gray rectangle beckoned through the comparative gloom.

Jasmine shuffled quickly through the confining space toward a broken iron gate that materialized out of the gray mist at the far end of the lane. Stacks of moldering wooden pallets and sheets of corrugated green plastic leaned against the intersection's far wall.

She shivered as the walls of stone inflicted a claustrophobic chill. Steps away from the lane's end, she halted with a gasp.

A dark figure dashed past the opening then hopped back, blocking the exit. Standing next to the gate hanging askew off one hinge, the shadowy silhouette with a backward baseball cap held a cellphone to one ear.

"Thanks," he said between breaths. "I got her."

Caleb. How did he …?

Jasmine swiveled her head, keeping Caleb in her periphery as she glanced at the rattling of chain links behind her. Akilah slipped through the fence flap, chuckling into her phone. She tapped the face of her phone, then held it sideways in front of her face, steadying it with both hands. Her cruel smile peered underneath the phone. "She's all yours, Cale."

They were following me?

Caleb's black cap and windbreaker dripped with dampness, sopping his sweatpants. His face was an inscrutable mask as he reached behind the brick corner and dragged a corrugated sheet of translucent green along the asphalt, scraping it across the gateway. In the chartreuse-tinted fog, a toothy predatory smile snaked its way across his face.

Jasmine's eyes locked onto a metallic glint on his right fist. Caleb spun a ring with a large "C" on the middle finger of his right hand. Jasmine strangled a gulp.

Crap crap crap—that was Nevaeh's.

"Howya doin', girl?" he said. The music of casual banter in his voice from the day before was gone. It echoed in her ears like a threat, resembling the snarl of a wolf.

"Leave me alone, Caleb," warned Jasmine with shallow firmness, that came out more like a frightened plea.

"Alone? A fine girl like you?" A fake smile widened to expose tightly clenched teeth. "You're so nayfa, mebbe I should give *you* my ring instead. Make you mine."

He held up his hand and looked at it with mock surprise as he sauntered closer. "Will ya look at that. Just like the one I gave to Nevaeh. Now, how do ya suppose I got it back? I don't remember her givin' it back to me …" Caleb stopped close enough for the fog of his breath to envelope Jasmine. It reeked of vape and weed.

"Oh, yeah, someone found it in your friend's trash."

Jasmine gulped again to stop the sudden urge to dry heave.

"What you doin' with Nevaeh's stuff? *My* ring?" The phony smile evaporated from Caleb's lips.

With his left hand he rammed Jasmine's shoulder against the wall. Ancient masonry crunched against her backpack, and small chips and pebbles danced around her feet. "You wanna be my ho? Is that it?" He held up his fist threateningly. "You want my ring? You wanna take Nevaeh's place?" He scowled, though a hint of sadness intruded upon the anger in his eyes. "Well, you got it, bitch."

Jasmine responded with a knee to Caleb's groin, but a twist of his hips deflected it.

A quick jab of his fist into her abs plowed the breath out of her. Her head snapped down as she gagged for air. He bore his full weight through his pelvis against hers. Bringing the heel of his right palm against the bottom of her jaw, he rammed her head against the wall. Wet stucco crumbled into her hair, and Caleb's grinning face began to fade and blur. She blinked and shook her head, trying to focus where she might hit or kick.

Sweeping the folds of the poncho to one side, Caleb grabbed the belt loops of her baggy jeans and yanked down.

Jasmine scrambled to pull her pants back up, but her hands clutched empty air. Straining against Caleb's weight pressing her against the wall, she opted to strike again. She poked her two foremost fingers where she guessed his eye might be.

Nothing.

A solid slap across her cheekbone blurred the last of her vision into a watery film. She bit her lower lip when she heard the rustle of Caleb's sweatpants sliding down. She caught a fuzzy glimpse of his pants bunched around his knees. Akilah giggled in a low sultry voice nearby—she must have closed in for a better shot.

"You *know* she wants it, Cale," she urged him on, followed by another lewd chuckle.

"You like it rugged raw? Let's find out."

"Do it Caleb! Make her beg! Then make her tell us what she did to Nevaeh."

Caleb pressed his left forearm against the base of Jasmine's throat, while his other hand clamped on her breast.

The "C" of his ring was the only thing on which her eyes could focus, sharp as a knife-edge. His hand slipped under her poncho and grabbed her chest again with renewed fervor.

"Lemme go. Didn't …" Jasmine gurgled. "Didn't do nothin'."

"Bullshit!" Akilah shouted. "You did *sumpthin'* to Nevaeh. Where is she? Didja *kill* her?"

Jasmine balled her hands up into fists, tried to flail at anything. Her back against the wall, she pushed against Caleb's chest. His strength flattened her meager leverage.

"Don't hurt me, or …" she said with a whining mewl. Jasmine squinted, trying to connect with what she made out to be Caleb's eyes. "Jack—"

She gagged when her mouth slammed shut. She tried to call his name again, but bit her tongue on the first syllable.

Why can't I say his damned name?

"He … he'll stop you," she gasped.

Caleb's blur of a head pivoted back and forth. "Jack? Who's Jack?" he laughed. "There ain't no Jack here."

"No one but us, Cale," Akilah seethed behind her phone. "Do it. Give her some of that fine dark rod. What are you waiting for?"

Jasmine wriggled, but could not squirm away. Caleb laughed, short and low. Jasmine gagged on the stench of his breath and taint sweat.

"Aw c'mon, Jazz. I ain't gonna hurt ya none." His breath came in heavy pants. "Gonna rock your world, baby girl," his hoarse whisper grated in her ear. She winced as he roughly kissed her neck.

Oh, God. This happened all the time in the Projects. Every week, there was talk in the halls—some girl getting turked. But that happened there, not here.

Not here. Not now. Not me!

Rage tried to well up in Jasmine, but its spark was extinguished by an overwhelming despair as heavy as the misty drizzle. The need to escape was smothered by the compulsion to hide.

To withdraw. To deny. To let the world's ugliness wash over her. *Not now. Not me. Not here.* I'm ... *not here.*

She squeezed her eyes shut, hoping that she might wake up in her sweat-soaked bed again. The will drained from Jasmine's arms, and they fell limp at her sides.

"But don't worry about getting knocked up. Cain't get preggo," Caleb heaved. He pressed his lips next to her ear. "Not if you ain't breathin' no more."

The sadistic grip crushing her windpipe vanished. She gulped a mouthful of fog rank with the taste of mildew, nicotine and weed. A slick curtain of Day-Glo snapped over her head, and the renewed pressure of Caleb's hand clamped on her neck. His thumb pressed mercilessly on her larynx before she could scream.

She gasped for air that would not come. Her world reduced to an ocean of orange and the taste of mildew and plastic.

Starving for oxygen, Jasmine's panic overrode her reason, her fear, her primal instinct to hide within herself.

Jasmine's arms pulsed with adrenaline, springing to renewed life. She clawed at anything and everything. At the tangerine nylon slickness smothering her face. At Caleb's hands crushing her throat and breast. At empty air, hoping to find his eyes, his mouth, or his groin.

Caleb's crude pawing at her breasts disappeared. Rough fingernails scratched as they tugged at her underwear, and an unfamiliar thick firmness pressed against her pelvis. She twitched her mound away from it. Her strangled scream echoed weakly in the poncho, funneled back to her own ears.

An ear-splitting crack resembling that of a wet bullwhip shattered her senses.

Caleb gurgled incoherently. The iron grip on her neck yanked away. He shouted something that started as a mishmash of obscenities, but it was silenced in mid-curse.

Above her head came the sickening munching, slurping, and crunching that invaded her nightmares. Jasmine's insides shifted and twisted into a knot of spasms.

She collapsed to her knees, planting her hands on wet asphalt. Tearing the poncho away from her face, she pawed for fresh air. A lungful flooded past her string of coughs and dry heaves. Her hand scrabbled against the poncho, searching for the belt of her pants, when she glanced to one side.

She froze, all except for her jaw dropping at the sight of Caleb's fist still clutching his ring disappearing down an immense gray gullet. With a whimper, she squeezed her eyes shut against the sound of massive claws scuttling across asphalt, brick, and stucco.

Another slash of something massive whipped above her head, and a gurgling high-pitched scream stabbed through the pounding heartbeats and panicked breaths roaring in Jasmine's ears.

She shook her head, and with the back of her hand cleared away the filmy curtain of tears and orange plastic. Lifting her head from the litter-strewn asphalt, she gawked at an enormous shape, the same dappled hue of the masonry, clinging impossibly to the wall.

From either side of its cavernous maw hung Akilah's form—legs kicking out the left side, head and arms thrashing out the right.

She struggled high above Jasmine's head, pounding her fists at a triangular mass of gray that seemed to shift in and out of existence as it flailed her body back and forth. Bobbing straight up from the other side of the ashen mouth, her legs kicked against open air, occasionally hitting stone. With her abdomen clamped between the thing's jaws, her shallow breaths had no room for a scream. She pushed impotently with both arms against the moving bulk of living stucco. Her cellphone clattered to the scree of blacktop, pebbles, and litter.

Mlinzi waggled his head, like a hunting dog with a bird in its mouth. Akilah's legs slipped down into the thing's maw, disappearing into the fleshy gray jaws that clamped again on her squirming torso. Akilah gulped a ragged breath and began to utter a cry for help. Her feeble plea was drowned out by the whoop of an ambulance announcing itself from the far-off street.

The indistinct mass of gray swung its thick neck, smashing the girl's head against a plywood sheet. The rotting wood splintered inward, muffling the sound of shattering window glass and breaking bone. Akilah hung silent and limp, until the creature unhinged its mouth. Her body tumbled in a heap against the wall, like a broken mannequin. Smears of blood traced from the shattered wood down the wall, ending where her head lolled against her chest.

Caleb's hat lay discarded in a puddle of water near Akilah's hip. The water swirled with sluggish eddies of her blood.

Clambering to her feet, Jasmine clutched at her pants, yanking them up to her waist. She breathed in panicked gulps drawn though clenched teeth. Her gasps filled the alley, her ears, her world. She splayed her hands against the wall, steadying herself as she inched sideways away from the horror staring back at her.

The monstrous hulk turned a shade darker, a shade redder. Its outline, as large as an SUV, hung pronounced against the sickly gray wall. Four massive legs terminating in formidable five-toed claws crunched through the stucco into the mason block underneath.

"God, oh, God," she cried in strangled shriek. "Damn, Jackson, what did you do?"

Mlinzi's conical eyes spun in their sockets toward Jasmine.

"*Mah lin zee. Koo lin da. Jassz-meen.*" The words slithered out of its quivering maw.

Tears flowed out of Jasmine's open eyes, as she softly wept at Akilah's crumpled form.

Two! Two dead! Another dying. Because of that thing. Because of me!

"*Kulinda*—Protect? Again, protect?" Her whole body trembled with nervous energy, holding the tattered rags of her will together. "Dammit, we had a … a truce! Bibi said so." Her breaths came in short bursts. "What have you done?"

His reptilian mouth unhinged and twitched. "*Caleb angeh enda kumwua Jassz-meen.*" His blood-tainted lips jerked with his words, like a poorly dubbed foreign film. "*Wewe ni salama.*"

Jasmine's throat was a dry as dust. "Oh, Christ. Not again. What the hell does *that* mean?" She clamped her hands over her ears, trying to block out *Mlinzi's* inhuman voice.

"What do I do? What the *fuck* do I do?" Her staccato words blurred together, increasing in speed and volume into an incoherent wail, reaching to attain the panicked scream that demanded a voice.

Mlinzi lowered his head over Akilah, shielding her broken body from the interminable drizzle. His wayward eyes stabbed directly at Jasmine. The weight of his stare filled her with a fear more consuming than any she had felt before.

She turned away, searching for a light, a human face, something she could run toward. Red and white pulses of an ambulance's lights softened by the mist bounced past the chain link fence that seemed miles away.

But *Mlinzi's* eyes swiveled like cannons, drawing her back. Shiny black beads nestled in their red scaly cones began to spin, began to grow and spiral, began to fill her vision.

First Akilah, then the alley, and the entire world disappeared—only *Mlinzi*'s eyes remained. They enveloped her with a blackness over-flowing with something deeper than sleep, and a foreboding that hinted there was something more final than death. From within the folds of darkness echoed a low hissing.

Jasmine recoiled from the monstrous voice, but its inexorable chant drew her back.

"*Kuwa na utulivu Jasss-meen. Kuwa na ...*" it droned in endless croaking sibilance.

The ground tilted, then spun under her. A dizzying vertigo, worse than standing on the highest bench of the bleachers, turned gravity upside down.

I'm gonna be sick. Get a grip, girl. Fight it. Fight ...

Mlinzi's ophidian voice crept inside her ear.

Part of Jasmine recoiled from the reptilian speech hissing inside her skull. Another part found it soothing, like a warm bath. Amorphous sounds, loathsome ululations, and tranquilizing murmurs coalesced into vowels and consonants, then finally into words.

"Be ... calm ... Jassz-meen," came *Mlinzi*'s measured words. "Caleb wanted ... kill Jassz-meen. You sssafe now." His hissing inhala-tions between words reverberated inside her consciousness. "Be calm, Jassz-meen," he repeated in a slow, soothing susurration.

After an unknowable number of inhales, heartbeats, and exhales, the reptilian hissing was gone from inside her. The ground was once again under her feet, and Jasmine could think.

The shock of death, violence, and gore was submerged under cool resolve. Fear had been swallowed up by an impartial acceptance.

It's over. I should be terrified. I was ... I know I was.

But now ... it's gone. Like it was never there.

She pushed herself away from the wall. A few faltering steps, and Jasmine stood over Akilah. She tilted her head, coolly examining Akilah like a scientist might regard a lab animal.

Blood oozed like strawberry jam down the side of the girl's face. Her chin bobbed slightly, raised by slow, shallow breaths.

The seed of revulsion and terror tried to sprout up anew inside Jasmine's chest, before she buried it handily with her newfound ice-cold lucidity. She refused to be reduced again to a heap of directionless emo-tion. Giving in to simpering helplessness would be almost as bad as surrendering to Caleb's repulsive touch.

"Man, you nailed her good, Jackson. But did you have to hurt Akilah so bad? It was Caleb that was going to kill me." She glanced at *Mlinzi*, uttering a dismissive harrumph at the satiated hue of green in which he had cloaked himself.

"Ssshe ... planned. Ssshe ... wanted." *Mlinzi's* back arched as he climbed a step closer toward Akilah. "Ssshe ... saw. Sstopped her ... sshowing otherss."

Jasmine bent down to assist Akilah, but stayed her hand inches from the fallen girl's head.

What should I do? If I help her, I might end up busting her up worse.

She shook her head as an errant thought slipped in the spaces between her calm logic.

Wait ... why should I help her? She wanted me dead. Raped and dead. She'll only come after me again.

She flexed her hand, forcing it away from Akilah, instead reaching for the phone lying next to her unconscious form. It continued to faithfully record the fuzzy blackness seen by its down-turned lens. Jasmine hit the "stop" icon, and a prompt appeared, "Share?"

"What ... will ... do?" *Mlinzi* hissed. "Help ... her ..."

"Is that a question or a command?" Jasmine asked.

Mlinzi tilted his head, each eye scanning opposite ends of the alleyway.

"Screw that, Jackson. Akilah planned this. You said so yourself. Help her? After what she did? And after what you did to her?"

She turned off the phone. Turning it end over end, she snapped off its back, and popped out the data card. She hitched the memory chip in her hand and wound up to pitch it into the fog. After a pause, her body relaxed as Jasmine held the chip in front of her again. She screwed up her lips to one side in a frown of concentration.

I got an idea what to do with this.

Her face contorted with effort as she broke the memory card in two. She tossed one half into Caleb's blood-soaked cap and pushed the other fragment deep into the back pocket of her jeans.

"Help her? I'm helping *us* instead," she replied, staring at *Mlinzi* without flinching. With a harsh downturn of her lips, she regarded the mammoth moss-hued hulk clinging to the wall and hovering over Akilah's helpless form.

Mlinzi lowered his head, shielding Akilah's head from the drizzle.

He returned Jasmine's stare with both eyes.

"What ... *you* ... do?" the giant lizard repeated. "She ... not kill ... Jassz-meen."

He really wants me to help her?

"Oh, all right, Jackson. If I must." She stamped her foot, and puddle water splashed all around her and Akilah.

Jasmine snapped the cover back onto Akilah's phone and dialed three digits.

"911—What is your emergency?" responded the tinny operator.

Jasmine drew taught her larynx, squeaking like a frightened child. "Some girl, she's bleeding bad and out cold. You gotta hurry. I think she might die."

"Where is the emergency?"

She rattled off their location, punctuated with a gasp when Akilah's form twitched. The unconscious girl's face stretched into a rictus of agony as her back arched and her twisted torso spasmed into rigidity.

"Hurry, she's doing something weird. I think she's having a seizure."

"What is your name?"

"I ain't gonna give you my name. Leave me outta this. Jane Doe."

She tapped the red phone symbol with harsh precision. *Nice phone. Loads better than the cheapo government-assist phone Ma gave me.*

Jasmine shook her head violently, rejecting the idea.

Nah, too much trouble. Too many questions if I'm caught with it.

She frowned at her fingerprints dotting the screen, clear as day for all the world to see—and the cops to dust. Wrapping the phone in Akilah's jacket, she methodically wiped off every surface of the phone. Just to be safe, she wiped off the chip in Caleb's hat as well. She pushed the phone into one of the jacket pockets, then tossed the sopping garment on top of Akilah's supine form like she was disposing of a used rag.

A rush of orange swooped past her eyes, with the flapping sound of plastic filling her ears as a flurry of runoff showered her head.

"Hey! Whaddyou ..." Jasmine protested as she swung her head upward. *Mlinzi's* tongue, the color of dried blood, scrolled back into his maw. The folds of her poncho crumpled in his lizard's jaws. He tore the plastic sheets out of his mouth, crushing it in his sluggish claw.

"Her ... ma-a-chine ... sssaw you," he rasped from his slavering mouth. His head turned toward the chain link fence at the end of the claustrophobic alley. "Other thingsss ... sssaw ..." He grabbed the poncho with his tail, holding it aloft. "... thisss."

"Other people?" Jasmine's gut crimped like it was sucked into a vacuum. A sudden image of herself in a police lineup flashed through Jasmine's mind.

"Other ... ma-a-chine-sss ..."

"Protector, huh?" Her shoulders twitched with a humorless chuckle, and her head shook with smugness. "Yeah, you protect real good, Jackson. But one thing I don't get. You ate Caleb. I guess you ate Nevaeh, too. Why not Akilah? She wanted me dead just as bad."

"Want ... and *do* ..." he hissed, his eyes flicking from Akilah to Caleb's hat. "Not ... the sssame."

After slinging her backpack over one shoulder and swiping damp chunks of stucco from her hair, Jasmine walked sullenly to the end of the lane that Caleb had blocked off. Brick and mortar behind her head crunched in cadence with her own footsteps. She halted a pace away from the corrugated sheet. Looking upward over her shoulder, she chuckled in disbelief at the faded emerald behemoth. The tattered rags of the poncho hung from the tight spiral of his tail.

"When did you start speaking English, Jackson?"

Why the hell do I think of a stupid thing like that now?

"I ... learn. From ... inssside you." *Mlinzi* climbed upward and backward, his tail and the poncho curling over the top of the building. As he rose, his green bulk dissolved into the fine mist drizzling down. One eye pointed at Akilah and the chain link fence beyond, the other at Jasmine. "What ... Jassz-meen ... learn?"

"I tried to warn Caleb. I *did*," she mumbled, clenching her fists. "I *really* did."

But I couldn't. Why was that? Why couldn't I say his name?

An implacable hand threw a switch inside her mind, and the cold logic returned. She faced *Mlinzi* and flexed her hands, letting them hang at her sides. Her face flattened into a mask of unfeeling stone.

"No more warnings. If treating people like shit is all these bastards respect, then that's what they'll get." She squinted and blinked, daring the monster to contradict her. "*That's* what I learned."

Mlinzi uttered a hissing grunt before resuming his upward climb. The faint sirens of a second ambulance approached, vying for attention over the first beyond the chain link fence. Jasmine shoved the green plastic panel to one side, pausing to survey one last time the wreckage of *Mlinzi's* intervention. She and Akilah were alone in the lane—*Mlinzi* had either camouflaged himself or climbed over the edge of the roof.

Hell, he's probably back in his cage by now.

Jasmine trudged through the broken gate and faded into the mist.

CHAPTER EIGHT

With each step, Jasmine's boldness diminished. The closer she came to the high school, her no-nonsense stride slowed to a trudge.

The hypnotic image of *Mlinzi's* eyes and the shielding cocoon of his voice faded with every emotionless glance from a stranger. Each passing kid's casual laugh into their phone, each effortless snark into their friend's ear, each repressed snicker from a nameless passerby, they all chipped away at *Mlinzi's* gift of cold, pragmatic serenity. Every wisp of exhaust-tainted fog wafting past her face recalled the reek of Caleb's breath, leeching away her confidence.

God, I was almost raped. Almost killed!

Knock it off, girl. You got this. Those little shits got what they deserved.

What's going on? A minute ago it all made sense. I could see a way through. I was ready to take on the world. Now I'm a scared little kitten.

Jasmine's world overflowed with streets crammed with people. All of them watching her, everyone judging her. A city full of potential witnesses—or worse, accusers. With waves of paranoia washing away the calm instilled by *Mlinzi*, she turned her head away from every street corner camera, every storefront, every ATM. The world seemed filled with blinking LED lights. Watching, always watching.

Why do I feel guilty? I didn't hurt anyone. It was all Jackson. He was protecting me.

Nevertheless, unrelenting tentacles of guilt squeezed her chest. She huddled her shoulders together against prying eyes and the clammy mist. Waiting at an intersection, she glanced upward, hoping she might catch a glimpse of a reassuring three-horned head peering over a rooftop.

Instead, a billboard of five uniformed people peered down. Each from a different branch of the armed forces, they commanded her and anyone else that glanced at them to "JOIN!"

What on earth was I thinking? I ain't no alpha bitch. Whatever Jackson did to me with those eyes, it's gone. I lost it.

The man in the Army duds reminded her of Dad. The guy might have passed for his brother—if her recollection of Dad's face could be trusted. The stern set of the Army grunt's jaw jived with the no-nonsense crackle of Dad's voice over the phone. But that seemed an eternity ago …

"… I only have a few minutes, Jazz. I wish I could Skype to you both. I'm dyin' to see your face, Sprout. Growin' up so fast, and I'm not there to help you …"

That phone call might as well have been a lifetime ago. She had dumped all her problems in a flurry at the voice on the other end of the phone—new neighborhood, new school, and no friends. If she could talk to Dad now, most of the problems would be the same, only worse—the pressure, not fitting in, and everyone out to get her.

What would he say? Probably the same as last time.

"Like I always say, one foot in front of the other. Other than that, I don't know what to tell ya, Sprout. Out here, most of the time it's easy to tell who your friends are. We wear the same uniform. Everyone else, all the locals—anyone of 'em could be your best ally or your worst enemy. Take our translator. He's from the neighboring province, so he blends right in. Couldn't tell him from the bad guys who'd blow ya up as soon as look at ya. But me and the whole squad, we trust him with our lives."

That didn't help two weeks ago, Dad, when we left the Projects. It sure as heck doesn't help me now.

And then, if you threw Jackson into the mix of her Mount Everest of problems …

Bibi was right. Even Dad would think I'm nuts. Hell, even I would think I have a screw loose.

A pack of unfamiliar teenagers jostled past her on their way to school. She didn't know them, and most were too absorbed in getting out of the cold drizzle to care about anyone but themselves.

Needles of anger pricked at Jasmine when one of the teens gave her a funny look, like she'd spotted Sasquatch. Jasmine squelched her rising fury to paranoid guilt with a sigh.

Another stranger's glance was a painfully common one—looking without seeing, tinged with careless sarcasm. The girl was obviously laughing at the soggy idiot without rain gear. At least she didn't give Jasmine a flash of recognition, or worse, accusation.

Good. Leave me alone, and we'll both be just fine.

She jogged the rest of the way to school, dodging and weaving as if avoiding a courtside defense squad. Her clothes grew as heavy as a soaked St. Bernard by the time she arrived—they smelled like one, too. Clinging to her skin, they sucked the last shreds of warmth from her. Entering through the closest entrance by the gym, her sigh of relief to be out of the rain was cut short when she spied Coach Garcia.

I shoulda known.

Budget cuts had pulled teachers into security duty for backpack inspection. But it was too late to remember that scrap of info now. And no amount of fading into the jabbering crowd funneling toward the doors was going to help. Jasmine considered going the long way around to another exit, but not before Coach locked eyes with her.

"*Dios mio,*" said Coach. She waved Jasmine forward with a commanding sweep, directing her to cut next in line. Jasmine slid her backpack onto the steel security table. Coach did a cursory dig into the pockets of Jasmine's bag, all the while pelting her with a flurry of worries, not waiting for any excuses or answers.

"Where's your coat? Did your Mama let you out like that? We got a game Saturday night. Are you *trying* to get sick? What's wrong with you, girl? Get in the locker room pronto. And dry off before you catch somethin' and spread it to everyone else."

Coach's hands were a blur as she zipped open the compartments and rummaged around their insides, then flipped back out to swat the air around Jasmine's head during her rant. It occurred to Jasmine that she could have smuggled in a full-sized *Mlinzi*, and Coach still might have missed him.

With the force of a cross-court pass, Coach hefted the pack at

Jasmine, who accepted it without a word. Ignoring the flock of juvenile titters around her, she scooted into the gym. She snatched a towel from the locker-room shelves and tamped away the damp chill, finally permitting herself the sigh bottled up for the past several minutes.

Gathering together the shreds of her determination, she headed toward her school locker.

Suck it up, girl. You got things to do. One foot in front of the other.

Jasmine huddled her bag close to her chest and kept her head low. She didn't want to see, or be seen. Drifting along with the streams of students, she floated past close-knit cliques clogging the hallways like rush-hour accidents on the interstate.

Strange, how this day, the crowded hallways left her less anxiety-ridden than the open streets. Maybe it was because the school's electronic eyes, unlike those in the city, were broken and incapable of scrutinizing her every move. It might have been the murmured lullaby of conversations, absent from the streets, that filled the halls with a strange comfort. Perhaps it was the whiff of lavender from one of the English teachers posted on hall duty, filling her senses with the memory of sitting wrapped in Bibi's toasty comforter.

Her sense of anonymous safety didn't last long. Adrenaline spiked her sense of impending doom the second she caught whispered snippets of gossip leaking out of the closely huddled posses.

"It's the second day that Nevaeh missed."

"Saw Nevaeh's mom bitchin' in Principal Moore's office. She went total spaz. She's wants Moore to call in the National Guard."

They clammed up when one of the group spotted Jasmine lingering around their personal space. She scuttled away into the milling throng until another conversation pricked up her ears.

"Maybe Nevaeh finally ran away with Caleb."

"Sounds right. I haven't seen him since yesterday, neither."

"Nah, he was hangin' out with Akilah last night. You know she's just itchin' for him to dump Nevaeh."

"Whoa. *They* doin' the nasty, now?"

"You kiddin'? Akilah doesn't take a crap without Nevaeh's or Trinity's say so."

"That's not what *I* heard, girl. Just yesterday the two of them …"

Annoyed glares from the gang focused on Jasmine when she hovered too close for too long. She ducked her head and shuffled away.

A sliver of *Mlinzi's* calm that had bathed her in cool serenity in the alleyway returned.

Everyone thinks Akilah and Caleb are together. They'll find Caleb's cap next to Akilah, and think he left her like that. Hell, the cops may even finger the bastard for Nevaeh's disappearance, too. Good—that's exactly what I need. And that gives me another idea.

She stood straight, nodding to herself with building confidence. A newfound reassurance filled her steps. They echoed crisply down the hallway, drowning out the hesitant shuffling of the other students.

The first bell rang, and the timbre of the crowd changed. The tightly wound groups scattered with rounds of hastily chattered "see-ya"s. Students began to funnel into nearby doorways for their home-rooms, while others scampered off to who-knows-where.

Jasmine muttered a small curse and dashed down the hall.

Gotta haul ass. Now—when everyone's distracted.

Diving into the nearest girls' bathroom, she ripped out a paper towel from the dispenser. She dampened the towel under the nearest faucet and slipped into the farthest stall. Folding the paper towel into a tight square, she slid the broken data card between the creases and slipped it back in her pocket. Back in the hall's thinning crowds, she turned the corner into the hall with Caleb's homeroom.

His locker has to be somewhere near.

Jasmine's eyebrows knitted together in consternation, and she stumbled to a sudden stop.

Trinity, backed up by some over-muscled Amazon with her hair done up like a lame copycat of Nevaeh's, was browbeating Madison. Trinity leaned over the chubby girl, nose to forehead, with a grin of pure malice.

Madison planted her pudgy back next to Caleb's locker, marked with his tag, an oversized letter C. Her thick knees twitched like her bladder was ready to burst. Her eyes danced back and forth, searching for an escape. Once, maybe twice, a flash of hate burned through her seizure of fear.

The she-Tarzan planted one arm tattooed with a black jaguar's snarling face on a locker door next to the girl's roundish head. The clang of the metal made the shrimp flinch.

Poor kid, I feel your pain.

Trinity smacked the center of the locker on the other side of her victim's head, making it thrum like a timpani. "Fat-ass Madison, how the hell did you *ever* get on my team?"

Her *team? Look who's making a power play now.*

"You sweat like a stuck pig on the court. It's a wonder we don't drown during practice."

"Go f—"

"No, *you* go f—," said Trinity, mocking Madison's feeble attempt to stand against her. "Listen up, Fatty-son. You think you had it tough before?"

Madison huddled her books against her stomach in trembling hands. "I already helped you out. I sent the new girl all those texts, including the head lice ones. What more do you want?"

That was you?

"Back me up for captain, and everything's cool. Otherwise, what do you think Nevaeh will do when she gets back, and we tell her you bailed on us?"

Not quite, Trin. I'm pretty sure she ain't coming back.

"And my big sister, Kimani, here," said Trinity with a toss of her hair at the Amazon. "She's getting anxious. You don't want to get on her bad side ... again." The bruiser inched closer behind Trinity, lowering her forehead until her unblinking eyes beetled straight at Madison. "She's captain of girls' wrestling, and she's worried that her little sister ain't getting the props she deserves."

Madison's eyes bored a hole in the linoleum.

"You think you'll do any better siding with Jizm? She's from the Projects. Can't trust anyone from that shit-hole." She nodded to the muscle looming behind her. "We're gonna make damn sure she goes down, and down *hard*. And anyone with her."

Madison raised her head with a look of surrender. A deep breath was followed by a hesitant nod.

Jasmine did a quick about-face and scrambled back to her locker, snarling under her breath. "And I was beginning to like that little shit Madison. Can't trust *anyone*."

Ricocheting off the buffeting crosscurrents of faceless kids, she slid along the last stretch of linoleum, nearly body-checking her own locker door.

Her nose crinkled in disgust, and her eyebrows pinched together. Slips of paper poked through the air slots of her locker door. Though every opening was crammed with crumpled trash, they were powerless to block the stench of cheap perfume. Jasmine unlocked the door in record time, flinging it open with a clang. An avalanche of paper slips spilled out of her locker around her feet.

She blinked, squeezing away tears from the overpowering wave of acetone and alcohol mixed with a musky stench that would have sent a skunk running for the hills. Discolored splashes of amber liquid streaked down her books and supplies inside the locker's cramped metal space.

Jasmine kicked at the slips littering the ground. Every one had an insult scribbled in block letters with bright red marker.

Skank. Slut. Whore.

Bitch.

She clutched at that last note lying across her sneaker. Her hand began to shake, but not with fear—righteous anger smoldered under her calm.

The "i" was dotted with a heart.

Of course. Trinity.

Jasmine blinked when a cold fire rekindled behind her sternum.

That! was the feeling from the alleyway she had lost. Under her breath she muttered, "Haven't you been paying attention, bitch? Your friends are getting scarce, and you ain't making any new ones."

That tears it. The bitch must pay.

The second bell for homeroom rang. She scooped her textbooks out of her bag, sandwiching the ones from her reeking locker in between. Ignoring the gasps, whoops, wheezes, and sneezes as she tromped past her classmates, Jasmine took her seat with a stern glower and dropped her pungent armful on her desk.

She willed the room to *not* exist—it became a gray featureless box. The students did not exist—they were lumps of inanimate clay. The teacher did not exist—his disembodied voice regurgitated monotonous mishmashes of information that made no sense and had no use in the real world.

A singular thread spun in her head, knocking aside everything else that dared intrude.

What was that goofy saying Mr. Wyatt had in yesterday's history class? "Revenge is a dish best served cold"?

Jasmine spent the rest of the day's classes concocting delicious Trinity-flavored retributions.

Each period was more mind-numbingly boring than the previous one. During lunch, she didn't sit with anyone, and no one saw fit to join her at the table. And that was fine with her, as she played with her food while staring off into her dreamland of endless paybacks.

The only thing that broke her wishful visions of justice was World History class. It was tough enough to withstand Mr. Wyatt's endless drivel about more notable quotes from famous people and the events that gave rise to them. The burning stares from Trinity, sitting next to Akilah's empty chair, was the cherry on top that made the class unbearable.

Just wait, dear Trinity. Yours is coming.

The last bell rang, and she was out of her seat like a shot, racing to get out of the room before Trinity.

The teacher's voice blared out like a tugboat horn, instructing his escaping students to pick up the day's homework sheet. "This homework on historical quotes is due tomorrow," he trumpeted after the kids who had already scampered out of the room. He barked out Jasmine's name.

She froze in front of Mr. Wyatt's desk while Trinity breezed through the doorway, sporting a demonic grin.

"Jasmine, I know you're having a hard time with my class." Holding a copy of the handout for her to take, he added, "I have a study group in this room after school."

"No promises, Mr. Wyatt. Not with team practice for this weekend's game," she mumbled as she snatched the paper from his hand and jammed it behind the front cover of her history textbook. Bursting out of the classroom, she hustled like an Olympic speed walker down the hall, making a beeline to Trinity's locker. Rounding the corner, the soles of her sneakers eked out a squeak as she backpedaled behind the end of a nearby row of lockers. She screwed up her eyes with bitterness at her target—Trinity yanked out her pack and jogged in the direction of the gym without a care in the world.

Taking a deep breath, Jasmine fished out the paper towel containing Akilah's broken data card from her back pocket.

I was gonna dump this in Caleb's locker. Now it's all yours, you bitch.

Sauntering nonchalantly toward Trinity's locker, she surveyed the halls—no one around whom she knew, and no one Trinity hung around with. As she floated past Trinity's locker, she rubbed clean the broken data card in the paper towel, aimed through one of the locker's air slots and squeezed. The bit of metal and plastic shot through the opening, rattling down the interior walls until it settled into something soft.

She tailed Trinity from a leisurely distance, pausing to hang out at a strategic corner where she could observe the entrance to the girls' locker room. One by one, team members strolled into the gym. Madison, looking like she had been through the wringer, was the last to stumble in.

It occurred to Jasmine this was the one time she appreciated having no friends, no one who would want to chat her up and draw attention to her. For once, being a nameless nobody was an advantage.

Jasmine checked her phone, tapping her foot with impatience. It was five minutes after practice was supposed to start, when she caught the vestige of Coach's whistle blast through the locker room's doors. "About freakin' time," she grumbled under her breath.

She slipped past the double doors, fading into the closest row of lockers while the slower team members tied their shoelaces. She changed into her team uniform quick as she could, hanging back behind the last of her teammates. Sidling into Coach's office, she picked up a piece of chalk, and an impish grin flowed across her mouth.

With her hand an inch from the Coach's board, she paused to mull a sudden thought. Her grin intensified to a wicked leer, and she switched the chalk to her weak hand. She scratched out a short sentence in a barely legible scrawl.

Jasmine slunk into the gym—a black ops agent couldn't have been smoother. Satisfied no one noticed her tardiness, she merged herself into the warm-up laps. She hardly had the chance to work up a sweat, when Coach blasted her whistle signaling the two squads to line up. With two missing members, Jasmine was first in order. She leaned back and looked down the line. There was Madison in last place, hands on knees, dripping with sweat.

Coach's face had the weirdest look. Jasmine expected her to lay into the team, complaining about Nevaeh's and Akilah's lack of commitment and team spirit.

Instead, Coach coughed. Her jaw trembled as she hemmed and hawed. She held a ball between her hands, then dribbled it absently a couple of times while she chewed on her thoughts.

"I'm afraid the school just received some bad news. Akilah was rushed to the hospital early today. She was beat up real bad in an alley on her way to school." Coach coughed again, wet with repressed emotion. "She's in a coma. The hospital don't know when she'll come out of it."

Jasmine glanced at Trinity. Like the rest of the team, her jaw hung slack at the news.

After a moment of silence, a chorus of questions surrounded Coach—how did it happen and who did it?

"The police are looking into it." Coach bounced the ball once more. "I'm calling practice off for today."

A morbid stunned silence followed her pronouncement.

"Keep Akilah in your thoughts tonight," said Coach. "We'll discuss at tomorrow's practice whether you are all still willing to play this weekend." She hurled her ball at the rolling rack of basketballs, knocking it over and sending its contents bounding in eight different directions. "Go on, hit the showers and go home," she yelled with a tremble in her voice.

Jasmine was the first into the locker room. Skipping the showers, she changed directly into her street clothes. She kept a silent smile, eavesdropping on the comments rolling over the wall of lockers.

"Wow. Both of them …"

"Who's gonna captain? Oh, no, not *her*," said a familiar voice. "Not Jizm."

Right back atcha, Trinity. You hard-ass.

"Whaddya worrying about *that* for? We should visit Akilah in the hospital."

"If *she's* gonna be captain, I'm not playin'," Trinity continued, ignoring her teammate's rebuke. "Neither should you."

The feeling's mutual, bitch. Enjoy it while you can.

Jasmine sat alone on the bench between two rows of facing lockers, watching and waiting until Coach entered.

Ms. Garcia clomped into her office, tossed her whistle on the desk and shuffled a few papers. She froze, staring at her chalkboard. "*¿Qué demonios?*"

Slinging her pack over her shoulder as she scooted toward the exit, Jasmine glanced with a smirk at the message she had scribbled in the corner of the board.

"TrINitY + CaLEb dId iT."

CHAPTER NINE

J asmine sat in front of the TV, curled up on the front room sofa. She splayed her history book, with its frayed and broken cloth spine resting lengthwise along her thigh. Her nose twitched from its fading remnants of cheap perfume as she rummaged through the assigned chapter.

She flattened the crumpled history homework handout for the umpteenth time, but it stubbornly sprang back to its crinkled shape. After completing a scribbled passage in her workbook, she paused to grimace at the last two assignments: match a list of famous quotations to the historical figure who said them, followed by a 1,000-word essay on any one of the quotes.

The quotes all sounded like the smarmy things grown-ups would say—filled with a double meaning that was supposed to make them sound oh-so-clever, but made little sense.

"Absolute power corrupts absolutely."

Whatever that *means …*

"Nothing ventured, nothing gained."

Whoever said that had a screw loose. Or never had it knocked loose for them.

The rest of the list was equally obtuse. But Jasmine's eyes rested on two that grabbed her heart and wouldn't let go.

"Revenge is a dish best served cold."

That sounds better every time I see it.

"The best lies have just enough truth."

At last. Something I can use.

She stared at the match-up list, chewing on her pen while she tried to untangle the puzzle of who-said-what. By the time the late-night news theme music rattled out of the television, she had abandoned the list entirely, proceeding to the second half of the assignment. What little concentration she managed to whip up for her essay was interrupted time and time again by the television newscaster blaring out a never-ending stream of sound bites, and snippets of flashy videos that yanked at her peripheral vision.

Page after page in her workbook was filled with disjointed thoughts and jumbled starts meandering off-topic before coming to a jarring stop. Her entries were peppered with whole paragraphs scribbled out, some of them eradicated to blotches of solid blackness.

Her head hitched up every time the terms "murder," "ambulance," "missing teen," or "young girl" squawked out of the TV. Once she ruled out the latest report of mayhem had nothing to do with the incident in the alley, she glanced again at the terrarium.

Jackson remained motionless, with his head tilted and his three horns pointed directly at her. His body was half green and half red, mimicking the skewed hues of the salvaged television. The chameleon's pebbled mouth crimped into a curious frown that approached disappointment.

Jasmine belted out a loud whoosh of exasperation. Her shoulders ached with tension that bulldozed its way past the nape of her neck.

This history crap is not for me. I'm gonna have to crib off of someone at school. But who?

The entire back of her skull was throbbing when Ma came through the apartment door.

She hummed a sprightly but aimless little tune to herself as she hefted two large bags into the kitchen. One overflowed with the night's treasure trove of stale coffee-store noshes, the other was loaded with *real* groceries. On her way to dumping her hoard on the kitchen table, she stopped to stare with concern at her daughter.

"What are you still doing up, girl? It's way past your bedtime. Not watchin' one of those stupid cop shows again, are ya?"

"Just the news. Wrapping up homework," Jasmine replied.

One bag tipped over, and a squad of bagels rolled across the kitchen table.

"Since when do you care about the news? I swear, that's *worse* than those messed-up cop shows you like to watch." Ma strolled into the front room and looked over her daughter's shoulder. "Uh-huh. Made lotsa progress I see."

She flicked off the TV and returned to the kitchen table, corralling the bagels into the breadbox drawer.

Jasmine bounded off the sofa, sending her book and papers tumbling to the floor. She snapped the TV back on, and froze for a moment, gritting her teeth. A pair of insets crowded the screen next to the newscaster's face—an old mug shot of Caleb and a girl's pixelated profile.

"… found in the alley, the teenage girl was rushed to …"

She planted her body in front of the screen, and hammered the volume button, dropping the audio to a whisper.

"… searching for the male, who is a suspect in both this violent assault and another girl's disappearance." A closeup of Nevaeh in basketball uniform, with her name and "Missing" captioned underneath slid in to join the other two photos.

Her hair is perfect, as usual … Well, was perfect.

"The latest victim remains in a coma, but doctors have not disclosed her prognosis. A second female is being questioned by police as a person of interest. The identities of both the victim and second female are being withheld, due to their age."

At last, Nevaeh, Caleb, and Akilah got their fifteen seconds of fame. Kinda.

A quick sequence of neighbors and local shopkeepers blabbed the usual montage of "whatta shame" and "nobody saw nuthin'." The newscaster's face returned, this time with a blurry time-stamped video still-frame, taken from streetlamp height, of a tall figure in a poncho ducking into a fenced-off side street. "Police are also asking for assistance. If anyone has information on the identity—"

Jasmine's arm shot out and clicked off the television faster than *Mlinzi*'s tongue, and with equal accuracy. She glanced as discreetly as possible over her shoulder in the direction of the kitchen. However, she couldn't suppress a guilty frown drooping the corners of her lips.

Ma was safely behind the refrigerator door, stuffing groceries inside. Jackson was still in his terrarium, but the twist of his leathern mouth appeared to lend an extra air of smugness.

"I'm so glad the rain stopped this afternoon. Did the poncho help?"

"A little," replied Jasmine. Her jaw muscles began to ache, and she rubbed the instep of one foot against the back of the other calf. "But …" Her mind seized up, not able to select which fiction to say.

"But, what?" Ma straightened up, with a cockeyed stare—one eyebrow raised, with her forehead tilted inquiringly toward her daughter.

Jasmine could almost hear the thunder rolling behind Ma's brow.

"Someone stole it. I thought I put it in my locker, but it was gone by the end of the day."

Ma exhaled her usual sigh of long-suffering. "You mean you lost it. You better hope we don't get rain again soon. I can't just conjure up a new jacket like that," she said, snapping her fingers. "Maybe after next payday, but not just right now."

The phone rang and Jasmine's shoulders relaxed. The inevitable lecture from Ma was postponed—hopefully forever.

"Now, who would be calling at such an ungodly hour?" She shoveled her armful of groceries into the fridge and reached for the phone. All the while, a train of sanitized expletives that wouldn't make a nun blush rolled past her lips, until she stopped in her tracks on its second ring.

Ma pierced Jasmine with a look of fear mixed with worry. "You don't think … Oh, dear God. Let Dad be all right."

Grasping the cordless phone from the wall and holding it close with a shaky hand, she ventured a cautious "Hello?" into the receiver. Quick as lightning, Ma stood ramrod straight.

"*Bibi!*" she squealed, holding her free hand over her heart. "Omigoodness, I know it's only been two days, but we were beginning to wonder … No, don't worry yourself about no time zones. How was your trip? Are you all right? Is Rendell and his family okay? How's his wife and baby? What name did they give her?" The cascade of questions rolled out of her like a machine gun of emotions.

Sheesh. First Coach, then Ma. Do all grown-ups do that—ask a ton of questions without waiting for an answer?

Ma paced an absent-minded circle around the kitchen table, first in one direction, then the other. She slammed the refrigerator door without a thought, and the bottles inside complained, their sloshing rattles penetrating the door's insulation. Her volley of questions was gradually replaced with staccato gasps and exclamations with each orbit around the table.

Without a word Jasmine observed her mother, trying to glean the slightest meaning from her gyrations and exclamations.

Ma halted without warning and sighed with relief so loud, it whistled. Holding the back of her hand against her forehead, she collapsed in the nearest chair.

"I'm so glad that's over, and ...? She's still ...? Oh, no. For how long?" Ma curled up tighter against the kitchen table with each breathless "Uh-huh?" whispered into the phone.

Jasmine's gut contracted with each utterance, cramping into a knot when Ma stood up from the table, handing her the phone.

"Here, Jazz. Bibi wants to talk to you."

Her throat went dry at the sight of Ma's eyes on the brink of overflowing.

"Be nice to her, she's gone through a lot," Ma whispered, before returning to her task of stowing groceries.

We both have.

She cradled the phone to her ear like a long-lost friend. Her voice shook like a timid church-mouse. "Bibi?"

"Ho-ho, little one! How have you been?"

Jasmine's face scrunched up in bewilderment. Bibi's voice was effervescent, like she was having the time of her life at a party.

She folded her legs up onto the sofa, settling in for a long talk. She tried to smile, but it wouldn't come. Straightening her back, she prepared her brightest carefree voice.

"I miss you so much, Bibi! What's happening? Is everything all right? How ..." She stopped herself. A sardonic half-frown creased her mouth, as she realized she was about to launch into her own rat-a-tat stream of questions.

"Like I told your *muuther*, I'm busy as a shepherd protecting her flock from hyenas. This evening I'm taking care of my *grahnt*-son while Rendell is away. Cheta's a good boy. But he is rightly named—he's a little cheetah all right. It takes everything out of me just to keep up with him. But my Rendell, he spends all his time between his work and the hospital. He hardly has time to sleep, while his wife and *beh-bee* daughter are still ..."

"Ohhhh ..." Her anguished sigh rattled in the phone earpiece.

"Ask your *muuther* to tell you. I don't want to repeat all that gloom again. But I need to tell you—I don't know when I can come back to your city. I'm afraid my son and his family are going to need my help for a long, long while.

"So I ask again, little one, how are you? Is *Jack-suun* behaving himself?"

A small boy's voice squealed with delight on the other end. Bibi's chuckle followed, replenished with her seemingly endless reservoir of innocent joy. "Bibi's on the phone, my little Cheta."

A simple "I'm okay," started Jasmine off, but a sigh slipped out. The steely, unyielding high school badass took a backseat. Deep inside, a part of her was busting to unload. "But it's been …"

Don't do it. Don't break down.

Cold logic smothered her kindling emotions.

You slip now, you'll be weak again. Pounded down again. And you'll never get it back. Keep your shit together, girl.

"I'm fine," she concluded with new firmness into the receiver, punctuated with an indignant "do-you-mind?" glare lobbed at her mother, who hovered over her like a news-hungry vulture.

"*Ai*, I could hear a whole story in that." Bibi hummed absently, and her voice took on a much more serious aspect. "What's really happening, *Jazz-meen*?"

She untangled her legs and clambered out of the sofa, scattering her homework into an even wider chaos on the floor. While she trotted to her bedroom, she rattled off a string of distractions to deflect Ma's inquisitiveness—"School's great," "History's a royal pain," "We have another game this weekend,"—until she secured the door behind her and sat on her bed. The receiver shook in her hands.

What do I tell her?

The TV news had unnerved her more than she expected. The picture of Caleb and Akilah's digitally blurred form flashed in front of her eyes again. The cacophony of emotion that she had managed to stamp down built up to a rolling boil. It all threatened to spill out—her stress, her grief, her turmoil of guilt struggling against her justifications. She clamped her teeth together until she could regain her brave front.

Let no one in. No one. Not Ma. Not even Bibi.

She spied two thin shadowy columns spreading from under the door. Like usual, Ma stood outside, with her shameless attempt to eavesdrop. Jasmine leaped from her bed and body-checked the door with just enough force to unambiguously inform her nosy audience that any curiosity was not appreciated. She scrunched down, crossing her legs once more, behind the far side of her bed.

"*Mlinzi* did it again." She surprised herself at how easily the news flowed out of her mouth, and how matter-of-fact it sounded. "He killed a boy and hurt a girl real bad."

An eternity of electronic background noise hummed in her ear. The beeps and boops of an electronic game were followed by a young boy's laughter. The noise fell away, diminishing with the hurried taps of Bibi's footsteps.

"He was going to kill you, no?" she said, half-whispered.

"Yes, after he ..." Jasmine peeked over her bed. The shadow of Ma lurking outside her door was gone. Even so, she dropped to a breathy whisper. "... after he woulda raped me."

"*Ai*, my child," she whooshed. "What a terrible world. Are you all right? Did he hurt you?"

"He punched me a couple of times. And choked me." Jasmine coughed when the memory of Caleb crushing her windpipe came rushing back. She swallowed a sudden urge to sob.

No you don't, Jasmine. No emotion, dammit. You start now, you'll blubber everything out. Let nothing out. Let no one in.

"But Jackson got him before he could ... y'know ..."

"Oh, I'm so sorry, my child." Bibi sniffled, her voice cracking with strangled sobs. "Who was it that *Mlinzi* kill—" She suppressed something that sounded between a cough and a cry.

"Caleb, Nevaeh's boyfriend. Remember, the one I told you was into drugs? One of Nevaeh's crew, Akilah, put him up to it. She blamed me for Nevaeh's disappearance. She thinks I killed her. Now Caleb's dead, too, and Akilah's comatose in the hospital."

"I'm so sorry," Bibi repeated while the intensity of sobs increased. "I never should have ... It's all my fault."

Jasmine shook her head, and her eyes crossed in disbelief. *It's Bibi's fault?*

"What do you mean?"

The sniffles stopped. A deep sigh echoed over the electronic distance. "I thought you needed help so bad, little one." A portion of her carefree bounce had returned—the happy rhythm and melody that made Bibi's voice hers. But squirming through her guileless light Jasmine detected a shadow of regret, a stain of sadness. "I should have kept him to myself. He *would* have stayed with me, if I didn't ask him to help you."

"I still don't understand."

Another chasm of silence followed by a forlorn sigh. "My child," she began, interrupted by a quick clearing of her throat. "When I showed him to you, I thought I would be there to guide you."

A tinge that sounded like guilt lurked under Bibi's words. A flash of memory wriggled into the forefront of Jasmine's mind—"The best lies have just enough truth."

Where did that come from? Bibi lying? I can't believe that.

"You can't handle him alone, not yet. For one thing, you have to be careful what you say to him. There's so much more I should have taught you as well. But I got called away, and now you're stuck with him. And *Mlinzi* will never leave you until he's ready." Another sniffle interrupted. "*That* is what is all my fault."

"But isn't that good, Bibi? He saved my life. Twice."

"Yes, yes. And I'm so thankful he did. But, my dear … oh, how do I put it?"

Jasmine's eyes danced left and right, up and down, as ideas flitted in and out of her head. A notion, a poisonous seed of icy logic, settled and took root.

Mlinzi won't *leave? That's actually to my advantage.*

The young boy's cheer of surprise shrieked in Jasmine's ear. "Bibi, come see," he chimed, followed by a squeal of laughter.

"Just a moment, Cheta." Bibi's sudden return to her ebullient sing-song almost gave Jasmine whiplash. It was muted and rang with a tight echo, like she was talking over her shoulder in a closet.

"I was scarcely older than you when Bibi Rakotomalala gave *Mlinzi* to me." Quick as it appeared, the bright façade vanished again. "But she was a wise woman of my people and understood so many things—things I could not. She cautioned me about *Mlinzi*, but I was too young to understand, let alone heed her. Things I only begin to understand now."

A hint of a sob throttled her voice. "*Ai*, child—there's so much I should have warned you about."

"Warn me about what?" Jasmine pressed, with a rasp of impatience.

Bibi's voice fell to a dire whisper, filled with foreboding. "His help always has consequences. Always."

"Yeah, well, I'll take being alive over any consequences."

"You think when *Mlinzi* took Mr. Fieldings and that other bad man, life was all roses for old Bibi?" Her breaths shortened and had the edge of urgency. "*Mlinzi's* not like us. He doesn't really understand us, our needs, our desires, our feelings. He's a force, a weapon. He never does anything halfway. He's like using a meat cleaver when a butter knife is called for.

"And then there's after. The looks. The questions. And I'm not just talking the police. Everybody—family, friends, soon even strangers —everyone around you looks at you different. They sense something's wrong—Wrong about *you*. He brings a taint with him, *Mlinzi* does. He gets inside you, child. He looks at you and sees deep inside you. But he leaves something behind."

"Yeah, he did something weird after he rescued me today. He nailed Caleb and Akilah, and I was freaking out. He looked straight at me, and he calmed me down." A small harrumph interrupted her train of thought. The image of Jackson's eyes whirling into a pit of blackness filled her with passionless calm again. "Made me see things more clearly," she mumbled, half to herself.

"*Ai*, it's worse than I feared."

Shit. I shouldn'ta said that.

"Then you know. You *know!*" Bibi quailed. "*Mlinzi* stains you. He doesn't mean to, but it's there all the same. And it sticks to you. It shows through. I didn't see it at first, but it changed me, almost took me over. It will change you, too, child. And the more it happens, the more you change—and not for the better. The people around you will see it."

Good. That's just what I'm counting on. Perhaps then they'll leave me alone.

Jasmine clicked her tongue and shook her head in annoyance. "So what do you expect me to do about it?"

"*Ai*, girl. Don't you see?" Bibi was frenetic, on the verge of panic. "Don't try to use him. You can't control him. The only thing you can do is, don't give him the opportunity. Be cautious. Avoid conflicts. Don't allow yourself to be placed in danger. Heed what you tell him, what you do around him.

"Maybe the best thing would be for you to do what I did—con-vince him to move on." A small gasp hissed in the phone. "*Ai*, on sec-ond thought, don't do that. Whoever got *Mlinzi* wouldn't know what to do with him. It would be far worse for the next girl than it is for you now. *Ai, napenda kuwa huko. Napenda kumchukua Mlinzi nyuma,*" she said, her voice pitching higher. Sobs poured out of the phone, her breaths and more spouts of gibberish coming faster and faster.

"Bibi? What the hell ...?" *She's so torqued, she's spilling her guts in Swahili.*

"*Ai,* I'm sorry." Bibi sniffled and blew her nose. "I said 'I wish I was there. I wish I could take *Mlinzi* back.'"

"Bibi, I'm doing just *fine,*" Jasmine said with concrete firmness. "Things are starting to go my way, and Jackson's a big help."

A gasp hissed in Jasmine's ear. "You ... you've changed, child. It's happened already. I can hear it in you. There's nothing for it. Get rid of him, child." Bibi's volume jumped so high, it distorted in the speaker. "Get *rid* of him! Pass him on to another."

Anger itched between Jasmine's shoulder blades and jumped up her neck. The hairs on the back of her scalp stood in defiance.

"Why should I do that? I finally can deal with these clowns. You yourself said they only pretended to be my friends. You don't know the half of it. They're my enemies. They tried to kill me. *Rape* me," she rasped with suppressed rage. "They got what they deserved."

Jasmine balked at herself. She heard the enmity dripping from her voice like blood from a knife. A small smile slipped out of her, as she breathed to rein in the hatred. "Now *I'm* calling the shots. And if they come after me again, Jackson and I will make sure they get everything what's coming to them."

"No, *Jazz-meen.* You don't know what you're saying," Bibi pleaded between pants. "Get rid of *Mlinzi,* I tell you. For your own good. Show him to another person who needs protection, who is in danger. That's how I passed him on to you.

"But it still won't be over. Whoever he goes to will need you. You may not know much about *Mlinzi,* but the next one will indeed need what little guidance you can offer. Until I can come back. But you must get him to move on. *Now.*"

Jasmine shook her head in annoyance, like she was suffering through a boring joke she had already heard a dozen times.

This is going nowhere. All right, humor the old girl, so she leaves me the hell alone.

"And how am I supposed do that?" she said with steady calmness.

A sigh of relief whispered from the receiver. "Good, good." Bibi cleared her throat and took a deep breath.

"Bibi Rakotomalala told me there are three ways. If he is summoned, he will come. That's how she called him so long ago. If I could do it myself, I would call him back to me. But I don't know how.

"The other is ask *Mlinzi* to help someone in need. Show him to someone who needs protection. If he sees the need, he will go. That's what I did with you, and that's what you need to do as well, child.

"You hear me? Show him someone who needs his help more than you, and he may choose to go. But for pity's sake, don't leave the next poor girl alone. You'll have to help her. We'll guide her together. I'll help by phone best I can, until I can return."

Get rid of Jackson? Yeah, like that's gonna happen. I'm the one who was targeted. No one needed help more than me against Nevaeh's gang. Now that he has those turds pared down, and the rest with their backs against the wall, they'll either leave me alone or come after me harder. And Jackson is just the protection I need.

Cheta's tinny voice in the background grew louder and sounded dire.

"So what's the third?"

"*Ai*, child—pray that you never find out. Just promise me you will pass *Mlinzi* on."

Anything to stop this lecture.

"Okay, yeah. I promise."

"Good, my child, good. Now, you will know *Mlinzi's* ready, when he—"

A crash sounded in Jasmine's ear, like a piece of furniture tumbling onto the floor, followed by a shower of tinkling glass. The boy's voice wailed into shrieks of pain, shouting Bibi's name.

"Cheta, are you all right?" Jasmine pressed the phone hard against her ear to catch the flurry of running footsteps. The boy's plaintive screams of panicked agony increased. Bibi drew in a sharp breath. "*Ai, mungu wangu!*"

It sounded like a curse. But Bibi *never* swore, as far as Jasmine recalled.

"*Jazz-meen*, I must go. I'll call back when—" The connection went dead with a foreboding click.

Picking herself off the floor, Jasmine walked into the kitchen, staring at the phone with a stern expression. She placed it back in its cradle and busied herself with collecting her homework. Stuffing the pile of books and papers in a haphazard array into her one-strap backpack, she almost collided with Ma.

She had changed her clothes for bed—one of Dad's camo flannel shirts under a threadbare nightgown tied loosely with an even more raggedy strap.

"You're right, Ma. Bibi and her family's got it bad," said Jasmine with a shrug of her shoulders. She set the pack next to the front door, and stretched her arms and back, letting out an oh-so-satisfying grunt. Even her ribs felt better.

She felt Ma's eyes following her as she trudged back to her room.

"I wonder how long she can hold it together," Jasmine added between yawns.

Ma scooped up Jasmine's arm in one hand, drew her close and stared. She craned her neck forward and squinted hard, her eyes darting over the entirety of her daughter's face.

Jasmine drew away in response. "What's with you?"

Ma shook her head rapidly, then rubbed her eyes with the other hand. "I dunno, I must be tired. These two jobs are wringing me out." She examined her daughter again, this time with skeptical eyes, then relented with a wan smile. "You looked strange there, for a second. Like someone else."

CHAPTER TEN

Jasmine woke refreshed, rousing herself out of bed a half hour before her alarm went off. The echoes of Bibi's dire warnings from the previous evening waned to an annoying memory, easily shelved into a dark cubbyhole.

A note from Ma greeted her on the kitchen table. The coffee shop started a new promotion—National Coffee Day or something equally silly—and a regular staffer had called in sick. No surprise that Ma jumped at the chance to grab a few hours of overtime before her day job.

"Good news! The bus strike is over. And don't forget your keys," the note ended with the last sentence underlined twice.

Jasmine took her time getting washed. She convinced herself it was a good omen that the shower was warm for its entire duration. Looking in the mirror, she fretted over the bruise on her neck that bloomed overnight. She attempted to blot out the memory using the makeup Bibi had given Ma. When that wasn't entirely successful, taming the rats' nest of her hair distracted her from the reminders of Caleb's violence. She twirled its frizzed cords playfully in the mirror, wondering how she might look in box braids like Bibi's.

Her fingers strayed downward and pulled one cup of her bra to the side. Jasmine gazed into the mirror, imagining how cool she would look with a tattoo of a chameleon over her heart. She chuckled at the thought of slashes keeping a body count below it, like some of Dad's Army buddies did on their arms.

Rifling through several drawers, she settled on a bright short-sleeve turtleneck—one of her best, and one usually reserved for special occasions. Tugging the collar so not to muss her perfect face, she adjusted it high to cover the marks where Caleb's murderous hand had throttled her. Drowning the ugly memories in contempt, she fluffed her hair back into shape.

While she luxuriated in her breakfast of a bagel, cheese, and—*gasp!*—real fruit, she leisurely watched her flip-phone hum with activity on the table. She read the stream of Trinity's rants and threats as she munched on her thoughts along with her breakfast.

> "Saw the news about Caleb & Akilah"
> "WTF"
> "It was you, Jizm, Wasn't it?"
> "Spent whole night answering stupid questions"
> "First coach and the rents, then the cops"
> "You sic 'em on me, slut?"

Poor Trinity. She can dish it out, but can't take it.

It was a no-brainer that somewhere, somewhen, somebody would drill her as well, about yesterday's events. It was all a matter of who would ask, how high up the food chain they were, and what her response should be. The real trick was how to get into Trinity's head.

Preparation was everything. Jasmine silently rehearsed, reviewed, and revised her spiel. She doodled with her index finger on the table to the right of her breakfast, the Formica serving as the blank slate where her plans took shape. Strategies, attacks, contingencies, and counterattacks formed invisible sketches before her on the table surface, while she grinned with satisfaction.

What if . . . She swished a small circle.

Trinity has two choices . . . She flitted her finger on the table in the shape of a Y.

How about I make . . . No, that'll only cause more problems . . . She frowned and swept away an invisible box with the side of her palm.

Or do this instead? Oh, yesss . . . Her knuckle rapped the table with a final punctuation mark.

Jasmine ate her last mouthful and hummed a spry little tune to herself as she cleaned up the table and counters. She checked the phone one last time before shoving it in her pocket.

"Snitch bitch"
"You ain't gonna lay this on me"
"We'll see who they believe"

Bring it on, Trinity. I'll be ready.

At the apartment door, she collected her keys and hoisted her backpack over one shoulder. She regarded Jackson with a chuckle and blew him a kiss. A sullen hue of tangerine zoomed down the length of the chameleon, from the tips of his three horns to the end of his tail lashed around his log.

"Bye-bye, Jackson, my little mood ring monster."

The outside air never felt so clean and fresh, washed by yesterday's rain and not yet sullied by diesel fumes. The streets were full of people, adults and students alike, though the kids no longer sneered at her with disapproving smirks of derision. Jasmine even caught the look of worried anxiety in the harried glances of students giving her a wide berth as they passed her by.

Wow. The Trinity grapevine is doing most of my work for me. They all think I messed up Akilah, and that's just the street cred I want.

After boarding the bus, she chuckled when one kid gave her a double take. The girl's expression of surprise dissolved into recognition laced with fear.

Hey, world. Say hello to the New Jasmine.

At the next stop, Madison waddled onto the bus. She hitched her pack high over her shoulder and ducked her head low, avoiding Jasmine's gaze as she squeezed down the aisle.

So this is what it feels like to be on top? I could get used to this.

Jasmine rose from her seat and followed the team shrimp. She knelt on the row in front of her target and smiled over her arms clasped on the back of the seat. She kept her Cheshire smile plastered immobile until Madison looked up from her phone.

"Hi ... Madison?"

"Yo, Jazz," Madison replied with a pinch of harried expectation. Her momentary glance became an extended stare, punctuated with blinks of wonder.

"I saw how Trinity was giving you a hard time yesterday. She's been bustin' my chops too, ever since I came to this crummy school." She rested her chin on her hands. "What if I can fix it so she leaves the both of us alone?"

Madison's eyes widened. She silently mouthed, "Really?" Her eyes zigged and zagged in search of unwanted ears among the occupied seats.

"Yeah, really. I have an idea to put Trinity in her place, but I'll need your help."

You fat backstabber.

Madison nodded twice, hunger in her eyes.

"Great. Text Trinity that you wanna meet her in the library between lunch and first afternoon period. Tell her you have the goods on me and Akilah. Nothing specific, just that's it's juicy. See you there, if you wanna join in on the fun."

They nodded at each other in silent agreement, and Jasmine returned to her seat. She seasoned her smile with a pinch of cruelty.

Hook and line—the sinker will come if both of them show up.

Once at school, Jasmine decided to stroll the long way to home-room, meandering along the hallowed hellish halls of learning. She bris-tled with anticipation, wondering what fresh experiences the New Jas-mine might encounter—like any antics around Caleb's or Trinity's lock-ers, or whatever spicy tidbits she could glean in the vicinity of Nevaeh's and Akilah's old hangouts.

The halls were abuzz, teeming with lines of students streaming toward their homerooms. Small cliques of second-rate queen bees and their posses formed tight circles in the stream's eddies, their heads bob-bing with eagerness while dishing and devouring the latest dirt.

Her mouth crinkled into the tiniest smirk as teachers' assistants broke the groups apart, sending them shambling toward their rooms. She sauntered through the diminished crowds, keeping an eye out for anyone from history class she could crib from. Hoping against hope, she scoured the masses to catch Trinity, perchance to maneuver across her path this fine morning.

Her crooked smile melted when she caught sight of three adults in the milling crowd. Huddled in a semicircle around a hallway locker were Principal Moore with her oversized glasses poised perilously at the end of her nose, a school security guard, and some lanky guy whose cheap suit and tan overcoat screamed "detective" loud as a gabardine billboard. She craned her neck and nodded her head with satisfaction. No doubt about it, it was Caleb's locker they surrounded.

The security guard flipped a dozen sheets back down on his clipboard and fiddled with the combination lock in the door. He swung it open with a clang, and the detective snapped on a pair of latex gloves. He dove in like a hound hot on the trail, disgorging the locker's contents into a garbage bag produced by the guard. Pausing as he pulled out a switchblade emblazoned with Caleb's trademark "C", he flashed a sneer while dropping the weapon into his own clear plastic bag emblazoned with the word "evidence" in capital letters.

Jasmine hugged the wall behind the distracted adults when they pulled out a book with a cavity carved out of its pages, filled to brimming with bags of white powder. The detective whistled low to himself and muttered, "Enough here to zonk out half the school. When we wrap up here, I wanna take a look at Nevaeh's locker as well."

"Shouldn't we lockdown?" asked Moore.

"That would slow us down. We're fighting the clock to find the missing girl, and she might be in danger."

"You've already searched Akilah's locker and now this one." Moore adjusted her glasses to focus her glower at the gaunt detective. "How many others do you need?"

"Wherever the trail leads me," he replied, his index finger pointing at a name encircled by rings of graffiti artwork on the book's inside cover. "And the trail says Nevaeh's locker is next."

"Why didn't you look there when her parents declared her—"

"Yesterday she was in Missing Person's inbox," he groused. He dropped the book and contents into another evidence baggie. "This says she's connected to the assault on Akilah. So *we're* looking. Now."

While the adults continued arguing around Caleb's locker, Jasmine traipsed down a T-intersection to her next destination. Her grin reasserted itself when she spotted a quartet of adults delving into the contents of Trinity's locker—another guard, Vice Principal Chatelain, Coach Garcia, and a female detective shrouded in a navy blue light spring peacoat.

Huh, they really do wear those, just like on the tube.

Chatelain adjusted his black tie with an audible snap. "Please continue, Ms. Garcia."

Jasmine sidestepped behind the nearest corner and leaned against the tiled wall. Playing the soul of cool disinterest, she kept an eye and an ear toward the foursome.

"I couldn't tell you who left the message, Detective," said Garcia. "I just found it on my office board yesterday, anonymous. When I saw the news last evening, with Akilah following that orange hoodie, of course I had to let Principal Moore know."

"You're sure you have no idea who wrote it," said Chatelain, folding his arms with a rankled glare at Coach.

"Nope. It was scribbled so bad, no way I could tell who it was from."

Jasmine mentally patted herself on the back for her chalkboard inspiration.

"Well-l-l, look at this," chortled the detective as she stood, examining a prize in her latex-gloved hand. She swiveled Akilah's broken memory chip between her thumb and index finger. "I do believe this is the other half of what we found in Caleb's baseball cap."

Jasmine's hand clamped over her mouth to stifle the giggle that percolated up.

The female detective snapped an evidence baggie open, sealed the chip inside, and stuffed the bag into an inside pocket of her coat. Turning toward the three staff, she said with a tone as flat as her expression, "I'm afraid Trinity has just graduated from 'person of interest' to 'possible suspect.' We'll have to detain her and resume questioning after we contact her parents. Where's her homeroom?"

The detective shut down the protest arising from Chatelain's lips by closing the locker door with a resounding bang. She pointed with one hand at the guard, while pulling out her cellphone with the other. "You stay here until we get a team to go through the rest."

She pressed her phone to her ear. "Fred, keep an eye out for the girl we interviewed last night. Yeah, Trinity Davis. We need her to go over her story again."

Uh-oh. If she can't make it to the library, I'll have to play this by ear.

Chatelain stood in front of the detective with his hands planted on his hips. "Where will you be taking Ms. Davis, Detective Bollard?" The detective was about to answer, but it was the vice principal's turn to commandeer the situation. "Her father works in a school in our district. I'm sure Principal Moore or the superintendent can have him here within the hour. I think it would be in everyone's interest if we can straighten this out with a minimum of disruption."

Phew—I think I'm still on track.

Bollard's smirk widened to an actual smile. "Fair enough. You fetch Trinity and her father. My partner and I will meet you at Principal Moore's office. In the meantime, I still need to take a look at Jasmine Price's locker."

Crap. They took Trinity's bitching seriously?

No problem, no problem. Time to muddy the waters some more.

Jasmine slunk behind the corner before trotting away. Resisting the temptation to run at full tilt, she forced her legs to walk with a calm, purposeful stride. The steady meter of her footsteps helped her reason out the situation.

Breathe, girl, breathe. Nothing's in there, so don't hang around your locker like you got something to hide. Just get what you need, go about business like it's a normal day, and get to homeroom. Maybe you'll catch a break, and—

Rounding another corner, she cruised smack into Trinity. Thinking fast, one of the plans doodled on the breakfast table popped into her head.

Jasmine rolled out her best cheerleader smile. "There you are. I've been lookin' for you all morning, girl. They let you out on good behavior?"

Trinity's eyes flared, ready to bore through solid steel. "That's a new look for you, bitch. Really getting into the ho vibe, ain'tcha Jizm? It suits you."

Jasmine deflected the lame insult with a wave of her hand. "Thanks! Nevaeh and yomama gave me good pointers. Say, girl, I need to crib off your history homework from yesterday."

"Why the fuck should I let you do that?" Trinity growled.

"Because I can do you a solid up front." Jasmine pointed her thumb behind her. "A couple of sherlocks are pokin' around the school, and one's digging in your locker right now."

Trinity's eyes sparked with panic for a moment, then resumed their stare of utter contempt. "How's that a favor, slut?"

"Not much. But here's what I *can* do." She cocked her hips and held out her hand. "They're on the lookout for you, and they didn't sound happy. So, I thought I could hold on to your history stuff, a-a-and ..." She cleared her throat as she looked past Trinity's shoulder. "... and anything you don't want them to find," she whispered. The sound of sharpening knives sliced sweetly between Jasmine's ears.

Trinity slapped Jasmine's hand away, and stormed past her. Jasmine clamped her arms close against her abdomen, fighting the urge to laugh out loud.

God, that was fun!

I knew she had nothin' to hide, but I just had to screw with her and set the stage. She'll find out soon enough what they did find, and that'll really mess with her head.

A deep breath, and she continued on her merry way to home-room. The first bell rang while she sorted her morning work out of her backpack. The tattered cover of her history text reminded her there was still more deviltry to be done before lunch. She made a quick scan of her locker, before stowing the rest of her stuff.

No new love notes from Trinity or whoever's left of Nevaeh's gang. Not that those dopes would have the guts or imagination to try anything new.

One last check of her phone before turning it off. Sure enough, there was fresh abuse awaiting her.

"ESAD, skank"
"Eat Shit And Die. In case ur 2 stoopid"
"You will SO pay"
"WTF in locker? I'm gonna"

"Aww, isn't that sweet?" Jasmine muttered to herself. "What was that last bit, Trin? Guess they caught you lurking a bit too close to your locker." She tried to contain her glee, but it was betrayed by a surpris-ingly loud snort.

Enjoy the third degree, Trinity. Go ahead, point the finger at me. I'll be ready by the time they finish with you.

Resisting the temptation to see if either of the goon squads was bearing down the hall, she closed the locker with unhurried innocence and glided into her homeroom.

Her homeroom teacher, Mr. Mason, droned on, babbling out the new day's line of announcements—assemblies, parent-teacher days, club events—all the stuff the administration cared about, but students never wanted to be bothered with. His uninspiring list came to an abrupt halt when the classroom door opened.

Vice Principal Chatelain stood in the doorway, beckoning the teacher over for a confab. After a quick exchange, they both stared at Jasmine with poker faces.

"Ms. Price, will you please come with me," said the vice principal, his imperious monotone echoing off the walls.

A hushed chorus of "ooh"s swept through the classroom, and Jasmine gathered her things. Once outside, the door clicked behind her with finality, and she found herself corralled by the vice principal and the lady detective.

With her hands burrowed into the pockets of her peacoat, the detective wore a curious half-smile, as if she couldn't quite remember how to be friendly.

"Yes, sir?" Jasmine ventured, hoping she didn't sound fake or smarmy.

"Morning, Jasmine," started Vice Principal Chatelain. "This is—"

"Detective Bollard," she said, seizing control of the conversation. Out of a coat pocket, she swept out her badge, deftly flashing it in front of Jasmine's face and dropping it back in her coat, all in a well-oiled motion that would have made a stage magician envious. "I'd like to ask you a couple of questions."

"Don't I need my Ma here?"

"Not yet," Bollard said with a practiced grin. "Having your vice principal here is sufficient for now. Besides, you're not in any trouble, you're just a ..."

"Person of interest?" Jasmine said with a drip of snark. She immediately regretted it the moment Chatelain flashed an annoyed frown.

"No-o-o," the lady detective dragged out, recovering with an amused smirk. "A potential witness." She stepped to the side and leaned against the wall of lockers. "Now where did you hear a fancy term like that?"

"Last night, on the TV news 'bout Akilah." Jasmine scanned Bollard up and down, getting the impression the detective thought herself a cat toying with a mouse.

"Uh-huh," Bollard mused as she chewed one side of her lip. "Do you know Trinity Davis?"

"Yeah, she's on the basketball team."

Bollard oozed haughtiness. "She's in a bit of trouble, and I'm hoping you can help her out."

"Uh, okay," Jasmine said with a guarded frown, hugging her books close to her midriff.

"Did you see Trinity on the way to school yesterday?"

"No," she hammered out with brusqueness.

"You're quite sure? The buses were on strike yesterday. How did you get to school?"

"I had to walk. In the friggin' rain."

"Which way?"

Letting her gaze wander, she rearranged her memories from the alley, substituting snippets with her doodles from the kitchen table. "I tried to get through a mess of construction on the main avenue. Took a shortcut through some alleyways."

"Did you meet anyone?" The thrill of the chase kindled in Bollard's eyes. "Say hello to any friends?"

Jasmine let a pinch of her anger rise to the surface. "*Friends?* No." She squeezed her books against herself even harder, forcing her breath short.

"But you *did* see someone." Bollard had an intensity in her eye, like the cat was ready to bite the head off the mouse.

Yeah, she knows I was there in that alley. She's waiting for me to screw up. And that's just fine. Time for the full-on act.

Jasmine hemmed for the slightest moment. "Yeah … I ran into Caleb." She hesitated, then squeezed her shoulders together, facing the detective with a deer-in-the-headlights expression, like she was afraid to remember. "He cornered me in some walkway between buildings near the construction. I could smell weed on him, and he kept twitching like he was stoked on that crap he sells." She hitched her breath with a man-ufactured sob.

"Cornered? Was Caleb looking for you? Why did he want to meet you?" The hunger in Bollard's eyes grew.

"He didn't want to *meet* me, he wanted something else. I knew what was goin' down. I seen it all the time in the Projects." She bared her front teeth in a weak snarl, then retracted back into the frightened innocent act.

That's it. Let out a little anger. It keeps it real. Use the right amounts of rage and fear, street-smarts and shock, and just the right mix of truth and fiction. Just like that quote from history class.

"He had his hand down his pants, and he was workin' himself hard. He was fixin' to bang out a home run with me."

Chatelain drew in a sharp breath, curling his hand under his chin. Jasmine ignored the distraction of the vice principal's indignation.

"He made a grab for me and punched me in the gut—hard. Then he shoved me against the wall and tried to choke me." Jasmine pulled down the collar of her turtleneck, exposing the sickly purple and yellow bruise. "Then he dropped his pants …"

She allowed another crocodile sob to slip out. "If that's the way Nevaeh likes it, she can have it."

"Nevaeh? The missing girl?" Chatelain blurted out, the disgust painted across his face supplanted by shock. "What about her?"

Bollard glared a silent command at the vice principal to shut the hell up.

"Don't you know? She and Caleb were screw– … hookin' up. The whole school knows that. She had his ring, and a whole bunch of other fine things." Jasmine permitted a little envy to slip out, just for show. "No way she could afford half the stuff she wore."

With a fresh rehearsed grimace, Jasmine retreated, her back against the wall under one of the school bells. Swallowing hard, she glanced at the concern and sympathy crimping the vice principal's eyebrows together.

"Shocking. You poor girl," Chatelain fussed, scanning the empty hallway for eavesdroppers. "Perhaps we should discuss this back at my office."

Bollard went stone-faced, raising her hand to delay the vice principal. "So what happened? Take whatever time you need, Jasmine."

"I tried kicking him in the nuts. He blocked and I made a break for it. Left his harpoon high and dry, and his pants around his knees. He grabbed at me. Ended up tearing off my poncho, but I kept on running."

Jasmine panted heavily, as if she were still sprinting away. She tried to affect a teardrop, but none would come. The corners of her books poked her breasts, reminding her to keep it short and move the focus away from herself. "Omigawd. Is that what happened to Akilah? Did Caleb fu– … Is that why she's in the hospital?"

"What was that about your poncho? What color was it?"

Yup, they found it. I wonder where Jackson left it?

"Orange. It was a nasty cheap plastic thing. I'm almost glad to be rid of it. Except that by the time I made it to school, I was soaked. Coach Garcia sent me to the gym to dry off."

"Sounds like you really had it tough. I'm sorry you went through that, but I'm glad you're okay now." The detective seemed confused, almost disappointed. And her consolations were devoid of any empathy. "We found your poncho—it was on top of a roof. You have any idea how it got up there? It looked like it went through a meat grinder."

Jasmine shook her head with a shrug of her shoulders. "Caleb sometimes has a knife on him, but I didn't see none yesterday. And I didn't dick around on no roof—I ran straight here."

"You didn't run into anyone else? Akilah or Trinity?"

They gotta have the same video Coach and I saw on TV, so they know Akilah followed me in a minute later. Wait—are they buying my red herring about Trinity?

"Maybe. I don't think so," she stuttered, her eyes whipping back and forth, pretending she was going through the file cabinet of her memory. "I just bolted the hell outta there. I wasn't paying attention to no one—except making sure Caleb wasn't following me." An awkward silence filled the hall, and Jasmine peered over Bollard's shoulder, staring at the memory of another one of her Formica doodles. "Wait, maybe I ran past … another girl from the team?"

"And who might that have been?"

Jasmine turned her head and squinted at the floor. "I don't know her name. Mary, Maddy … something like that. She's on the second string, kinda short and fat. Most of the team don't talk to her much, except for Trinity."

Tough luck, Madison. Under the bus you go. Maybe Trinity was right, not to trust me. But fair's fair—you turned on me first.

"Wait, what does all this have to do with Trinity?" Jasmine asked with feigned innocence. "Did Caleb go after her too?"

Out of her coat's other pocket, Bollard pulled a small notebook with a pen speared through the spiral binding. She dashed off a few quick scribbles. "No, she's fine. Just trying to piece together who was where, when Akilah got hurt." Bollard jammed the pen back in the pad's spine. "Do you have a boyfriend?"

"At *this* school? No way. Ma and me moved outta the Projects a few weeks ago." She scrunched her textbooks closer. "Not sure I want one after this. Boys are the same all over."

Bollard and Moore exchanged glances, their faces twitching like they dare not show any reaction. "What about your dad? Where's he?" asked Bollard.

"He's Army, serving in Afghanistan."

"Have you talked to your mother yet?" inquired Chatelain.

The bell above her rang, and Jasmine cringed under the intensity of the harsh metallic clang. Along the length of the hallway, doors swung open and the rooms' student hordes spilled out. Dozens of surprised eyes peered at her, as the students gave the Inquisition their space.

"All right, that's enough for now," Chatelain interjected, stepping to interpose himself between the two. "Any more questions will have to be in my office."

"'Scuse me, ma'am," Jasmine said, placing a tentative hand on Bollard's wrist. "You didn't answer my questions—how is Trinity mixed up in all this?"

"You seem awfully concerned about Ms. Davis, Jasmine." Bollard's hungry smile returned.

Jasmine flashed a glance of surprise, like she slipped up. She then hung her head, staring at her feet, keeping her lips taut.

"C'mon, Jasmine," Bollard patiently urged. "We're only trying to help, and you look like you need to tell us something."

Lowering her voice, she parsed out her words in her best angry tremolo. "Before class today, she wanted me to hold something for her. But I wouldn't take it. She texted all sorts of trash about me last night and this morning, and then she wants me to do her a favor?" She clamped her teeth together and hissed, "No fuckin' way."

She exhaled, suppressing the legitimate rage that threatened to burst out. "Sorry, I shouldn't have said that."

Bollard tilted her head back in wary silence. "No, that's all right. What did she want you to take?"

"I didn't see. Didn't *wanna* see. All I know, it was small, in her fist." Shaking her head, Jasmine decided to change the topic. Feigning concern by tenting her eyebrows, she looked imploringly between the two adults. "Jesus, who cares about Trinity—what about Akilah? Was it Caleb who beat her up? He didn't, y'know ... *do* her? There wasn't much on the tube."

"I'm sorry, we can't say much beyond what was already on the news," the detective explained as she put her hand on Jasmine's shoulder. There was no compassion in her touch. "Akilah was badly injured in that walkway you cut through. She received a concussion, one severe enough to put her in a coma. But, at least I can confirm she wasn't sexually assaulted."

Bollard squeezed Jasmine's shoulder tighter. "I'm sorry to press, but we need to be sure of one thing. Caleb didn't ra—"

Chatelain coughed loud enough to be heard halfway down the hall.

"He didn't complete what he started?" said Bollard.

"Would you like to see a doctor?" chimed in Chatelain.

"*No*, and no." said Jasmine, as flat and hard as an anvil.

"Okay, you're the boss." Bollard tapped the pen against her lips, scrunched up tight in thought. "Oh, just one more thing. You said you're on the basketball team. Coach Garcia tells me you're one of her best. How high can you jump?"

The boarded-up window, splattered with Akilah's blood, flashed in Jasmine's memory. The impact crater where *Mlinzi* caved in her head had to be at least twelve feet off the ground.

Bollard's nuts if she thinks I can jump that *high.*

Jasmine was on the verge of blurting out that damning little tid-bit, before she snapped back to her senses.

Dammit, Jasmine, shut up—Bollard almost tripped you up.

She mocked a look of confusion at the detective. "With a running start, I can skim the hoop." She shook her head, leveling a pleading look played straight at Bollard. "Wait—what the hell did Caleb *do* to Akilah?"

I should get an Oscar for this performance.

"Sorry, I *really* cannot say," she said, striving to be heard over the flood of students. "Thanks again, Ms. Price. We'll be in touch if we have further questions."

Down the hall, Bollard's partner in the tan overcoat—Fred, Jasmine deduced—emerged from the nearest intersection and beckoned Bollard toward him.

"Excuse me," Bollard mumbled, giving the vice principal a polite nod before turning to leave. Chatelain stepped to fill the void left by Bollard, blocking Jasmine's escape.

"Ms. Price, you've been through a terrible experience. Are you sure you don't want to talk to a doctor?"

"I'm sure."

"Do you want to see our counselor, at least? I think you should talk to Mrs. Ainsworth, and I can take you to her now if you—"

Jasmine squirmed away, stretching to peer over Chatelain's shoulder. She strained to catch any morsel of information in the detectives' conversation, but she couldn't hear diddly over the crowd's hubbub and the vice principal's fretting. All she could spy past the stampede of students and Bollard's peacoat was a jerk of Fred's thumb pointing in the direction of Caleb's locker.

"No thanks, Mr. Chatelain," Jasmine said with a dour expression. "Maybe later."

"I really think you should, Ms. Price. In any event, I must notify your mother."

"Fine," she snapped, glowering at the floor. "You do that. But no shrink, and no counselor."

Jasmine's shoulders relaxed and she sighed, regaining control of her voice. "You're right, sir. It was bad in the alley. But it's nothin' new. Like I said, that crap happened all the time in the Projects. I thought it would be better here."

She faced Vice Principal Chatelain, finally releasing the bile that had been building since he and Bollard ambushed her. "But it *ain't*. And it ain't *me* who needs a shrink. It's this whole fuckin' school."

Jasmine stomped away without asking permission, dissolving into the crowd. Glancing sidelong after the detectives as she passed their corner, she clamped the inside of her lips flat with her teeth, preventing the twist of a smile from squirming out.

If they're stumped by the bloody window in the alley, they must be going nuts over Jackson's claw marks on the walls.

They'll scratch their heads for a while and have no choice but to pin it all on Caleb. And Trinity's in for a rough ride, to boot.

Meanwhile, I still have work to do.

CHAPTER ELEVEN

Jasmine stalked the aisles between bookstacks. She forced her breathing to slow down—it had been a headlong rush between periods to grab her keys, phone, notebook, and history textbook from her locker, then haul ass to the library.

Wiping one finger along a chest-high shelf, she uttered a snide *humph* at how much dust had accumulated. Her other hand thumped the side of her leg in quick cadence, like it was impatient to dribble a basketball. It wouldn't stop until she shoved it into her pocket. She clenched her fist around her key fob, pressing her thumb against the ends of her keys, searching for the sharpest point.

She turned the corner around the end of one bookstack, keeping her attention surreptitiously on the entrance to the library. The aluminum doors, mostly large windows filled with heavy-gauge crisscrossed wires, were closed. Paired with anti-theft panels, they gave the large L-shaped reading area the gloomy aspect of a prison.

Opening her history textbook, Jasmine leaned against the bookcase, where she could observe the doors, yet not be seen from the hallway outside. She lazily flipped the book's pages, pretending to read while she stared at the entrance.

One door opened, and Madison took a halting step past the panels, her eyes darting to and fro. Twitching like an overgrown Chihuahua, Madison jostled her way past the stacks, halting one by one, searching for a friendly face. Jasmine withdrew to the end of the aisle, pacing herself to remain one rack behind her target.

Trinity sashayed into the library like she owned the place. Spotting Madison, she waved her over, directing her to meet at a table around the L-bend, farthest from the entrance. Jasmine closed her textbook, tapping it against her chin with every step as she circled around the back of the stacks toward their table.

"So, whaddya got for me?" Trinity said, leaning across the table over her own history text, hungry for the down-low.

Madison replied with a sheepish frown.

"C'mon, what's the dirt on Jizm?"

Jasmine tossed her books onto the table with a resounding slap. "Well, hello, girlfriends. Glad you could make it," she said, her smile sloshing over with cruelty.

Trinity glanced at Madison with dismayed surprise, but then blasted a ferocious snarl at Jasmine.

"What the f—," Trinity began with a loud voice, which she clamped down to a whisper. "What do *you* want, bitch?"

Jasmine chuckled at the daggers shooting from Trinity's eyes. "What do I want, Trin? Well, for starters, I want you to stop calling me that." She slipped her hand into the pocket of her jeans again, finding the sharpest key and grasping it firmly. She cocked her hips, leaning against the table inches from Trinity.

"I'm gonna do lots worse than just call you names," said Trinity, rising out of her chair. Her hand arched like a cat's claw, her nails angled to dig.

Jasmine's hand flashed out of her pocket and formed a fist. With the key's teeth protruding between her index and third fingers, she slashed across Trinity's upper arm.

Trinity's eyes bulged, and she drew in a sharp hiss. Jasmine shoved her back down into the seat. Trinity clamped her hand across the beads of blood that dotted her skin.

"Another thing I wanted, *darlin'*, is to show you that I give as good as I get. Remember those scratches you and Nevaeh gave me late last week?" She pointed the key at her own arm, then leveled it at Trinity's eyes. "Be glad you didn't scratch my face."

Trinity leaned forward with a tiger's snarl, looking to leap out of the chair. Her hands spasmed into fists.

Still brandishing the key like a diminutive knife, Jasmine pushed the thumb of her other hand against Trinity's forehead, pressing steadily. Madison goggled at the pair as Trinity discovered she could not stand up, unable to leverage her weight against Jasmine's piddling slight pressure.

With difficulty, Jasmine repressed a victorious chuckle at this little trick Dad had taught her after he returned from basic training. "Sit down and stay down."

"You are *so* off the deep end, Jizm."

Jasmine shoved Trinity's forehead back with a jerk using the butt of her palm. "I said no names, sweetness."

"The cops are comin' after you, after what I told 'em," Trinity grumbled.

"Says you. Vice Principal Chatelain, Detective Bollard, and I had a nice long chat this morning before Moore and Bollard's buddy Fred grilled you. That's right, I know all the players. They believe *my* story about what Caleb and Akilah were up to."

She paused, staring with a smirk into Trinity's hateful eyes. "And more. I had them eating outta my hand. Hell, Chatelain has a soft spot for me now." Jasmine burbled like a pouting toddler, saying, "He thinks I need counseling, to overcome the terrible experience I suffered."

Trinity's eyes betrayed her fear, and confusion was written across her twitching forehead.

"You're the one boxed in, Trin. Your friends are gone—Akilah's a basket case, and Nevaeh and Caleb are outta the picture."

"What did you do to them? Where are they?" An edge of panic seeped into Trinity's voice.

Jasmine eased her palm away from Trinity, while she studied the point of the key between her fingers of her other hand. A tangled half-up, half-down smirk wrinkled her mouth.

Come to think of it, what did *happen to them, once Mlinzi changed back to Jackson?*

"I honestly don't know," she pondered, followed by a shrug of her shoulders. "And I don't care. But you do the math, Trinity. Cross me, and you're next."

Jasmine aimed the point of the key momentarily at Madison. "Or maybe you. After all, I'm from that 'shit-hole' in the Projects. No telling what I might do." She mugged a crazy look, crossing her eyes, and raising her lip in a goofy snarl.

Madison's jaw dropped, and her eyes widened with the recollection of that hallway encounter. "You heard," she whimpered.

A few tables away, the librarian patrolled past the group. She darted a suspicious glimpse in their direction as she trundled her overloaded cart of books into the stacks. Jasmine nodded at her, flashing a polite smile. It evaporated just as quickly, the moment the librarian disappeared.

"One word from me, and the cops are all over your ass," Trinity scowled.

"You can't bullshit me, Trin. The cops ain't your friends. I *know* what they found in your locker. On the other hand, one word from *me*," she parroted, "and they're all over *both* your asses. I already told 'em I saw someone when I ran away from Caleb." She gave a quick nod at Madison. "Right now, they think it's you."

"Me?" Madison blurted out, barely managing to maintain a hoarse whisper.

"I might change my mind if they ask me too many questions, Trin."

"They won't fall for that," Trinity replied, attempting a brave front, but the fierce rebellion that once burned inside her faltered.

"Is that so? What are they gonna think, when they get around to looking at your cell phone records? They do that, y'know. Even if you erase them from your phone, they can still dredge 'em up. They do it on cop shows all the time.

"They'll find all those nasty-grams Nevaeh, Akilah, and you two clowns had sent, picking on poor li'l-ol-me. Especially today's gems, where the two of you were planning to jam me up." Jasmine tapped the table with the key. "Right here in the library."

The heads of both girls at the table sunk between their shoulders, like guilty turtles diving into their shells.

"Sonova …" Trinity breathed. Madison sniffled, staring bug-eyed at the table.

"You know what they *won't* find? Nothin' from me. No insults, threats, and no gossip. Nothin' except questions about homework that were never answered. Why, as far as they're concerned, the evidence says *I'm* the victim in all this." Jasmine leaned in, wearing a grin leaving no doubt how much she relished applying the screws. "And if those dunce detectives haven't made that connection yet, I'll be sure to remind them, if you jokers sic the cops on me."

"Enough, enough," Madison sobbed, on the verge of bawling. Her body trembled with every stifled blubber.

"You made your point," grunted Trinity. "What do you want?"

Jasmine slipped her key ring back into her pocket, pulling out her flip-phone. "Three things. For starters, you're both gonna vote for me as team captain. And get the rest of the team to go along." Jasmine grinned at the sound of Trinity's teeth grinding.

"*Fuck!*" Trinity spat through clenched jaws. "Whaddya want to be captain for, anyway?"

Just because you *want it so bad, Trin.*

"Second," she continued, ignoring Trinity's tense protest. She popped open Trinity's book and swiped the handout folded inside the front cover. "You are gonna let me copy your homework. Just because I asked so nicely this morning."

Trinity's cheeks puffed in impotent fury while Jasmine snapped pictures of both sides of the paper with her phone. "Don't worry, I'll make a few changes on mine, so Mr. Wyatt won't catch on. I'm not as stupid as you."

Anger boiled in Trinity's eyes.

Jasmine noted the time on her phone before stowing it back in her pocket. "And third—well, I'm sure I'll think of something."

She beamed a saccharine grin at Madison and winked at Trinity as she scooped up her own books. "But for now, catch you at history class, girl."

The first bell rang as she sauntered out the library doors.

Getting the assignment done was more difficult than Jasmine expected. Snatching covert glances at her phone under the prying eyes of the study hall monitor was difficult enough all by itself. The poor resolution of its camera, and the crack in its screen made the going tortuously slow. Not to mention that half of the essay made little sense to her, even after rewording it.

An unbidden thought stalled her pen in the middle of cribbing the essay. Jasmine surveyed the classroom, reaffirming a detail that froze into a heat-sucking lump in her stomach.

Madison was gone. The two other students who were on the basketball team had vanished as well. Jasmine tapped her pencil against her teeth, trying to vacuum up the vague shreds of memory over the past half hour. She shook her head when she pieced it together—they all had gotten library passes.

Trinity better not be up to her old tricks, if she knows what's good for her.

She glanced at the clock winding down the period and threw herself back into scrawling the last of Trinity's drivel, tweaking it into something that sounded like her own. Despite the aggravating mountain of distractions conspiring against her, Jasmine managed to finish the homework before the bell announcing the start of history class.

She waltzed into the classroom, dropping the paper into Mr. Wyatt's tray while beaming a smug grin at her classmates. The teacher interrupted writing his outline at the blackboard, turning toward Jasmine. She found the vague surprise wrinkling his brow, as he glanced back and forth between her and the completed sheet, to be supremely satisfying.

But then, a troubled hitch crowded out Jasmine's short-lived smile. Trinity's seat was empty.

Jasmine sat at her own desk, wary as a cat perched in a tree, waiting for her prey to walk through the door. Her taut lips were hammered into a frown by the sight of Trinity's nonchalance as she waltzed into the classroom. She plopped her homework into the tray as the bell rang and swept into her chair with the grace of a ballerina and the smile of a saint.

Okay, what's she up to now?

Jasmine's mind whirled at the possibilities, and her finger sketched a fresh set of plans on the surface of her desk at a fevered pace. The invisible flowcharts of strategy piled upon her desktop while Mr. Wyatt droned away with his hypnotic monotone.

The history class bell rang, and Jasmine jerked up straight in her chair, out of her daydream filled with scenarios, what-if's, and reprisals. The stratagem doodles only she could see evaporated into nothingness.

Half of the class had already skedaddled out of the room, anxious to exit the school as quickly as possible. Trinity was a blur that zipped out the classroom door. Jasmine scrambled to collect her books and belongings, and made a sharp dogleg up her aisle and past the front desk, only to be blockaded by the history teacher.

In one hand Mr. Wyatt held the sheaf of homework pulled from his tray. With the other he pulled out a single sheet, holding it close for examination. "I must say, Jasmine. I'm impressed that you handed in today's assignment on time. That's an unexpected improvement. Though I was convinced that I was boring you again today."

"Sorry, Mr. Wyatt. I guess I was distracted by …" she hemmed, "a meeting with Vice Principal Chatelain earlier." She shifted her weight and rubbed her instep against her calf. "But, I finally got into the quotations last night. That one about revenge was really interesting."

"I see." He nodded and flipped her sheet over, scanning the other side. "So why did you write your essay on Lincoln's 'You can fool some of the people some of the time'?"

"At the time, it seemed … easier." Jasmine eked out a nervous smile and an apologetic shrug of her shoulders. She stumbled out the door with a harried, "Sorry, Mr. Wyatt. I'm gonna be late for basketball practice."

Yanking out her pack from her locker, she wedged her books into the bag, filling every cubic inch that wasn't already crammed with fresh gym clothes. In the crosscurrents of human traffic, she cut a zigzag path to the gymnasium. Strutting into the locker room, she reveled in the surprised glances from the team members who were seeing the New Jasmine for the first time. Trinity and Madison regarded her with unblinking eyes devoid of emotion.

She smiled a satisfied grin to herself as she piled her belongings into the locker nearest Coach Garcia's office. A myriad of gasps and gawking stares surrounded her.

"That's Nevaeh's locker," whispered one of the second squad members. The walls of metal and masonry echoed the breathy rasp, until it bounced back from every corner of the locker room.

Jasmine changed into her uniform, secured her locker and fairly skipped into the gym. She shot a series of perfect three-pointers as the rest of the team sputtered out onto the court.

After putting the team through the usual laps and warm-up drills under her watchful eye, Coach whistled the teammates into order and eyed each squad. After shuffling one or two members between the groups, she stood to face the team. Her legs planted wide and her hands clasped behind her back, she closed her eyes and inhaled deeply.

"I know this has been a rough couple of days for everyone, and we keep our friends in our thoughts and prayers—for Akilah's quick recovery and Nevaeh's safety."

Jasmine's neck muscles pulsed, strangling the urge to laugh, throttling it down to a guttural hiccup.

"But I think we still have enough *fuego* to play Saturday's game. Let's do this for Nevaeh and Akilah. Whaddya say?"

The team waffled with a stumbling response, urged to a vigorous cheer after a second shout from Coach. Jasmine's response remained lukewarm.

"Right. We have a job to do, so let's get down to brass tacks. I'm sure we all hope for Nevaeh's quick return, but in the meantime, we need a new captain. Any nominations?"

Trinity stewed under scrunched eyebrows at the squads. The girl next to Madison piped up, "Is that fair? What if Nevaeh comes back? She's gonna be captain again, right?"

Coach shook her head with a frown. "No. You've probably heard the news. The police now say she may be in trouble. Even if she came back safe and sound, it'll take time for her to sort everything out with the authorities. Then she'll need time to readjust after her experience, catch up with schoolwork and everything else. We'll reassess when she gets back—but in the meantime, I'm sure Nevaeh would want what's best for the team, and ask someone to fill in."

That's laying it on thick, Coach. Either that, or you really didn't know Nevaeh.

Trinity's shoulders slumped. Jasmine tilted her head a smidgen to the side, firing her a burning under-the-eyebrow stare.

Trinity grunted through gritted teeth, "Jasmine. I nominate Jasmine."

A heartbeat later, Madison repeated her name in a whimper.

The pause after hearing her name seemed to last forever. Coach finally said, "No other nominees? Okay, show of hands. Who votes for Jasmine as captain?"

Jasmine bored a hole in the floorboards with her eyes, though taking the entire team in her peripheral field of awareness. All hands rose —eventually. Jasmine made mental notes of the laggards.

Good girl, Trinity. Sit. Stay. Roll over. We'll get to "beg" later.

Coach clapped her hands once. "Perfect. I think you've all made an excellent choice. Now to the matter at hand." She began to pace up and down the length of both squads, keeping her eyes riveted on Jasmine. "Our game Saturday night against Crosstown is a critical one. I expect you to give it your all." With each sentence, her voice grew in volume and intensity. Though Coach was on the verge of shouting down the rafters and blasting out every girl's eardrums, her speech washed over Jasmine like a cloudburst, loud and refreshing.

She bounced on her toes during the pep talk, barely able to contain herself. Scanning over her new team with Coach's every exhortation for courage, heart, and team spirit, Jasmine smiled inwardly at Trinity's taciturn slouch and Madison's dour expression of submission.

Wrapping up her overly long repetitions of "Are you ready? I can't hear you!", Coach blew her whistle one last time. "Captain Jasmine, put your team through the drills."

She eagerly sent the squads through their paces—alternately running laps around the court, interspersed with passing and shooting drills. Boundless energy filled every inch of Jasmine's body. But her intensity didn't seem to catch on with her teammates. Rather than inspiring and reinforcing, Jasmine's vitality sapped the spirit from the other girls like a leech. They stumbled, they flagged, they fumbled.

What's wrong with these slackers?

Trinity jogged past Jasmine with the energy of a sloth.

"C'mon, move yer saggy butt," Jasmine charged with unabashed sarcasm. Another girl trailed Trinity with even less enthusiasm. "Flank your opponent, dammit," she chided, her frustration mounting with each order.

Madison attempted a jump shot, but her feet barely left the floor. "How could you miss an easy shot like that, Fatty-son?" The girl next in the loop was even more pathetic.

Nothing seemed to click. Trinity let a girl from the second squad zoom right past her. "Block her like you mean it, you pussy." Her orders were met with flashes of anger, lasting glowers, and pained resentment, not just from the intended target but from everyone around her.

Coach's whistle trilled, and she flagged Jasmine over. She planted her fists on her hips.

"*Caramba!* What the hell you think you're doing, *Captain*?" she snarled low and hoarse. Chewing on stern bitterness, she snatched the ball from Jasmine's hands. "Girl, these are your teammates, not a chain gang. If anyone is allowed to yell at my girls, it's me. *Got it?*"

She shoved the ball into Jasmine's chest, forcing her a step backward. "Now, *you* move it like you mean it."

Jasmine turned and jogged back to the team, muttering a chain of curse words to herself while gritting her teeth like she wanted to bite through railroad spikes.

Coach blew her whistle once more and shouted with her best drill sergeant bellow, "First squad, V-cut drill. Fill-in squad, ten laps."

First squad weaved back and forth, each member taking their

turns at passing, shooting, and rebounding. Each round, Jasmine grumbled a terse compliment. The flimsy encouragements left a sour taste in her mouth, making her jaw clench in rebellion. Sweat built on Jasmine's brow, boiling off from the festering anger radiating underneath.

On the other squad's fifth lap, opportunity fell square into Jasmine's lap. It was the perfect storm to vent her frustration at a convenient target—Coach distracted, Jasmine fast-dribbling the ball in position for a long pass, and Fat-Ass Madison huffing and puffing behind the pack.

She took the shot, rifling the ball directly at the back of Madison's head. Her aim was perfect.

Madison tumbled into the bleachers like a rag doll. Crumpling face first into the lowest bench, one leg wedged between the first and second rows. She cried out, rolling onto the floor on her backside. Curling into a fetal ball, she rocked back and forth, clutching her knee. Bleats of agony whined in quick breaths through clenched teeth.

Coach blasted her whistle and pointed at the team members nearest the locker-room door. "You, get the first aid kit just inside the door," she barked. "And you, get ice packs from the fridge in my office." The two girls zoomed out and popped back into the gym on the second beat of the swinging door. Both squads inched together in a circle around Coach and Madison.

"Okay, okay. Show's over. Everyone hit the showers," Coach commanded as she wrapped the compression bandage around the twisted knee.

"And *you*," she shouted under fierce eyebrows aimed straight at Jasmine. "Get cleaned up and wait in my office."

The team sulked into the locker room. Silent accusing eyes stared at Jasmine. Mumbled curses merged into a stream of grunts that cascaded over the lockers.

"What're you looking at?" she scoffed at anyone and everyone. She popped open Nevaeh's—now hers—locker at the end of the row and began to strip.

The hairs on the back of her neck stood up.

She glanced over her shoulder, then wheeled fully around in surprise. Her face at first screwed up in consternation, until she recognized the Amazon hulking behind her.

Kimani?

Only now she was wearing gym duds with a faded wrestling logo across her chest, and her ridiculous Nevaeh hairdo bunned up tight. The black jaguar tattoo on her forearm gave a silent roar as the muscles underneath flexed, and her fists clenched.

"What the fuck," Jasmine spat. "When did *you* get in—"

Her outburst was cut short by a kidney punch from behind, sending her sprawling into the grasp of the gargantuan. The she-berserker spun Jasmine around, slamming her into the wall of lockers and pinning one arm below her shoulder blade. Before she could search for who struck her from behind, a towel whipped around her head. Dingy white cotton filled her vision and the stink of old soap and diluted bleach filled her nostrils.

The iron grip on her wrists behind her spun her away from the locker, and a mix master of muffled "C'mon"s surrounded her.

"Hey, your dad's a grunt. Ain't that right, *Captain?*" There was no mistaking the poison in Trinity's voice. "Well then, you should know what an Army blanket party is."

Blows rained down from all angles. Some were soft like a sneaker, some were harder like a plastic bottle of shampoo, others were rock hard. They crashed down in rapid succession, each preceded by the telltale swish of a towel wielded like a sling—pounding every limb, every muscle, every joint, every inch below her neck.

Jasmine tried to cry out. "Jacks—"

A hard hit to her abdomen.

She sucked the air into her lungs again, through the filter of damp terry cloth. "*Mlin—*"

A harder hit to her shoulder blade.

Where is he, dammit?

A pair of blows to the back of one knee. The joint screamed in agony and gave out. Jasmine slumped with her arm still forced behind her, twisted to a socket-wrenching angle. She yanked one arm away and flailed blind, hoping to find support on the bench between the rows of lockers. She tottered and crumpled to the floor with one last blow aimed at the back of her head. Gray whirlpools of vertigo rushed in. Hands clutched at her, stripping off her sports bra and panties.

Out of the swirling bleach-infused cotton fog, the image of Caleb's hungry leer flashed in front of her.

"No!" she gasped plaintively against ribs that remembered their old injury, aggravated by the new ones.

A command to shut up was reinforced by another *whomp* of a

painfully rigid but nameless object wrapped in a towel. Jasmine bit her lip, forcing herself to silence.

Rough hands dragged her along the floor, her feet jouncing against the pebbled dimpling of rubber mats. She struggled in vain when her legs were lifted off the floor. Unseen hands gripped her shoulders, arms, and legs as she was carried toward the sound of running water.

The towel whipped off her head, and she was heaved like a side of beef. Bouncing once on the hard floor, she slid on slick tiles until she came to rest under a thin lukewarm spray of a shower. Every square inch of her body screamed, wishing to be under the balm of that tepid water.

Her world continued to spin as she raised her head. She squinted at two figures: a tall, burly blur looming in the shower entrance, and a shorter slimmer chuckling shadow.

Jasmine groaned as she tried to gather her aching legs underneath her. She blinked again, trying to muster a scowl at the two fuzzy blobs. As the smaller blur fidgeted with something in her hands, she muttered to the larger, "Go on, Sis. Beat it before Coach sees you."

A stabbing flash of whiter-than-white paired with the sound of an electronic shutter assaulted her senses. A swarm of starry afterimages flooded her shredded consciousness. After a few blinks, the remaining shape coalesced into a single figure standing over her with a menacing gloat.

Jasmine struggled to push herself to the wall. She yelped when the shadow kicked her legs wide apart. A second flash blasted her blind again, and a shutter echoed in the stalls.

An eternity of blinking, and her vision stopped strobing. Trinity leaned against the wall near the shower's entrance, cellphone in hand.

"You think you're such hot shit, Jizm. You think you got me over a barrel, bitch? Give me any trouble, any reason whatever—sic the cops on me again, or take what's mine again, you even look at me funny—and this," she chuckled with delight as she patted her phone, "your tits, your bony ass, your va-jayjay, your *everything* goes out to the whole world."

She laughed once, picking out a soiled washrag between two fingers from the used hamper. She flung it square in Jasmine's face. "As far as Coach and anyone else is concerned, you slipped and fell while taking a shower." With a chuckle of cold derision, Trinity turned and walked away.

Jasmine collapsed back on the floor, letting the water roll over her. She barely made out the far-off cry.

"Hey, Coach! C'mere quick, Jasmine fell in the shower."

Where the fuck were you, Jackson?

CHAPTER TWELVE

C oach slammed the wall phone in its cradle. Turning toward the two students in her office, each absorbed in their own futile efforts to stifle their moans, she folded her arms and released an exasperated whoosh like a steam pipe about to burst. With an expression of frustration, she leaned against the open door.

"Nurse Genesee is gone for the day. The two of you are stuck with me, until someone picks you up, or you feel you're ready to go."

Madison, still in team uniform, slouched in her seat along the wall opposite Coach's desk. With her foot propped up on a second chair, she grunted with effort while rubbing her shin. Wrapped in three layers of extra-wide elastic bandage, blue ice packs, and knotted towels, her tree-trunk knee looked like it was encased in a cotton pressure cooker.

Jasmine reclined in Coach's chair, fully dressed. She rested her head on a single ice pack set on the crown of the chair, and her knee swathed in another cocoon of frozen blue chemicals and towels. Peering under stray dangling locks of mussed hair, she regarded her backpack crammed behind the office door. Longing to retrieve her pocket mirror, she wondered how much of a mess her face was—and if the old or new Jasmine would stare back at her.

Pushing off from the wall, Coach stood in front of the two girls.

Facing Jasmine, she didn't just fold her arms, she *clamped* them together, her fingers digging into her elbows with a death grip.

"You sure you're okay, Jasmine? You still refuse to let me call a doctor, EMT, or anything?"

"No. I just ..." she hesitated, stifling a groan. "Just slipped in the shower, Coach."

How the hell can talking hurt so much?

"Yeah, right. And I'm the Easter bunny." Her arms twitched, and her fingers dug in deeper. "If you ask me, it's mighty suspicious that you had your ... *accident* while I was busy with Madison. Well, you managed to dress yourself, so you obviously got enough ..." She shook her head and raised her hands in frustration. "I dunno *what* it is you got."

She prowled over to her desk and tapped Jasmine's chair leg with her foot twice.

"Move it. I need to get something."

Jasmine obliged with agonizing care, and Coach rolled out the bottom drawer, pulling out a manila folder.

She flipped though the team rosters, picking out a sheet. Bringing out her cell phone, she skewered the girls with a glower that would freeze molten glass. Her focus oscillated between phone and paper as she dialed the number. With her phone nailed to her ear, she said, her temper subdued, "Stay put. Not a peep outta either of you. Or believe me, I'll—oh, hello? Is this ...?"

Huddling her head close to the phone, Coach slipped behind the office door jamb under the sole light left on in the vacated locker room.

The girls stared at each other. Madison's jaw twitched, and her brow furrowed. Her mouth opened and closed twice, like she was struggling with a decision—what to say and how to say it, despite Coach's admonishment. Jasmine once more longed for her backpack behind the office door, wishing she could reach her own phone. One eyebrow rose in thought.

The blanket party must have been what Trinity spent all afternoon arranging. And that damned Mlinzi hung me out to dry.

Jasmine pictured a tantalizing scene with her tearing off *Mlinzi's* tail and beating him with it.

Coach paced past the doorway, her stern expression streaked with stark shadows under the ceiling light. She gripped the phone like she was ready to crush a soda can and dialed a second number. Casting a harsh shadow under the cone of light, she grimaced at her charges, then after the slightest of moments frowned at the phone.

"Hello, this is Coach Garcia with a message for Mrs. Price." After a few terse mumbled sentences, she abruptly turned back to her office, rattling off her office extension and her cell phone numbers. She clicked her tongue with a harrumph and searched her sheet for a third number.

She dialed and the phone in Jasmine's backpack vibrated to life. Coach shot a confused look at the pack behind the door, then jabbed a finger on the face of her phone, terminating the call.

"Jasmine, what's your mother's cell number?"

"She doesn't have one." She pointed at her backpack behind the door. "She gave me hers when we moved here."

Madison cocked her head, with an expression like she had just eaten a lemon.

"You wouldn't happen to know her work number?"

"She just changed her second job, and she's probably on her way there. I didn't put her new number in my phone yet." Jasmine stifled a twitch in her cheek when she remembered her cell's recent-call list would have it from Ma's interview.

"Well, isn't that just dandy," Coach complained.

What message did Coach leave Ma? I'll have to deal with the fallout when I see her. Unless I beat her home, and I erase—

Coach crammed her phone back into her sweatpants. "Madison, your mother is on her way to pick you up. And you've had that ice on long enough. Let's see if we can get you ambulatory."

After shoving the manila folder and its roster back in its drawer, Coach scratched her head for a moment, then left the room without a word. Amplified by the acoustics of the emptied locker room, the scraping and shuffling of large objects scuttling across concrete drifted through the office doorway. The perplexing sounds soon ceased, and Coach reappeared, holding a dilapidated pair of crutches with the school initials painted on their wooden struts.

She propped one against the open door next to Jasmine's pack and handed the remaining crutch to Madison. Undoing the knotted towel, she collected the blue packs and tossed them into her fridge. Coach finished wrapping the swollen knee in an elastic bandage, adding, "Once you get home, put some ice on it and rewrap it. Now, hop up on that foot, and let's see how it is."

Madison fumbled with the crutch and clambered with effort out of her seat. She hobbled her first step and hissed a sudden intake of breath, her face scrunching up in expectation of another stab of pain. After a pair of hesitant steps, a mild balm of relief swept over her entire bearing. "It's … it's not too bad, Coach."

"*Bueno*. Your mother should almost be here by now. I'll get your street clothes and walk you to the bus stop to meet her. While *you*," she punctuated with an accusing finger pointed at Jasmine, "sit tight and don't move from that spot. Or I'll personally see that you spend two weeks' detention with Vice Principal Chatelain."

Madison tottered to the door, leaning on it while Coach vanished between rows of lockers. She turned to Jasmine and whispered, "Yeah, Nevaeh was bad. So's Akilah and Trinity. But *you're worse*. At least with Nevaeh, I knew what—"

Coach reappeared, corralling Madison toward the gym, but not before shooting one last glare at Jasmine. Madison hobbled away, showing Jasmine a pout overflowing with the wariness of a trapped animal.

Their voices disappeared behind the squeaks of the swinging doors leading to the gymnasium. Jasmine leaned forward, squelching a groan that sprang from the small of her back. She pulled open the lower drawer and slid out the manila folder. Extracting an earmarked page sticking out from the pack, she examined it until she found what she hoped for—Trinity's contact information.

Ignoring the cell phone entry, she stared at the home phone, mouthed the numbers to herself, and closed her eyes, repeating the sequence until it was firmly imprinted in her memory. Sliding the folder back undisturbed, she closed the drawer and settled back in Coach's chair. She closed her eyes and mouthed the sequence in silence, stumbling over stubborn echoes of Madison's "*you're worse*" interrupting her concentration.

Dammit. I don't need anyone's pity. Least of all yours, Fat-Ass.

Coach once again stood in the doorway with her fists riveted to her hips. She parked herself on the corner of the desk, her face a conflict of emotions, concern overriding them all.

Coach started in soft confidence, with a nod toward the shower. "Now just between us, Jasmine. What happened in there?"

"I … fell," she repeated without conviction.

Coach crossed her legs and folded her arms. Her face was a stop sign of sarcasm. "Says you. Who *made* you fall?"

"No one," Jasmine stonewalled, her eyes focused on the stark circle of light on the floor through the open doorway.

"Uh-huh." Coach stood and paced around the far side of the desk, her eyes roving over the roll of names on her blackboard, divided according to squad. Two names were crossed out—Nevaeh and Akilah. Question marks were next to two others—Jasmine and Madison.

"C'mon, Jasmine. I ain't stupid." She circled the room twice more, keeping a bead on Jasmine with a look that smacked of Madison's disappointment. "I want to help you, but I can't if you don't help *me* first." Coach ceased stalking the room like a caged tiger and leaned her full weight against the open door again. Jasmine's backpack crumpled under the pressure.

"Treat me like a grown-up, and I'll treat you the same. That's one of the things grown-ups do—deal with things straight up, and with each other the same way. At the least they should, even when it's unpleasant. And you should know by now that's how I do it.

"So here's how it's gonna go down." She thrust a thumb into her chest. "I tell you the truth, and I expect you to tell *me* the truth. One of those unpleasant truths is … I know you nailed Madison on purpose."

Jasmine sat up to voice her protest, but instantly regretted it when everything south of her neck screamed at her.

"Don't bother denying it, Jasmine. I said we grown-ups deal in truth, remember?" Coach leaned away from the door and resumed her slow-motion laps around the desk, with her hands behind her back and her whistle bouncing in the hollow between her breasts. "Some of your teammates told me so. But no one snitched about who worked you over in the shower. Don't bother denying that either. The way you're sitting tells me you got the royal treatment, but good."

She halted directly across from Jasmine, looking down at her like a judge presiding over her court. "I wouldn't be surprised if the whole team was in on it. Not the most promising start for a team captain." She clamped her arms again, thrusting her chest at Jasmine. "But *truth* be told, I think you might have deserved it."

"What?" Jasmine blurted, feigning indignation. She grimaced in a feeble attempt to ignore the pain.

"Truth, remember?" Coach pointed in the direction of the gym. "I *told* you to treat our girls like teammates, not your personal slaves. But, no. You had to lord it over everyone. Had to show 'em who's boss." She began to pace again. "Well, guess what, Sunshine? You ain't the boss. *I* am."

"But I … they were …" Jasmine stuttered.

"I'm not finished," Coach barked loud as a foghorn, making the blinds rattle against the window. She puffed out a long breath with her eyes closed and pulled down the edge of her sweatshirt. "I'm not sure how you got the whole crew to vote you for captain, but now it's plain to me what they *really* think. And after your performance out there today, I gotta agree with them." Coach was breathing heavy, like she was in the middle of a street brawl.

"You demonstrated that you know *nada* about the quality of leadership I expect from a captain," she halted directly in front of Jasmine, and began counting on her fingers. "You took out your frustration on a teammate, you dumped on the entire team, getting them so riled that they beat the snot out of you. And now I'm out two more players for a total of four. Madison puts up a brave front, but she's in no shape for practice tomorrow. She might not even be able to play for the rest of the week. And one look at your sorry carcass, and I know you ain't, either.

"Congratulations, Jasmine, the team's down to four people. I now have to inform everyone that we forfeit Saturday's Crosstown game." She paused, glaring a hole into Jasmine's forehead. With her voice barely above a whisper, she added, "And when we have enough able bodies on the roster again, I'll choose a new captain."

Jasmine's jaw dropped for a moment, before she clamped it shut again. She slouched deeper into her chair, not caring about the groan that escaped.

Coach's shoulders sagged, the last of her energy spent. A pensive frown cast a shadow on her face, replacing her anger with melancholy. "You're not gonna tell me who did this, are you?" she inquired rhetorically, waving one hand to indicate Jasmine's entire body.

"Your everything goes out to the whole world."

Shut up, Trinity.

Jasmine's eyes began to water. She scrunched her eyes shut, attempting to stop the flow and silence the echo of Trinity's voice. Neither the tears, nor her mouth would obey. "I couldn't see. They wrapped a towel around my head."

"The whole world."

I said shut up!

Coach put her hand on Jasmine's shoulder—lightly, as if she were afraid she might aggravate some hidden injury. "Finally, some truth. So it wasn't a fall after all. How bad they do you over?"

Jasmine attempted an answer, but all that came out was a sob. Coach dug into her pocket.

"That's it, I'm calling a doctor."

"No." Jasmine looked up at Coach with tired eyes.

"Why not?" she demanded.

Jasmine replied with burning silence.

After a pause and a sigh that seemed to last an eternity, Coach relented. "All right, it's your call. But what about the rest? Who started it?"

Jasmine chewed on her thoughts.

"The whole world."

She shook her head once, silencing Trinity's threat.

Coach retook her seat on the desk corner. "The school requires me to report *something* for your and Madison's *accidents*. What I report, I'll leave up to you." She scrutinized the indecisive battle of emotions washing across Jasmine's face. "Just consider this—if it wasn't a fall, Principal Moore will demand the entire team be disciplined, not just the person who engineered it. Personally, I think forfeiting to Crosstown is gonna hit the whole team hard enough." Coach leaned over Jasmine, planting her hands on her knees and searching for the slightest clue what was going on behind her student's eyes. "But it's up to you. You want to lodge a complaint, or do I report it as a fall?"

"A fall." She spat out her reply, with her tears forced back. "And you can't let them—let *anyone*—know I told."

"You haven't told me much of anything."

"Doesn't matter. It'll just get bad. Real bad."

"I see," she sighed with a shrug of her shoulders. Jasmine couldn't tell if it was in relief, resignation, or dread. "Okay, I'll hold back for now. I'll report two ... accidents. But if you change your mind, my door is always open. Or if things get worse, I won't have choice. I'll *have* to report everything."

Coach grabbed Madison's chair, scraping its back legs on the floor. She placed it facing Jasmine and sat with her fingers interleaved in front of her chin.

"Okay, truth time again." Coach hemmed as she flexed her steepled fingers. "I was honestly surprised when Trinity nominated you. Before today, I didn't think you were interested. Why did you suddenly want to be captain?"

Jasmine chuckled and was rewarded with a stick in her ribs. "You're not the first person to ask me that today."

"Well?"

"They wouldn't have liked my answer."

Coach blinked.

Aw crap. Too much truth.

"I mean, I didn't *have* an answer then. I still don't now."

"Who asked?"

"I'm tired, Coach. Can I just go home?"

And stop being nice to me. It's hard to lie when you're nice.

But I have to. I must. Or else "the whole world" sees.

"Yeah, in a minute, Jasmine. I can see you're not gonna tell me anything you don't want to. Though I can guess who asked." Coach untangled her fingers and put her hand on Jasmine's good knee. "Whoever has it out for you, just lay low for a while. Swallow whatever resentments you still got, and deal with it. Just remember, if it gets too tough …"

Jasmine glowered at the crack in the concrete floor and growled, "Don't worry, Coach. You can bet I'll take care of that little—"

"Whoa, hold it right there, girl," she barked, followed by a quick mutter. "*Dios mío.* Sometimes, I swear I don't know who it is I'm talking to."

Coach's chair squeaked as she sat erect with a commanding grimace. "So far, nothing you've said is leaving this room. But you go *vigilante* on me, and that promise goes right out the window. I look out for *all* my girls, got it, Ms. Price? And Moore and Chatelain will sure as shit bring down the hammer—right on your head."

She flicked Jasmine's forehead lightly, snapping her attention away from the floor. "*¿Comprendes?*"

Coach stood and shuffled her chair to the side. "Now, stand up. Can you walk?"

Jasmine handed the ice packs to Coach Garcia, and levered herself out of the chair, one arm and one leg at a time. She staggered forward two steps.

"I can make it," she rasped.

"Yeah, I can see that plain as day." Coach Garcia grabbed the remaining crutch and handed it to Jasmine. She pulled out her phone, and redialed Jasmine's home. Half a minute passed before she rattled off a second message, her terse sentences signaling her patience was burnt to a frazzle.

"Still no one. C'mon, let's get that knee in an elastic bandage. Then I'll ride the bus with you, and see you make it home. Then your mother can try to convince you to get some real medical attention."

Jasmine's body telegraphed it had discovered new boundaries of pain by the time she made the bus. A few blocks down the line, and she thought she heard her phone ring in her backpack. She shoved it far as she could into the seat, hoping Coach didn't hear it.

Screw it. Whoever it is, it can wait.

After fifteen minutes of bouncing over potholes in a barely upholstered seat, followed by hobbling down two more city blocks, her arms and legs felt like they were about to snap off.

She lumbered to her front door, her crutch clicking with every step. Coach patiently shadowed her footsteps, her arm looped through the backpack's remaining strap. Jasmine stopped, pivoting on the rickety crutch to barricade the front steps.

Coach clicked her tongue in exasperation at her phone. "Answering machine again."

"I can take it from here, Coach."

"Yeah, you look like you're ready to tackle the Himalayas." Coach swung the backpack to her side and started up the steps. "Besides, your Ma still isn't home yet."

Jasmine held out her free arm. "No, it's cool. I stay with Bibi, one of Ma's friends, until she gets home."

When did it become so easy for me to lie?

Regarding the girl standing rock steady on the crutch, Coach blocked her way. Her shoulders, cocked at an angle that screamed skepticism, relaxed when she released a sigh of frustration.

"Okay, but if you have any problems that you and … Bibi can't handle, you call a doctor." Coach clicked the backpack strap around the handle of the crutch. She waved one last time as Jasmine hobbled through the front door, watching until she had lumbered up the stairs to the first landing.

With each step, the pain raced up her limbs. Once she attained the second landing, out of view of the front door, she leaned against the wall with a groan. Up her arms through her shoulders, and up her legs past her hips, the pain collided somewhere under her breastbone. To top things off, the crutch had rubbed her armpit raw. The backpack banged against her good knee with every step until both joints creaked louder than Bibi's.

She eased open her apartment door and dumped the crutch and the rest of her belongings into an unceremonious heap on the floor. Shuffling a tortuous stagger toward the sofa, she prayed she could make it before collapsing. Her jumbled thoughts zinged into focus when she caught her first glance of the terrarium.

Jackson sat on his log, radiating waves of gray and orange.

"You sonovabitch," she mumbled. "When I can move again, I'm gonna …"

Jasmine flopped face first onto the sofa, raising her head to glower again at the traitorous lizard. She let her head plop back with a groan into the cushions when Ma materialized with phone in hand, rounding the kitchen doorway.

She did not look pleased.

CHAPTER THIRTEEN

"Good glory, Jasmine. What have you been doing?" trumpeted Ma as she barreled out of the kitchen. She loomed over Jasmine, shaking the cordless phone like she was trying to strangle a cobra. "First the TV, the police, and now all these phone calls waiting for me the minute I get home? As if I don't have enough to worry about!"

Jasmine didn't budge from her face plant on the deliciously soft throw cushion.

"AwcmomMa. Ijuss gobbak fomskool," mumbled the sofa.

Jasmine's neck emitted a sandy grinding sound as she rolled her head to unearth one bleary eye from the pillow.

Ma was midway into her wardrobe change—wearing her hotel pants, and her shirt with its coffee shop logo half-buttoned. Her phone dropped to her side as she gaped wide-eyed back and forth between the crutch abandoned against the apartment door and her daughter's bandaged knee.

"What is going on? What's this about you getting injured at school? Are you all right?"

"ImvyneMa."

"You're fine? What a week. Each day you're in worse trouble than the day before. You're gonna put me in my grave. What have you got to say for yourself?"

"Skoolsux. Jaxomsux. Evvybuddysux."

Ma flashed her hands at Jasmine in mock surrender. "No, never mind. I don't wanna hear your excuses. Let me tell you about *my* day.

"I'm at the tail end of my shift at the coffee shop, dealing with all the crack-o'dawn customers, and outta the blue, I see you on the early morning news." Ma gestured at the muted TV, its two-toned red and lime green screen tuned to a local station. "Every ten minutes they flash a blurry photo of someone—just *your* size. In a poncho—just like the one you said you *lost*. Going into some funky alley—just like the one down *our* street. The news was asking for help in identifying 'the mysterious figure.'

"I begged the boss to use his office phone, which got his nose bent outta shape. He's screwy that way, but that's neither here nor there."

Ma shook the phone at Jasmine again, ready to crush its plastic case.

"I tried calling your phone, but no soap. Just as I'm about to leave, the police tracked me down at work, calling my boss on his phone. If he wasn't happy with me before, he sure as shootin' was ticked off now.

"Then two detectives stopped by my day job, asking me all sorts of questions, while my work piled up. Asking questions about you, your friends—Nevaeh, that poor girl Akilah, and whatshisname, Caleb?— and that danged poncho. So many questions, and they wouldn't say why. Not until I pushed back.

"Even then, all they said was that there was 'an incident,' and you and Akilah were attacked. They said you were all right, but they couldn't tell me anything more. But they sure hinted something worse went down. You coulda knocked me over with a feather. For pity's sake, Jasmine, what's wrong with you?"

Jasmine stared in disbelief at Ma. Somewhere deep inside herself, righteous indignation bared its teeth, and she could hear the howl of a wolf. She wanted to howl out loud, too.

You're kidding me. You're making what happened at the alley my *fault?*

"The police kept digging at me for details, but I told 'em I was in the dark. But would they let it drop? No, they kept at me so hard, my boss thought they were going to arrest me—*Me!* But they left me hangin'. Said I should get the details from the school or *you*. Public servants, my left foot.

"Lord, my boss was so steamed at me when they left, it took the rest of my shift to get him off his high horse, fretting all day long about his hotel's reputation and all that nonsense. Like *I* was responsible for all your mess. And then he docks me two hours' pay, for the time with the cops. We can't afford that!"

Ma rocked left to right on her legs, like she was warming up for a slow-motion boxing match. "So, you didn't lose that poncho after all, did you? What happened to you and your friends yesterday?"

"They're not my friends, Ma." Jasmine's eyes fluttered as she rolled onto her side. "And I didn't lose that stupid poncho—it was taken. When I was in that stupid alley."

Ma flicked an angry hand toward the silent TV. "Am I gonna see your mug on tonight's news? Cripes Almighty, girl. I don't know what upsets me more, the fact you were mixed up somehow in that poor girl's attack, or that you lied to me about it. When were you gonna tell me about all this stuff? As if there wasn't enough bangin' around my head all day long, the bosses and my co-workers at both jobs kept givin' me the hairy eyeball."

Ma's yowling bounced around Jasmine's head until it was shouldered aside by the crescendo of blood in her ears. She planted her hands on the sofa and shifted her legs, each movement accompanied by a groan shouted into the drowning silence of the pillow. Pushing off the arm of the sofa, she hefted herself into a sitting position. Through gritted teeth she began, "But Ma, you don't underst—"

"The hotel boss gave me a dressing down, wondering out loud in front of the whole crew if the hotel should keep me on." As her grievances piled up, Ma's voice inched higher, transforming into a chromatic opera of screeches, accompanied by her arm flailing with increasing energy. "I was never so embarrassed in all my days. Dagnabbit, girl. How long is this gonna go on? We can't afford losing even one hour's pay."

"Ma, will you calm—"

"Then I come home and there's a boatload of messages left for me from your principal, vice principal, the cops, your coach ..."

I don't know how much more I can take. All the crap I've been through, and I now I gotta listen to Ma climbin' on her cross?

Jasmine's stomach joined the chorus of bodily complaints, burning a caustic hole in her gut.

Ma cinched her eyes shut for a moment and took a deep breath. Her voice dropped an octave, and her words were more measured.

"Christ crying in a bucket, Jasmine. I love you, I wanna help you, and I'm trying to understand all this crud thrown at me all at once. Believe me, it's taking all my willpower not to go medieval on your butt. What the Sam Hill is going on?" Ma managed to light her fuse again, and inhaled in preparation to release another string of rants.

Jasmine set her jaw, hunkering down behind the pillow to fend off another fire-hose spout of raving vitriol. The simple act made her wince and yelp in pain.

Ma's fighting stance broke, her arm dropped, and her voice quailed. "What the devil? What happened to you? You said you were fine."

About time, Ma. Thanks for noticing.

Jasmine rested her chin on the pillow. Her spine crunched like it was filled with gristle, and every muscle and tendon in her limbs complained like they were about to tear. "I could sure use a whole bottle of Tylenol."

Chewing her lower lip, Ma fumed into the bathroom, returning by way of the kitchen. She filled the teakettle and blammed it down on the stove, before filling a glass of water. Entering the front room, she launched into a mother's habitual sermon of righteous indignation.

"What on earth goes on at that school? Coach Garcia's message said you took a bad fall, though she didn't sound quite convinced. Where was the nurse? Why didn't your coach give you anything?" She stopped in front of the couch, holding out the pills in one hand and the glass of water in the other.

"The nurse was long gone, Ma. She's only there for half a day as it is. And Coach isn't allowed to give any meds. All she could do was bandage and ice my knee and loan me that old crutch," Jasmine said, nodding her head in the direction of the heap next to the front door. "She wanted to do more—take me to a doctor—but I wouldn't let her."

With the speed of an injured sloth, Jasmine took the glass and pills from Ma.

"Why not, for pity's sake?" She lowered herself gingerly onto the couch next to Jasmine, wringing her hands.

"It wasn't that bad."

Ma dismissed Jasmine's denial with a roll of her eyes.

"Relax, Ma—no concussion or broken bones, at least. Besides, could we afford a doctor? Or an ER visit? I seen the Army copays sheet." Jasmine tilted her head back and gulped everything down. She hacked, nearly swallowing down the wrong throat, when Ma pulled down the neckline of her turtleneck.

"Not that bad?" Ma harrumphed. "Is that where you got that whopper of a bruise?"

"That was from yesterday, in the alley. Didn't those detectives tell you? I gave the whole story to some lady detective named Bollard."

"Bollard—that's one of the people who nabbed me at my hotel job. And no, neither of them told me. Weren't you listening? All she said was that you were attacked in the alley and managed to escape. She was real skimpy on the details, like she was holding something back, or ..."

Ma folded her arms, twisting sideways to face Jasmine directly, though her attention was divided, periodically eyeing the television. "Or is it that the police think *you're* holding something back? What trouble did you get yourself into?"

"Yeah, I don't think Bollard likes me. But like I told her, it was all that gangbanger Caleb."

"Well, this explains why the TV news ain't flashing that poncho picture no more." Ma planted her shoulder against the sofa back, this time her full attention focused on her daughter. "Okay, I'm listening. What did you tell Bollard?"

Jasmine wheezed as she sank behind the pillow again, squeezing it like a teddy bear. She rolled out the half-true half-false ordeal—just like she had rehearsed early that morning. Just like she had rattled off to Bollard. Glancing at Jackson, she frowned at his sudden shift to the shade of green when she mentioned Caleb.

Ma's eyes flitted left and right, like she was watching a movie depicting every scene in Jasmine's tale. She remained silent for a long while after the story wrapped up. She shook her head, rubbing her fore-head with the heel of her palm.

"Criminy, it never stops, does it? What did we do to deserve all this?"

We? We?! *Weren't you listening, Ma? I was almost raped. Killed. Me.*

"We finally scrape enough together to get out of the Projects. We're here for less than a month, getting settled in, making friends like Bibi—not botherin' nobody. Then it all goes to heck. First I lose one of my jobs. Just as Bibi helps me get back on my feet, I come home one night to find you at her apartment, a nervous wreck after getting mixed up in some street to-do. Then Bibi, the one friend we got who's as close as family, leaves to take care of her own catastrophe. Then you almost get caught up in that mess in that blasted alley. And today you come home looking like a ton of boulders fell on you."

Drop it, Ma. Drop it, or I swear …

"Oh, you thought I was going to forget about that? I gotta agree with Coach, you didn't take no tumble in no gym shower. What really happened there today?"

"I'm telling you, I slipped on the wet tile and fell." Her shoulders tensed, and a bolt of misery shot up her neck.

"Coach didn't buy that malarkey, and neither do I. Are you going to lie to me again—*again*? Spill it, Jazz. Do the schoolkids blame you for what happened to Akilah?"

"Yeah, that's about as good a reason as any. But don't make waves, Ma. Like I told Coach, it'll just make things worse."

"Worse? Worse how? That school is supposed to protect you."

"Ma, just drop it, okay?"

No such luck. Ma was firing up for another lecture.

I swear, I'm just about to lose it.

"What about all those anti-bullying programs, safety awareness, and counseling for … for …"

Good God, she's afraid to say it.

Jasmine blurted out her own sarcastic laugh. As punishment, every muscle and bone made her instantly regret it.

Hit a dog enough, and it will stop cringing and bite instead.

Something inside Jasmine commanded her to bite.

"That unicorns-and-rainbows crap doesn't do a damned thing, Ma. It's a coat of paint to hide the shit underneath. It's window dressing to make parents feel good and leave the school the *fuck* alone."

"Jasmine!" Ma barked. "You know what I think about language like—"

"Christ, Ma. Give it a rest," bellowed Jasmine.

The dam broke.

"It's a real *shit* show out there. Or haven't you figured that out yet? You're pissing and moaning about how all this is affecting *you*? God damn it! What the fuck about *me*?

"I almost got raped. *Raped!*"

Ma flinched at the word.

"I almost got *killed*. Don't you fucking *get it*? Why is everyone treating *me* like the criminal? I'm just trying to get by—to *survive*. And now you're bent outta shape about my fucking language? I'm not a little kid anymore, Ma."

Jasmine hunkered the pillow down and close, shoving her breasts upward. "It's a long time since I been skipping rope and playing with dolls. Jesus, you think we move out of the Projects, and everything's just peachy? News flash—It's just as fucked up here. I'm trying to deal with grown-up problems, but no one is showing me *how*."

It was Jasmine's turn to flail her arm, wanting to slap the world outside her window. To hell with the pain it brought. "Dad's off in Crap-istan, Bibi's bailed on us, and ..."

Jasmine glowered at Jackson. She bit her lip to prevent blurting out, "*and left me with some damned monster lizard.*"

"And you're never home 'cause you're busy with your two fucking jobs." Puffing like a wounded animal, Jasmine mumbled at her pillow, "I sometimes wonder if you prefer it there. Away from me."

She recoiled, frowning at the line she crossed.

Hell, I didn't just cross it, I beat it with a tire iron and ran screaming over it.

Ma drew her hand back to slap Jasmine.

Crushing the pillow against herself, Jasmine relented when her knee and ribs reminded her of the Army blanket barrage they had suffered.

Halting in mid-swing, Ma instead dropped her trembling arm across herself. Ma sat in abashed silence, her jaw muscles twitching and her eyes brimming. She leaned forward, and enfolded Jasmine in a loving embrace.

No, dammit. Stay mad at me, Ma.

Jasmine groaned again, but she couldn't stop. She coughed and groaned open-mouthed until her face became wet.

I'm not ... Dammit, I'm not crying. She slammed her throat shut, holding her breath so she wouldn't sob again. *Dammit, I'm not crying.*

A sob shook Ma's entire body. "I'm sorry," she heaved in a hoarse whisper. Her forehead, bowed next to Jasmine's ear, bobbed with each slow, blubbered word. "I'm ... so sorry."

She shuddered with a moist cough and sat up once more, meeting Jasmine eye to eye. "I get so wrapped up in my life, feeling like I'm doing this all by myself, I forget that you're in the same boat. Out there all alone, doing what *you* need to do, all by yourself. I forget that we have each other—that I can lean on you. But most importantly, I'm supposed to be here for you to lean on *me*. I don't show it enough, but it kills me when I can't be there for you."

No, Ma. I can't lie if you're like this. Be pissed, so I don't have to tell you the truth. About Trinity, Akilah, Caleb, Nevaeh … About Jackson. About me.

Jackson had one eye trained on her, the other on Ma. His leathery hide transposed from its vibrant green to a wretched maroon, like an apple that had rotted into slush.

The teakettle whistled low and soft, rising to an annoying banshee. Ma sniffled, and grabbing a throw blanket from the couch, she herded Jasmine to the kitchen table. "Bibi left us some of her white whisper tea and honey. I think we can both use some right about now."

Jasmine gathered the moth-eaten blanket about her. Before she sat down, she scooped a handful of ice cubes out of the freezer, wrapping them in a dishtowel. While Ma fussed with the tea, Jasmine limped to her seat, cocooning herself in the blanket and nursing her knee with the makeshift compress. She immersed herself in the delicious combination of warmth and coolness: warm where she wanted, cold where she needed.

But an express train of images, like railroad cars filled to bursting with cargo, rolled around in her skull, destroying what little calm was afforded by the solitary moment of silence:

Nevaeh's alley ambush—her wind-up before punching her ribs;

Caleb's ring front and center on her fist;

The nightmare flash of slick umber wrapping around Nevaeh's head;

Mlinzi wrapped around the length of Bibi's couch;

Caleb's lust-filled leer;

His lifeless hand disappearing down a stucco-camouflaged gullet;

The dark and brooding *Mlinzi* hunched over Akilah, like a pit bull guarding its territory;

Madison and Trinity cowering in the library;

The silent snarling jaguar on Kimani's arm;

Trinity and her Amazon sister looming over her in the shower;

A burst of blinding white.

An avalanche of nervousness ran straight down her arm. Her finger twitched, tapped the table, and began writing plots, plans, invisible blueprints, hurried attempts to decide what to do next. It scribbled with increasing speed, until Ma set a steaming mug in front of her. The sweet aroma crowded out the storm building in her thoughts, and her hand stopped sketching her schemes and scenarios.

I can feel it start to crumble again. But it won't be anger this time. I could lie to everyone else. I can't lie to Ma—not now, not like this.

Ma sat, and with her elbows propped on the table, inhaled the tendril of mist curling up from her mug. A tired smile erased the worry that had stretched her lips taut, and she quaffed a deep draft of tea. She let go a deep sigh that drained the raw tension from her shoulders, exhaling all her uncertainties into a wispy cloud.

"Jazz, you know you can always talk to me. Believe it or not, I remember what it was like to be your age. There are things you'll tell me, and things you won't. Things you'll never tell me or any grown-up, no matter how much we try to drag it out of you." Her benign smile grew, until even her eyes reflected a smidgen of serenity. "Other than Bibi, have you made any friends yet? Is there someone—anyone—at school you can talk to?"

"No," Jasmine replied. Cupped in her unsteady hands, the mug trembled, its contents resembling a turbulent beige sea. "I've tried, but they all still treat me like an outsider. I thought I had a friend—a girl named Madison. She was picked on, just like me. But when push came to shove, she stabbed me in the back."

She tested the tea with a tiny sip that sloshed into a loud slurp. She exhaled her own cloud of mist, but it did not bring a smile, did not relax her muscles, did not help the scores of aches and pains. "I think Coach was probably the closest thing I had to a friend."

I'm losing it. Gotta think of something soon, or I'm gonna spill my guts. Everything including about Jackson. And then I'll be in some real shit.

"Had?"

"She's royally ticked off at me. Nothing was going my way today, so I took it out on Madison. So Coach ..." Jasmine let the sentence trail off with a paltry shrug.

"She *did* sound upset, when she left all those messages," Ma mused, looking at the ceiling. "Maybe that's what I should do now—call her back. But I'm sure she's not at school at this hour."

"No, she saw me home after practice."

Change the subject. Make a distraction. Do something, anything.

"There, you see, Jazz? She's not mad at you. She was surprised or upset, maybe even a little disappointed. But she's not mad at you any-more." Ma took another swallow of tea and rose out of her chair, stretching her arms wide and high with a satisfied grunt.

"Let me call her cellphone back and get to the bottom of all this." Dropping her arms, she glanced at the clock on the stove. "Whoops— gotta do it now, before I get ready for my night job."

How the hell do I get out of this? Echoes of Trinity's threat invaded again, drowning out her own voice.

Ma picked up the receiver to dial, only to be startled when it rang in her hand.

"You see," Ma said with an embarrassed chuckle. "That's proba-bly Coach Garcia now, checking to see that you're all right. Hello?" Her brow wrinkled in bewilderment. "Yes, that's me. Who's this?"

Her face transformed into an inscrutable wall, except for her eyes hinting at a fearful panic. She searched for the support and sanctuary of her chair. Her legs quivered until they buckled, and she collapsed in her seat. Her eyes piercing Jasmine with desperation, she whispered into the phone, "Oh, God … Yes, I'm … I'm still here. Is … is he gonna be all right?" Ragged gasps came in rapid succession.

Dad?

Ma's questions didn't come in their usual torrent. They were sepa-rated by long agonized pauses filled with blank stares of naked shock, peppered with shallow breaths, soul-wrenching shudders, and a succes-sion of "Oh, God"s.

"How bad?" Silence. "How … how did it happen?" More silence. "He's where? *Where?*"

Dad's in trouble. Big trouble.

Jasmine chided herself about how coolly she came to that realiza-tion.

Ma leaned hard against the table, cradling her forehead in one hand, knocking over her mug of white whisper tea.

Jasmine lurched out her chair, ignoring the pain that stabbed her knee. She unwrapped the dishtowel from her leg, lobbing the ice cubes into the sink. She sopped up the spreading liquid moments before it spilled onto the floor.

Ma sobbed, her body quaking with every gasp. "I … understand. You'll call when he's out of surgery?" Another tattered sob. "Thank you, Major. I'll be waiting."

She spasmed into another racking whimper, fumbling with her

thumb to shut off the phone. Failing miserably, she dropped the phone on the table. She paid it no heed as it tumbled over the edge, clattering on the floor.

Jasmine stood behind her, wondering what to do. She had the nagging suspicion that the answer was right in front of her, and that the other Jasmine—the Jasmine who could feel, the Jasmine who wouldn't hide in lies—would instinctively know how to respond.

Unsure of herself, Jasmine placed her hands on her mother's shoulders, sliding them down until her arms crisscrossed below Ma's neck. She squeezed with the gentlest of touches, fearing she might crush what was left of her mother's heart.

"What happened, Ma?" Jasmine ventured, her voice a ragged whisper.

"Ambush. An IED?" Each sentence ground out, as though it was forced out of her by the lash of a whip. "Some sort of bomb. Half his squad gone. Tore up his arm and leg. Shrapnel in his neck. Don't know how bad yet." Her body shook with a sob filled with a lifetime of hurt.

Wanting to say something simple, some wise adage or magical phrase to make Ma stop crying, Jasmine opened her mouth to speak. She searched over the space of a dozen heartbeats, but the words of comfort would not come.

Ma collapsed into her own folded arms on the table, slipping from Jasmine's weak embrace. From the Formica came whispered moans of, "I told you. It never stops. Oh, Damon. Oh, Jasmine. What did we ever do to deserve this?"

Jasmine's hands clutched empty air. She dropped her arms at her sides and bit her lip, still puzzled. Helpless to reason out what it was that must come next, she simply stared at Ma's simpering.

What would Dad tell Ma? What was that he always says?

Staring into the corners of her memory, Jasmine muttered in a subdued whine, "C'mon Ma. One foot in front of the other."

Ma pounded one fist on the table. "No!" she shrieked. "You do *not* get to say that!"

Jasmine jumped back, her eyebrows leaping halfway up her forehead. Ma propped her head with the heel of her palm, while the other fist shook a fraction of an inch above the table.

From the floor, the phone sang out its urgent *at-at-at* of a disconnected line. Jasmine bent from her back instead of with her legs to pick up the receiver, not wanting to exact another jolt of punishment from her weary knees.

She dumped the phone into its cradle on the wall and wandered aimlessly into the front room. Glaring at the terrarium, she lowered her head, her eyes burning under an angry brow. She bobbed her head this way and that, scanning the log, searching the leaves and flowers. The only sign of life in the cage was a small cadre of ants dismantling a slimy gray lump stuck on the front pane.

Where is that damned lizard?

As if in reply, from under the broad leaf of an African violet sprang a jet of pink flesh, slapping against the glass and glomming half of the ants. Jackson emerged from between the fleshy leaves of the violet to regard Jasmine. He smacked his pebbled lips and turned a dull green.

"Was that you? Did *you* do something to Dad?" Jasmine demanded in a threatening whisper.

Jackson tilted his head, thrusting out his lower mandible. If he were human, Jasmine thought he would have seemed indignant.

She beetled her brow one last time at the indifferent lizard, before storming out of the front room. Making a beeline for Ma's bedroom, she tore a work uniform from their hangers in the closet. She unceremoniously draped the barista apron and pants over the chair next to Ma at the kitchen table.

Before she realized it, she wrapped her arms around Ma again in a hug and heard Bibi's words spill out of her own mouth. "We have each *uuther*, and we never give up."

Jasmine's hand snapped up to cover her mouth, and her eyes blinked in confusion.

Did that come out of me? I only wish I really meant it.

Ma scrubbed her eyes with the back of her forearm.

"What ... what did you say?"

Bibi's words once again had worked their magic, just as they had when Ma lost her job. They threw a lifeline down into Ma's dark well of self-pity.

"C'mon Ma. I know it sucks. I'm worried about Dad, too." She sat across from Ma, wincing with a groan when her knees shouted at her for finally giving them a rest. "But sitting here, halfway around the world, crying about it don't help nothin'."

Ma sucked in a trembling breath, her eyes regarding Jasmine with the look that predicted another parental tirade. But Jasmine beat her to the punch.

"Yeah, I'm in trouble. Bibi's in trouble. You're in trouble. Dad's in trouble. But what are we gonna do about it? Cry until we're dust? Spend another hour lecturing me?

"I don't have the time for that, and neither do you. I got homework to do, and you got real work," said Jasmine, flipping the legs of Ma's work pants to drive home her point.

"Believe me, Ma, I could feel sorry for myself all night long about all the crap that's happened today—this whole damned week. But I can't afford it. Are you gonna sit there and blubber all night long? You can't afford it neither." Jasmine wanted to talk about a brighter future, like Bibi so often did. But her jaw would fall off trying to say "hope."

Ma's face screamed astonishment in perfect silence, but the tortured lines on her face mellowed into a grimace, like she held a mouthful of vinegar. She swallowed with a loud guttural *glug*. Her fist rested on the table, no longer shaking.

"We just deal with it, do what we can." Jasmine held Ma with unblinking eyes. "Then hunker down and wait for the next thing. Good or bad."

She stiffened in case Ma took Dad's words badly again. "One foot in front of the other."

Ma pushed herself up from the table. She took her clothing from the chair and shuffled off to her room. The back of her shoulders told Jasmine that her spirit took a shellacking, but was not completely defeated.

"You sure paint a gloomy picture, Jazz," she said, her voice fading away like a wind of desolation.

"After this week, what else?" Jasmine muttered to herself.

She was drawing with her finger aimlessly on the kitchen table, unable to recapture her invisible plans before Ma returned.

Freshened up and her work duds clean and crisp, Ma swirled her jacket about her before slipping it on. She marched to the fridge and collected her brown-bag supper. Her eyes, pools of regret, never left Jasmine.

"How did I miss you growin' up?" She zipped up her jacket halfway and shoved one hand in its pocket. "You got both my work numbers now?"

"Yeah, Ma. I already got your hotel job number. And you called my phone a couple of times from your night job's *stupor*-visor, right? I'll add it to my contacts list."

"You still got a ton of explaining to do when I get back home. And I wanna hear anything you wanna tell me about that horrible … about the alley. But you're right—that waits 'til tomorrow. One foot …" Ma choked on the words. "Until then, you promise me."

The veins stood out like mountain ranges on Ma's hand, and she wagged her finger at Jasmine's nose. "You stay put. If that phone rings, you call me. If it's that Army major with more information about Dad, you call me the second you finish. If it's the police, you tell 'em to call me, and hang up. Anyone else, just tell 'em you'll call back." Her voice warbled with restraint. "But you promise me, girl. Promise me you won't leave this apartment tonight."

"Yeah, Ma."

"'Yeah Ma' don't cut it." She bit the words, like she wanted to inflict pain on them. "You *promise* me."

"I won't leave the apartment tonight," she echoed, mimicking the mechanical tone of a robot.

Ma nodded her head sharp, like that could put the whole world in its place. Without warning, she stooped close and gave Jasmine a hug. She squeezed tight, much tighter than her usual toodle-oo, until she trembled.

Jasmine stiffened—half to bolster herself against the yelp of whatever injury Ma aggravated, half because she drew a blank on how to react. Too late she raised her arm to coddle Ma's waist—she was already out of the kitchen, tramping toward the front door.

Her voice echoed as she admonished her daughter through the closing doorway. "Remember, you promised. Stay put and call."

"I—" The deadbolt closed with a metallic click. "… will."

Jasmine fixed a bagel with a fruit spread from the coffee shop leftovers and headed for her bedroom. She spewed a few crumbs out her mouth between bites as she passed by Jackson's cage. "And *you* … you just stay outta my face for the rest of the night."

Jackson was preoccupied eyeing the remaining ants in his glass box.

In her bedroom, she heaved the window open. Traffic horns and the murmur of the growing night crowds milled in the streets far below. She straddled the windowsill and planted one foot on the fire escape. Wolfing down the last of the bagel, she pulled out her cell phone and pointed it down the street.

"Technically, I haven't left my room," she said with a smirk.

The phone indicated a marginally stronger signal, and even a few wi-fi connections. Jasmine smiled at one that was open for public use, and connected to it—Parker's Corner Store.

She pulled up an online phone directory. Jasmine closed her eyes, and muttered to herself, dredging up a familiar combination—the number from Coach's manila folder, burned with unfading hatred into her memory—the number of Trinity's home phone. Nodding to herself with satisfaction, she punched in the number for a reverse search. The address appeared with some hesitation as it competed with a slew of online ads. A flurry of fingers on the phone's minuscule keypad, and a map materialized on its screen at a tortuously slow rate.

Jasmine *tsk*'d and sighed great heaves of exasperation while she waited for her ancient phone to deal with bucketloads of digital information. She was a hair away from hurling the phone down to the street when Trinity's location and a route from Jasmine's apartment popped up.

"A bit far from here, but it's one block from my metro bus line," she said to the night air with grim resolve. She closed the phone and slipped back into her bedroom. She wanted terribly to face Trinity, to see her expression when confronted on her own doorstep, but her legs and ribs reminded her it was not meant to be. Not tonight.

Okay Trinity. You've won the day, but the war is far from over.

CHAPTER FOURTEEN

A dreamless, sleepless, miserably uncomfortable night. Not even the luxury of a hot shower—or at least the mercy of a shower that didn't blast out ice water—helped her situation.

No matter which way Jasmine lay, those parts of her body that pressed against the bed complained. They ached mildly at first, but the closer her exhaustion pulled her toward slumber, the louder the hurt screamed until it roused her back into the world of alertness, commanding her to roll to a new position.

Hurt, toss, turn. Hurt, toss, turn.

All. Night. Long.

Ma returned from work in the small hours of the morning. Jasmine had rolled with her back to the door as soon as she heard the front door squeak open on its rusty hinges. She shifted once more to take pressure off her ribs, which promised to make her sorry if she didn't scooch immediately. She squeezed her eyes shut moments before Ma poked her head into the bedroom.

A little over an hour after Ma shuffled into her own bedroom, Jasmine lumbered out of bed. She flicked off her alarm minutes before it would have beeped. Quiet and slow, and with the occasional wince, she changed out of her nightshirt.

She balked at her image in the mirror when she stripped down to her panties. Every violence done to her over the past week was recorded on her skin. Purple and yellowed splotches covered her entire torso and limbs, making her look like a leopard with blood-bruise spots.

She rummaged through her wardrobe, selecting clothes for the day. It was warm enough to wear short sleeves, and on any other day it would have been a no-brainer to wear her favorite jeans and a loose T-shirt. One look at the bruises on her throat and arms made the decision for her. She selected a high-necked short-sleeve tunic and her long-sleeve sweatshirt hoodie—the best combination at hand to cover everything up.

Jasmine held up her jeans in front of herself in the mirror and frowned. No amount of washing could get that food coloring stain out. Yesterday's baggy pants smelled yucky. She held up her only other pair of jeans, a somewhat older pair.

There was no question they were out of the running. Fashioned for a younger form that hadn't yet filled out in all the right places, it would rub everything that hurt below the waist raw. She'd be a walking blood sore by the end of the day. Loose sweatpants were the choice forced upon her.

After laying out her things on the bed, she tiptoed into the bathroom. She bathed the night before, so that she wouldn't rouse Ma this morning—and she grimaced at the present she left for Ma in the toilet bowl, the moment she realized flushing ran the same risk.

Sorry, Ma, but I'm not ready to start the day with where we left off from last night's hug-a-thon.

She scooped up all the armaments of getting "on point" and spirited the armful of toiletries into her bedroom. Arranging them on her desk that became her makeshift vanity, she stared at her reflection in the mirror for a full minute.

Trinity's gonna be strutting around like a peacock today. But if I go back looking like the old Jasmine, she and everyone will know I've been put back in my place. That ain't gonna happen.

She fussed with her face and hair, dipping once more into the supplies that Bibi had given Ma.

Something in her reflection looked off.

Dab this, pluck them, straighten those, primp that. Nothing worked, even though her face was unbruised.

Jasmine clicked her tongue at the clock. If she was going to catch her bus, she would have to wrap this up. She grimaced at her reflection one last time.

Something *still* didn't look quite right. Too much around the eyes?

"Last chance, Jasmine," she whispered at her reflection. "Take a sick day, or tough it out? Yeah, right. Like I have a choice."

If she curled up and nursed her wounds, Trinity and her minions would never let her get back up. She'd always be the Wannabe Who Was Whupped.

And fair game to get whupped again.

Slugging down a couple of painkillers with a gulp of water straight from the tap, and grabbing a plain bagel from the breadbox, Jasmine was a silent whirlwind as she whisked out to the front room. She grabbed her backpack and the forlorn crutch leaning against the closet door and shot one last angry frown at Jackson.

Hanging upside down from the terrarium's wire mesh lid, both his eyes were riveted on her.

"You're still on my shit list, you stupid lizard," she hissed as she closed the door behind her.

With the crutch under her arm, she faced a challenge merging into the pedestrian flow in front of her building. If she didn't feel the eyes of everyone on her before, gimping along sure helped her stand out in all the wrong ways. She stewed, imagining how stupid she must look, with her face all done up, set against cheap-ass grunge clothes and a crutch.

She glared upward at Jackson once more for good measure when she passed under his terrarium. Though she couldn't see him in their stories-high apartment window, she was sure he was watching *her*.

The glances and giggles from other kids converging on the bus stop reinforced her paranoia-laced mood. No two ways about it, she was going to ditch the crutch as soon as possible, and to heck with the hurt.

Jasmine pushed a determined sigh through clenched teeth. The regular seating was packed, except for seats between morbidly obese people. She plopped herself down on one of the seats reserved for handicapped and leaned her head against the crutch.

Jasmine snatched furtive glances at the crowd. Heads bobbed with every bump, heave, and sway of the bus. School kids peppered the bus's forest of hair, hats, and earbuds. She wasn't quite sure what to feel about the absence of Trinity and her gang.

No doubt, they'll be itching to rub it in at the first opportunity. Gotta keep my eyes peeled.

The monotonous drone of the diesel engine lulled Jasmine into a Zen-like state, filling her with a rare tranquility. It was almost like the times she fell into "the zone" when losing herself in basketball. She felt she was able to observe the entire bus at once—relaxed yet tantalizingly alert.

The bus lurched to a stop. Jasmine watched with a warrior's stoic wariness as Madison lumbered onto the bus, leaning heavily on her own crutch.

Madison's eyes latched onto Jasmine as soon as she reached the top step. Her face filled with uncertainty, vacillating between surprise and anger. Then all that pent-up emotion was erased by a stern blankness. She sat down with a whooshing exhale of relief into the handicapped seat facing Jasmine across the aisle, and adjusted a brand-spanking-new neoprene knee brace.

Madison ventured a cautious glance across the aisle at Jasmine. It was followed by a wide-eyed double take.

The color drained out of Madison's face, and she shook her head so hard her jowls waggled. "What the f—? You got a glass eye, a stroke, or sumpthin'?" She continued her gawping, until Jasmine couldn't stand the scrutiny anymore.

"*What!*" she barked over the thrum of the diesel engine.

Madison rubbed her bloodshot eyes. "Maybe I shoulda stayed home."

What the heck spooked her? Or is she trying to mess with my head?

The two regarded each other like a fencing match. Look, don't look. Glance, look away. Don't let your opponent know that you're looking.

After staring at the floor for half a city block, and her jaw muscles bunching with indecision, Madison planted her flag and faced her adversary.

"Look, I'm sorry you got hammered yesterday. I had no idea that fight was gonna go down in the locker room. But I'm on Trinity's shit list, thanks to you." There was a splash of acid in her accusation.

Jasmine swayed in her seat, hugging her crutch like a shield.

Madison rapped her brace with her knuckles "What did I ever do to you?"

"You and Trinity ganged up against me, among other things. Like those shitty texts you sent."

"Are you friggin' serious? All she wanted was for me to vote for her as captain."

"Damn straight. You *know* I wanted it." Jasmine stamped her crutch on the floor. The thump was drowned out by the screech of air brakes.

"Big friggin' deal. I don't get why you two are so bent outta shape for something so *stupid*."

"Never mind *why* I wanted it," Jasmine snapped. "I wanted ..." She stumbled over own her words.

Suddenly, she *did* feel stupid. Getting angry over something so petty, so ridiculous as a dinky title and position. And to top it off, in her heart of hearts, she *knew* she didn't want it. Her only motive was to keep it from Trinity.

"You were there when Trinity dissed your old home, the Projects, right?" said Madison. "Then you gotta know I didn't have a choice about it."

She flicked one hand toward the ceiling, her eyes glancing at an imaginary giant. "I was jammed up against the lockers. Her big sis, Kimani, was gonna pound the crap outta me if I didn't do what she wanted."

The two girls slouched their shoulders in sync. Their eyes met each other and widened. Madison had the same look in her eye as when they left Coach's office yesterday.

It wasn't pity, was it? Not then, not now either. Then what ...

"How does it feel to be on the receiving end of Kimani's love taps?" Madison leaned into her crutch as the bus turned at an intersection. "I've been there. Though I didn't have everybody gang up on me."

Jasmine shrugged her shoulders, as though she didn't know what else to do.

"I got worked over when Nevaeh, Akilah, and Trinity first asked me to send those shitty texts," said Madison. "I refused, and Kimani went to town on me. They asked again. I had no choice." She moved her crutch to her side and pouted. "So I sure as hell wasn't gonna go another round with that she-Tarzan, just because you two were in a pissing match for captain. That nutcase was expelled once already from school for jammin' up some kid and breaking his leg. And that was *before* she bulked up for a year in some gym."

Jasmine's stomach burned, and she wanted to puke.

"Captain, huh?" Madison harrumphed, full of spite. "Did you really have to nail me on the head and screw up my knee, just for that? The doc says I'm gonna be stuck with this stupid brace for a week."

Jasmine swallowed the rising bile back down. "I, uh … Madison, I …" She stared at the rubber aisle runner, then bit her lip with a guilty frown.

The bus shuddered to a stop, its air brakes doing an impression of a trumpet getting squished. Madison grasped the steel pole next to her and leaned into it, using the bus's deceleration to stand up. Steadying herself with the crutch, she slung her backpack and shot that curious look at Jasmine one last time.

"Yeah, I didn't think there was gonna be a 'sorry' anywhere in there."

By the time Jasmine clambered out of her seat, Madison was gone, along with the rest of the students hustling their way out of the bus.

Jasmine grabbed her backpack and slung it over the shoulder that ached less. By the time she wended her way through the school security queue, her knee was begging her to sit down again. Ignoring the complaints it barked with every step, she took a detour through the gym instead of straight to her homeroom. Her nervous stomach ceased churning when she dropped off her crutch at Coach's office door. She counted her lucky stars that Coach's office was dark, and that she avoided another lecture.

From the gym, then her hallway locker, she whooshed out a steamboat whistle of relief when she collapsed in her homeroom seat. Slouching deep between her desk and chair, she sought the refuge of self-imposed silence amid the chorus of random conversations around her. Even so, she would not allow herself to truly relax.

She observed the entire rowdy crowd around her, losing herself in the shouts and laughter that thankfully never brought up her name. She allowed herself a half-smile, as she monitored the entire panorama of her class.

Is this what Jackson does all day long—just sitting and watching? So how come he didn't help me yesterday, dammit?

She barely heard the homeroom phone ring—eavesdropping on the hushed conversation between three girls in a grinning huddle across the room demanded all her attention.

"Party tonight—and e-e-everyone's gonna be there," said one girl.

Another girl flashed a sour-persimmon frown in Jasmine's direction. The others dipped their heads in a shared giggle.

Jasmine's placid smile morphed into a wry "what-else-did-you-expect?" smirk.

"Where and when?"

"I am *so-o-o* there."

E-e-everyone—except me, of course.

Jasmine looked up with lazy eyes at her homeroom teacher, Mr. Mason, who had thrust a hall pass under her nose.

"Ms. Price, take this and …" he looked at her with cautious concern. "Hey, are you all right? What's with your eyes?"

Jasmine blinked, and he came into sharp focus.

"The school nurse wants to talk to you," said Mr. Mason as he took a step back and cocked his head, never taking his gaze off Jasmine's face. "You sure you can make it? You looked out of it for a second there."

"Yeah, I'm fine. What does Ms. Genesee wanna see me for?"

"You'll have to ask her." Mr. Mason waved the slip of paper at Jasmine again.

"What about my first period class?"

"Don't worry 'bout it. Nurse Genesee's clearing it now. Take your things with you."

Jasmine snatched the hall pass and corralled her belongings. She flashed a petulant frown, more for the benefit of the classroom gossips than for herself.

An eerie self-conscious awareness shivered up between her shoulder blades as her footsteps echoed from both directions in the empty hallways. Around every corner she turned, Jasmine imagined Trinity laughing just out of her sight.

She had left her homeroom with a brisk step, but by the time she reached the nurse's hallway, the pain in Jasmine's knee yowled at her like a wounded kitten, and her limp had returned. Her mind was a jumble with a dozen "what-if"s. They all boiled down to a single one by the time she reached the nurse's office.

Did Coach leave a message on the nurse's phone last night? Even if she didn't, I'll bet she did this morning. This has to be about yesterday's beatdown. And Trinity still holds those damned photos over my head.

Knocking on the half-open door, she ventured a tentative "Hello?" into the room.

"Come in," sounded a voice from within the office.

Jasmine stepped in, leading with her head craning forward to find the source. Nurse Genesee rounded her desk into view, followed by a woman Jasmine hadn't seen since her first day at the school. The lady pushed her glasses up the bridge of her nose and snapped shut a three-ring binder crammed with official looking documents. Jasmine spied the word "Procedures" on the cover of the binder.

Jasmine hunched her shoulders, clutching the spines of her books tight in her hand. "Mrs. ... Ainsworth?" she said, scrunching her eyebrows together.

"Hello, Ms. Price," she replied with a cursory nod.

With a cautious raised eyebrow that perturbed what she hoped was an otherwise perfect expression of innocence, Jasmine regarded Nurse Genesee. Jasmine said, "Mr. Mason said you wanted to see me?"

"Yes, Ms. Price. Coach Garcia said you had an ... accident after practice and was concerned because you had refused medical attention. Have you seen a doctor since yesterday?"

Jasmine replied with a cautious, drawn-out, "No?"

With a muffled harrumph, Mrs. Ainsworth sat behind the nurse's desk. "Nurse Genesee, I'll remain in your outer office. You talk with Ms. Price in the examination room, while I inform her mother." Setting her binder in the center of the blotter, she picked up the desk phone, though never taking her eyes off Jasmine. Her expression was firm and clinical, as if she were determining if a dollar bill was counterfeit.

"Examination?"

"Jasmine, if you'll come with me?" The nurse ushered her into the examination room. Jasmine stifled her limp as best as she could.

Leaving the door ajar, the nurse swished a security screen behind her, obscuring the stone-faced Mrs. Ainsworth as she dialed the desk phone. Nurse Genesee showed Jasmine a practiced smile and adopted a disarming bedside demeanor. "How are you feeling today, Jasmine?"

She responded with an "okay" devoid of enthusiasm.

The nurse yammered away with small talk that failed to register on Jasmine's attention scale. That was, until the class bell rang. Soon the murmur of students in the hallway filtered through the walls.

"Leave your things on the chair, and please remove your sweatshirt."

"What?" She instinctively huddled her books close to herself with both arms.

"Take off your hoodie," the nurse repeated in patient syllables.

"W-why?"

"Since you have not been to a doctor since last night, Principal Moore thought it prudent that I give you a preliminary examination." She snagged a stethoscope and inflatable cuff from a rolling metal table and took a step toward Jasmine. "We'll begin with your blood pressure."

"I'm fine. I don't need no exam." Jasmine clutched her arms tighter.

Nurse Genesee shook her head, and took a stance blocking the door. "Please, Jasmine. Don't be difficult. You said you didn't seek medical help, so the school is left with the responsibility to follow up on an incident occurring on our grounds." She pointed to a spot behind Jasmine. "Now leave your books on the chair, take off your sweatshirt and, hop up on the table."

Jasmine stood her ground.

The nurse tilted her head forward, leveling glaring eyes under stern eyebrows straight at Jasmine. Her pleasant bedside manner was gone.

"Ms. Price," she hammered. "Neither you nor I have a choice in this. I'm *required* to do this. Mrs. Ainsworth outside will back me up, as will Vice Principal Chatelain if he needs to be involved. Do you get my drift?"

Jasmine sulked at the nurse and unceremoniously dumped the pile of books on the plastic seat. She unzipped her hoodie, peeled it off like she was shedding a second skin, and lobbed it onto the chair.

Mounting the padded examination table like it was an electric chair, she regarded the nurse as though she were the warden about to throw the switch.

Nurse Genesee's eyes lingered on Jasmine's exposed forearms, then skewered her directly with a look of concern.

Jasmine suppressed the urge to follow the nurse's gaze, fearing it would only draw more attention to the scratches and bruises on her arms.

The nurse's momentary frown disappeared behind professional dispassion. She wrapped the cuff around the upper arm that was less bruised, and repeatedly squeezed the bulb.

"So, tell me about this accident."

Jasmine winced with every pulse of the tightening cuff. She thought the bone underneath was about to break. "I fell in the gym shower yesterday."

I'm so tired of repeating Trinity's lame-ass lie.

The nurse uttered a noncommittal "uh-huh" as she wrote in her tablet. She poked a lighted cone into Jasmine's ear canals. While she stuck another probe into her ear to take her temperature, Nurse Genesee asked in a monotone, "Did you hit your head? Do you have any dizzy spells?"

"No," Jasmine replied. She glanced down at the nurse's tablet. The top paper had a diagram of the front and back of a hairless and sexless human body splayed out. A few circles were drawn on its arms, accompanied by scribbles and arrows pointing to them.

Nurse Genesee scrutinized Jasmine's hair, pausing at the back. She probed the scalp, and Jasmine flinched when her fingers found the bump on the back of her head. The nurse plied the hair apart for a closer look.

"You didn't get that last night—it's not fresh. How did this happen?"

Crap. Got that when Jackson killed Nevaeh.

"Uh, practice at the beginning of the week." Jasmine tried not make it sound like a question.

Another notation, a large circle with an arrow and more scribbles went around the head on the drawing.

"Look straight ahead." Nurse Genesee shone a strong light into one of Jasmine's eyes, then the other.

"Hold your head still and keep your eyes on this." She held up her index finger, making broad passes to the left and right. "Your eyes are okay."

Then why were Madison and Mr. Mason spazzing out about them?

Jasmine wished there was a mirror somewhere in the room.

"Coach Garcia said no concussion yesterday. And you seem all right this morning." A few more notations went onto the tablet.

The nurse placed her stethoscope all over Jasmine's chest and back, each time paired with an emotionless command. "Deep breaths." "Hold your breath." "Breathe normally."

Jasmine let her focus roam, until she felt a finger pull at the neck of her tunic. The jarring vision of Caleb in the alley blinked in front of her with full force. Jasmine's arms twitched upward, and her hands tensed into claws ready to tear at his face.

She forced her forearms back down flat on her thighs and took a deep breath. The room's antiseptic odor whisked away the memory of mildewed poncho and Caleb's rancid vape breath from her nostrils.

"Those bruises around your neck are *not* from a fall. And they're older. How'd you get them?"

After a short pause, Jasmine answered with grit in her voice. At least she didn't have to lie about this one. "Didn't Moore or Chatelain tell you? Caleb tried to rape me a couple of days ago."

"Yes, I was told," Genesee muttered through a pained frown. "I'm sorry you went through that. Where else did he hurt you?"

"Nowhere."

Nurse Genesee pulled out a pocket ruler, measured the larger bruises, and added a few more circles, arrows, and notes to the drawing on her tablet. "I'm sorry to ask, but I have to. Did he—?"

Jasmine hammered out her reply before the nurse completed her sentence. "No."

Her jaw clenched when the nurse, devoid of empathy, said, "Please lift up your shirt. Just up to your chest."

Oh, God, she's gonna see it all—everything that happened yesterday.

"Do I have to?" Jasmine squeezed her elbows against her sides.

"Ms. Price." She stepped back and stuffed the business end of the scope in her frock pocket. "I appreciate you've been through a lot. Believe me, I do."

Planting her fist on one hip, she said, "But either I do this here, or I ship you out, and a hospital doctor examines you. And that'll be a *full* examination." Marching out the words like an assembly line, she added, "If you get my drift. Your choice."

With an exasperated sigh, Jasmine inched the hem of her tunic upward.

"Higher, please," said the nurse.

Jasmine hefted it higher, stopping just under her bra. The nurse's stiff composure cracked, letting a small "oh" slip out when she saw the minefield of bruises around the entire circumference of Jasmine's midriff.

"These are fresh. Did you get these, during your ... fall?"

"Yes." Jasmine clamped her jaw tight and glared at the floor. She wanted so bad to tell Nurse Genesee, tell Mrs. Ainsworth, tell *anybody* the whole truth. But if she spilled her guts about the beatdown and the photographs to a single grown-up, Trinity or one of her minions would hear about it sooner or later. Then her ass would be in a sling—and literally for everyone to see.

The nurse regained her composure, blank professional stare and all. "This injury's older than the rest as well," she said, measuring the yellowed welt over Jasmine's ribs. "How did you get this?"

"Got elbowed during basketball practice. Late last week."

"The same day you got that bump?" The nurse emitted another tired sigh as she added a swarm of circles and notations to her tablet. "Okay, you can lower your tunic."

While she wrote, she engaged Jasmine in small talk—questions about her classes, or if there was anything exciting happening in her life. The hairs on Jasmine's neck lifted when the nurse slipped in an inno-cent-sounding question—"How are things at home? Everything all right?"

"Just fine. Ma works her butt off day and night."

The nurse responded with another indecipherable nod.

"Lift up the cuffs of your sweatpants, please?"

Jasmine was about to protest once more, but the no-nonsense glower of Nurse Genesee brooked no excuse. With a cranky sulk, she scrunched the sweats up to mid-calf.

"Past your knee, please. I need to see where Coach Garcia ban-daged last night."

The nurse leaned sideways and gently prodded and squeezed not just the offending knee, but each and every bruise—spending extra time measuring the largest and darkest patches around the sore knee. Jasmine gritted her teeth, squelching the groan that longed to wriggle out.

"It's fine. I walked to school today."

I feel like I'm getting violated all over again—but in slow motion. I gotta get the fuck outta here, or I'm gonna scream.

Another noncommittal grunt from the nurse. "So this accident in gym yesterday—how many times did you fall down? Or did you fall down a cliff into the shower?"

Jasmine shot a double take at the nurse. It was weird to hear sar-casm from such a deadpan expression. Her exasperation couldn't be silent anymore. "Look, what is this all about?"

Nurse Genesee took her time, calmly finishing her notations in the tablet. "Ms. Price, I can tell this was no fall. And there's more injuries than can be accounted for by mere basketball roughhousing."

She softened her tone, and the edge in her stare blunted. "Or the attempted rape the other day." With a frown and a shake of her head, the nurse held the tablet against her chest. "I'll be plain. Who's been doing this to you, and how long has it been going on?"

Jasmine clamped her hands around the edge of the table. "I'm tellin' ya, basketball gets tough sometimes. Ask Coach."

She knows something doesn't add up. But I still can't tell her. Just let me go, please?

The room was dead silent, even the coursing of students behind the walls had died down.

Nurse Genesee finally broke the standoff, with a brusque "Really."

It didn't sound like a question.

Jasmine pulled the cuffs of her sweats down and straightened out her tunic. Facing Nurse Genesee straight on, she kept up her stoic face. "Really. Are we done?"

"For now." The nurse pulled out a slip of yellow paper and handed it to Jasmine. "Coach informed me that basketball is canceled until further notice. This note will excuse you from Phys Ed for a few days as well. Are you *sure* you want to go back to regular classes?"

"Yeah, I'm sure." Jasmine snatched the note and stuffed it in her books. Grabbing her hoodie, she stormed out past Mrs. Ainsworth. She ignored the final plea from Nurse Genesee as it faded behind her.

"Come back or call if you need ..."

The rest of the day was filled with dreary repetitive lessons, preparing for tests that measured knowledge for which Jasmine could see no earthly use—peppered with the slings and arrows of snickers that always came from behind, knowing smirks from classmates, and snide looks from teammates. The most irritating were the smug leers from the growing throng of kids that used to be Nevaeh's flunkies, but now had fallen under the thrall of Trinity.

The end of the day culminated with the final insult that was history class. A split second after Jasmine parked her rear end into her seat, Trinity made her grand entrance.

Jasmine couldn't stop the knee-jerk reflex of a sneer on her face, so she forced her head down, aiming her snarl harmlessly at the desk in front of her.

Mr. Wyatt's class droned on.

And on.

And on, with the second half of historical quotes from President Bleah, Pope Who-Cares, or was it Queen Get-Lost? "One small step for man ..." "Real courage is when you know you're licked, but you begin anyway." "The enemy of my enemy is my friend."

Already exhausted from fighting the growing pain in her knee and the day's continuous stream of slights and taunts, Jasmine could hardly keep her head from thwacking her desk.

She blinked back into dismal alertness when Mr. Wyatt strolled down one aisle and up the next, handing out sheets of paper—yesterday's graded homework.

A sidelong glance, and Jasmine caught the "A+" on Trinity's handout.

At last—I should get a boost in my history grade.

Her reverie was shattered when Mr. Wyatt handed her a paper emblazoned with a "D." Her essay was circled in red with the dreaded annotation, "See Me After Class."

Proud-as-a-peacock Trinity smiled at Jasmine with smug satisfaction.

Jasmine tried not to think about the grade through the rest of the class. Nonetheless, despite the interruptions of discussion topics, Trinity answering questions with overblown enthusiasm, and a fresh homework handout, Jasmine fell into the prison of repeating Wyatt's mantra "After Class" to herself in silence.

The blessed relief of the school day's last bell finally arrived, and the students blasted out of the classroom as if shot from a cannon. Trinity sauntered out with a smarmy grin, humming a *neener-neener* to herself.

Jasmine methodically collected her materials and hobbled with a sullen expression up to Mr. Wyatt's desk.

"Jasmine, you and Trinity are on our basketball team, right?"

"Yeah."

"And you're good friends, ri—?"

"No," came Jasmine's firm response.

Mr. Wyatt's eyebrows flicked with bemused surprise. He folded his arms and leaned forward like he was about to plow into a football scrimmage. "Glad to hear it. Because the next time I see something that isn't your own work, it's going to get an F."

Shit. Nothing is going my way today.

He sat on the edge of his desk, and relaxed his arms, clasping his hands together. "I hear that the next basketball game is canceled. And by the look of that limp, you're not going to be in practice for a while.

Which means you'll have time for the after-school makeup session we talked about. Have you given that any more thought?"

Jasmine mumbled an apathetic "Kinda."

"Well, *kinda* put some action behind that thought. Next session is Monday. Be there. I wouldn't want you to flunk my class. Makes us both look bad." He stood and coughed loudly to announce this audience was over. "Now, scoot."

Jasmine lurched to her locker. Most of the other students had already fled the premises to run to their buses, their meetups, or anywhere else but the school building.

A pink postcard, folded in half, fluttered to the floor when she opened the locker door. She bent to pick it up, but snapped up straight when something pricked her finger. She gaped at her open hand. A thin crease of blood darkened her fingertip. She flipped the card over with a pen from her notebook.

Taped to opposite edges of the card were razor blades. Between them was a message, a collage of printed words pasted together from various magazines.

"No one Want s YOU here. Eat sh It AND Die."

Trinity's goading me. She's trying to make me lose it, so she has an excuse to nuke me with those photos.

"That ain't gonna happen," she mumbled to herself. *But I ain't gonna let this go unanswered neither.*

She penned a reply in block letters, avoiding the blades.

"You First." She resisted the temptation to dot the "I" with a heart.

Sarcasm would just confuse the bitch.

Avoiding the razors, she refolded the post card and pushed it through the vents of Trinity's locker.

The bus ride home was quiet, even soothing in its own rumbling, stop-start sort of way. The ache of her knee faded into her body's chorus of pains as she climbed the last steps to her apartment.

She was tired—too tired to fight with Ma, too tired to fume over Jackson.

Jasmine opened the door and stopped in her tracks when she faced three adults—Ma, a kindly-looking woman with a plastic badge on her jacket, and Detective Bollard.

"Hello again, Ms. Price."

CHAPTER FIFTEEN

B ollard greeted Jasmine with an expression that was more sneer than smile. The detective still hadn't mastered the art of appearing friendly.

"You got a warrant?" Jasmine snarked with all the swagger she could muster.

"Didn't need one. Your mother graciously let us in."

Looking past the two intruding visitors, Jasmine fixed her mother with a "what-were-you-thinking" stare. "Ma, what's going on?"

Ma's eyes bored holes in the backs of the visitor's heads. "Detective Bollard and Ms. Stevens from Family Services are here to talk to us. Someone is playing a nasty trick on—"

The fair-haired lady in the pants suit stepped forward. A county photo-ID badge dangled from her lapel. She gripped a leather-bound notebook emblazoned with the county seal with enough force, it might have contained state secrets.

"Ms. Price—can I call you Jasmine?" Badge Lady didn't wait for an answer. "You can call me Abby. I'm afraid we received a call this morning, informing us you've been assaulted on a regular basis, and—"

"I already been over this with the school nurse. It's nothing, just basketball getting outta hand, y'know?"

"Yes, Jasmine, we *did* get the report from Nurse Genesee, as she is required to do." Ms. Stevens held up the notebook, like it was all the proof she needed. She moved over to one end of the sofa, inviting Jasmine to sit on the other end. "But this is a little more complicated. Even before we received her report, we got a phone call on our Abuse Hotline."

"You had to bring the cops, too?" She shot Bollard a glance brimming with contempt. Bollard replied with another plastic smile.

"Not every time. But Detective Bollard, who's already familiar with your situation, requested to come along."

Ma gritted her teeth as she inhaled, gearing up for one of her epic rants.

"Mrs. Price," Bollard interjected, all pretense of humor gone. She raised one arm in a firm gesture deflecting Ma toward the kitchen. "Can I bother you for a glass of water or something to drink, please? I believe Ms. Stevens would like to speak with your daughter for a moment … alone."

"How much longer is this going to take, detective?" Ma's voice faded into the next room. "I have to leave for my night job soon."

The cushions exhaled a complaint of dust as Jasmine plopped herself down. "What phone call? Who from?"

"Sorry, Jasmine, but the tip line is anonymous." Stevens's mouth scrunched up and her eyes squinted just a bit, as if she were weighing options. "But I don't think I'm going out of bounds by saying the caller sounded like someone your age. Maybe one of your classmates is concerned for you?"

"Like I told Bollard, I don't have any friends at school."

"Nobody? Not a single one?"

Jasmine shot a caustic glower at Jackson, who was engaged in a leisurely climb onto his log. His tongue made a casual slimy pass over his lips.

"Maybe my guardian angel called it in." Jasmine snickered and shook her head with a mocking smirk. "Besides, like I said, I gone over all this with the nurse. She and Bollard told you about Caleb and what he tried to do a couple of days ago, right? Everything else was from basketball."

"I'm sorry Jasmine, but the call alleged that there's something more to the matter of your injuries."

Wait—Someone snitched on Trinity? Oh, crap, I am so sunk. The stupid bitch will think it was me *that spilled my guts, and she'll ...*

Jasmine broke out in a cold sweat.

"And when the nurse's report corroborated it," Stevens said, pulling out the top inch of one sheet from her leather notebook, "we had to investigate."

"No, it wasn't ..." Jasmine's tongue went dry, sticking to the top of her mouth. She swallowed with difficulty. "No one at school."

"So it wasn't basketball, after all?" Stevens almost pounced out of her seat.

"No—*Yes,*" Jasmine stammered. She pressed the palm of her hand on her slick forehead. "I don't wanna talk about it anymore."

Stevens set her jaw and surveyed the room in thought. "Is everything okay at home? Do you get along with your mother?"

"Yeah-h-h," Jasmine replied, her voice trailing upward in suspicion. Unable to guess where Stevens was going, she read her expression, searching for the smallest hint.

"What about when you and your Ma argue? Do things ever get out of hand?" Stevens leveled a dead serious stare at Jasmine.

"What?!" Jasmine held her stomach. She wanted to hurl, but she managed to thrust out the inside of one forearm, displaying the damage to Stevens. "You think *Ma* did all this to me? What the hell are you smoking, lady?"

"I'm sorry, Jasmine, but I have to ask. The caller alleged parental abuse."

The cramp in Jasmine's stomach turned to a fevered burn.

So it wasn't someone else snitching on Trinity. Then who the hell called it in? And why?

Jasmine blinked when an epiphany smacked her right between the eyes.

Fuck! It was Trinity herself who called it in. She's trying to trick me into spilling my guts.

Stevens dove into a checklist of questions, delving into how well Ma was taking care of her—did she withhold any necessities like food or heat, did she become physical, did she cause any of the bruises, did she ...

"No," Jasmine interrupted, striking her fist on the arm of the sofa with a dull thump. "None of that. Ma *ain't* the problem, you stupid ..." She finished her sentence with a mangled "augh" as her eyes began to well up. She turned toward Jackson again, her eyes demanding a response from him.

You're supposed to help me, to protect me, you stupid lizard. How the fuck did you get me backed into this shit stain of a corner?

Stevens followed Jasmine's gaze toward the terrarium. Jackson whirled both his eyes toward them in return.

"That's an interesting pet—a chameleon, right? They're rather expensive, aren't they. Wherever did you get it?"

Jasmine planted both her arms in her lap as she continued to look plaintively at the lizard. "A gift. From Ma's friend, Bibi. She's our down-stairs neighbor. He's not a gift, really. I'm looking after him while Bibi's away."

"And this Bibi? How good a friend is she?"

A tired smile crept over Jasmine's face. "She's like a grand-mother." *Or the weirdest fairy godmother on the whole planet.* "We visit each other all the time."

"How often? When your Ma is here, or when she's away? How does Bibi behave when she visits?"

Jasmine swiveled her head back at Stevens, flashing a glower that drew a "don't-you-dare" line in the sand. "That's *sick*. Bibi's the nicest person I know. Besides, she's been outta town for most this week. What *is it* with you people?"

Ms. Stevens, with a taut downturned mouth, closed her notebook. "To be perfectly honest with you, Jasmine, we really didn't suspect your Ma, nor your friend. But we're required to investigate fully."

Her eyes softened, with almost a motherly touch. "It's not uncommon for people to call in false accusations, just to cause trouble. But since it was paired with the school nurse's report, we had to follow up."

Jasmine shook her head. "Who would—why would someone jam up Ma?"

Stevens gave a quick shrug. "Maybe someone is trying get back at your mother. We've seen it happen before. Do you know of anyone like that? Can you think of anyone who wants to cause problems for your mom?"

"I dunno." Jasmine slowly shook her head, staring at nothing. "I really have no idea."

Oh, yes, I do!

"Ms. Stevens, what if someone's trying to get back at *me*?"

Stevens scrunched up her mouth into a half-smile, half-frown.

"Who? Someone who thinks you're abused? I'm not sure I see how such a person would be trying getting back at you."

Well, I sure as heck can see it. The more I think about it, this sure feels like Trinity twisting the knife, by siccing these goons on Ma.

Jasmine lurched out of the sofa and stormed into the kitchen redolent with the scent of white whisper.

Ma and Bollard were sitting across from each other at the Formica table, each with a mug of Bibi's favorite tea. Ma's finger tapped a nervous drumbeat inches away from the cordless phone resting on the table.

Jasmine frowned at their icy silence. She grabbed a glass of water and the bottle of painkillers, still on the counter from this morning. After downing the medicine, Jasmine rattled the plastic bottle of pills at Bollard.

"Wanna check to make sure they're legal?"

"Already did." Bollard sipped from her mug with a veneer of smiling serenity.

The phone trilled, and Ma jumped so hard, Jasmine thought she might overturn the table. She snatched the phone and barked a no-nonsense "Hello," followed by a second, more fearsome one.

Jasmine stared at the phone with apprehension.

Dad?

Ma barely contained her fury as she held up the receiver in front her face. "Don't you bozos have anything better to do? God da—" She thumbed the off button and planted the phone back on the table with enough force to make both mugs rattle in place. "Freakin' telemarketers," she grumbled.

Ms. Stevens placed herself in the arch between the kitchen and front room, content to observe in silence.

Jasmine slammed down the bottle and fumed in silence at the detective. "I don't care what your stupid anonymous snitch said. My Ma didn't do nothin'."

Bollard's screen of false friendship was replaced with another one of frank politeness. "We know, Ms. Price. We had a nice long talk before you got here. And Ms. Stevens completed her Family Services inspection—checking for cleanliness, safety, availability of food, and so on. While I—"

"Speaking of food, I'm starving." Jasmine leaned against the sink. "What do we got, Ma?"

Ma took a sip from her mug, struggling to regain her composure. Her shaking hand rippled the surface of her tea, sloshing droplets on the table. Her eyes further betrayed her inner turmoil, flitting between the phone, Bollard, and Stevens.

Clearing her throat, she replied, "There's a couple of sandwiches from the shop in the fridge, Jazz. Have one with a fruit cup, and a banana muffin from the breadbox. I'll take the rest to work for my supper."

Jasmine marched to the refrigerator and plucked out the plastic containers. A half-sheet of yellow paper fluttered on the door as she slammed it shut. She frowned at its county seal, and a column of carbon-copied check marks and X's next to a bullet item list. Ripping open the plastic triangle with the coffee-shop logo, she munched on a stale turkey club in annoyed silence.

"And on that topic, Detective, are we finished here?" Ma swigged down the last of her white whisper. "I really have to get dressed for work."

Bollard stood with stately formality. "Yes, Mrs. Price. For now."

Stevens and Bollard dawdled their way to the door with a drawn-out string of pleasantries. Stevens handed Jasmine a card before Ma hurried them out the front door. "If you want to talk, call me. Anytime, you hear me, Jasmine? Anytime."

"As if," Ma grunted at the locked door. "I hope you'd talk to me before *that* Nosy Nellie."

She wheeled in place to face Jasmine. "So spill it. What brought those two knocking at our door?" She folded her arms and cocked her head.

"More grown-ups sticking their nose into business they can't do nothin' about."

"That don't cut it, Missy." The crinkle at the end of Ma's frown told Jasmine she wasn't going anywhere until she gave a satisfactory answer.

Jasmine sat on the arm of the sofa. "The school nurse gave me an examination today."

"I know. Some high-handed know-it-all called," said Ma, affecting a snooty accent with a waggle of her head, "to 'officially inform' me."

"That would've been Mrs. Ainsworth, one of the school counselors. They were doing what they had to do because of my accident at basketball yesterday."

Ma sniffed in disbelief. "And I'm still waiting for the lowdown on that so-called 'accident.'"

Jasmine ignored the rebuff. "Ms. Stevens said it was some kid who called the abuse hotline. I'll bet the school officials knew about the call, too."

"You see, Jazz? You *do* have friends at school. They're concerned about you, just like me."

"No, Ma. You don't *get* it," Jazz grabbed clumps of hair at her temples and tugged theatrically. "If I had *friends,* they'd know about my accident. They wouldn't make a call like that. They weren't concerned, and they weren't trying to help me. Whoever called it in, did it to make trouble.

"They wanted to hurt me—to hurt *us.* Why do ya think Bollard and Stevens left so quick? Even those two lamebrains figured it out—it was a setup.

"I'm tellin' ya, Ma. That school is just as fu– ... just as messed up as the Projects. I said the same to Vice Principal Chatelain's face."

The phone chirped where Ma left it on the kitchen table.

She shot a glance at Jasmine, her worried look mixed in with a stony, "We're not finished," before she hustled to beat the second ring.

"Hello?" Anger started to tense in her shoulders. "Hello.? Dammit, if this is another ... Oh, Major. Thank God, it's you."

Ma huddled over the receiver, her voice suddenly muted. Jasmine inched closer, hoping to catch tidbits of the tennis match conversation. When she was within reach, she tugged at Ma's arm to angle the receiver between both their ears. Ma yanked the phone away and held up her free hand, as if she were trying to shield her daughter from something worrisome.

Ma's nods and scattered "uh-huh"'s punctuated the tinny voice leaking between the gaps between plastic and earlobe. Jasmine clenched her fists hard. Her nails threatened to draw blood from her palms, until Ma finally exhaled, whispering, "Oh, praise God. What? Excuse me Major, could you repeat that?"

Ma blipped the phone's speaker button and held the receiver between herself and Jasmine.

"Your husband is out of surgery, Mrs. Price, and the doctors say his prognosis is excellent. The pressure on his brain has been relieved, and as soon as he is fit for transport, he'll be airlifted to our medical facility in Landstuhl, Germany. There he'll get the best of care, and he may even begin physical therapy within a week."

Jasmine throttled the urge to shout down to a hoarse whisper. "What did he say? His brain?" She stepped back, steadying her suddenly rubbery legs against the kitchen table.

Ma hit the speaker button again with lightning reflexes and thanked the Major for the news. Between a fresh peppering of "uh-huh"s, she managed to beam a relieved smile at Jasmine, as if all the concerns of their world were washed away.

"How soon until I can talk to him?" The smile vanished as quickly as it had appeared. "I see. No, no—I understand. These things take time." Her watery eyes latched onto Jasmine, filled with a mother's patience. But she managed a wan smile and a nod. "Yes, Major. That's just like Damon—PFC Price—says. 'One foot in front of the other.'"

A few more effusive thanks into the receiver, and Ma hung up the phone. She leaned against the refrigerator, looked skyward and mouthed a silent prayer of thanks. She launched herself away from the appliance the moment the cooking timer clanked away on its cracked plastic bell.

"Lord, if it isn't one thing, it's another." Ma bolted to her bedroom. After disembodied commands echoed down the hall at Jasmine to do her homework, Ma reemerged, stuffing her barista apron into her handbag.

"And try to at least do one of those chores on that county checklist? If Little Ms. Nosy comes back, I want to show them we're making progress on her 'suggestions.'"

"I don't think she's coming back, Ma," Jasmine said before pouring another glass of water to wash down the dry-as-desert sandwich.

"You don't know that for sure. You never dealt with any government do-gooders before. I have, and I know how they think. Social services is the worst. The next time you're in any trouble—any hint of trouble at all—they're back like a shot." She snapped her fingers in front of Jasmine's nose.

"So, you're going to be a good girl tonight. Right, Jazz?"

Jasmine nodded with a pout. *Only Ma could make a question sound like an order.*

"Do your homework, and something from the list to keep Stevens off my back. And sit on that phone, just like last night. Call my work if there's any more news about Dad."

"No worries, Ma. Basketball's canceled forever. There's a party tonight, but I wasn't invited. Not that I would want to hang around any of those bimbos."

"Oh, I'm sorry, Jazz. That stinks. I know it hurts now, but you'll find friends soon enough." With a tired smile that seemed it could melt away any injury, Ma caressed Jasmine's cheek. The moment of connection didn't last long. "I promise, we'll talk tomorrow."

Ma slipped on her rain slicker, then shoveled a small brown paper bag from the fridge into her workbag. While wrapping her head in a bright yellow, green and black bandanna, she said, "But I gotta say I'm relieved. It's for the best that you stay home. At least for tonight."

A peck on the cheek and Ma whooshed out the door.

We'll see about that.

CHAPTER SIXTEEN

No sooner had Ma deadbolted the front door, than Jasmine washed down another round of painkillers and scurried to her room. She opened her window and leaned out, scoping out the alley. The chill air had a clinging quality that made her skin shiver.

Less than a minute had passed, and there zipped Ma, bustling along in a breathless jog with her workbag clutched firmly to her side. Long after she crossed the intersection and disappeared behind a brick wall laden with a fortress of utility meters, Jasmine remained stock-still —watching, waiting, thinking.

Trinity crossed the line, dragging Ma into this with that parental abuse crap. I gotta make her back off. And get those damn photos outta the way.

She slipped once more into that comfortable place of calm observation. It seemed to come to her more easily with each successive instance.

A thrill ran through her body as, without moving, she monitored the entire stretch of the alley—from its far end disappearing in a left-elbow turn, to the intersection with the traffic-laden main drag. The sensation was accompanied by the smug superiority of a predator, like a lioness over her territory.

But how? Do I reason with the bitch, butter her up, keep her off balance

with a full-court press, or just smack some sense into her? If I could count on
Jackson, I'd love to see her …

The lack of sleep and long hours of adrenaline-spiked alertness
throughout the day's trials weighed heavily on Jasmine's eyelids. She
caught herself nodding off, followed by a shaking of her head to snap
herself back to sharp attentiveness.

A bus trundled past the intersection. Ma, wearing her neon-bright
bandanna, was in the second to last seat, staring at nothing through her
window. A pallor of endless sadness and worry dominated her face.

"About time," Jasmine muttered to herself.

Now I gotta move it. Have to catch Trinity, before she goes to that party
everyone but me's invited to.

Jasmine grabbed a pile of clothes from the chest of drawers and
lumped them on her bed, plumped her pillow, and drew a blanket over
the whole arrangement.

Just in case Ma gets back before I do. This always works in those stupid
TV cop shows.

She closed her bedroom window, snatched up her keys, and
whipped on her hoodie with a bullfighter's flourish. She pressed up
against the front door's peephole. No one in the hallway or the stairs—
no busybodies that might report to Ma about her daughter's mysterious
comings and goings. She likewise scoped out each staircase from the
landing above before she descended it.

Pulling her sweatshirt's hood over her head, she walked at a brisk
pace to the metro bus stop, Not too many people had ventured out this
evening. Even the regulars around Parker's broken-down bodega were
unaccounted for. That riddle was soon explained by the fickle mid-
spring weather, as the tendrils of a cool and thickening fog crept down
the darkening streets. By the time the next metro bus rumbled along,
Jasmine's sweatshirt had dampened enough to adhere to her frame.

Leaning her head against the pillar between the bus windows, Jasmine watched the gray misty world roll by, muting the pulsing neon
signs and traffic signals. She settled into the mode of watching everything on the sidewalk as it scrolled by—faceless amblers and joggers
that emerged out of gray nothingness, only to disappear into the mist
behind.

A blur of school colors caught Jasmine's eye. She huddled close
to the metal spar between the windows, and cupped her hand against
the window, blotting out smudgy reflections that got in the way.

Kimani marched up the street, her arm swinging an oversized gym bag. Large enough to sink a battleship, it had the Amazon's familiar snarling jaguar emblazoned on the side, ringed with the name of her gym.

Well, whaddya know, Madison was right. Wouldn't be surprised if she moonlights as a bouncer someplace.

A relieved smile snuck onto Jasmine's mouth.

That means I have a better chance of talking sense into Trinity—alone.

With a whiny blast of air brakes, the bus heaved to a halt. Jasmine stepped into the fog and turned down the nearest intersection. The fog reduced the world around her to a claustrophobic sphere that dimmed lights and swallowed sounds. She paced herself along the sidewalk, noting doors, glass transoms and mail slots, counting the progress of their street numbers.

With the passing of each doorstep and building entrance, Jasmine's struggle on how to approach her nemesis intensified—soft sell, hard sell, reason or violence? It all boiled down to one gut-twisting thought.

Whatever it takes to get rid of those photos.

Her phony excuse for a smile switched to grim determination when she stood facing the number that was Trinity's address. An apartment building not unlike her own, though nowhere near as dilapidated, it blocked her way with a security door.

I would love to trick her to buzz me in, but I don't know any of her new friends' names. And I don't think she'd open for Madison.

Backpedaling to a poorly lit alley across the street, she leaned against the farther corner, once she assured herself there was no one and no thing to disturb her.

Time slouched by as she hunkered down to wait in shadow. When her stomach growled, she pulled a banana muffin from her hoodie's pocket. She devoured it and tossed the wrapper on a nearby dumpster filled to overflowing. The weight of her hoodie pulled on her shoulders as it soaked up more mist-sodden atmosphere.

Watching both her alley and the street with ease and perfect stillness, she had a clear view of the tenants that came and went. Jasmine pressed herself further into the wall's shadow when the occasional pedestrian strayed too close to her perch, or when a car's headlights pieced the gloom.

Trinity shouldered open the door into the evening fog.

At last.

Her makeup and hair were flawlessly on point, and she was dressed in colorful clothes way too racy for school—but perfect for an all-night rave. Jasmine sniffed at the irony—at this moment, though dressed picture-perfect to impress the world, she was alone and absorbed in the confines of her cell phone.

"Okay, I'm on my way. I'll see you in a few," she warbled in a sing-song voice. "Save the vodka for me—Dad always checks my breath, especially after the school dragged him in the other day. Later."

No sooner had Trinity popped a breath mint into her mouth, than her phone played a hip-hop ringtone. Pausing on the last step, she thumbed the phone's screen. A carefree grin splashed across her face as she held the phone to her ear. "What's up? Yeah, I'm headin' there, too. Oh, and wait 'til you get a load of what I got. Some nasty cool pix of Jizm after my crew whupped her butt." She laughed a cruel chuckle and crossed the street. A car's horn spat out a blast as it veered around the heedless girl. The auto roared away, drowning out Trinity and the expletives the driver shouted at her.

"What? I said no. I don't wanna send them just yet. I'll show them to you at the party. I wanna see your reaction, when you get a load of Jizm like you never seen her before. Okay, later." She blipped the screen and sauntered without a care in Jasmine's direction.

That bitch! She's gonna share those damned pictures of me anyway.

The hairs on the back of Jasmine's neck stood at adrenaline-stoked attention. She bent her knees and pulled her hand into the cuff of her sweatshirt.

Trinity strolled past with a bounce in her step. Her finger was poised above the screen to scroll down though her list of contacts, when Jasmine's arms shot out from the dark.

Her sleeved hand clamped over Trinity's mouth. The crook of her other arm wrapped around Trinity's neck, dragging her into the shadow.

Trinity tried to bite down on the fingers muffling her cry. She only succeeded in getting a mouthful of soggy sweatshirt. Flailing at her attacker's stranglehold, she let fly her phone. It clattered against a dumpster stuffed with bags of garbage, broken drywall, splintered lumber, and PVC plumbing.

Jasmine spun, flinging Trinity against the wall. She scooped up the phone and faced Trinity, who charged at her with claws extended.

Jasmine ducked into a crouch, then exploded upward with a sharp elbow into the center of Trinity's midriff.

Trinity staggered back, doubling over with her butt against the dumpster. Her arms were clamped around her gut as she gasped for air.

"You fight like a girl, Trinity. I fight like the *Projects*, remember?" Jasmine said between huffs. She taunted Trinity, waggling the phone in front of her face. "You and me, we're gonna have a little talk. Behave, and you get this back in one piece."

The screen pulsed to life and Jasmine blinked, not quite believing her luck—the phone was still unlocked. She paged the screen with desperate speed in search of the photo gallery icon.

Trinity coiled her legs underneath herself and bounded up like a rocket. Charging at full bore, she planted the corner of her shoulder in the center of Jasmine's rib cage. Both girls grunted when Jasmine was driven back into a wall of concrete block.

Stars splashed everywhere, obscuring Jasmine's vision when the back of her head smacked the stone, next to the almost-healed lump from her encounter with Nevaeh. She swung blindly, using the phone as an improvised set of brass knuckles.

Trinity's irritating laugh receded, and Jasmine lurched forward in stumbling pursuit. She squinted hard, trying to peer past the multicolored stains that swam in her vision like an oil-slicked stream.

A sudden swoosh accompanied a blur of white. The thrum like that of a plastic drum reverberated between the walls of the alley. Searing pain rifled from Jasmine's wrist up the length of her arm. The phone flew out of her hand.

She champed down, stifling a yelp. In a futile attempt to halt the pain, she clutched her hand close to her chest.

Another blur of grayish white flew out of the darkness, and a low plastic whoop careened down toward her side. Jasmine rolled away from the thrum whipping toward her. Ignoring the smack of pain, she managed to latch her good arm around the plastic tube when it glanced off the side of her ribs.

Jasmine wrenched the PVC plumbing out of her assailant's hands. She shook her head, stumbling a retreat to the support of the wall behind her.

A scrabbling of something hard against the concrete skittered above Jasmine's head. Crumbs of crushed masonry sprinkled down on her shoulders.

I know that sound. He's here.

"That tears it, Jizm," Trinity sneered with primal malevolence. "You blew it big time. You are *so* toast."

Blinking furiously, Jasmine concentrated on the garish form that was the source of the mocking scorn. A face emerged from the fading splashes of undulating color dancing in her eyes. Trinity's eyes glowed a ghoulish electronic blue, lit from underneath by her phone. She grinned with malicious glee as she tapped and swiped at the screen with her index finger.

A car with a barely street-legal engine paired with a muscle muffler raced past the alley with a deafening testosterone-fueled roar. Trinity held up her free hand, shielding her eyes against its burning blue-white xenon high beams.

Her phone beeped once.

"What are you waiting for, Jack—?" Jasmine called to the heavy scraping above her head. Her throat slammed shut, as though a claw squeezed it tight. She pried her jaw open again, crying, "Mlin— She's gonna—"

Trinity blinked and squinted, interrupting her task on the phone. "What the—who the fuck are you talking to?"

With a yawp of desperation, Jasmine propelled herself from the wall at Trinity, wielding the thick tube like an axe in both hands. She swung down with her full weight. The PVC whistled like a vuvuzela and struck the phone with a satisfying crack.

Trinity screamed, curling her hand in agony. The phone slammed against the asphalt. The darkened screen glinted from a jagged crevice splitting its full width.

Trinity dodged as Jasmine swung again. The PVC whistled low as she whiffled through thin air. Trinity began to laugh—a cruel, sadistic howl. She beamed an evil smirk that gave her the appearance of having fangs.

"Too late, bitch. It's already gone out." Trinity danced away, weaving backward with a brazen smart-ass smile that begged to be hit, and hit hard. Her smile vanished, transforming into a wary snarl when she backed into the dumpster with a dull metallic thump.

With a scream that cried for blood, Jasmine swung the hollow club, going for a home run. The force of the recoil almost popped the plumbing out of her hands when she connected with Trinity's hip.

One of Trinity's designer heels broke, and she slammed against the dumpster. She crumpled into a whimpering heap. She clawed with one hand against the cold slick metal, and held up the lamed hand in a pitiful defense against the next blow. Her eyes grew as large as golf balls, swinging from Jasmine to the concrete wall behind her. She mouthed something, but her words were lost in the rush of blood in Jasmine's ears.

"You ... goddamned ... *cunt!*" Jasmine shouted, each word shot out between ragged, heaving breaths. "I just came here to talk, you fucking idiot. But *no*—you had to ..."

She hoisted the PVC above her head with both hands. Her arms trembled with fury.

"I'm gonna fucking ki—"

The crack of a something heavier than a metal cable flooded the alleyway. Jasmine let out a cry of surprise as cold, slimy flesh wrapped around her wrists. She spun around, dragged by an irresistible force. Her hands spasmed with shock and the PVC tube clattered to the ground with a staccato beat like oversized plastic castanets.

Mlinzi's head, transformed into a bloody red, seemed to emerge straight out of gray masonry inches above Jasmine. Great horned claws gripping and crunching holes into the stony bricks turned the same angry crimson.

Jasmine stared straight into *Mlinzi*'s slimy maw. Twice as wide as her shoulders, its umber flesh filled her vision as the glistening tongue drew her closer. Her jaw opened wide to scream. All she could summon was a simpering whine.

A sound not unlike great sheets of slime-covered Velcro being pulled apart assailed Jasmine's ears and made the bones in her forearms ache.

The mucus-covered flesh slipped from her wrists.

A huge claw clamped on Jasmine's shoulder. *Mlinzi*'s eyes pivoted wildly, then zeroed in on Jasmine's head. Inches from her nose, his pebbled lips quivered, and from his gullet hissed words that seemed to echo from the depths of Hell and back.

"You ... kill ... her ..." The stink of rotting flesh gusted out of the slavering mouth, and Jasmine held her breath to stop herself from spewing banana muffin.

"I ... kill ... you."

Mlinzi's claw squeezed her shoulder hard, and the joint ached like it wanted to pop out of its socket. With a hiss that spattered globs of slime on her hoodie, he shoved Jasmine aside.

Kill.

That's *why he didn't save me in the locker room. He comes only when death is in the cards. He comes to kill the killer.*

So why didn't he …

She gaped at *Mlinzi* in abject fear. Her legs turned to jelly, and she stumbled over the PVC plumbing, landing on her rump. She wrapped her arms about herself and began to sob, sputtering between heaves of her chest, "Oh, God … What have I … I was going to …"

Unbidden, the memory of Bibi's warning ricocheted around her cranium—her cryptic response when asked the third way to be rid of *Mlinzi.*

"Oh, child. Pray that you never find out."

Jasmine ground the heels of her palms into her eye sockets and wiped away a flood of tears. She whispered to herself, "Oh, God, I'm sorry. I am *so* sorry."

Clambering down, *Mlinzi's* body curled as it hugged the right-angles between wall and asphalt.

Trinity twisted into a fetal ball, her legs kicking spasmodically, trying to push herself into some nonexistent cubbyhole in the metal behind her. Her eyes grew larger than before, and she gibbered in disjointed vowels at the monster slithering toward her.

Mlinzi halted halfway across the alley, his hind legs still gripping the wall and dissolving into its texture, seeming to flow out from the structure.

From the side, Jasmine watched with morbid curiosity as his eye began to spin in its socket. She tried to collect herself to stand, but she plonked back down when the asphalt underneath her no longer felt as solid as it should. She cowered against the tug from the depths of the black whirlpool that threatened to drown her in *Mlinzi's* eye.

"Be calm … Trin … it … ty."

Jasmine shook her head, and clamped her eyelids shut. So hard that tears squeezed out. The ground regained its firmness.

No, don't look. If I saw both his eyes, I'd probably be drawn in. I can't let Mlinzi in my head again, or I'm lost for good.

Guttural hisses, grunts, and groans came out of his fetid mouth. No attempts at words, just sounds. They rang in Jasmine's ears with a peculiar familiarity, though she could not precisely recall having heard them before. Yet his grating ululations filled her with that strange calm she first felt standing over Akilah's limp and bloodied body—that buzzing stillness that erased all fear, all emotion.

Jasmine clamped her hands over her ears. She began to hum to herself to blot out the whispers of *Mlinzi*'s hypnotic sibilance. Stamping down panic when she couldn't think of a single song to blot out the monster's scraping hiss, she resorted to the first thing she could recall. She focused her being on it, repeating it over and over, cleaving to it for dear life, or be sucked down into blackness.

Absolute power corrupts absolutely.

After she lost count of the repetitions, Jasmine stopped her murmuring, spread her fingers the tiniest amount and listened. The hissing had stopped. She dropped her hands with tentative indecision and peeked open one eye.

Mlinzi stood between her and Trinity. His massive head had turned toward Jasmine, its angry red gone, darkened to streaks of dull sienna. One eye swiveled to stare at her.

Trinity's eyes were half open, staring into nothingness. Her mouth had gone slack, and spittle dribbled out of one corner with each torpid breath.

"What did you do to her?" Jasmine said in a breathy whisper. Trembling as she stood, she stepped forward to stand beside *Mlinzi*'s throat.

"Made her … forget."

Jasmine still had the urge to shiver whenever that unearthly voice slithered out of that quaking mouth. She picked up the broken phone. Poking the screen and pressing the buttons that lined the bent frame, the cracked screen refused to come to life.

"Forget what? Everything that happened?" She shook her head at the broken technology. "How am I going to find out who she sent my photos to?"

"Assssk her."

"But—you just made her forget."

"Ssshe forget … me."

Regarding the half-prone form splayed against the dumpster, Jasmine squatted down and examined Trinity's face. Her eyes were still half-closed and unseeing.

Another sweep of reflected headlights swung through the width of the alley. The girls' shadows pivoted around their owners on the ground. Jasmine wasn't sure if one revolved around *Mlinzi*.

"Trinity. Can you hear me?" A shiver rippled up Jasmine's neck when Trinity's eyes turned toward her, only half-open.

"Yes," came the distant reply, accompanied by a rivulet of foamy drool.

Jasmine knelt, placing her hands on her knees. "Just now, you sent those pictures, didn't you—those pictures of me in the shower?"

"Yes," she replied. Trinity's head lolled to one side, but her emotionless eyes remained fixed on Jasmine, staring through dangling locks of magenta-tinted hair.

"Who, Trinity? Who'd ya send them to?"

"Just one. Only time for one." Sentences were separated by languid breaths.

"Who, dammit? *Who?*"

"Didn't see who. Headlights blinded me. Could've been sent to Hailey, Chloe, Laisha, or ..." Slobber spattered out with each consonant.

Dammit. I don't know any of those names.

Trinity sucked in a gurgling breath. "Wanted to send out to everyone. Didn't know how."

An incredulous frown exposed Jasmine's gritted teeth. "You don't know how to use your own damn phone?"

"Phone isn't mine. One of Caleb's burners."

Jasmine glanced cross-eyed at *Mlinzi* in confused skepticism.

"She's bullshitting me, isn't she?"

"No," the humongous lizard growled.

"Crap, this just keeps getting worse and worse," she grumbled under her breath. "I had a decent shot at getting rid of those pictures. But now I'm screwed. *Screwed,*" she said, screaming the last word.

Jasmine glowered at the hulking lizard. "This is all your damned fault, you shithead freak. What's to stop me from squishing your little head, when I get you back in your box at home?"

Mlinzi's closest eye ratcheted to stab at her.

"Many ... tried." The stony eye swiveled back onto Trinity. "They ... failed."

Jasmine tried to ignore the cold stony fear that solidified in her bowels. She crossed her arms, trying to reassure herself that some control in the midst of this clusterfuck could somehow be regained. "How can I trust anything she says?"

Mlinzi hummed a long sonorous tone and rasped a gurgling hiss at Trinity's head. Turreting his eyes back to Jasmine, he uttered, "Ssshe ansssswer ... truth. Ssshe do what ... you asssk."

She did a double take at *Mlinzi*, then focused again on Trinity.

"Okay, Trinity, spill. What the hell were you doing with Caleb's phone?"

"Stole it, when he dumped me for Nevaeh," came her slow, measured syllables.

"You—and *Caleb*?" Jasmine blurted a raspberry. "That's rich. You're *Nevaeh's* top sidekick."

"Was biding my time. Waiting to fuck her up good for what she did to me."

"Why not just sic your sister on her?"

"Simple pain not good enough. Wanted to get in her head and make her suffer."

Just like you been doing to me the past few days, bitch. Revenge may be a dish best served cold, but you're made of ice.

Jasmine tamped down the urge to launch a bile-filled screaming torrent that would have blistered Ma's ears. She breathed quietly, as Trinity's motives began to soak in.

"Then you came along, Jasmine," Trinity continued in her ghastly monotone. "You fit the bill perfect."

"What are you saying? *You're* the one that got Nevaeh on my case?"

"Yes," she replied.

She expected Trinity to sport another vindictive smile, but her half-asleep face remained devoid of emotion. Jasmine stamped her foot on the asphalt, obliterating a dewy puddle beginning to form. "But why —and why *me*?"

"Sooner or later, Nevaeh stole everyone's boyfriends. Every single one she ever had. That was her power trip." Trinity drew in a breath and gurgled a cough. "Show us that she could take away anything from anybody. It was easy to make her think you were going to do the same to her—to steal Caleb."

"No way I'd hook up with that creep."

"Nevaeh didn't care. She had a jealous streak a mile wide. Caleb was hot, had cash, the best dope on the street, and a hard-on for you."

A sickly grin creased Trinity's face. "That was the best part of the plan—the *fun*. Send your pictures from his phone? Get you outta my hair, and Caleb would get jammed up for child porn, too." A single laugh escaped from her, spewing phlegm down her chest.

"Da-yamn, that's cold," Jasmine mumbled. "But something I don't get—why did you stay pissed off at me? Why did you keep dumping shit on me after Nevaeh was …"

Don't say it. Don't say 'killed.'

"… after Nevaeh disappeared?"

"I wanted to be on top—the queen bee."

"What, the stupid basketball team again?"

"No. *Everything*," Trinity said with a rise of temper in her voice.

Mlinzi droned a rumbling hiss at her.

"Everything," she repeated, her anger faltering back into mesmerized compliance.

"Whaddya mean, everything?"

"You were getting too big, too much notice. More popular than me. Your street cred popped when the rumor spread you wasted Nevaeh and fooled the cops. You got in my way. And Caleb still trusted me, the dumb fuck." Spittle coursed down her chin, when a ghost of a smile lifted one corner of her mouth. "Easy to maneuver him and Akilah to come after you. *Too* easy."

The veins in Jasmine's neck twitched. She lunged from her kneeling position and grabbed Trinity, jerking her bobbling head close.

"You … *You?*" she screamed as she shook the pliant body with trembling violence. "God *damn* you! You almost got me *raped*. Got me *killed!*"

Jasmine thrust Trinity's listless body against the dumpster. With all the strength at her command, she pummeled Trinity's cheek with a right cross. Offering no defense, Trinity's limp body crumpled prone to the ground.

Panting on the border of hyperventilation, Jasmine jumped up and staggered back a step. The broken phone crunched underfoot. She leaned against the nearby wall and wept—a single anguished howl, and a strangled sob on its heels. The rest of her tears fell in silence.

Seizing control of her breath, she pushed herself away from the wall, standing erect with her eyes closed until she swallowed her tears and forced her quaking rage to stop. Opening her eyes, she picked up the phone, and popped open the case.

Here I am, doing this crap again? I am so fucking tired of all this cloak-and-dagger drama.

She pulled out the memory chip, the battery, every bit of electronics she could pry from the device. She whipped the remaining husk of a phone at the dumpster. A resounding metal clunk, and pieces of it showered over the unflinching Trinity.

"*Mlinzi*, what did you say? 'She will do as I ask'?"

"All ... you command." The behemoth's wattle inflated as he grunted a sinister growl at Trinity. "Thisss day."

Oh man, part of me wants to ...

Jasmine snorted back the salt, tears, and snot that clogged the back of her throat. She spat it at the wall, dismissing along with it a rush of thoughts—a slew of dirty stunts she could order Trinity to perform as a righteous punishment. Instead, she selected the one thing, the singular burning desire that crowded out all else.

She bent at the waist and shouted, her hands clinched into trembling fists in front of her. "Leave me alone, Trinity, you bitch. Ya hear?"

Her voice escalated into a screech. "Just—leave—me—the fuck —*alone!*"

A homeless man trundled his cart past the alley. His shaggy face glanced at Jasmine, then at Trinity. With a rheumy cough, he huddled over his precious cargo and wheeled it away with renewed haste.

Jasmine's eyes followed the shambling man, then returned her attention to the situation at hand.

Mlinzi was gone.

The venom of Jasmine's hatred spun in her gut and stabbed upward. Her abs twitched, then spasmed.

Jasmine dashed to the side of the dumpster, hiked herself up on tippy-toe over its edge, and puked. After a cough and spit, she grudgingly wiped her mouth on her cuff, then scraped off the retch and *Mlinzi*'s slime onto the rusty lip of the dumpster.

The heavy mist coalesced into a light drizzle. Jasmine hitched the hood of her sweatshirt over her head and backed away from Trinity.

She lay there, not moving a muscle except for her slow, measured breathing. Not even her eyes twitched when a raindrop plinked directly into it.

Would serve her right, if someone like Caleb came along, and did to her ...

A sudden sob racked her body. The tension in her neck evaporated, and with a sigh weighted with shame and guilt, her shoulders slumped.

Not even Trinity deserves that.

"Trinity. Go home. Go to bed." Jasmine watched in silence as Trinity pushed herself off the ground, her colorful clothes rumpled and soiled with her mucus, along with drab bits and pieces from the alleyway and the dumpster.

"And take your damn phone with you."

Trinity complied. The only sound she made was a grunt when she bent over and scraped it off the asphalt. Shuffling on one good heel and favoring a bruised hip, she slogged across the street with all the slow determination of a zombie. A lone couple sauntered past Trinity and paused to marvel at the shipwreck of a human being that limped across their path. She climbed the stairs, punched a few numbers on the security pad, and disappeared into the building entrance.

Jasmine grimaced at the drizzle that weighed her sweatshirt down even heavier than before. She began her slog back to the metro stop, pausing at each storm drain along her route to toss a piece of Caleb's phone electronics into the sewer.

Once home, she sighed with relief that Ma was still at work.

She didn't waste a moment, not even to pause and scowl at the gray and brown mottled Jackson hugging his log, safe in his terrarium. All she could think of was to take the hottest shower she could stand before the hot water ran out.

Afterward, she tried to eat some food, but the aroma of the remaining banana muffin made her stomach flip-flop. Jasmine paid little attention to much else—only plowing the laundry off her bed onto the floor and crawling under the covers registered on her brain.

Her fitful sleep was filled with nightmares about teachers and classmates laughing at photographs of her naked self that spilled out of every phone, tablet, and computer at school.

CHAPTER SEVENTEEN

J asmine's alarm squawked its jarring klaxon. She rolled out of bed, shambling through the fuzzy twilight between her last fading dream and the growing morning light.

She rapped the top of the alarm and was jolted awake by sharp pain. She wondered for a moment why her hand hurt so much, until she recalled how loud her knuckles cracked when she plowed her fist into Trinity's cheekbone.

Returning from the bathroom, she spied Ma sprawled out on the sofa, purring with a muffled snore. Still dressed in her barista clothes, she clutched the kitchen phone to her chest. Even fast sleep, she wore an expression of worry stirred with hope that Jasmine knew so well.

Still waiting for that call from the Major.

She tiptoed back into her bedroom and steeled herself to face the routine of painting on the fake Jasmine. Pulling the chair from her desk that doubled as a vanity, her eyebrows flicked up when a shopping bag slid onto the floor.

She popped open the bag. It contained a new spring jacket and pair of jeans.

New. From a real store. Not from a rummage sale or a charity thrift shop—but *new* from a *real store!*

Jasmine tore the pants out of the bag and slipped them on in record time. She hopped on tiptoes in front of the mirror, turning this way and that. Looking over her shoulder to assess her posed booty, she shot herself an ear-to-ear grin. They fit like a dream.

As she removed the store tags, a flurry of thoughts rolled through her racing brain.

These are great! And not another crappy poncho, too!

Man, how does Ma find the time to do all her stuff?

Out of the blue she surprises me with how much she does for us.

For me.

Or is she trying to make up, butter me up so I'll talk?

She shook her head with guilty regret, trying to shake off that last rambling accusation.

Dammit, Jasmine. Why do you always think the worst of people?

She thumped her temple with the heel of her palm several times, trying to push out the stream of like-minded worries that tagged along with her easy reflex of suspicion.

Dressed, primped, and brushed, she paused once more in front of the mirror. The urge to admire her reflection was elbowed out of the way by the unwanted flood of realities from the previous night.

Trinity would be waiting for her. Or would Jackson's sway still keep her in check?

And then there were the photos—those damned photos. Even if her nemesis had a mindset to behave, it was still doubtful Trinity would lift a finger to assist her—even if it were possible to delete that photographic genie and its electronic bottle. Jasmine peered over her shoulder at the unkempt bed behind her and imagined herself crawling back under the covers.

"Real courage is when you know you're licked, but you begin anyway," echoed the quote from a famous someone in her head, delivered in Mr. Wyatt's nasal drone.

He'd be happy I finally remembered some things from his history class.

Slinging on her new jacket and her backpack, she stole through her bedroom door into the kitchen. Opening and closing the breadbox with a cat's stealthiness, she shot a naughty-child grimace in the direction of the front room. She stuffed the remaining banana muffin into her pack, thankful the aroma didn't throw her gullet into reverse this time. Satisfied Ma was still asleep, she gulped a swig of fresh milk from the refrigerator carton.

She spied a sheet of paper on the table, a note from Ma.

"When you're ready to talk, I'll listen. Wake me before you leave for school."

Jasmine pouted, adjusted her backpack, grabbed her keys, and stole out of the apartment.

Thanks Ma. We will talk—soon, I promise. Just not right now.

Walking to the bus, she called her home phone. After a single ring, Ma answered with comical overtones of sleepiness mixed with panic. Jasmine took in a deep breath and rifled out with the speed of an ambulance-chaser commercial, "Hi, Ma. Thanks for the pants and jacket. They're great. On my way to school. We'll talk when I get home." Her finger homed in on the "end call" button with the speed and accuracy of a guided missile.

Jasmine relaxed her head on the back of her bus seat, and stared at the seat in front of her, trying to imagine what the day ahead held in store. She passed the time, falling into her habit of drawing plans only she could see on the back of the worn-out Naugahyde seat in front of her. With a dismissive click of her tongue, she wiped away her invisible schemes when the bus lurched to a halt at its next scheduled stop.

Enough of this crap. Look at where all my scheming got me. Look at where all Trinity's scheming got her. Just stick with "one foot in front of the other."

Jasmine glanced over at the person who hovered in the aisle, then locked eyes with her.

Madison, still wearing her knee brace, paused above the empty seat next to Jasmine. She wore a poker face of pure granite, while her eyes measured Jasmine from head to toe.

"Nice jacket," she commented flatly, before she swiveled and plopped down in the open seat. Jasmine was forced to scoot over an inch to accommodate Madison's size, made even more ungainly by her brace and backpack.

The bus trundled back up to speed. The mismatched pair of girls stared straight ahead. A silent tension vibrated between them over the duration of several city blocks.

Madison heaved a stern sigh, like she had come to a difficult and painful decision. She slipped her cell phone out of her jacket and began to tap away.

Jasmine focused on the seat ahead of her again, having resolved to not intrude on her traveling companion's personal space. She turned

her head when Madison coughed, then coughed once more with atten-
tion-demanding firmness.

Madison held her phone close to her chubby chest. In a voice that
was as enigmatic as her expression, she said, "Don't get the wrong idea,
Jasmine. We still ain't friends." She sniffed wetly and coughed with a
gurgle, then discreetly angled the phone toward Jasmine. A pronounced
tremolo of emotion racked Madison's voice. "But no one deserves what
Trinity did to you. Not even you deserve *this.*"

Jasmine could only guess if she was upset by rage or disgust. Or
was it her unwelcome pity again?

Her eyes goggled at the screen and her jaw dropped, quivering in
disbelief. The picture of her, naked, thrown in a disjointed heap on the
shower floor, filled the screen—except for a text box that asked,
"Delete?" Madison nudged it toward Jasmine, inviting her to do the
honors.

Her index finger approached the phone, quivering with anxious
energy. Jasmine stabbed at the "Yes" button. One eternal heartbeat
later, the picture blinked into nothingness, replaced with the second
damning photo. Another "Yes," and the money shot was gone.

The bus pitched forward to the wheezing screech of air brakes,
and a handful of students on the bus rose from their seats. Madison
stood as well, leaning to one side, placing most of her weight on her
good knee.

She looked down at the thunderstruck Jasmine with a renewed
glacial dispassion. "I don't know who else got that stuff from Trinity,
but I want no part of her trash." A caustic frown intruded on her face,
pulling down the corners of her eyebrows as well.

She turned to hobble away, but was yanked to a halt when Jasmine jumped up and grabbed her wrist.

"Madison, I think you were the only one that got those pictures,"
Jasmine said in hushed tones with eyes that couldn't face her unexpected benefactor. "Watch out for Trinity. She sent them to you by mistake. She doesn't know you got them. She'll never forgive you if she figures it out."

"How do you—? Never mind. I don't wanna know." Madison
tried to turn away once more, but Jasmine gripped her forearm with
earnest.

She summoned the courage to look Madison in the eyes, and
muttered a soft but heartfelt, "Thank you." After a moment she added,

looking at Madison's knee, "And, I'm sorry."

Madison nodded, her stony silence unperturbed. She hobbled off the bus, with Jasmine trailing a few somber steps behind.

Before climbing the steps of the school's main entrance, Jasmine paused. Turning toward the street, she settled into her comfortable contemplation and observed everybody. The throngs of students in front of her, past her, behind her—the circles of girls flirting at the boys, the gangs of boys lusting back.

Any one of these faces might be the next one of Trinity's allies who picks up the torch of "Let's dump on Jasmine." She tried in vain to recall the laundry list of names Trinity rattled off the previous night.

All this crap, just because two girls tied themselves up in knots over a gangbanger who was lower than scum?

She wondered how Ma and Dad managed to find each other, steeped in their generation's version of raging hormones and toxic drama.

She climbed out of herself when a pair of girls, one on either side, sneered at her with surprised "eww"s that oozed with disgust in stereo. She blinked a few times and replied with a quizzical "mind-yer-own-damn-business" glower at the closer girl.

Jasmine sighed heavily and cast her eyes heavenward—she knew that she should be happy, that she should be relieved that the tatters of her reputation weren't entirely flushed down the toilet. Instead some dread still filled her heart, like everything was a heartbeat away from going catastrophic. Like she had forgotten something that would bite her in the ass.

By habit, she checked her backpack pocket. She expected her keys to be absent, forgotten back in the apartment like she so often had done before. But no, they were there.

How did I get here, into this mess? How could I not see almost everybody yanking me around like a puppet? Nevaeh, Akilah, Trinity—even Mlinzi. And I bought into it. I shoulda steered clear, but instead, I tried to play their stupid games.

Bibi tried to warn me, and I ignored her. Two people are dead, one's in a coma, and Trinity could still be a zombie for all I know.

So what right do I have to be happy? Maybe I deserve whatever retribution comes next.

Trudging up the last stairs, Jasmine meandered through the hallways to homeroom. Turning a corner, he eyes locked on the river of jostling bodies navigating around a threesome huddled against the wall. Madison, with her back against lockers, faced Trinity and her big-sis bouncer Kimani.

Aw, crap. Déjà duke—where have I seen this shit before?

Except it wasn't quite the same. Kimani seemed to have a lost look about her, like she was off her game. Jasmine suppressed a chuckle when she got close enough to spy Trinity's swollen cheekbone that no amount of makeup could hide.

"Don't deny it, Fatty-son. I checked with everyone in my posse. You *have* to be the one who got it." Everything above Trinity's neck burned bright beet red to match her inflamed cheek.

However, the most noticeable change in this little rerun was in Madison's demeanor. She wasn't shivering or cringing. This time, she was a rock that stood, implacable against the raging Sea of Trinity. There was even a hint of a proud smile on her lips when she muttered something that Jasmine couldn't catch from that distance. Trinity's face exploded in a burning crimson of astonishment.

"Whaddya mean you *deleted* them?" she roared. "You stupid cow, if you think I gave Jizm a hard time, you're gonna wish you'd never been born. I'm gonna—"

"Leave her alone, Trinity." Jasmine announced. She marched up and planted herself by Madison's side. "She's with me."

At first, the two sisters gawped at her, like two hyenas who had just stumbled into a lioness protecting her cub. Madison faced Jasmine as well, her granite disposition crumbling into blinking surprise.

But the Davis sisters shrugged off their initial shock a split-second later.

Trinity's mouth slammed shut, though her eyes still burned with an inferno of enmity. Her arms slapped to her sides as if a giant hand had gripped her entire body.

Kimani stepped forward and grabbed Jasmine and Madison by their collars. The black jaguar tattoo on her forearm snarled from the muscles bunching underneath. Disgust tainted the edges of her rage. "Listen, bitches. The two of you are in for a world of—"

"Leave 'em alone," Trinity trumpeted, turning the heads of everyone across the width of the school hall. "Now, Kimani. *Now,* dammit! Just—leave—her—the fuck—*alone.*" She champed her jaws together in a snarl that might have shattered her teeth down to their roots.

Hearing her own words from the previous night echoed from

Trinity's lips, Jasmine's bowels twitched as she struggled to keep her brassy "in-charge" face and her wits about her.

Trinity wheeled in place and marched away, leaving a nonplussed Kimani whirling her head back and forth between her targets and her sister. One grunted expletive later, the Amazon dashed after Trinity, bowling over a succession of unlucky students in her path. Her cries of "What the hell? What's going on, Trin?" faded into the crowded murmur of whispers and sniggers.

With her fist, Trinity pounded the door of her own locker across the hall. She growled something at her older sister, whose confusion morphed into shock. Even over the crowd, Jasmine could hear Trinity terminate the conversation with a stern "Just *do* what I tell you."

Madison regarded Jasmine with suspicious wonder. She swallowed, and ventured a quiet, "Uh, what just happened?"

Trinity flung wide her locker door, banging it open with all of her unfocused animus. An avalanche of curses poured out of her mouth, when books and sheets of paper tumbled onto the floor about her feet. Her last profanity was cut in half when she spied, picked up, and unfolded a pink card.

The color drained out of her face, and she peered at her sister with a lost, pleading, forlorn look.

Kimani was oblivious, continuing her barrage of complaints. "I still don't get it. Say the word, and I'll pound both of those shit balls into … Hey, where you goin'?"

Trinity spun on her heels like a robot, the pink note crumpled in her hand. She marched down the hall, toward the nearest girls' bathroom.

Jasmine felt something squeeze her heart—something important that refused to come entirely into recollection.

Kimani followed hot on Trinity's heels, her hands gesticulating wildly then bunching into fists, and her mouth still spewing an avalanche of profanity and questions. She failed to notice the drops of blood that dribbled from her sister's hand onto the floor.

An icicle of recollection stabbed at Jasmine's heart. "Stay here," she said to Madison in a shaky whisper.

She plodded with determination toward the restroom. But each step became more difficult and slower, as she waded deeper and deeper into a quicksand of apprehension. She froze mere feet away from the doorway, blocked by the towering figure that barricaded her way.

"I don't care what Trinity says, Jizm." Kimani grabbed Jasmine by both shoulders, hefting her off the ground with ease. Every vein on her neck bulged. "No one does that to my little sis and gets away with it."

Jasmine replied with silent dread.

A voice gurgled past the bathroom entrance. "What the fu—?"

Then another voice screeched, "Oh my God ..."

A chorus of confusion emanated into the hall, all echoing the same phrases.

Kimani's head jerked toward the growing frenzy. Spitting her own curse, she shoved Jasmine against the wall and dashed toward the commotion.

The crescendo of voices built, cascading out of the bathroom. An inarticulate scream rang out from the bathroom, amplified by the tiled walls like a ceramic megaphone. A screech that sounded like something between Kimani and a wounded animal shouted, "No!"

All heads in the hall within earshot of the cry turned, and a hushed confusion spread down both directions of the hallway.

A moment later, a herd of screams blasted out of the bathroom, followed by a panicked stream of whimpering and crying girls. Some charged out fully dressed, some with clothes partially undone, some with makeup smeared across their faces.

Out of the restroom reverberated a single anguished roar of "Oh —my—*God*," with a ragged texture as if the vocal cords that uttered the words were tearing themselves apart.

Kimani tumbled out of the room and collapsed onto her hands and knees. Her arms were dripping in blood up to her elbows. Her back arched, and her stomach disgorged, splattering everything it held onto the floor.

A pit opened in Jasmine's stomach, heart, and soul. She shuddered, repulsed by the scene in front of her, reviled by the prospect of what caused such a blind panic.

But she had to see. She had to know.

Ignoring the whimpers of the students around her, and the orders barked from teachers emerging from their homerooms, Jasmine rushed in.

Paper, soap, abandoned purses, and toiletries were strewn across the sink counters, spilling onto the tiled floor. Water flowing from several taps squeaked to a stop, as one by one they timed off. A hand dryer wheezed, blowing the whiff of sewer to Jasmine's crinkled nose. She looked down the line of toilet stalls, her eyes backtracking a line of bright red footprints leaving the scene. She gasped at the pool of blood spreading under the metal walls of the farthest compartment.

Jasmine scrambled to the open door and froze at the edge of the red morass, gazing at the tableau of violence and ruin.

Trinity lay lifeless, her torso facing forward, draped on its side over the toilet seat. Her jacket was discarded next to the toilet.

Blood seeped out of two long cuts. One along the length of her forearm sliced straight through her blouse sleeve. The other ran across the entire expanse of her throat from ear to ear, staining her raspberry-tinted hair a vivid crimson. An explosion of blood splatter lined the stall where Trinity exhaled her last.

Her uncut upper arm was plunged into the glistening gore-soaked toilet bowl. In death, her hand still gripped a mass of feces and toilet tissue. Her face was a slopped, slathered wet mess. Obscene streaks and sticky smudges of brown encircled her lips. A turd sat pretty as you please, half-chewed in her mouth.

Her other arm angled down from the toilet to the floor, a criss-crossed network of red rivulets from her forearm feeding the sticky red pool. Its hand clutched a rusted razor blade, with shreds of tape and blood-soaked pink paper still dangling from it.

Jasmine sobbed, unable to catch a full breath.

She could not take her eyes off that lost face. Or those vacant eyes that stared at their doom. She followed Trinity's line of sight, focused unblinking in death on the wall above the tissue dispenser. Above the holder sat the folded pink card, covered in blood that obscured all but one phrase of mangled print.

"Eat sh It AND Die"

Next to it, scrawled on the metal wall was Trinity's final response in excrement.

"Me first."

Jasmine clamped her hand over her mouth and lurched to the bathroom sink. She heaved and heaved. Nothing came except a trickle of gall. She pounded on the water tap and washed out her mouth. Finally able to breathe, Jasmine swiveled her head up from the sink and wheezed open-mouthed at the mirror.

Her breath and blood froze at the thing that gazed back at her.

Jasmine's right eye stared directly into the mirror. Her left eye had a mind of its own, pivoting up then left, scoping out the entrance as one teacher, then another, followed by a security officer, charged breathlessly into the room. She witnessed every nuance of horror that contorted their faces.

One teacher snapped an order at Jasmine to get out.

She paid no heed. Another of the adults planted gruff hands on her shoulders and manhandled her toward the exit.

Her left eye snapped forward, while the right swiveled across then downward, using the row of sink mirrors to peer back at the tableau of blood and shit sprawled behind her.

Jasmine plastered her hands over her face and screamed. Beyond a simple scream of fear, she poured her entire reservoir of guilt, hatred, anguish, and self-loathing into a wail of pure delirium.

CHAPTER EIGHTEEN

"Why am I here?"

Jasmine toweled off her face and flashed nervous glances of distrust at Mr. Chatelain and Mrs. Ainsworth.

Last thing I remember was ...

The counselor sat in a plush rolling chair to the right of Jasmine, along the rounded side of a long table shaped like a football with the ends cut off. Her ever-present binder lay flat in front of her. On Jasmine's left, at the head of the table, brooded the vice principal, fingering a bottle of imported sparkling water.

"We've been trying to get a hold of your mother," Ainsworth started, her eyes hungry to pop open Jasmine's head and peer inside. "We wanted to have a chance to talk in the meantime, before—"

Chatelain expelled a polite harrumph behind a raised hand.

Jasmine swiveled in a similar chair between the two adults. The leather chair yielded, easing the kinks out of the nervous tension that jangled her spine. But her skin itched under the heavy gaze of her chaperones/guards/wardens.

She took a quick swig from the bottle of expensive water set before her. Running her hand under the lip of the table, her fingertips touched polished wood—not the expected rough stubble of particle board. If this was a detention, it was the most luxurious one she ever had.

Alternating columns of glass brick and polished metal separated the school board council room from the adjoining hallway. Vague blurs of people—some standing, others bustling about—hovered about a door in the center of the glass and steel sections.

The wall performed its job of muffling voices rather well. Jasmine couldn't make out anything uttered by the amorphous forms behind them. Her reflection on the smooth glass blocks highlighted the streaked and mottled mess on her face.

From the table in front of her, she snatched the cotton towel already damp with sweat, tears, and smears of makeup. She found the cleanest corner and dug its fibers again across her forehead and neck beading anew with pinpricks of sweat, before scouring out the last stubborn motes of rouge and eye shadow.

"You've experienced something no one should witness," said Ainsworth, attempting a note of empathy that somehow still missed its mark. She reached out her hand to take a reassuring hold of Jasmine's, who retreated, curling into the folds of her seat and pulling her hands into her lap. "We're here to help you, Jasmine. You must believe that."

Except that they weren't helping. And she didn't believe them.

All their platitudes and consolations—"It will take time to get over the hurt," and "This is hard on us all"—fell on Jasmine's ears as pre-programmed psycho-babble from a textbook. And they were speechified with the sympathy of a school lecture.

"Please, Jasmine," said Chatelain. "You mustn't blame yourself. You were just in the wrong place at the wrong time. It wasn't your fault."

Jasmine's blood hammered in her veins, exacerbated by Chatelain's too-general-to-be-useful aphorisms. "How would you know?" she grumbled.

"You're right. We don't," Ainsworth countered. "That's why we're asking for your help to figure this all out."

Two colorless shadows paced behind the glass bricks. They engaged in animated discussion, though their lowered voices remained unintelligible drones.

"Such a terrible thing to happen," mused Chatelain.

"It affected you so terribly," Ainsworth added. "Trinity must have been a good friend—"

Jasmine's hands bunched into fists. "She was *not* my *friend!*" she howled. "Why does everyone think that?"

Chatelain and Ainsworth exchanged surprised glances, and there was a deafening pause in the argument behind the door.

Jasmine's burning gaze met that of her segmented reflection in the glass brick, as she examined herself for eyes that went askew. She watched herself trace a light border around her lips with her fingers, wondering if she should expect a rough pebbling to emerge through her skin. Or if her skin might change color while she peered at herself in the glass.

Am I the good Jasmine, or the bad Jasmine?

"I don't want to be here," Jasmine huffed, folding her arms across her chest. "Can I go home?"

"Not yet, Jasmine," Chatelain said with a foreboding twist of his eyebrows. "The other witnesses to Ms. Davis's sui– ... her demise are making statements to the police. I'm sure they'll want to speak with you as well."

Jasmine's jaw trembled at the mention of Trinity's last name. She pressed further into her seat, surprised at her own irritation at hearing it spoken without a lick of emotion.

"The police?" Jasmine asked with a slight shake of her head, before her eyes planted a bead on Chatelain.

They're here already? How much did I miss?

"Well, of course, Jasmine. A death has occurred. We have little choice in the matter," Chatelain replied. "Though given your agitated state, we requested Detective Bollard to hold off until after the EMTs released you into Nurse Genesee's care, after she examined you, and after we have this chance to talk."

Jasmine squeezed her legs together involuntarily. Her eyes darted back and forth, searching her memory. A gray blank wall stood in her way. "She examined me? EMTs? I don't remember any of that."

"Yes, she and a student calmed you down—Madison, I believe? She and Nurse Genesee convinced the emergency responders not to sedate you."

Ainsworth paused to hunch over the table, probing Jasmine's inward stare. "You really don't remember?"

Chatelain folded his hands on the table. "When they arrived, you were so agitated that it took two teachers and a police resource officer to hold you still. They had quite a time preventing you from hurting yourself or anyone else."

Nightmare flashes of blood-soaked tiles, feces-smeared walls, blurred wisps of grown-ups' faces, swirled together with Madison's voice, echoed distantly over the space of a heartbeat in Jasmine's mind. She rubbed her wrists that ached with strains that she herself could not recall.

"I hope we won't upset you, but we must ask. But can you think of any reason why Ms. Davis felt she had to resort to such a terrible thing?" Chatelain duplicated Ainsworth's action, placing a sympathetic hand on Jasmine's. His skin felt hard and dry, like a crocodile's claw. "Take your time. We're just trying to understand—"

Ainsworth chimed in again. "And at least make sure you are lucid enough before—"

Voices escalated behind the wall, to the point where distinct words pierced the door's wood. One indistinct shape behind the mottling glass was nose to nose with the other. Detective Bollard's voice was a barely muffled bullhorn behind the door.

"I've been patient long enough, principal. Your teachers and that lamebrained resource officer of yours tracked so much crap around that damned bathroom, it'll take a week for the crime scene unit to sort it all out. And your counselors are so concerned over managing the fallout and covering your school's butt, the witnesses have been coached to the point where it's making my job damn near impossible. I will see Ms. Price now."

A muffled, single-word protest later, the door handle twisted.

"*Now*," she bellowed.

The door swung open. Detective Bollard, her knuckles white from their iron grip on the handle, beetled a pair of no-nonsense eyebrows aimed at Principal Moore behind her.

Bollard's partner, Fred, trailed behind the pair, his wrinkled tan trench coat wagging behind his lanky frame. He leaned a shoulder against the doorjamb and crossed his arms.

"Hello again, Ms. Price," said Bollard. Her usual sardonic sneer was absent, replaced by an expression devoid of emotion. Only the dying remnant of passionate anger in her breathing betrayed her otherwise calm demeanor. She doffed her navy blue peacoat and folded it crisply over the back of an empty chair before sitting in the overstuffed seat across from Jasmine. She placed her spiral notepad on the table, removed its pen from the binding with the deliberate precision of a surgeon, then dashed a mad scribble on a fresh page.

"You don't need to tell Detective Bollard anything you're not comfortable with," Ainsworth began. She was shut down by a rap of Bollard's pen on the table.

"Principal Moore explained the situation to me. As I hope she did to all of you. You are here as a courtesy to Ms. Price, but please do not interfere—"

It was Jasmine's turn to interrupt. "Don't I need a lawyer here? Or at least my Ma?"

"My, you *are* the expert, aren't you?" Bollard regarded Jasmine with cold eyes and a severe mouth. "You are a witness, Ms. Price, not a suspect. You don't require a lawyer or parent, though the school has notified your mother," she said, shooting an inquiring glance at Moore. "Correct, Principal?"

"We have not been able to contact her yet," Moore said after a hesitant clearing of her throat. "The hotel supervisor is being rather uncooperative."

Jasmine suppressed a snort.

Bollard spun around to her partner, still pretending to be a door. "Fred, see if you can light a fire under that bozo's butt." Fred dug out his phone, disappearing behind the door jamb with a smile like a little boy opening his birthday present.

Returning her attention to Jasmine, Bollard continued with all the compassion of a robot with a human voice. "If she manages to make it here, we'll see. As I said, her presence is not required. School staff will suffice in the meantime. I need to get your side of the story, before anyone ..."

Bollard machine-gunned a withering stare at the three school staff. "... conflates your story." Her commanding tone would have silenced the rowdiest of classrooms. Chatelain took an unhurried draught from his bottled water.

"Con ... flate?" Jasmine tripped over the word.

Bollard rolled her eyes with indifference, looking for a definition. "Mmm, mix someone else's story in with your own." Telegraphing another glare boring into Ainsworth's head, she laid down her pen with a solid click, parallel to the edge of the notepad.

"Where were you when Ms. Davis ..." Bollard pursed her lips with a half-frown. "... when the incident in the girls' restroom happened?"

Jasmine's skin itched again at the all-too-formal mention of Trinity's name. "Don't you know already? Didn't anyone else tell you?" she said with a sarcastic huff.

"Yes, I've talked to several of your classmates. And I've been over the whole messy scene. But like I said, Jasmine, I want *your* side of events. What *you* saw and heard."

"She's a bit flustered," said Ainsworth. "Her memory is still a bit patchy. You can't remember much, can you Jas—"

"Fred," Bollard snapped, pivoting in her seat. Her partner had already resumed his position, making sure the door frame didn't collapse. "Would you be so kind as to escort Mrs. Ainsworth outside? Since people in this room seem to be light on the definitions of words, please explain to her the meaning of 'interference in an investigation' and what the penalties are if she continues?"

With a smirk dripping with *schadenfreude,* Fred beckoned with his first two fingers at Ainsworth.

The counselor's cheeks puffed with indignation, until Moore silenced her with a nod of her head. She stormed out of the room, trailed by Fred and his fluttering coat. Ainsworth's cherished notebook pouted alone and forlorn on the table.

"Well, let's see if we can help you remember." Bollard placed her elbows on the table and interlaced the fingers of both hands. "When did you first see Ms. Davis—?"

"Her name was *Trinity,*" spat Jasmine. Grinding her teeth at herself, she could not figure out why she was so upset on behalf of the girl that had been the source of all her misery.

"Fair enough. When did you first see Trinity this morning?"

"In the hall," Jasmine began slowly. "She and her sister were dumping on Madison."

"Her sister …" Bollard flipped back two pages on her notepad. "Oh, Kimani Davis. Yeah, she's a real piece of work. And a long juvie sheet to boot. So why were they picking on Madison?"

"She did me a solid early this morning. Trinity didn't like it. Madison needed help, so I stepped in."

"You stood up to Trinity *and* Kimani?" Bollard's eyebrows twitched. "Impressive." She wrote a line in her notepad. "How did you convince them to leave you and Madison alone?"

"I told Trinity to back off."

"And?"

"That's it. I told her that Madison was with me, and to lay off. Kimani still wanted to pound the crap outta us, but Trinity yanked her leash."

Bollard focused a squint at Jasmine. "Y'know, Kimani's not too fond of you. She believes you pushed Trinity into suicide."

"Detective, I thought you said Jasmine was not a suspect," complained Chatelain. He clutched his bottle of water and took a wary gulp.

The corners of Jasmine's mouth went south so hard, her lower lip folded back. Her languid breath was followed by a barely audible, "Kimani's right. I *did* tell Trinity to do it."

Chatelain coughed a rheumy wheeze, spluttering water on the table in front of him.

"You *what?*" blurted Moore. Bollard's hand snapped out, commanding Moore's silence, though her eyes never flinched from Jasmine.

"Wow, Jasmine. Seems if someone messes with you, they don't stand a chance." Bollard's smirk reappeared in full force.

Jasmine was firmly convinced this was the detective's comfort zone, and being in a confined room facing her prey was her natural habitat.

"First, Nevaeh goes missing, then Caleb. Akilah's still a vegetable in the hospital, and now Trinity." Her gnashing grin spread nearly ear to ear. "Heck, you're a one-girl wrecking crew. Who's next? Or perhaps I should check with Missing Persons about any open cases you might've left behind in the Projects?"

Principal Moore bolted upright out of her chair, sending it rolling against the wall behind her. She planted both hands on the table and glowered at Bollard so hard, her glasses slid down to the tip of her nose. "That's *enough*, Detective. This line of questioning has gone beyond simple gathering of evidence. If you want to question Jasmine further, I'm afraid I must insist it is with her mother, and quite possibly a lawyer, present."

"Relax, Principal Moore." Bollard tried to allay the school staff with a wave of her hand. "Jasmine's in the clear. Several independent witnesses place Ms. Price in the hall when Ms. Davis ..." Bollard paused, searching for the softest words, then shrugged her shoulders in surrender. "When Trinity took her own life."

Bollard swiveled her attention once more on Jasmine. "But there are a few loose ends, that no one else can seem to explain. I'm merely trying to get a handle on them." She turned her pen end over end in her hand. "Jasmine, what do you mean, you told her to do it?"

"You saw the card in the stall, right?"

"The pink one." Bollard nodded.

"The letters pasted together? That was Trinity." She pointed at Bollard's pen. "And the writing on it? That was me."

Jasmine's jaw muscles ached from holding a scowl for so long. "Trinity had it in for me since day one. She was behind all the stupid pranks and bullying. She goaded Nevaeh, Akilah, and everyone else to dump on me. She was behind all the other cyber-bully crap, too. She's the one who manipulated Caleb to try to rape and kill me."

Moore's jaw went slack.

"And she was behind the beatdown I got in the gym."

"So Coach Garcia was right," snapped Chatelain in surprise. "Jasmine, why did you lie to her and Nurse—"

"Vice Principal," barked Bollard, as strident as a pit bull in the ring. "Would you care to join Mrs. Ainsworth outside? I can arrange that."

Chatelain's eyebrows angled harshly, and he exposed his lower teeth in a stark frown. He forced himself to silence with another swig of water.

"I lied because Trinity held a knife to my throat," said Jasmine. "If I told anyone what happened in the locker room, she promised to …"

Don't tell them about the pictures. They're gone. Let 'em stay gone.

"She was going to make it even worse," she whispered toward the table.

Bollard rubbed her chin once and began her reply with a hum. "Yeah, we can talk about that later. All right, Jasmine—you were saying before? What about the pink card?"

"That was her latest stab at me. She doctored the card with razor blades to cut me, and slipped it into my locker yesterday." She flashed her scarred index finger at Bollard. "I wrote my reply and shoved it, razor blades and all, back into her locker."

Jasmine's grimace melted into weak despair. "You saw what she spelled out. She told me to 'Eat shit and die.' I wrote her back, 'You first.'"

She sighed with a whine, and her shoulders sagged. "So she did."

Chatelain's face blanched. He exchanged glances with Principal Moore, who turned her head with eyes shut. "You mustn't blame yourself, Jasmine," he offered in a hoarse whisper. "It wasn't your fault."

Jasmine pounded the table, the force of her fists propelling her to her feet.

"Don't you get it? It *was*," she screeched, followed by a trembling breath. "It was," she forced through the sliver of grief that cracked her façade of anger, before collapsing again in her chair.

"I didn't mean it," she sobbed. "It was just something to piss her off. I didn't think she would actually *do* it."

She leaned her forehand into her hand. "But that was before Jack —"

Her breath caught in her throat. "I didn't know that *Mli*—"

Say it, dammit. Say that damned lizard's name.

Jasmine choked on the words. She tried again, only to feel a burning sensation crawl up her esophagus. Sweat needling over every square inch of her face, she stared again at her distorted reflection in the glass block wall.

Are my eyes straight? I can't tell.

Jasmine wailed, folding her arms in front of herself on the table. Grasping the damp and smeared towel, she buried her face into its dark safety, sobbing with abandon.

Principal Moore rose from her seat to stand beside Jasmine, squeezing the girl to her side with one arm. Jasmine shivered off her touch and wiped the dampness from her face. Moore warned off Bollard with a motherly stare.

Bollard closed her notepad, sliding the pen into its spiral. She stood, gathered her peacoat, and turned a sullen face toward Principal Moore. "I'll have a patrol unit escort Ms. Price home, and arrange for a counselor from Family Services to meet them there. If Jasmine's mother happens to show up here, tell her everyone's waiting for her at home."

Detective Bollard faced her partner, still leaning against the door frame. Fred pouted and shook his head. With a sigh, Bollard pointed an impersonal thumb at Jasmine. "We'll resume this ..." She glanced with a piteous frown at Jasmine's listless form, and her arm flopped to her side. She shrugged almost imperceptibly. "... sometime later."

CHAPTER NINETEEN

The police cruiser crawled through city streets clogged with the stop-start of the lunch hour snarl. Curled in the back seat, Jasmine tried to hide in her thoughts.

Jerking stops, a radio voice spouting harsh syllables distorted beyond comprehension, and the random staccato of automobile honks repeatedly bounced her back to the here-and-now. During the rare stints when the sounds merged into the background drone, her recollections of the horrific tableau of blood and muck in the girls' restroom filled the void. Like a scab that itched to be picked, peeled, and bleed anew, the red memory would not leave her be.

A burly officer drove the car with his wrist dangling over the steering wheel. He glanced with disdain over his shoulder through reflective aviator frames at Jasmine every time the car came to a halt. His partner broke her silence a block from their destination.

"Give it a rest, Doug," she harped. "It's not like she's gonna bolt anywhere." She twisted in the shotgun seat to face Jasmine with an empathetic smile through the steel grate. "Ya doin' all right, kiddo?"

Jasmine continued her pout unperturbed.

With a flick of his wrist toward the windshield, Doug groused, "Oh look, Emms. Another clown begging for a ticket."

Doug firmly applied the brakes, and the tires complained with a short screech. He double-tapped a dashboard-mounted control box crammed with an array of LED buttons. The car's siren whooped a short blast.

Jasmine looked through the cage separating the back and front seats in time to spy a mid-size U-Haul with one set of tires hiked up on the sidewalk, pulling away from the curb. The driver's thick arm gave a curt wave out the truck's side window, thanking the cops for clearing his lane.

"Lucky that joker caught me in a good mood," Doug snarled between gritted teeth. He swerved his vehicle toward the spot vacated by the scofflaw, next to a fire hydrant.

"Aww, too bad, Doug," Officer Emily teased with a playful lilt. "Ya missed handing out a nice birthday present to someone." The cruiser pitched to a stop when Doug slammed the shifter into park, leaving the vehicle not quite parallel to the curb.

A bunch of teens lazed around the front of Jasmine's apartment building. With the arrival of the patrol car, two goons with their heads wrapped in bandannas fumbled to pinch out their hand-rolled smokes. They hid their remnants, while another whooshed out a large vape cloud of the legal stuff. The group scattered, the bulk of them headed in the direction of Parker's bodega.

Jasmine locked eyes for a moment with one of the younger toughs wearing a jacket sporting a letter for the school wrestling team. The sleeves were bunched up around his elbows, revealing a tattoo of a black jaguar with fangs bared. He raised a leering eyebrow at her before he took out his cellphone and skulked down the block after his friends.

"You drop off the kid, Emily. I'll stay here and check in with Central …" He swiveled his head, surveying the rest of the neighborhood. "… and make sure our ride doesn't end up stripped fer parts."

With a roll of her eyes, Emily gave a mock salute and swiveled her hips out her door. She screwed on her cap, its back resting firmly on the top of a hair bun. Doug flipped another illuminated switch, and Jasmine heard the rear door solenoids clunk, their solid weight thumping through the floor and her feet.

Emily swung open Jasmine's door. "How you holding up, kid?"

"Okay," she replied with zero enthusiasm.

"Wow, she speaks. All right, let's get you home. What floor you on?"

"Fourth."

"No elevator, of course," said Emily with a ladle of uptown snark as she assessed the tall building's exterior. "Yeah, well. Coulda been the top floor."

Without a reply and with her eyes downcast, Jasmine got out of the cruiser lugging her backpack. Dragging her feet along the pavement, a movement of color in the first-floor window caught her eye. Jasmine dismissed it with a shake of her head.

Once through the entrance, Jasmine shuffled toward the rear stairs, halting at the first door of the hallway. "Wa-a-it a minute," she mumbled. She tilted her head in the door's direction to listen.

Something heavy was being dragged inside.

What the …? No one's supposed to be home.

Officer Emily halted a step past Jasmine, turning and putting one hand on her belt behind its holster.

Jasmine's spark of uncertainty that someone had broken into the empty apartment was allayed when she caught a whiff of lavender mixed with wintergreen liniment. A relieved smile spread across her face before she pounded on the apartment's door with abandon, making it shudder in its frame.

"Bibi!" she yipped. "You back home, Bibi?"

The rattle of a security chain and deadbolt preceded the squeak of the opening door.

Jasmine melted in the warmth of Bibi's beneficent smile, and dove into the palette of earth tones and turquoise that was Bibi's frock. She wrapped her arms around the slight woman's frame, plowed her face into Bibi's bony shoulder, and drank in the scent of shea in her hair.

"Hello, little one," said Bibi with the reassuring purr of a mother lioness.

"Oh, Bibi, I missed you," gurgled Jasmine as she struggled to keep the dam inside from breaking.

"So, you are home early too," fussed Bibi behind her smile. She lifted Jasmine's chin with a gentle plying of her hand. "All the children are out today—I see them outside my window. Is today a school holiday?"

Officer Emily took a tentative step forward, one eyebrow cocked at an inquisitive angle. "And you are … Mrs. Price?"

"Oh, ho," Bibi blurted with a chuckle. "No, I'm Mrs. Fieldings, a friend—"

"She's my grandmother," said Jasmine, squeezing harder. A flicker of surprise on Bibi's face was shoved aside by a beaming grin.

"Well, Mrs. Fieldings, there's been an incident at the school. We're here to bring Jasmine home."

"*Ai*, no. An incident?" Bibi held Jasmine at arm's' length, digging her fingers into the girl's shoulders, and her smile disappearing into a curl of concern. Her searching gaze met Jasmine's, already dampening with a hint of apprehension. "What happened, Officer?"

"A student, a friend of Ms. Price's, took her own life."

Jasmine ground her teeth together the moment the officer spouted the same stupid assumption that everyone else made.

She is not *my friend, dammit* ... Was *not my friend.*

Her red anger was quashed with jet-black guilt. She lobbed her backpack into the nearest corner of Bibi's apartment.

"She saw the aftermath of the unfortunate event. The investigating detective assigned us to escort Ms. Price home and stay with her until her mother or a grief counselor arrives." Officer Emily stepped between the two women and peered sidelong at Jasmine in a vain attempt to pry her away. "Is her mother home? I'd like to take Ms. Price to her now."

"No, I think she is not. I stopped by their apartment the moment I arrived, while my son unloaded all these boxes."

Jasmine peered over Bibi's shoulder, and her jaw dropped, trembling. A lopsided tower of folded cardboard boxes was surrounded by stacks of old newspapers, packing tape dispensers, and rolls of packing material in the center of the room. The center table was shoved to one wall, heaped with various knickknacks already cocooned in bubble wrap.

"No one answered, so I slipped a note under the door."

Jasmine's voice cracked, reflecting the condition of the dam holding back her grief and renewed sense of abandonment. "You're *leaving?*" she gasped. "You can't! You have to take *Mli*—" Her teeth slammed shut so hard, she almost bit her tongue.

Dammit! Why can't I still say his name?

"Oh, Officer," Bibi said with a singsong lilt and a dismissive wave of her hand. "I think it will be fine if you leave *Jazz-meen* with me until her *muuther* arrives." She resurrected her brilliant grandmotherly smile. "She and I have much to talk about. Besides, I think helping me pack will be the best therapy for her right now."

"Where are you going, Bibi? Why are you leaving us—leaving *me*?" Jasmine whined.

"Now, now, little one. You cannot believe I *want* to leave you, but I must. The world does not revolve around you alone." The wizened woman showed Jasmine a knowing smile and tapped her on the nose like a naughty puppy. "Like I told you on the phone last time, I must go where I'm needed most. Though my daughter-in-law is on the mend, her *beh-bee* is still—"

A double whoop of a siren filtered through the apartment's windows, and Emily's walkie-talkie sputtered to life with a squelch of static. "Emily, we caught a 211," barked Doug's distorted voice. "A bodega down the block. Drop what you're doing and get your butt down here."

Emily tilted her head toward the mic. "But what about the kid?"

"Central sez go, we *go*," squawked the unit in reply.

She retreated a tentative step, her hand clutching the shoulder microphone. "10-4, Doug. Be right there." With wary eyes, Emily's glances shuttled between the two in the doorway. "You two gonna be okay?"

Bibi scooted her away with a flick of her hand. "You go, Officer. My son, Rendell, took his moving van to collect a friend, and should be back any minute. *Jazz-meen* can help me pack my things until her *muuther* arrives."

Emily fixed Jasmine with an officious glare. "Stay put until I get back." Her thick-soled shoes clomped heavily, fading as she ran toward the entrance.

Bibi closed the door, and her smile evaporated under the weight of the wrinkles around her mouth and eyes, growing into deep fissures of age-worn concern. She hugged Jasmine once more, then herded her toward the couch.

"*Ai*, child. *Mlinzi* killed again? What a world, that a young girl must see so much ugliness."

Jasmine sat with shoulders slumped, gazing upward into Bibi's eyes. She hoped she would find understanding, if not forgiveness. "No, Bibi. It wasn't him this time," she said, her voice an anemic whisper. "It was me."

"*You?*" Bibi's wiry legs twitched and gave out underneath her. The sofa creaked when she plopped down into it, facing Jasmine.

Bibi's eyebrows scrunched together with a flare of disbelief. Huddling next to the cringing girl, she placed both her hands over Jasmine's in her lap. Bibi's knobby hands were angular yet pliant, covered with skin like mocha parchment, yet warm like a savanna sun.

"How could that be, child?" She scrunched up her eyes. "You promised me." Her hands squeezed, coaxing the truth out of Jasmine.

It spilled out of her in stops and starts, disjointed bits and fragments. Jasmine described a jumbled jigsaw of images and scenes: every wrong did to her, and every transgression that she inflicted on others over the past few days. Her words tumbled out of her faster and faster, frequently interrupted by shudders invoked by her phantoms: what Jackson said, what she did, and the red, brown, and black carnage they had driven Trinity to inflict on herself.

Bibi nodded with understanding at some points in the tangle of Jasmine's story, crumpled her brow in confusion at other details scrambled into the mix, scowled with unexpected anger at the mention of the social worker's visit, and shrank with empathy at the bloody aftermath.

Bibi pressed the fingertips of one hand gently against Jasmine's cheek when her sobs outnumbered her words.

"*Ai*, child. You talk so fast, I can hardly keep up." She closed her eyes and massaged the bridge of her nose. "And so jumbled, I am not sure what happened first."

With a solemn breath, she spoke dispassionately, as if she were reading the daily newspaper. "Caleb tried to rape and kill you, while Akilah filmed it. *Mlinzi* killed him, then savaged her. That much you told me over the phone. The next day, the detectives got involved. You used the police to threaten Trinity and her friends. You compelled your schoolmates to make you team captain or else—"

"It sounds stupid now, but it seemed so important to me then." She shrugged her shoulders and directed her pleading eyes at Bibi again. "I didn't even *want* to be captain. I just wanted to keep it from Trinity."

Bibi nodded, but held up her palm to silence Jasmine. "But Trinity being Trinity, she would not stand for it. She and her sister hurt you in the gym. She took—what is the word … compromising?—photos of you in the shower. With that sword dangling over your head, she made life unbearable. She did so many things to knock you back down. She even told you to take your own life—*Ai*, what a horrible girl."

"And I threw that pink card right back into her locker, with my answer, 'You first.' I might as well have slit her throat myself," Jasmine rasped, failing to swallow the taste of bile that burned at the back of her throat.

Bibi closed her eyes again and shook her head like a heavy pendulum. "No, my child. You could not foresee what was to become of that. How could you? Something so small, something so in-noc-*you*-ous," she said, struggling with the word.

"I just wanted to get rid of those damned pictures," Jasmine whimpered, the rising bile eroding her voice box to grating sand. "But she went back on our deal, and was going to show them to everyone, just because she could. Even after I put up with all her crap.

"I had to stop her. But I got so royally pissed, I lost control—no, that's a cop-out. I wanted to kill her." Her eyes flashed with self-loathing, and she held her breath to stifle a sob. "And I almost did. But *Mlinzi* stopped me."

Jasmine wanted to uncork every bottled-up emotion, confess every sin, yearned to bear her soul to Bibi. But fear and shame clogged her throat. Tears started to brim at the bottom of her eyes, and she snuffled back her flooding sinuses.

"He hypnotized Trinity to forget that night and commanded her to 'do what I ask that day,'" she wailed, before her voice tore with grief. Her rheumy eyes pleaded with the ceiling, half expecting Jackson to appear and leer back down at her.

Jasmine convulsed with a gut-wracking sob. "Oh, God! 'Do what I said?' 'That day?' I didn't even think. I never intended her to do something so ..."

"Such sadness." Bibi clasped Jasmine's hands again, and peered past Jasmine's eyes, boring deep into her soul. "But it was not your words on the paper that were to blame for her death. No, it was something else."

Something else? Then it's not my fault? It's not ...

Jasmine recoiled, and her heart shriveled.

Bibi's eyes held none of the absolution she hoped to find. Instead, they were filled with a pained sorrow tainted with something far worse—the same damnable look of disgust mixed with pity that Madison often displayed.

Except now, it stabbed like an accusation.

"Don't look at me like that, Bibi. I don't want your pity," said Jasmine through clenched teeth. She slipped her hands out of Bibi's and rubbed them together to squelch the sudden cold that drenched her fingers. "I thought you, of all people, would understand the hell that Jackson put me through."

"I do, child. More than you know."

Bibi stood up, graceful as a ballerina. She smoothed her frock with a single swipe, elegant in its economy of motion. "But it's not just pity, my child." She drifted into her kitchen, and after the sounds of pouring and a clink of a spoon, Bibi returned with a fresh steaming mug of tea. The scent of white whisper and honey made Jasmine's stomach growl.

"It is disappointment."

After a long draught with eyes closed, she took her seat again. Jasmine could only stare with mouth agape at the reclining slender woman, until indignant disbelief shoved aside her remorse.

"Disappointment?" she stammered. "Whaddya mean? Didn't I kill *enough* people?"

"No, that's not it at all, child. And don't give me your att-*tee*-tude."

Jasmine's reflexive wall of rebellion stood firm. "I said I'm sorry, okay? But you don't know what it was like. I've been in a world of shit, and you weren't there to help. You say you know what it was like, but you don't. You *don't*." Her chest heaved, like she was catching her last breath before being dragged underwater. "And there's nothing you can say to make me feel worse."

"Is that so?" Bibi leaned back, fixing Jasmine with judgmental eyes. Her lips pursed to a bloodless shade, and her jaw worked in silence before she found her words. "Little one, this is going to be hard for you to hear, but it is just as hard for me to tell you. And it will haunt you for the rest of your days."

Bibi's deep breath of resignation occupied the silence between the two.

"You believe your thoughtless words on that paper killed that poor girl? Not quite, my child. You doomed Trinity long before then."

Bibi took another sip, and set the mug on a small table, pushing the faded photograph of her younger self and Mr. Fieldings to one side. "I am disappointed—but not because of those unfortunate words on that silly piece of paper. They were not what killed Trinity. I'm disappointed because you *lied* to me, *Jazz-meen*. You *deceived* me."

Jasmine drew in a sharp breath, and defensive excuses welled up in her throat. But they shrank into nothingness when Jasmine's heart stopped. Crushed under her own guilt, her heart knew the truth—it refused to beat again until she faced that horrible reality.

"I told you—I *begged* you—to pass *Mlinzi* on to another. And you told me you would." Bibi rapped a gnarled knuckle on her own temple. "Maybe I was foolish. Maybe, if I could have faced you eye to eye, I would have seen the lie for what it was. But I believed I had persuaded you not to rely on him anymore." Bibi angled forward, her unrelenting gaze refusing to release Jasmine.

Jasmine's blood turned to ice with a sudden fearful thought—the image of Bibi's eyes going off kilter.

"But no, child, you made no attempt to get rid of him. Quite the opposite. You made *Mlinzi* your champion, your knight in shining armor. Even after I warned you that he was as subtle as a meat cleaver. Despite all that, you crafted your plans against Trinity. Despite my warning that he could not be controlled. Despite my—"

"*Stop it!*" Jasmine clamped her hands against her ears. "Stop it," she repeated in frail gasps of defeat.

Bibi pressed on, relentless. "I tried to help you the best I could, the only way I could, and you turned it away with a lie."

"Oh, God, Bibi—You're right." She squeezed the tears out of her eyes, tried to swallow the knowledge, and gagged on the bitter taste her admission left. "You're right."

Pressing her hands against her temples with all her strength, she curled them into fists, hoping they might smother the truth she quailed against. Or squirt out any desperate idea on what to do next.

Soft warm hands eased her fists away from her temples.

Jasmine's eyes snapped open. Her whole body twitched, making the sofa legs rattle the floor.

Bibi exhaled, as though she were crushed under the weight of the world. "I said I was disappointed with you," she said, her soothing calm having returned, eradicating her moment of fire. "But not only because you misled me."

She licked her wrinkled lips, unsure of her words. "I had hoped you would be smarter than me, stronger than me," she said, barely a whisper. She reached for her mug and emptied it. Placing it back on the table, she exchanged the mug for the black-framed photo of her and Mr. Fieldings. "Not make the same mistakes that I ..."

Bibi probed the picture with longing eyes filled with an empty chasm of sadness that made Jasmine's heart ache. She trained her eyes once more upon Jasmine—but they didn't throw accusations at her. Instead, they were filled with their own tears, brimming with a sense of pleading and guilt.

"Mistakes? What mistakes?" Jasmine ventured, all attempts at defensiveness gone. "Mr. Fieldings, and that gangsta with the gun, they got what they deserved. They were going to kill you."

Jasmine's hands slipped around Bibi's. They were shaking.

"Yes, my child. *Mlinzi* knows. He comes when death is near."

Jasmine swallowed to stop the quailing in her voice. The vile taste of gall was gone. "I finally learned that when I faced Trinity in the alley. *Mlinzi* only comes when the one he protects is about to be killed. And I got the bruises to show for it." She hugged herself to ward off the phantasms of pain from the army blanket party and Trinity's PVC tube.

"Yes, little one. But there's more than that. There's—"

"There's something I gotta know, Bibi." Jasmine rubbed her wrist with urgency, rekindling the memory of *Mlinzi* holding back her murderous vengeance on Trinity. "Why am I still alive?" she croaked scarcely louder than a whisper. "He killed Nevaeh and Caleb to protect me, and almost killed Akilah for her part in it."

Jasmine raised her palms face up, imploring Bibi for reason. "So why am *I* still here? I wanted Trinity dead, and I was ready to do it, too. But *Mlinzi* stopped me." She strained at the sudden clinch in her throat. "By all rights, it's me who should be dead. *Me!* But *Mlinzi* spared me. Why?"

Jasmine blinked as more questions flashed in her mind. They tumbled out of her mouth, like a slot machine that hit a big payout. "Why was I able to resist him when he hypnotized Trinity? And why can I say his name now? I couldn't say his name all day long, but now … And why—"

"Stop it, child. I don't know!" Bibi trumpeted, blaring through a grimace that signaled her patience was at an end. Angry tears poured down her cheeks.

Jasmine held her breath, staring. The unbreakable Rock of Gibraltar was crumbling before her, exposing a side she scarcely believed could exist.

After a moment, Bibi sucked in a breath to calm herself, leaning back again into the cushions. "I told you before, I didn't pay attention to my *bibi*. Oh, how I wish I had. She tried to tell me about *Mlinzi*, but I didn't listen, and now both you and I are paying for my willfulness and the ignorance it left me with. I may not know much about him, but I hoped to teach you what little I could. As for the rest … as for *my* sins

...

"You think you were the only one *Mlinzi* turned on? You think no one else suffered as you?" Bibi placed the picture frame face down on her lap. "It was soon after *Mlinzi* took Mr. Fieldings. My young Rendell was just beginning to walk, and with my husband gone, we were forced to move to a place as bad as your 'Projects.'

"Then Mr. Fieldings's sister came into our lives, under the pretense of being helpful. But things changed quickly.

"Of course, I could never tell her what really happened to my husband. Even though I couldn't say *Mlinzi's* name to her—just like you—here and there little truths slipped out. About what Mr. Fieldings did. To me, and to Rendell.

"It was soon apparent she never believed me, for reasons I shall never understand. In her eyes, her brother could do no wrong. If he had hurt me, I must have been my fault or my clumsiness. Even when I showed her little Rendell's faded bruises, she would not accept the truth about what type of man her brother had become. It was somehow my fault. In her eyes, I was not a good *muuther*, unable to look after my child. Worse, she accused me—saying that it was *I* who had taken out my frustrations on my precious one. She spread terrible rumors, and her serpent's tongue soon turned her entire family against me.

"And she did worse. Just as Trinity did to you, she told lies to whatever social worker would listen to her. But it wasn't just one day. Week after week, a new accusation and another inspection. Then one day I got a summons for family court."

Bibi lifted her eyes heavenward. "Where in the world did she get the money to hire a lawyer? I couldn't fight her—I certainly had no money for such a thing. She was intent on taking my Rendell away, and there was little I could do to stop her."

"That's terrible," said Jasmine. "But a grown-up? She's just as bad the skanks who bullied me."

"Yes, little one. Some bullies never grow up." Bibi's fists clenched, their veins pulsing dark blue. "I resolved enough was enough. And just like you, I decided to confront my tormentor in her home. That was a terrible mistake."

Bibi trembled in her seat. "Before I knew it, matters got out of hand. I screamed at her, describing down to the tiniest detail exactly what her brother had done, and what a monster he was. She became incensed and threw things at me, even with little Rendell crying at the kitchen table. She was a mad woman, throwing one plate so wild that it almost hit my sweet Rendell. Then, another dish cut me when it shattered near my head against the wall. I saw my own blood, and looked at my child.

"My blood was all over my little one." Bibi rubbed her hands over her arms, as if all the warmth had left the room. "I wanted her blood in return. In that moment, in my heart of hearts, I wanted that evil woman gone from this world. I picked up a shard and wielded it like a knife, ignoring the cut it sliced into my palm."

She opened her hand to examine it. Jasmine gaped at the faded scar that ran from the base of her thumb across her palm.

"I was inches away from driving that makeshift dagger into that witch's cold heart." Bibi's chest was heaving with quick shallow breaths. "But *Mlinzi* appeared, he intervened. I don't know if he knocked her out, or if she simply fainted. But his tongue wrapped around my wrist, holding it fast like manacles of iron. I was a mouse crushed in the python's grip. But a miracle occurred. He let me go and spoke to me."

Her eyes drifted to the ceiling again. "I still have nightmares where he warns me again and again ... '*Ikiwa unamwua, nitakuua.*'"

"You kill her, I kill you," Jasmine whispered back, needing no translation.

Bibi nodded without a word and squeezed her eyes shut, forcing a tear down one cheek. "Just like that, *Mlinzi* disappeared. My sister-in-law was hypnotized, collapsed in the corner and staring at the ceiling. I went to grab little Rendell and run, when my heart froze. My little one had stopped crying, because he had the same empty stare."

She wiped her face with both hands, like she was sweeping the ash of memories away. "That's when I knew what had to be done. I had to be rid of *Mlinzi*. And my little Rendell could never know.

"I watched, I listened, I learned. I became everybody's friend— but not because I really wanted to. For years I waited and searched for some poor soul who was in dire trouble, someone who *Mlinzi* would accept—someone who would become his next protected.

"But the waiting was terrible. Every time that Rendell came home from school with a bump or bruise or a black eye, I feared *Mlinzi* might bond to him, and the nightmare would start all over again. But thank goodness, he never turned blue."

With her shaky hand looped behind Jasmine's neck, Bibi pulled her close. "Months became years, and I forgot the horrors. Until *Mlinzi* turned blue for you. I am so sorry it was you, *Jazz-meen*. Yes, yes—I am happy you're alive, but I am ashamed at how *Mlinzi* treated you so shabbily, and far worse than I ever could have dreamed.

"You see, unlike the others I exposed to *Mlinzi*, I *liked* you and your Ma. I grew to love you both. Your *muuther* is the daughter I never had, and you ... well, I guess now I have *two grahnt*-daughters."

She attempted a wisp of a smile, but it melted into pained wistfulness. "But my mistake was that I forgot—No, I hid the truth from myself. I was so concerned with my own family, I failed to help the family right in front of me. I didn't think to shield you and your Ma from *Mlinzi*, the way I protected my son."

Their foreheads touched, and Jasmine closed her eyes as well. "Can you forgive me?" Bibi whispered. After they exchanged deep breaths, Jasmine pulled back.

"What happened to your sister-in-law? Did she ... take her own life?" She swallowed, fearing what the answer might be. "Like Trinity?"

"No, but I don't know whatever became of her. She never bothered me again after that day." A strange grin flickered across Bibi's face, like she was caught red-handed doing mischief. "Though I did hear later from friends that she was scared to death of me."

"So why, Bibi? Why did *Mlinzi* spare me, you ... us?"

"*Ai*, if I knew, I would tell you, little one. But we shall never know for sure. Whatever the reason, Bibi Rakotomalala took it with her to the grave. She has been gone these many years."

"Gone? How do you know she's gone? You've never been back to Tanzania," Jasmine fidgeted with her fingers. "Have you?"

Bibi shook her head, a stoic frown emphasizing her thin jowls. "No. But one day," she began, a wistful wind blowing through her voice. "*Mlinzi* turned coal black and remained motionless for a full day. I knew then my *bibi* was gone."

Bibi blinked, and her maternal smile returned, as if everything was in its place and all was right with the world. "You ask why you could not say his name? You're saying it now, aren't you? And I can name him to you, as well. My guess is he won't let us say his name in front of those he has not touched.

"As to why he spared us?" she asked with a shrug. "That's the biggest of my *bibi*'s secrets. It has puzzled me for years. Maybe he has a conscience of sorts, or some strange code he must live by. Maybe he's required to give the one he protects a warning. Maybe he sees the future. Maybe he needs us alive to move on. Who knows?

"So, child, you ask why he let us live? When we were so deter-mined to kill, and so richly deserved his punishment?" Bibi's shrug was replaced with her innocent smile. "I'm just glad he did. All I know is on that day, I resolved never to give *Mlinzi* or myself another chance to find out."

She stood, set the picture frame on the table beside her son's graduation photograph and collected her empty mug. "Oh, he still pro-tected me—remember that bad man who broke into my home? But I shall never call on *Mlinzi* again. Nor will I ever allow myself to gaze into his eyes again.

"And neither should you." she said, tapping a fingertip on the top of Jasmine's head in rhythm with her words. Bibi sauntered back into her kitchen, humming over her empty mug. "I don't think I have to worry about you anymore, little one. We've both had our bad patches with *Mlinzi*, and we've both learned our lessons, no?"

"That's for damn sure," said Jasmine, punctuated with fervent determination. She shook her head, though her eyes were downcast, staring at a lost screw on the floor. "I never want to see that stupid lizard again."

She blinked with a sudden thought. Sure, it was a long shot—but what was that screw-loose quote from Mr. Wyatt's history class?

Nothing ventured, nothing gained.

Jasmine bolted out of her seat with a look of optimism. "I know! I'll bring Jackson down with his terrarium, and you can pack him up and take him with you," she blurted with innocent enthusiasm.

From the kitchen echoed Bibi's cavernous reply. "*Ai*, child. Haven't you been listening? You *know* that will not work. He'll just pop back into your room, your home, your life. Just like he did when I came to America.

"How many times must I say this, little one? He's *yours* now." Bibi emerged from the kitchen, her Look stifling the gripe that welled up inside Jasmine. "Until the day you die, or you find someone who needs him more than you. And don't forget, *Mlinzi* has to agree and accept. He will not go unless he agrees."

Jasmine's pressed her lips thin with consternation. "Oh great," she grumbled. "How do I get him to do that? And how do I tell when—or even *if*—he agrees?"

"Oh, for pity's sake, little one. Does everything I say go in one ear and out the other?" she good-heartedly sniped with a roll of her eyes, before her smile of infinite patience asserted itself again.

"Child, remember the day I first showed *Mlinzi* to you? He was on your arm, and turned a brilliant blue? Like a sapphire glinting in the sun he was," she said, a haunting melody in her voice. "*That's* how you'll know. He was that same color when my *bibi* showed him to me when I married. After so many years, and showing him to so many others, I had almost forgotten that color. Until he accepted you that day."

Jasmine clicked her tongue. She felt she was offhandedly given an arduous and eternal task—like cleaning every toilet in the city. Until another flash of inspiration struck, bringing a faint sliver of hope.

Maybe, just maybe, there is *someone.*

Bibi returned from the kitchen, with two fresh steaming mugs. She offered one to Jasmine, who held up her hand and begged off, retreating a couple of steps toward the door.

"Not just yet, Bibi. If I can't get rid of Jackson, I can at least get rid of the new Jasmine—the fake Jasmine—I pretended to be. I have all your makeup and other stuff you gave to Ma. I sure as heck will never want to use it again. As far as I'm concerned, it's yours—pack it up and take it with you. I want that gunk out of my hair—literally."

"*Gunk*? *Ai*, I feel I've been slighted," Bibi said, her arms akimbo in mock indignation. "Doesn't your Ma need it for work?"

"I've had the stuff for days, and she hasn't missed it." Jasmine's eyelids flicked wide as she splayed her fingers over her mouth. "Omigod—*Ma!*"

"What is it, child?"

"You've been gone all this time, how could you know?" She cradled her forehead in her hand, as though it was her turn to have a migraine. "Her jobs are terrible, and her bosses are such pricks. One has a fetish about his phone, and the other's a stickler for his hotel's rep —aw, who gives a flying ... Not to mention all the grief I've been putting Ma through. But the worst ..."

Jasmine paused to take a trembling breath, her eyes riveted on Bibi's worried frown. "Dad was injured in Afghanistan. He was hurt kinda bad, and we still haven't heard how he's doing after the surgery and transport. We've been waiting for the phone call with the latest news since last night."

Holding back a wince of panic, Jasmine practically leaped through the door. "Ma was counting on me to watch the phone. I gotta go and see if there's a message."

Bibi called after her, but Jasmine's pounding heart drowned out the words. She dashed down the hall and bounded up the three flights of stairs to her floor. Though her legs felt wondrous, running after a day of sitting through endless hand-wringing misery, anxiety still crimped her heart to the point where it wanted to tear itself apart. Halting in front of the door, she dug in her pockets for the keys. An exasperated grimace snapped into place.

"Dammit, they're in my backpa—"

A sinuous arm swooped down in front of her.

Jasmine's head snapped to one side, as the arm whipped around her neck. A wiry bicep pressed under her right ear, and a rock-hard forearm rippling with its jaguar tattoo wrapped around her throat. She tried to tuck her chin under the crook of the arm, but the clinch was too strong. The forearm clamped under her left ear, and she felt a hand pushing her head forward into the hollow of the arm. She wriggled, trying to squirm her body around, but it was held fast in a flawless sleeper hold. She tried to inhale and scream, but little air would come.

A contralto voice hissed into her right ear.

"After what you did to my sister, I'm gonna make you pay."

Kimani!

Jasmine grabbed the arm, planted her feet against the wall and twisted. She tried to yank the arm away from her neck. Failing to move Kimani's arm the slightest fraction of an inch, she wriggled futilely, gasping for breath as the edges of her vision dimmed. "Can't ... breathe ..."

"Oh, it'll be quick." The vice of flesh squeezed her neck, then loosened ever so slightly. "Or it'll be slow. Haven't made up my mind yet. Trinity was so screwed up last night. I never seen her like that before. And now she's ... What the fuck did you *do* to her?"

"Sorry," Jasmine croaked. "Wasn't me. It was Jack—" She gagged on the name. "I never meant ..."

"Shut up, bitch." The arm ratcheted tighter once more. The flexing muscle under the tattoo made the fangs of the jaguar lunge for Jasmine's jugular.

Everything beneath Jasmine's knees submerged into a river of tingling numbness.

"Even if my sister didn't whisper your name over and over like a fuckin' nutcase last night, I knew it had to be you."

Jasmine reached her right arm behind her, grasping and clutching to find her attacker's face or anything soft to rake at.

Kimani tensed behind her, nimbly ducking her feeble counterattack. "Knock it off, you fucking ho. Or I'll snap your neck right here," she growled with earnest. "It'd be so fuckin' easy to kill you."

Jasmine heard the grinding of gristle in her neck.

"Screw it," Kimani spat. "You're dead. For Trin."

Jasmine's eyes bulged, trying to peer through the shrinking iris of darkness that encroached on her sight. She spied a swirling movement on the wall and tried to draw a gasp that wouldn't come.

Out of the painted masonry grew three horns. Their tips turned red, becoming a more furious crimson the further they protruded.

"Don't, Jack—" she rasped. Reaching toward the pair of soulless black eyes on either side of the horns, she cinched her eyelids shut and spent the last of her air. "Don't ... kill ... her."

"Kill *me*? Whaddya talking about, you stupid—" Kimani gasped and retreated, her own back thumping into the wall behind her.

Hanging from Kimani's noose of bone, sinew, and muscle, Jasmine swung like a puppet with its strings cut.

Keening like it emanated from the bottom of a black chasm, Kimani shouted, "What the fu—"

Kimani's scream dwindled into strangled silence before darkness flooded Jasmine's entire being.

CHAPTER TWENTY

Jasmine's eyes snapped open, and she jerked forward with a sudden gasp.

"Kimani!" she croaked, followed by a series of asthmatic wheezes and racking coughs.

Her hands clutched at thin air, grabbing for the choking arm that was no longer there. She winced at the headache that jabbed a spike into the base of her skull. It ebbed away almost as quickly.

"Whoa, kid, chill. You all right? Who's Kimani?" thrummed a deep baritone.

Looking around, Jasmine found herself seated on the floor with her back curled away from the cold wall. An indistinct figure knelt before her. With the back of her right hand, she wiped away the tears and mucus that blurred her vision. Her fingers rang with electric numbness as they clumsily rubbed her face. The dull rhythm of her heartbeat pulsed down the length of her limbs.

A middle-aged man with a chestnut complexion and a low-fade buzz-cut scored with a wavy pattern patted her hand. "You Jasmine?" he asked, the rich timbre of his voice filling every corner of the hallway.

"Yeah," Jasmine said through a ragged cough, yanking her hand out of his grasp. "Who're you?"

"Rendell. My Mama—Mrs. Fieldings—sent me up here. We heard a commotion coming down the stairwell. Sounded like a real battle royale. Then some woman ran down the stairs past our floor, screaming bloody murder. Mama called the cops and scooted me up here to check on you."

"You—you're Bibi's son?" she said, followed by coughs.

His voice carried no trace of her Tanzanian accent, nor any hint of the street. He was much older than his graduation photo, and beefier than he appeared in the snapshot Bibi showed them over their kitchen table days ago. There was a facial resemblance, but not enough for Jasmine to guess he was Bibi's son.

A door opened halfway down the hall, and a grizzled old man stuck his head out the door for a moment, ducking back inside like a frightened meerkat after Jasmine blinked at him in surprise.

After a whole week of insanity, now *a neighbor bothers to poke around?*

"*Bibi,* huh?" said Rendell. An awkward grin spread across his face. "Well, if Mama's your grandmother now, I guess that makes you my … niece?"

Jasmine could see Bibi's smile reflected under those high cheek-bones.

He stood from his kneeling position and held out his hands. "Can you stand?"

"Dunno. Kimani had me in some sort of headlock." She pressed against the floor and wall, determined to stand on her own. Her legs refused to cooperate.

She cast a worried gaze at the walls across from her and behind her.

No blood. Good. What the heck did Mlinzi do?

Her small whoosh of relief was cut short. Three fresh sets of helter-skelter rake marks were dug into the mason block hallway, expos-ing deep gouges of gray under the pallid beige paint.

Jasmine glanced up and down the hallway, ignoring the sudden surge of dizziness. She smacked her hands on the floor, hoping it would stop the hallway from spinning.

"Who's this Kimani you keep talking about?"

"Some 'roid-rage bitch from school. Did you see her? Where'd she go?" Jasmine coughed, and the headache came back for an encore.

"Like I said, we saw a woman zoom down into the basement. That could've been her. Is there an exit down there?"

"No, there ain't. Help me up," said Jasmine, extending her hands in compliance.

Rendell gripped her hands in his and pulled Jasmine to her feet. "Is this your place here? Let's get you inside, where you can get some ice on—"

"I could use some water," said Jasmine, "but I left my keys downstairs." She pitched toward the staircase, with Rendell in anxious pursuit.

He swiveled himself in front of Jasmine once they reached the first of the steps. Grasping her right hand and descending backward, he guided her while keeping his own balance against the banister. "Take it slow. If you fall, I'm gonna have to carry your butt downstairs. And I'm already stiff from clearing out our guest room for Mama's stuff."

"Bibi's really moving out, isn't she?" Jasmine said, dejection in her voice.

"Yeah, and it's about time. The missus and I have been begging Mama to move out of this place and live with us ever since we had Cheta. He and Mama just dote on each other."

So why didn't she move out sooner? Oh, yeah—the 800-pound chameleon in the room.

"You taking everything?" Jasmine asked, daring to hope despite all that Bibi said.

"Keepsakes and her things from the old country, and whatever else we can fit into her room. What we don't take, you're welcome to. Otherwise it goes to charity or the dump." He chuckled to himself. "Mama tells me you're taking her chameleon. Good riddance to—"

Jasmine stumbled over her feet, doubling over into Rendell's arm. He caught her as handily as folding laundry. "Whoa, careful, girl."

"You know about *Mlinzi?*" she sputtered, followed by a hiccup with the realization she had said his name out loud.

Of course, I can say it. He may have only been two years old, but he was zapped by that stupid lizard.

"Sure. Mama loves the thing, but he gives me the creeps. She's had that critter forever, which is one of things that wigs me out about him—they're only supposed to live ten years, tops. I'm surprised she's finally letting go of the little monster."

Jasmine chortled out loud in disbelief and signaled that she needed a breather on the third floor.

He doesn't have a clue! Probably better that way.

"I'm really sad to see Bibi go," she said. "But she's explained about your family, and that—oh, good grief, where's my head at? Your family!" she panted, putting her hand to her mouth. "Last time I spoke with Bibi over the phone, it sounded like Cheta had a really bad accident. Is he all right?"

"Now *that* was one cruddy day. My boy pulled a dresser on top of himself. Mama—*Bibi*—got Cheta all bundled up, then our neighbor zipped both of them to the ER. That night, the whole family was in the hospital for one reason or another. Thank goodness, Cheta's injuries were minor, and he bounced back fast. Kids do that, y'know—I swear they're made of rubber. He's doing a sleepover tonight with the neighbor's kids while my friend and I move Mama's stuff."

"What about the rest of your family? Bibi told me a little, before my own cruddy day got in the way. Make that a totally crappy day."

A shadow fell over Rendell, slouching his entire body. He slipped a high-end cell phone out of his pocket, taking a few seconds to scroll his screen. "The missus is still resting in the hospital, but she's out of immediate danger. But the doc told us there's an 'abnormality' that …" he paused, with a catch in his throat. "She lost a lot of blood that night, but the docs pulled her through."

He turned his phone to show Jasmine a picture of a small brown wrinkled mass of flesh, with a pink band around her tiny wrist. A bundle of tubes stuck out of her body as she lay asleep—or unconscious— in a clear Lucite box. Behind the tiny life crouched a worried Rendell wearing a surgical mask and cap. His massive gloved hand stuck through one of the box's portals, stroking the preemie's side with one finger.

"The abnormality is what caused the birth to come premature. It was touch and go the first two days of this little one's new life, but she's over the worst of it now. However, the doctors still can't tell us if she's gonna …" Rendell's face screwed up into a sullen scowl that he struggled to override with a hopeful grin. "We're going to name her what Mama called her—*Shujaa*. It means warrior, a fighter."

"Looks like she's earned that name already," Jasmine said with a wan smile of empathy.

Rendell pocketed his phone. With solemn faces, they resumed their silent push-pull trek down the stairs.

On the second-floor landing, Rendell asked, "Do you need another break?"

Before Jasmine could respond, shouts bounced up the shaft of cracked masonry, rusted metal railing, and peeling linoleum. She tilted her head, trying to untangle the cacophony of voices: a guy spouting every profanity known to humankind and then some; a girl gibbering nonsense on the verge of raging panic, and a man and woman shouting commands over the fracas.

Rendell and Jasmine leaned over the creaking banister to peer down the central shaft into the basement. Ill-defined shadows flailed and swept across the floor, thrown from the sole light that graced the basement stairwell. A wide shadow swung across the concrete, then the entire floor went dark with the tinkle of breaking glass.

"Goddammit punk, siddown," roared Officer Doug, his voice bounding up the stairs. A single grunt from the gangsta was paired with the sound of a body slam. "Christ Almighty, making me chase you down from that crappy bodega. You're already under arrest for theft, and now I'm adding assault and battery to that. What the hell did you *do* to her?"

"I didn't do nuthin'," came the teen's immediate shout of protest, reverberating up the walls. "She called *me*. She wuz talkin' bat-shit crazy. When I got here, she was already hurt bad."

Jasmine pulled away from Rendell. Grabbing the rail with both hands, she wobbled down the stairs to the landing between floors. Rendell caught up to her and held her fast around the shoulder, though he couldn't prevent her from craning her head toward the scuffle below.

"She called *you*?" shouted Officer Emily. "That's some feat, with a broken arm."

The distinctive zip of handcuffs being applied filtered up the stairwell. The whimpers of the girl were drowned out under the static of Doug's walkie-talkie.

"Central, we're gonna need a bus. Female suspect with a broken arm, multiple compound fractures. And get a second car to our location. The others are still at the 211." After the squawk of a static-filled acknowledgment, he said in full bluster, "I'm gonna stash this hump in the car. You gonna be okay with her?"

"Yeah, she's not going anywhere," replied Emily. "Not with that bum knee to boot."

The pair of arguing males stomped out of the basement. Doug shoved the teenager in cuffs up the stairs, and Jasmine blinked with recognition—it was the gangbanger with the jaguar tattoo loitering in front of her apartment building.

He was the one on the phone, watching my place. He must've called Kimani when I arrived.

Jasmine shuffled to the edge of the landing, watching them parade out toward the first-floor hallway.

"Hey, kid. Jasmine, right?" Doug said, yanking the boy to a halt. He shot a momentary glower at Rendell. "Hey, bud, you the guy who called in the 911? If she was assaulted, you shouldn't be moving her."

"No, Officer—Mrs. Fieldings called it in. As for Jasmine here, I couldn't've stopped her if I tried," Rendell responded with a shrug and a smile that was pure Bibi.

An inarticulate yowl exploded from the basement, following by rapid scuffling of both sneakers and heavy shoes.

If the girl weren't hunched over, she would have towered over Emily. Despite a grossly swollen knee, the girl limp-bounded up the stairs, still managing to outdistance the female officer. All the while she uttered streams of curses, cackles, and drooling mumbles though every exhale of exertion and pain. Stumbling to a halt the moment she came into view, she fixed Jasmine with a stare of a mind lost to madness.

"Kimani?" Jasmine gasped.

Thank God she's alive! But what the hell did Mlinzi do to her?

Kimani's arm hung in front of her. The wrist bent inward at an impossible angle, and the white shade of bone pressed under the skin of her forearm's tattoo. Both arms were ringed with blood bruises, as though giant handcuffs crushed her arms. The skin around her neck was rubbed raw and red, like she had been lassoed by a hawser inches thick.

"Hey, Jasmine, you okay?" exclaimed Officer Emily. She grabbed Kimani by the shoulder and the waist of her pants. "Did this girl attack you? Or was it the kid with Doug?"

Jasmine grimaced and bit her lower lip. Her nod was more like a nervous twitch. "Just her."

Kimani's face pulsed with anger in response, and she crouched to pounce.

"Cool yer jets," Emily shouted, yanking Kimani back.

"Monster!" Kimani gibbered through fierce tears. "She killed my sister. Trinity … with that thing. Red hate … It obeys her. Dinosaur … dragon … It wanted *me*. Jasmine, you … *You're* the monster!"

Maybe once, Kimani. Not anymore.

Snapshots of fury, fear, and bewilderment streamed across the face of the broken Amazon in rapid succession. "It hides. Everywhere. It's coming—don't you see it?"

Her head snapped up and down, back and forth, her wild eyes searching every dark corner around her. "It's coming for *me*!"

Kimani tensed to bolt again, but instead simply crumpled against the handrail, as if all the will were sucked out of her. "The walls. It's eyes ... It's eyes ... they see everything. They see ... *inside*!"

"Okay, Jasmine. You hang out with Mrs. Fieldings for a while." Emily flashed an annoyed smirk at the back of Kimani's head. "I gotta get this upstanding citizen to the ambulance. I just hope it has rubber padding." She corralled the simpering hulk, wrestling her though the doorway like a broken tree trunk.

Kimani lurched down the hall, struggling to turn her head over her shoulder, continuing her spouts and accusations mixed with nightmare. "She did it. Killed them all ... I know it! No, not there! It's waiting for me ..."

"What in the world was all that about?" mused Rendell aloud.

After a drawn-out sigh, Jasmine shook her head. "I could probably tell you, but it's a long story."

She guided herself down the stairs, her feet becoming more sure of themselves.

CHAPTER TWENTY ONE

"Are we finished?"

Sitting on her bedroom chair, Jasmine crossed her legs and arms, tying herself into a knot.

Next to the door sat Ms. Stevens, on a chair borrowed from the kitchen table. She tapped a pen on the county seal of her leather-bound notepad. "Not quite. These things take time, Jasmine. Especially after all that has happened today—first Trinity, and then her sister, Kimani. I'm concerned about you. It's a lot for you to absorb. I need to know how you're coping."

The door was ajar, its latch bolt an inch away from the strike plate. The bedroom window was hoisted up and open, and the sounds of the street below filtered through the screen.

Jasmine turned her head to concentrate on everything except what Ms. Stevens was saying.

The hustle and bustle of Rendell and his friend bounded up the alley's walls, as they lugged Bibi's belongings into the moving van. They chatted and laughed between grunts while hefting furniture and rear-ranging boxes. In the hallway, Ma paced back and forth between kitchen and bathroom, yammering at lightning speed into the phone, alternately arguing then pleading with Dad's medical staff at the overseas Army hospital.

Ms. Stevens straightened her pleated skirt while seated, accompanied with an exaggerated cough that snapped Jasmine's focus back on her. "I'm sure your mother and Bibi are concerned as well. So much anger and violence around you. So much that was directed *at* you—take for example, this latest assault. Kimani was hurting from the sudden loss of her sister. She was confused, and was wrong to think that you —"

"We've been over this, Ms. Stevens," Jasmine said with the force of a brick wall. "Kimani thinks I'm responsible for Trinity's death. And she's right. I *am* responsible."

"Now we *know* that's not true. And we're all trying to help you see that. Your mother, Bibi, and I, we're *all* trying to help you." She crossed her legs as she added a notation in her pad. After the final swoop of her pen, she fixed Jasmine with a clinical stare. "Jasmine, I can only imagine what you've been through. But I can see it's been a lot."

And I can see half-baked attempts to gain my trust miles away.

"We're just ..." Ms. Stevens pursed her lips, choosing her words. "We're concerned you might make the same mistake as Trinity."

Jasmine refused to budge in her chair. "Don't worry, I won't. You've asked me a dozen times. And warned me a dozen different ways. I am *not* depressed. And I am *not* going to off myself like Trinity."

Mainly because it wasn't suicide.

Ms. Stevens inhaled a long, slow breath, never taking her eyes off Jasmine. The sounds of Rendell and the street from the window and Ma on the phone from the next room filled the emptiness from opposite directions.

"I'm not going to try to force anything more on you today. But I will return Monday, and every day until school reopens or you're ready to go back. Do you still have my card?" Not waiting for an answer, she slid another one out of her notebook and placed it on Jasmine's desk. "Call me if you want to talk. I'll come anytime."

Ms. Stevens stood, closing her notebook with a resounding clap. "You are strong, Jasmine. But you don't have to go it alone. Even if you don't want to talk to me, talk to your mother. She loves you. She will listen."

Jasmine's frumpy glower twitched. She directed her gaze past her bedroom door in the direction of the kitchen.

Bibi said almost the exact same thing to me a few days ago. There, over the kitchen table. Though it feels like it was a lifetime since then.

"I'll try," trickled out of Jasmine.

Try, and fail. Jackson won't let me tell her everything.

The doorknob jiggled, and Ma shouldered the door wide open. Her face brimmed with a contagious look of excitement.

"Excuse me, Ms. Stevens." Ma raised the phone in front of herself, in an attempt to emphasize her urgency. "There's a family issue that's come up, and I—"

"That's quite all right, Mrs. Price." She tapped her business card lying on Jasmine's desk once more. "Jasmine and I have finished for today."

Ricocheting glances of concern between Jasmine and Stevens, Ma clamped her hand over the phone mouthpiece. "Is my daughter all right?" she said, uncertainty warbling in her voice.

Stevens placed a hand on Ma's back, corralling her into the hallway. "We've made a lot of progress," she continued in a hushed voice. "But given everything your daughter has been through, I'm sure you can see the need for more counseling."

I can still hear you, ladies.

"I'll stop by again Monday to check up on your daughter and continue our discussions. But be advised, it's quite possible she may require further sessions after school reopens. But we will have arranged for professional grief counselors on site by then."

Jasmine stared at the floor and shook her head with annoyance.

They couldn't handle my counseling. The only person who can is downstairs, and she's leaving.

She followed the pair into the front room as Stevens made her polite goodbyes to Ma. Both women bravely shined counterfeit smiles that seemed like they might hide mountains of fears festering underneath. The moment the front door clicked closed, Ma rammed the phone against her ear.

Jasmine inched closer to her mother, watching her expression blossom from politeness to boundless mania.

"Hello, Doc. You still there? Hello?" Ma said, the tension threatening to rip her vocal cords to rags. She almost screamed into the phone, when she cut herself short. She punched the speaker button on the receiver and held it up for Jasmine to hear.

"Babe, is that you?" came a slow whisper that carried the weight of a ponderous fatigue.

Jasmine's mind froze, filled with hope grappling against disbelief.

"Damon!" The phone danced in Ma's trembling hand. "Yes, Honey, it's me. Jasmine's here too."

"Dad?" whispered Jasmine. "Where are you?"

"Hey there, Sprout. It's so good to hear your voice."

Ma and Jasmine dared not to breathe, hanging on every syllable.

"Dad, how are you feeling?" Jasmine knew it was an incredibly stupid thing to say, but it was all she could think of. She wanted to hear his voice say everything was going to be all right.

"Was knocked down for a bit." A wheeze crackled over the phone. "But better now."

"When are you coming home?" Jasmine cried, her cheeks becoming wet.

"That's up to the docs here." Another labored breath. "Patience, Sprout. One foot ..." the sentence faded away.

The two women completed his sentence in unison. "In front of the other."

They both choked an anxious giggle and hugged, squeezing the air out of each other. Wails of suppressed grief and relief spilled out of the pair. It was only when a series of beeps sounded out of the speaker that Ma pushed away.

She wiped her face, blinking to press out the last of her tears. "Hello. You still there, Hon?"

"He's resting now, Mrs. Price," came a woman's voice with a Southern accent.

"Oh, doctor. Thanks so much for the news, and letting us hear Damon's voice. We've been going out of our minds with worry."

"I understand. I'll call tomorrow with an update. Hopefully, PFC Price might join us on the call again. But there are some details that we need to work out today. If you can be by your phone in about an hour, our division director will contact you about his recovery plan, reevaluation and reassessment."

"Recovery plan? Reassessment?" Ma shrieked, her face twisted in confusion. "He's been injured, almost killed. When's he coming home?"

"I'm sorry Mrs. Price, I've said too much already. I really don't want to speak out of turn."

"That sounds like something's wrong," Jasmine muttered under stern eyebrows.

Ma held up her hand to silence Jasmine, while twitching her head with a silent "no."

"My staff and I are working with the Director, to find the best solution for your husband's recovery. Things are a bit up in the air now, so I don't want to raise any expectations unnecessarily."

Ma clamped her hand over her forehead, as though she were preventing it from splitting open.

"What's that supposed to mean?" she nearly screamed. "Is Damon all right? Is he gonna—"

"He's recuperating and doing as best as can be expected, Mrs. Price. That's all we can say for now. Please be patient," urged the doctor with calm perseverance. "The Director will call you as soon as he has news—within an hour, maybe two."

A muffled voice burbled behind the doctor's, and the rapid beep of a medical monitor obliterated the background buzz. "Now I must go. Another patient requires my attention."

The two paced around the front room, until the questions burst out of Jasmine.

"What happened to Dad? Is he going to be all right? What the heck did the doctor mean, 'raise expectations'?" Her throat threatened to clamp shut before she eked out, "He's not gonna … die?"

Ma's shoulder muscles snapped taut. "No, of course not. The Major told me the other day the operation was successful. And if Dad was doing poorly, they wouldn't have let him on the phone."

"Unless they knew that was the last time we would hear him." Jasmine tried not to wail through a tortured grimace.

"Don't even think that!" Ma cried, her fists at her sides. "Besides, you heard your father. 'One foot in front of the other.' He says that when it's bad, but not when it's gonna get worse."

"He only started it. We finished it," Jasmine muttered with expectant eyes.

"Jazz," Ma scolded, stamping her foot fiercely. "You know what I mean."

She paced once more around the room for good measure, then placed the receiver back in its cradle. "Okay, now scoot. Go on, get out of here." She thrust her hand toward the front door. "I gotta stay here for the Director's call. If you stay here, you're just gonna get in my hair, and we'll be at each other's throats before you know it. And neither of us needs that right now. Why don't you go downstairs and help Bibi and her son pack? Get rid of your nervous energy. Something to get your

mind off of school, Dad, and everything else." She punctuated the suggestion with another flick of her wrist.

Jazz helped herself to a glass of water. "I don't wanna see her
go."

"Neither do I. But we don't have a say in these things. Just like
with Dad." Ma stopped pacing and rubbed her hands together.

"Look Jazz, when I'm feeling messed up," she said, leveling
earnest eyes at Jasmine and exhaling a self-depreciating chuckle. "And
when I'm not being a self-absorbed ass, I help someone. Like how I got
a certain someone new pants and a jacket?" Folding her arms slowly,
she added, "Helping someone makes me feel better. And it sure makes
them feel better too. Don't you think Bibi would love to spend time
with you before she leaves?"

"Yeah, I guess." Jasmine wasn't sure if Ma's sweetness-and-light
suggestion would work, but she knew she couldn't stay cooped up in
the apartment.

Ma's right, we'd be picking at each other until someone explodes.

She shot an annoyed glance at Jackson. He sat on his log, the picture of serenity as he cleaned his eyes. Jasmine repressed a shiver.

And if we did, I don't wanna think about what you'd do.

Jasmine walked down the hall, trying not to look at the gouges in
the cement block and the floor left by Jackson. Descending the stairs,
she could hear lively conversation and a spout of laughter coursing up
from the ground floor.

Once in Bibi's apartment, she got her marching orders from the
old woman with the eternal smile. Wrapping odds and ends, packing
them in boxes filled one hour. Helping Rendell to move those boxes
occupied another. Despite the initial cloud of dismay hovering over her
disposition, Jasmine soon found herself smiling at Bibi's small talk, the
jokes and barbs traded back and forth between Rendell and his friend,
and fond reminiscences between proud mother and embarrassed son.

Rendell and his friend had rounded the corner, maneuvering
Bibi's disassembled bed frame out the door, when Jasmine started to
wrap Bibi's *mbira* in bubble plastic. Bibi caught Jasmine gently by the
shoulder.

"Oh, no, child. Please don't wrap that." She unsheathed the
instrument and handed it with both hands back to Jasmine. "I want you
to have it, to remember me by."

Jasmine pursed her lips flat, pushed away the petty and ungracious thoughts that jumped to the forefront.

"I know what you're thinking," Bibi said with a wink. "But you won't have *Jack-suun* forever. So please, keep my *mbira*. And think kindly of me from time to time?"

She hugged Jasmine with all her might.

Much to Jasmine's own surprise, she returned it in kind.

Out of the blue, Bibi landed a playful swat on Jasmine's rump, before pointing to a threesome of wooden slats leaning against the wall. "Now you hurry after Rendell and take those runners. They're what hold the box spring, and they should stay with the rest of the bed. It wouldn't do if everything was packed up and there was no room for all of my bed's pieces."

Jasmine wrapped her arms around the load and waddled her way down the hall, threading the planks with care through the open doors to the street. As she handed them to Rendell on the loading step, her attention was distracted by Ma's distinctive scream.

Her voice wailed like an ambulance siren, bansheeing out each story's open-grated hallway window, until she burst out of the front door.

Ma's head spun like an owl's as she searched for her daughter. Once she spied Jasmine standing at the rear of the truck, she ran. Her bolt of speed diminished to a trot by the time she hugged Jasmine with one arm—the other was occupied, still grasping the silent phone.

Jasmine coaxed Ma out of her bear hug when she could no longer breathe. She goggled at Ma's expression of utter glee.

"We're leaving. We're *leaving*! I don't know how the Major arranged it with the Director," she panted, "but we got housing near the medical base. Where Dad ..."

Another gasp and a swallow, and Ma calmed down. "Where Dad is recuperating. Our passports are green-lighted for priority, and we can leave in one week."

Her voice bounced right back to megaphone volume, and her eyes shone like beacons. "Oh, Jazz, we're out of this city!"

Jasmine shook her head as she tried to piece together the flood of information thrown at her. "But wait, Dad's still in—"

"That's right, Germany!" she exclaimed. "And we're going on the Army's dime. Dad's reassigned there after he completes therapy." She bounced on the balls of her feet with giddiness. "Germany—Ooh la la!"

"That's French, Ma. And we don't speak German," Jasmine countered with flat disbelief.

"Who cares? Perfect time to learn!" Ma planted a wet kiss on Jasmine's cheek and gave her another bone-crunching hug. Jasmine was convinced she heard the housing of the phone crack, before Ma released her with a whoop and dashed back into the apartment building. Her enthusiastic voice soon poured out of Bibi's window at bullhorn volume with the news.

Jasmine followed, stumbling along in a perplexed daze, stopping at the bottom of the stairs.

At the top, Detective Bollard leaned against the split and weather-worn concrete side rail, flipping pages in her pocket spiral notebook with a deliberate, unhurried pace. She glanced at Jasmine, with a mock look of surprise and a glib smile, as if to say she had four aces up her sleeve.

"So, I hear you're leaving our fair town. I guess that gives me one week to figure out why you're always at the center of trouble around here." Bollard glided down the steps, until she stood next to her prey. "Unless there's something you want to get off your chest."

It took every ounce of Jasmine's determination to withhold the scowl that wanted out. "What, are you tapping our phone now?"

"No, Ms. Price," she chuckled. "I think everyone within a city block heard your mother's news."

"So, you're following me."

"If I had the time, I'd love to. I'm here because Central notified me about this latest incident involving you and Kimani. And *voilà*, here I am. So what can you tell me?"

Bollard's dangerous smile intensified. Something dark inside Jasmine wanted to slap that smirk all the way to Germany.

"There's nothing to tell, Detective. Nothing you probably don't already know from the cops that brought me here."

"Yeah, I got the officers' reports. I want to hear your side of the story."

Jasmine folded her arms in defiance. "Kimani came after me. She put me in a full-nelson, sleeper-hold, stranglehold—whatever it's called —and I blacked out." She looked up at her floor high above and rubbed the back of her neck. She flinched when she heard one of her vertebrae click back into place. "Next thing I know, the cops are stuffing her jerk boyfriend in their cruiser, and fitting Kimani for a straitjacket."

"That's old news. C'mon, Jasmine. There's got to be more to it than that. We *both* know it. What *really* happened?"

Jasmine stared Bollard straight in the eyes.

"I can't tell you."

Bollard's smirk evaporated. "Can't? Or won't?"

"Honest, I can't."

Even if I wanted to, which I don't.

From the eroded concrete rail behind Bollard, another voice asserted itself. "Maybe *I* did it."

Madison limped out onto the open sidewalk. Her knee brace clicked as she cocked her generous hips to one side and planted a hand on the outermost one. "Maybe *I* killed Kimani."

Bollard recovered from her surprise and rolled her eyes with an impatient scowl. "Beat it kid, Kimani's not dead."

"Then why you givin' Jazz grief? She didn't do nuthin' to Kimani. How could she? Kimani's got at least forty pounds on her." Her voice ramped up and soon its echoes rattled windows across the street. "And she didn't do nuthin' to Trinity, Akilah, or Nevaeh, neither. Or that douche bag Caleb."

Madison's voice built to the perfect combination of pitch and volume that made Jasmine's eardrum convulse in pain.

God help her kids, if she ever has any.

"They *all* been doing shit to her. And as far as I'm concerned, every one of them got what they deserved. So maybe I *did* do it. *All* of them." She harrumphed, crossed her arms in front of herself, and waggled her head, daring Bollard to doubt her.

"Stop wasting my time, kid. Madison, was it? Scram."

Bollard turned back to Jasmine. She leaned in, her voice hushed. "I can't touch you for Trinity. But the others are still open cases."

The detective shoved her pad into one of the pockets of her peacoat. "You may have everyone else fooled, but something doesn't add up. And you're always smack dab in the middle of it all. But I still got a week, Ms. Price. Who knows what else I'll turn up? Maybe Nevaeh and Caleb didn't run away. Maybe we find their bodies in some dumpster in a nameless alley. Maybe Akilah wakes up and fingers you. In any event, you'll be the first one I'll let know. And even if I can't figure it out before you leave, just remember, there's no statute of limitations on murder. And Germany extradites murderers."

Jasmine stood stock-still, not caring if she was the picture of the long-suffering victim, or had the taint of guilt all over her face. Bollard's mind was made up, one way or the other.

Standing erect with a frown that would make a hanging judge jealous, Bollard took a step back before adding, "Enjoy your moment of glory while it lasts, Jasmine. But my head, heart, and gut tell me something is wrong with you—*very* wrong. You may have your classmates fooled, your family fooled, the school and child services fooled. But not me. And sooner or later, everybody screws up. You're gonna mess up, too."

Maybe, if what you were chasing was human. But what if it isn't, Bollard?

Bollard's jaw shifted from left to right, like she wanted rail on, but thought better of it. She shoved her hands into her pockets, turned on her heels and stormed away.

"That lady has one serious bug up her ..." Madison finished her thought with a click of her tongue.

"Madison," Jasmine ventured meekly. "Thanks for that." The second she spoke it, she grimaced at her own awkwardness—it sounded more like a question than a real expression of gratitude.

"Was nuthin'," Madison huffed, her eyes nailed on Bollard until she turned the corner. "Something about her I just don't like."

"Yeah, she's a hard-ass. But she's just doin' her job," Jasmine said with a sigh. She tried to work up a smile for Madison, biting her lip in the process. She just couldn't seem to get in the groove. Maybe like Bollard, she forgot how to be friendly. "So whatcha doin' here?"

Maybe I can get Jackson to take a look at Madison, as long as she's here.

"Actually, I just wanted to thank you for standing up to Trinity and Kimani for me, before she ... before ..."

"Yeah, I know."

"A-a-and," Madison drawled while she tapped the bottom step with a toe. "I wanted to see how you were holding up. Everyone's texting like crazy about what you saw in the school bathroom. Or what they think you saw. Some of it's *wa-a-ay* out there." She gave Jasmine another dose of that look, caught somewhere between pity, disgust, and fear.

Jasmine ignored it. "And you?"

"I wanted to look too, but I didn't wanna. Y'know?" Madison gave her shoulders a quick up-and-down shrug, and her whole chest bounced. "But man, all the crap Nevaeh and her crew put you through, topped off with what happened this morning? Then you get the third degree from Chatelain and Moore and bull-dyke Bollard? And then Kimani comes gunning for your ass? Man, I don't know how you hold up."

"Yeah, thanks. It was kinda ..." Jasmine sighed. "I don't know how to describe it right now. Maybe later we can talk."

Like maybe after you see Mlinzi, then I can tell you everything. If he accepts you.

"Naw," Madison backed away one step. Her face went blank and serious. "We're still not friends. I just wanted to say thanks for standing with me, and make sure you were okay."

"Yeah, about that. I should thank you for standing with *me*, too. When I lost it in bathroom. They told me what you did for me."

After a firm nod, Madison wheeled about and limped away. But not before a wet glint rose from her eyes.

Yeah, not all friends are all huggy-kissy. I was wrong about Madison. She's a strong kid.

I was gonna try to give Jackson to her. Maybe she won't need Jackson's help after all. Either way, I got a week to figure it out.

A strange laugh percolated out of Jasmine, followed by a sardonic grin. She mumbled to herself, "If Bollard shows up again, maybe I'll show Jackson to her instead. Wouldn't that be a kick in the pants if he turned blue?"

CHAPTER TWENTY TWO

The girl with a butterfly tattoo half hidden by a breezy cotton blouse sipped from a steaming demitasse across the table from Jasmine. Pinpricks of sweat under the unusually hot early autumn sun made the blue and green ink come alive with jeweled wings across her deep mocha skin.

How on earth can she drink hot coffee in this weather?

She pushed a dainty plate holding a slice of cake toward Jasmine.

Jasmine munched on her salad and eyed the *konditorei* confection with suspicion, as trickles of pedestrians ambled past the open-air cafe. Were it not for the occasional auto, bike, and streetcar, Jasmine could convince herself she were in a countryside park instead of downtown.

"Go ahead, Jazz, try this little bit of heaven. Besides, what Coach Müller doesn't know won't hurt him." She took a polite sip of her espresso, followed with a playfully wicked grin. "Or your diet."

Jasmine flashed an annoyed wrinkle of one eyebrow at the girl across the table. "No worries about that. This city's nice enough that I don't mind walking."

The girl dabbed a napkin at a crumb that fell on her kaleidoscopic butterfly.

"Y'know, Charlotte," said Jasmine, "I once thought about getting a tatt of my own. A chameleon. Right about the same place too."

"Why didn'tcha, girl?"

"I slept on it, and decided it just wasn't me." She glanced at her friend's hair—relaxed, and glossy blue-black in the sunlight. Jasmine nodded to herself with a petite wrinkle of a grin, content with her decision to have done her own hair up in box braids.

Wiping off her salad fork, Jasmine sliced off the corner from the wedge of icing, fillings, and chocolate. She popped it in her mouth, and within moments her eyes rolled half-closed as she hummed with delight.

"Mmm, Charlotte," Jasmine said between smacking lips, "that's hella good. What's this called again?"

"*Mozart-torte*. Chocolate sponge, cream, nougat, pistach– ... You're not even listening, are you, girl?"

"Yup," came Jasmine's crumb-filled reply before she plowed in a second forkful.

A shadow crossed the table, and a tall blond hunk leaned over the table and gave Charlotte a peck on the cheek.

Jasmine's mouth spasmed as it tried to do five things at once—chew, swallow, spit, talk, breathe.

Sonuva– ... He's with Charlotte? No wonder he's been avoiding me.

"Already finished with socc– ... I mean *fussball*, angel?" Charlotte returned the youth's greeting, and flashed Jasmine a playful taunt of a smile.

"*Ja*. May I join you?"

"Sorry, Jazz. I don't think I introduced you. Anton's a freshman at Kaiserslautern University." With a sly tease, Charlotte taunted, "That's on the other side of Landstuhl."

"I know my own city," Jasmine shot back. She imagined herself kicking Charlotte's shin under the table.

"And Anton," Charlotte said, just before pulling her dessert dish back with the tines of her fork, "Jasmine here's my best friend. My father and hers are in physical rehab together at Landstuhl Medical."

"Pleased," said Anton with a continental bow. "Excuse me, I shall get myself tea and join you presently."

Jasmine couldn't resist the temptation to follow Anton's receding form. She flushed with embarrassment after another audible "mmm" escaped her lips.

Charlotte wriggled her shoulders with an exaggerated shiver.

"Aren't they the sexiest things when they're freshly washed and still just a little sweaty? And that accent …"

Jasmine clinked her fork on the half-empty glass of iced tea in front of her. "Down, girl." Her annoyed frown curled into a sassy grin. "You did that on purpose, you little so-and-so. You saw him behind me and set me up."

"Even a blind person could see how you undress my man with your eyes every time you look at him. Hell, you practically rape him," she said with a snicker.

Jasmine stomped down the twist in her gut. Though it was months ago, any reminder of what nearly happened to her in that dark alley still made her want to scream.

Don't tear Charlotte's head off, Jazz. She doesn't know.

Put it behind you. It's in the past.

Caleb is long gone. Dead and gone. He can't hurt you anymore.

"So hands off, girl." Charlotte crossed her arms, pretending to examine her nails. "Or we're gonna have words."

"Don't worry, Shar. He's all yours," said Jasmine, pushing her salad plate to the side. "For now. Though he's gonna be the first one I call when you break up." She snorted at Charlotte's mock dismay, before they both shared a giggle.

The two sat back in their seats, with feigned smiles of utter inno-cence plastered across their faces, when Anton pulled out a chair for himself. He took a long drink from a red chai in a to-go cup.

"Don't forget, Charlotte," said Anton, clueless that he had been the subject of discussion. "If you still wish to shop for your father's gift, we should leave soon. The stores will be mobbed this afternoon."

"Why, what's today?" inquired Jasmine. Attempting to regain the image of a ladylike demeanor, she dabbed crumbs from her mouth with a napkin.

"There's nothing today," said Charlotte. "But tomorrow's Unity Day, and all the stores will be closed. Guess this is your first one?"

Jasmine responded with a perplexed frown.

"It's the holiday celebrating when East and West halves of our nation were reunited." Anton took another pull from his lid and shrugged his shoulders. "I can take it or leave it, but the older folk really get into it."

A chorus of rhythmic shouts rang out across the street. A large group of men ranging from gangling teenagers to roly-poly burghers marched past, climbing the hill waving tri-colored flags. After a few cheers and fist pumps, they broke out into a miserably out-of-tune sports team fight song.

Something about 'They see our team, and piss their pants'? Oh, brother, that's *real class.*

"And to make things more interesting, there's a big *fussball* league match today." A twitch of worry scrunched the bridge of Anton's nose, when stragglers behind the group were harangued by two policemen in padding and helmets. "Now those are the types you must watch out for," he said in a hushed voice.

Jasmine glanced past Anton, trying not to gawk. A pair of skinheads stumbled and yelled at the police between swills of beer. She squinted with a tilt of her head at the rowdies, not at their shaven heads, or their necks and arms festooned with tattoos, but at their heavy steel-toed boots.

"What's with the pink shoelaces?" she asked, trying to suppress a chuckle.

"If their laces are white, they are just everyday—*ach*, what is the word—white supremacists," said Anton, disdain staining each word. "The pink ones take pride that they were arrested for violence. Red are worse—they boast that they have spilled blood."

The two girls sat in wary silence—snatching a peek, then forcing their eyes on their food in front of them until the miniature parade turned the corner. Under sharply angled eyebrows, Anton's gaze never faltered, skewering the boisterous pair.

Jasmine marveled at the wonderful contradiction. Here sat the perfect blonde-haired blue-eyed poster boy for those racial-purity dunderheads, yet he made no attempt to hide his disgust for them.

"All right, we should be fine now," said Anton, standing and moving to pull out Charlotte's chair. "But nonetheless, we should go, Shar. Before the square gets too crowded, no?"

He gave an inviting look at Jasmine. "Care to join us?"

Charlotte's cheeks flustered and her widening eyes shouted at Jasmine, *"Don't you dare!"*

Jasmine's mouth wrinkled with a wry grin, as she pushed back her own chair. "No," she began before a chuckle slipped out. "I've got some … errands to run for Ma. You two have fun. See you at the rehab later, Shar. Nice meeting you, Anton." She took a final stab at Charlotte's torte and gulped it down.

Jasmine strolled to a waiting streetcar but paused, looking at the azure sky dotted with puffy clouds as she mulled her alternative. She did an about face, deciding a long constitutional was the best penance for her chocolate transgression. After several blocks, she switched to the east side of the boulevard to avoid the relentless sun as it climbed higher. Once she judged sufficient calories were burned, she surrendered to the increasing humidity and jumped on the next streetcar, riding until the stop nearest her neighborhood.

In front of her home nestled in its row of townhouses, she dug for the house keys in her tote. Madly searching the chaos of her bag, she could almost hear Ma say, "Some things never change."

She was about to put the elusive key into the door when she paused once more, stepping back off the front stoop. Eyeing the front of her residence, she shook her head with a bittersweet grin.

How did I get here? I don't deserve to be this happy.

We got a nice place in Army housing, I'm finishing up my last year in a good school near the base, and Ma's got work that she loves. Dad's doing great with therapy and raring to return to non-hazardous duty here on base, though that's still months away.

And I've got friends that are real *friends.*

She scanned the clear blue sky, searching for the errant meteor that would spoil the perfect day any minute now. Suppressing a small snicker at her idle imagination, she ended her aerial search at the front window. The louvered blinds were lowered and half-closed, choking off the late morning light from Jackson's new terrarium.

Jasmine's snicker blossomed into a full smile, recalling the tizzy Ma was in, when she discovered Jackson halfway through unpacking their meager belongings in their new house ...

"*Fuck!*" Ma screamed in an octave Jasmine had never heard before. "What the *hell* is that critter doing here?"

"Now, now, Ma. Four-letter words are for four IQ's."

As soon as Ma could be pried off the ceiling, it was rather simple for Jasmine to convince her to keep Jackson. Pelting her with a flotilla of arguments quickly wore her down.

"After he survived the trip hidden in our luggage?" "He's been here for days already." "Turning him over to quarantine is pointless now." "I found a used terrarium, cheap." "Bibi will be heartbroken if anything happens to him."

She knew her barrage was successful when Ma conceded with the universal code words that signaled parental capitulation. "We'll see …"

Jasmine dropped her keys and handbag on the nearest end table. She shivered and sighed with relief as the cool living room air enveloped her. She called for Ma twice while strolling toward the bedrooms, then meandered into the kitchen when there was no answer. Predictable as ever, a scribbled note lay on the butcher-block kitchen table.

"Don't forget, I'm heading to see Dad in rehab after work. Join us for supper in the commissary—he can walk that far now!"

Jasmine whispered a small "wow" to herself, and an easy grin splashed across her face. She hummed her way back into her bedroom and grabbed a small plastic container from the windowsill. Returning to the front room, she removed the *mbira* from the top of Jackson's terrarium. Plunking a few playful notes on the thumb piano, she set it aside and removed the screen lid. Popping the corner off the container, she shook a small parcel of wriggling mealworms into the tank.

"Okay, Jackson, come'n get it," she said, searching the maze of moss, flowers, and budding plants for his telltale eyes and three horns. "Where are you hiding now, you little coin purse?"

Jasmine's heart froze on the last word. Reaching into his enclosure, her hand trembled an inch away from Jackson.

From horn to tail, the chameleon was jet black. The diffuse glossiness that usually dappled his pebbled skin was reduced to dull flatness. As far as Jasmine could tell, he might have been carved from a large lump of coal.

"Jackson?" Her eyes flashed wide with dread. "*Jackson!*" she cried with urgency. Jasmine waved her hand over the creature's head, then squatted down to look him eye to eye.

Jackson remained frozen, like a statue of onyx.

A queasy pit of fear stabbed in her abdomen. Jumping up, she scrambled for the front door and delved into her tote. Finding her phone, she fought down waves of panic as she scrolled through her contacts.

She punched the screen and paced the living room in near frenzy. Each ring of the phone kicked her apprehension up another notch. She whimpered with frustration until the voicemail's outgoing message finished with a beep.

"Bibi? Rendell? It's Jasmine. If you're there, pick up. Please, *please* call me as soon as you can. Jackson went all—oh, never mind. Just call me? I need to know everything's okay."

She paced even faster, each lap punctuated with a glower at the phone's screen in hopes to persuade it to ring. And with every pass by the terrarium, she examined Jackson for any sign of movement, or any hint of color.

Don't think it. Don't think it.

She scurried back into her bedroom and tore open her desk's drawers. Planting herself into the desk chair, she burrowed into paper tablets, piles of loose sheets, dried-up pens and crumpled Post-it notes.

There's gotta somebody in their city I can call. I think I saved the number for their old hospital back when—

Jasmine yelped when her phone rang. Dropping everything, she fumbled for the phone with both hands.

"Hello!" she said, trying to keep hysteria at bay.

"Jasmine," responded a familiar baritone, though tinny with distance. Distraught and subdued, the voice cracked with emotion. "It's Rendell. I'm sorry I didn't pick up. We ... I haven't been taking calls right now. But the missus saw it was you." Over the speaker whispered a long heavy-laden exhale, the type that built one's courage. "I'm afraid I have bad news."

Oh, no. God, no. No no no ...

Jasmine listened, saying little. She nodded her head, with nary a mumble or grunt after each detail.

Bibi was gone.

The end was peaceful and painless, but she was gone.

Jasmine responded through a haze of shock, not quite sure of what it was she said in response to Rendell's news.

He said his goodbyes. Jasmine dropped the phone, trying to remember if she expressed her condolences, trying to recall if she asked after his children Cheta and Shujaa, hoping she at least said something remotely sympathetic.

She wandered in a sleepwalking daze before collapsing cross-legged in front of the terrarium. Her head hung low, chin touching her chest as she breathed through her mouth.

Her eyes—her entire being—fixated on Jackson. Unyielding as stone, not even his eyes twitched from their forward-facing position.

Her forearm suddenly ached down to her wrist. Jasmine glanced down, wondering when she had grabbed the pad of paper from her desk drawer, or when she clutched it in a shaky grip.

Written in stops-and-starts, as bad as her old history homework, were her abortive attempts to write a letter to Bibi over the past weeks.

Stray sentences thanking her for all she had done. Promises that she would take care of Jackson and do her best to guide whomever he chose next. Rivers of reminiscences. Dozens of sentences that never seemed to hit the mark, never seemed to reflect what she truly felt, never expressed her gratitude, never …

And now, would never be read.

Jasmine poured out the grief of a thousand tears.

Wiping the streams from her cheeks, she sniffed back the wetness, then stumbled to the bathroom in search of tissues. Staring back through the doorway at the immobile Jackson, something akin to envy came to mind.

How do you feel, Mlinzi? Do you feel like I do? Are you sad, alone, suddenly lost? Is this a sign of respect? A reaction driven by instinct? Or just some mystical reset switch?

With a delicate touch, she pried Jackson's stiff room-temperature form out of the terrarium. When his tail thumped against the glass, she eek-ed with a small grimace and an absurd expectation that Jackson might chip or crack like fine china.

Do you feel at all?

Looking down at him, she petted his soft but rigid leathern form once, then twice, like a puppy orphaned in a storm.

No response.

"No, I guess you don't. But I do." She placed him back on his perch under an African violet in full blossom, then replaced his lid and Bibi's old *mbira*. She thumbed all the tines in a row one last time.

"I can't stay here, Jackson. I gotta get out, be among people. People who I can talk to." Her shoulders slumped with a forlorn sigh. "And I gotta tell Ma, face to face. A phone call won't cut it."

With the tissue, and another clean one for good measure, she wiped her face in front of her bedroom mirror, until she no longer resembled a crying clown. She dumped her phone in her handbag and left the house.

Walking in silence, saying nothing to passing neighbors, she boarded the local streetcar and its connection to the rehab. Immersed in quiet reflection, she wondered how best to break the news to Ma, and how she might hold herself together during the ordeal.

The blazing sun retreated behind clouds marching across the sky from the northwest. The carriage shuddered when a sudden gust whipped across the tracks. Jasmine cast a worried glance upward through the window at the graying sky, regretting she didn't have the forethought to bring a jacket.

The walk from the station to the rehab was dominated by cool breezes that promised the snap of autumn was just around the bend. For reasons she didn't question, the humid-turned-dry air and the simple act of walking refreshed her body and brightened her spirits. Jasmine hoped it would sustain her when she delivered her weighty news.

Barely though the front door of the rehab building, she heard a voice she couldn't quite place.

"Jasmine? Over here," rasped a girl in a red bandanna and dark sunglasses. Huddled behind a table, she waved frantically at first. It was reduced to a subdued beckoning when she grimaced, twitching with a wince that the kerchief and glasses could not hide. Beside her stood a tall blond-haired youth with his back toward her. At her approach he turned, his face distorted with a shiner on one side and a swollen bruise on the opposite cheekbone.

"Anton?" sputtered Jasmine. "Charlotte?" She skittered over to the table and knelt in front of her friend.

Straggles of frizzed blue-black hair stuck out from underneath the bandanna at odd angles. Jasmine plucked the glasses from Charlotte's face, revealing a purple welt under one eye. Charlotte snatched back the sunglasses, cramming them back on her face before curling into a quivering ball.

"Good God, girl, what happened?"

"Oh, Jazz, it was awful," she sobbed, her voice ripped to shreds. "We were minding our own business. I had just bought a bicycle bell for Pop's new walker. I figured he and your dad would both get a laugh out of that. When we left the store, a bunch of skinheads ambushed us."

"What—" Jasmine blurted. "They wouldn't dare! Didn't those *polizei* have their eyes on them?"

"It was not the same ones," said Anton. "The ones you saw had white shoelaces." He put his arm around Charlotte, who squeezed her eyes shut and leaned against him. "These *scheissköpfe* didn't. I guess they didn't approve of the idea of one of their own kind being familiar with a black girl." The look of disgust he had shown before at the cafe coursed across his face again like wildfire.

"The crowd got the attention of the police, but not before those damned bootboys whaled on us both." Charlotte ensnared Anton's arm with both of hers. "They punched and kicked. I screamed bloody murder. Anton tried to protect—"

Her voice went dry as sawdust, and a rickety cough cut her short.

"But there were too many of them," said Anton, completing her sentence.

"And they had red shoelaces!" Charlotte exclaimed through a grimace. She rasped a wet cough that announced that she probably belonged in a hospital ward as well.

"So what are you doing here?" Jasmine flustered at her friends. "Have you contacted the police? Why aren't you at the hospital?"

"No! We're fine," Charlotte said in an angry whisper, followed by another coagulated cough.

A worried Anton rose from his chair. "Jasmine, could you watch Charlotte for me? I need to get her some water." Once behind Charlotte, he signaled to Jasmine and silently mouthed "doctor."

Jasmine nodded and slid into the chair next to her friend. She hugged Charlotte for all she was worth.

Another cough. Charlotte covered her mouth with a tissue, wiping away the sputum. A sob gave way to a body full of shivers.

In a gravelly voice she rattled, "But that's not the worst. They said they knew who we were. They knew where I lived. And that they …" A gasping breath punctuated each sentence, until she looked at Jasmine with pleading eyes filled with terror. "That they would come back and *finish* the job."

Charlotte grabbed Jasmine's wrist, her grip fierce with panic. "Jazz, they had red shoelaces! They're gonna kill me, I know it!"

Jasmine clasped gentle hands on Charlotte's shoulders and coaxed her friend to face her.

Eye to eye, Jasmine said with a patient smile, "Hush, girl. Things will be fine. You can stay at our place for a day or two. While you're there, I'd like you to meet a friend of mine."

THE END

A REQUEST

I need your help.

Authors not picked up by major publishers live and die by the engagement of *you*, the reader.

Please file a review?

Regardless of the number of stars you give this book, your feedback is valuable. Online stores and media adjust their advertising and promotions depending on the number of ratings that books receive.

Please file a review?

If you would, write a sentence or two in addition to rating 1-5 stars. I *do* read your comments. They influence the direction of my writing.

Please file a review?

If you've had the patience to read all the way down here, you're in luck! Readers who review my books on Amazon are entered to win an autographed copy of my next book ... Just like the lucky someone who has already won an autographed copy of *this* book!

Won't you *please* file a review?

Thank you.

Pssst ... Did you remember to file a review?

SAMPLE QUESTIONS FOR DISCUSSION

STORY

- What are Jasmine's strong points, and what are her flaws? How did they change after *Mlinzi*?

- What do *you* think Jasmine should have done with *Mlinzi*? Pass him to Madison? To Bollard? To someone else? Create a story where she shows *Mlinzi* to that person.

- What are Bibi's strengths and weaknesses? With all the demands placed on her, might she have handled *Mlinzi* better?

- With which character do you identify? Why?

GENERAL

- Many cultures have creation myths. Tanzanian folklore has characters like *Buibui* (spider), *Buku* (rat), *Fisi* (hyena), *Jogu* (crow), *Keema* (monkey), *Kobe* (tortoise), *Mwanaume* (ape), *Nyoba* (serpent), *Simba* (lion), and *Sungura* (hare).
  Create a story describing how *Mlinzi* (chameleon) came into existence.

- Have you recently been bullied?
  With whom did you talk about it?
  Why or why not?

ABOUT THE AUTHOR

Christopher D. Ochs's foray into writing began in 2014 with his epic fantasy *Pindlebryth of Lenland: The Five Artifacts*. He combined his knack for telling stories in the Lehigh Valley Storytellers Guild with his writing style to craft *If I Can't Sleep, You Can't Sleep*, a collection of the mirthful macabre.

His short stories have been published in several anthologies: *GLVWG Writes Stuff, Write Here Write Now, The Write Connections,* and *Rewriting the Past,* by the Greater Lehigh Valley Writers Group; along with *Untethered,* Finalist in Killer Nashville's Silver Falchion, and *Once Upon a Time,* by the Bethlehem Writers Group; and last but not least, *Meanwhile in the Middle of Eternity* by Firebringer Press.

His current literary projects stirring in the cauldron include: many more short tales of the weird; a couple of sci-fi/horror mashups; an e-book prequel and the second installment of the *Pindlebryth* saga ... and maybe another *Jackson*?

Chris has too many interests outside of writing for his own damn good. With previous careers in physics, mathematics, electrical engineering and software, and his incessant dabbling as a CGI artist, classical organist, voice talent on radio, DVD, audiobook, podcast and the *Voice of OTAKON*, it's a wonder he can remember to pay the dog and feed his bills. Wait, what?

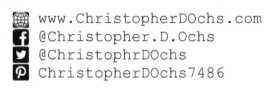

www.ChristopherDOchs.com
@Christopher.D.Ochs
@ChristophrDOchs
ChristopherDOchs7486

CPSIA information can be obtained
at www.ICGtesting.com
Printed in the USA
LVHW091603280821
696353LV00008B/656